W9-CCL-770

RECEIVED
JUN - 9 2006
By

Also by Morgan Llywelyn

*Published by Ballantine Books*

DRUIDS

RED BRANCH

*the*

# GREENER SHORE

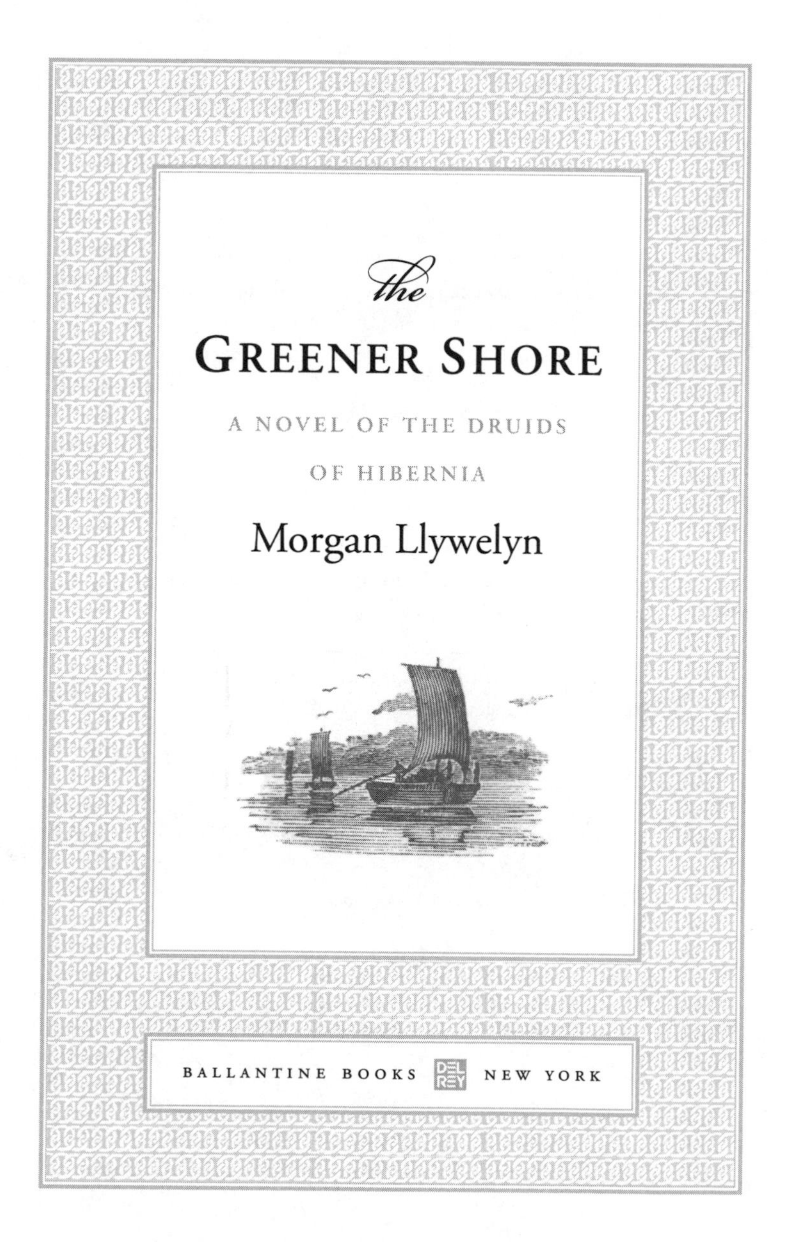

*the*

# GREENER SHORE

A NOVEL OF THE DRUIDS OF HIBERNIA

Morgan Llywelyn

BALLANTINE BOOKS DEL REY NEW YORK

*The Greener Shore* is a work of fiction. Names, characters, places, and incidents are the products of the author's imagination or are used fictitiously. Any resemblance to actual events, locales, or persons, living or dead, is entirely coincidental.



Published in the United States by Del Rey Books, an imprint of The Random House Publishing Group, a division of Random House, Inc., New York.

Del Rey is a registered trademark and the Del Rey colophon is a trademark of Random House, Inc.

ISBN 0-345-47766-9

Printed in the United States of America on acid-free paper

www.delreybooks.com

2 4 6 8 9 7 5 3 1

First Edition

*Text design by Laurie Jewell*

*for Sonia*

## Phonetic Glossary

*Ainvar:* AYN-var
*Aislinn:* ASH-lin
*Anicius Bellator:* An-ICK-ee-us Bell-AYT-or
*Anluan:* AN-luah
*Bean Sídhe:* Ban-SHEE
*Briga:* BREE-ga
*Cairbre:* KAR-breh
*Caman:* Cam-AWN
*Carnutes:* Kar-NOO-tays
*Cas:* Kosh
*Cathal:* KA-hul
*Cohern:* KO-ern
*Cormiac Ru:* KOR-mick Roo
*Damona:* DAH-mona
*Dara:* DAH-ra
*Deisi:* DAY-sha
*Dian Cet:* DEEN Ket
*Eoin:* OH-in
*Eriu:* AYR-yoo
*Fíachu:* FEE-ah-koo
*Filidh:* Fil-EEE
*Fír Bolg:* Feer Bohlg
*Glas:* GLAHS
*Goban Saor:* GO-bawn Sear
*Gobnat:* GOB-nit
*Goulvan:* GOOL-van
*Grannus:* GRAN-us
*Éber Finn:* EEB-ar Fin
*Éremon:* EE-re-mon
*Keryth:* KER-ith
*Labraid Loingseach:* LOW-ree LOYNG-sha
*Lakutu:* La-KOO-too
*Lorcán:* LOR-kawn
*Mac Coille:* Mok-KIL-eh
*Maia:* MY-uh
*Mahon:* MAH-hun
*Morand:* MUR-an
*Niav:* NEE-uhv
*Ongus:* AHNG-us
*Onuava:* On-you-AY-vah
*Probus Seggo:* PRO-bus SEGG-oh
*Rígan:* REE-gawn
*Seanchán:* SIN-chawn
*Senta:* SIN-tuh
*Slea Leathan:* Slay LOWuhn
*Sulis:* SOO-liss
*Tarvos:* TAHR-vos
*Teyrnon:* TEAR-nun
*Túatha Dé Danann:* TOO-ah deh DAN-uhn
*Vercingetorix:* Ver-kin-GET-o-rix

# *the*
# GREENER SHORE

# Prologue

Everything is lost.

The sea is so wide. There is no end to it and no beginning. Strange gods rule the waves. From time to time Ainvar thinks he hears their voices, but they speak a language he does not know. He cannot impress them with magic, he cannot placate them with sacrifice. He can do nothing but wait.

Once Ainvar's extended family had numbered in the hundreds, yet theirs had been but one clan among many in the tribe of the Carnutes. The Carnutes of Gaul were part of the vast Celtic world that stretched from the river Danube to the edge of the Great Cold Sea. The far-flung tribes spoke many versions of their mother tongue and practiced a variety of customs, but all had two things in common. Every tribe was ruled by a warrior aristocracy led by a chieftain. And every tribe treasured its druids.

From his seat in the stern of the boat, Ainvar the druid frequently turns to look back. Every time he does this his heart breaks anew, but he cannot help it. The land he loved is far behind him now. He sees only an endless army of waves rolling on, rank after rank.

Like the Romans. The relentless, remorseless, rapacious Romans, against whom the power of the druids had proved insufficient.

DRUIDS COMPRISED THE INTELLECTUAL CLASS OF THE CELTIC PEOple. Although some came from humble origins, in tribal society the druids were equal in rank with the nobility.

In every generation a few boys and girls were born with special talents. These gifts usually revealed themselves early in life. At that point the chief druid of the tribe began training the youngsters in the disciplines necessary for acceptance into the Order of the Wise. Neophytes were apprenticed to other druids whose gifts were similar to their own. After being fully trained, a druid was supported by the tribe in return for the free gift of his or her abilities.

Druids served in a number of capacities. Their principal obligation was to maintain the harmony between the visible and invisible worlds. They also kept the laws of their race and were the only members of a tribe exempt from battle.

AINVAR HAD FOUGHT CAESAR WITH HIS HEAD, NOT HIS SWORD. HIS was a long and noble head packed with the wisdom of centuries, accrued since before the before and added to in every generation.

But the sword had won. A lust to dominate and a thirst for power had won.

Where was the justice in that?

TRIBAL WARFARE HAD BEEN THE CELTIC WAY OF LIFE FOR UNTOLD generations. As with stags in a forest, success in battle was the way in which leaders proved themselves. Chieftains competed for the best land or access to the most profitable trade routes. When the women joined their men in battle, they were reputed to be fiercer than the males.

The Carnutes had proudly styled themselves "The Sons of War and Thunder." Their territory was considered to be the very heart of Gaul.

They have all but ceased to exist.

ONLY A SCORE OF AINVAR'S CLAN SURVIVE; A HUDDLE OF REFUGEES IN two open boats, lashed by the indifferent waves, at the mercy of forces beyond the control of druids. The sacred land that nurtured their mortal bodies and their immortal spirits has been conquered by a man to whom nothing is sacred. Julius Caesar slaughtered the people who worshipped the land—but not because he hated them. He did not even know them. They were simply in his way.

THE VESSEL'S SQUARE SAIL FILLS WITH A RISING WIND. THE SAIL IS emblazoned with the emblem of the Order of the Wise, but it means nothing to Ainvar anymore. The potent symbols he trusted all his life have failed him.

He feels as if his body has been torn open and his entrails ripped out.

Druids read the future in entrails. The odious Caesar was only interested in spilling entrails for personal gain. He left the bloody ruin of an entire nation strewn across the lovely face of Gaul.

FROM HER PLACE IN THE PROW BRIGA KEEPS AN EYE ON AINVAR. HER heart aches for the tall, gaunt figure crouching in his cloak as if it were a cave. The others assume he still mourns the slaughtered tribes, but Briga knows that her husband's unremitting melancholy has a more specific source. The chief druid of the Carnutes cannot forgive himself for failing to save Vercingetorix, chieftain of the Arverni.

Vercingetorix is a wound that will not heal.

The spirit housed in Briga's body is much brighter. The moment she stepped into the boat, she tidied away regret like domestic debris and turned her face toward the horizon. It was part of Briga's nature to open herself to possibilities.

When she suggested that Ainvar do the same, he made a bitter shape of his mouth. "Let the past go? How can I let go of something that's entangled with my spirit like mistletoe on an oak tree?"

Since then Briga has kept her own counsel. Patience with their men is one of the many gifts of women.

AINVAR STRUGGLES TO KEEP FROM LOOKING BACK. HE IS SO FILLED with pain that to add one drop to the total might cause it to overflow. To distract himself he tries to think of something else, yet within a few heartbeats he is mentally running through the names of the loved and lost. Until he comes to Vercingetorix.

There he stops. With the loss of Vercingetorix, everything stopped.

THE BOAT LEAPS WITH THE LIFT OF THE WAVES. IT RIDES UPWARD, upward toward the distant sun as if offering its passengers as a sacrifice, hangs suspended for a timeless moment, then swoops sickeningly downward into a deep dark trough of sea.

The boat always comes up again.

Nature, instructor in all things, is making a point.

## *chapter* I

THE SUN IS THE SYMBOL OF THE GREAT FIRE OF LIFE, CREATED BY the Source of All Being. I remind myself of this whenever the glare of the sun makes me squint.

I, Ainvar, salute the Source of All Being.

The Source of All Troubles is Caesar the Reprehensible. I should have recognized that from the beginning. I keep going over and over events as if by tumbling them in my hands like pebbles I can change their shape. I cannot. Even a chief druid cannot redraw the Pattern.

But I can see it. Oh yes. Looking back, I can see it so clearly. At some crucial point the tribes of Gaul must have disrupted the harmony of the Pattern, thus precipitating catastrophe. Which means that at some crucial point the druids failed.

I failed.

At first the Gauls had welcomed traders from the tribes of Latium as they had welcomed the Hellenes before them. The Latin language was not beautiful to the Celtic ear, being hard and abrupt rather than musical, but we shared the vocabulary of trade: a nod, a grunt, a slap of hands. In this manner arrangements were concluded and goods exchanged. Gaul offered salt and iron and grain; the speakers of Latin brought wine and olive oil and luxury goods from the Mid-Earth Sea. Traders from each side were able to provide enough to satisfy the other side. Everyone benefited. For a while.

Then one tribe, the Romans, proved they did not understand the concept of Enough; they wanted More. Their traders brought warriors to stand at their shoulders while they made unreasonable demands. The Gauls swatted the more importunate traders away as one swats a fly. The Romans kept coming. Tendrils of a poisonous weed, they extended their reach until at last we realized their true and deadly intent. Led by someone called Gaius Julius Caesar—a figure of walking excrement that needs three names to make it feel like a man—the Romans meant to steal everything from us, even the land on which we lived. Our sacred Mother Earth.

If I close my eyes I can still see the glorious victories we won; the desperate battles we lost. And then the final battle. And the subsequent destruction of all we held dear.

The destruction of the Great Grove of the Carnutes blew us away like chaff on the wind.

I chew on my memories as if they were food, but receive no nourishment from them. When I dream, I dream of the lost skies of Gaul.

Free Gaul, which bled to death to fatten Caesar's purse.

MY WIVES REFUSE TO TALK ABOUT THE PAST. FOLLOWING BRIGA'S lead, the other two keep their faces turned to the west and their eyes on the future.

Onuava is a tall, strong woman, with a lion's mane of fair hair. Her first husband was Vercingetorix, chief of the Arverni. His name meant "King of the World." Such a man is not born once in ten generations. The tribes of Gaul made him their leader when they needed him most, and lost him to merciless Caesar when they needed him even more. Onuava was carrying his first son in her womb when they dragged Vercingetorix away.

After Keryth the prognosticator foresaw the death of Vercingetorix at the hands of his captors, I made Onuava my third wife. Although we were as different as fire and water, Rix and I were, are, and always shall be, soul friends. I was obligated to offer my fullest protection to his family. Since then I have even learned to love Onuava, at least as much as her proud and prickly nature will allow.

My second wife is Onuava's opposite. Lakutu is small and dark, docile by nature and Egyptian by birth. She was already past her prime when I first saw her. Lakutu is old now, yet from time to time a mischievous child peeks out of her black eyes.

There are intriguing rumors concerning certain mysterious rites practiced in her homeland. Although Lakutu has learned our language, she conveniently forgets it whenever I question her about those rites. Egypt's child keeps Egypt's secrets. In her head my second wife holds knowledge to which I cannot gain access, and that is her power over me. Druids love a mystery.

Briga is the youngest of my three wives in age, but senior to them in rank. The daughter of a prince of the Sequani tribe, she was the first woman with whom I celebrated the marriage ritual. According to our custom Briga had to give permission for me to marry Lakutu, and then she and Lakutu had to give permission for me to marry Onuava. Such permissions usually are granted, because each additional wife serves the wife who is senior to her.

In practice, Onuava serves no one, but that was to be expected.

My Briga is a small, sturdy person with hair like dark flax. Her most interesting feature is her voice, as soft and hoarse as the purring of a cat. Her speech still bears the musical lilt of her native tribe. The Sequani are Gaulish Celts like ourselves but they speak a different dialect, one that they share with remnants of our race who have never left the Blue Mountains. I love the sound of it on Briga's lips; the exotic echo of an older time.

Many women are more beautiful, yet from the beginning Briga drew me like no other. I did not know the body but I recognized the spirit within. It spoke to me through her blue eyes, as clear as those of a child. Her spirit was a member of the tender network that surrounds me through all my lives. Each of us has such a network, stretching from the distant past into the far future, making us Part of the Whole.

Briga knows me better than I know myself. And loves me anyway.

The first time I lay with her I knew what the Source of All Being experienced at the moment of creation.

Because Celtic law allows a man of high rank to have more than one wife, the Romans called us savages. Yet who is the savage? A chieftain—or a druid—can offer the status and protection of marriage to as many women as he can support. I have traveled in the land of the Romans and seen how they live. The depraved men of Rome have only one wife at a time, but use any number of concubines and prostitutes. These poor creatures must suffer whatever indignities are heaped upon them. When their sexual attraction fades, they are discarded.

By purchasing Lakutu I had saved her from such a fate. When Vercingetorix and I came upon her, quite by accident, in a Roman slave market, she was already well-used goods. After another year or two the Romans would have had her cleaning out latrines. They would have thrown away a truly exceptional spirit.

All my women are exceptional.

While she was married to Vercingetorix, Onuava and I had worked powerful sex magic together. To assure her husband's election as commander-in-chief of the united armies of Gaul she had opened her body to mine. The power of the ancient ritual pleaded for Rix in the Otherworld and enabled him to fulfill his Pattern.

No other man in Gaul could have formed the Arverni, Bituriges, Ruteni, Nitiobriges, Gabali, Senones, Sequani, Parisii, and Carnutes into a confederacy to defeat Caesar. And he almost succeeded. That knowledge torments my dreams and miseries my days. With the splendid and shining Vercingetorix leading the united tribes of Free Gaul, we defied the despicable Caesar and his army of clanking dwarfs and very nearly won.

Clanking dwarfs. A perfect description that illustrates one of the differences between Celts and Romans. Our warriors were taller than the invaders by the length of a man's forearm. In battle they did not hinder their bodies with armor or imprison their heads in iron. Free and unencumbered, the warriors of Gaul faced whatever the day brought. They were celebrated for their courage, which resulted from the teaching of their druids.

No person who understands that an immortal spirit inhabits the mortal body need fear death.

In my youth Menua, our chief druid, who had been trained in the greatest of all druid schools, told me, "Dying means only a change of direction in a long life, Ainvar. Death is not the last thing but the least thing, a cobweb we brush through."

Death brings us back to the dawn of life so we may start afresh without the burden of memory. Examples of this may be observed in nature, where nothing is wasted. Living spirits, sparks of the Great Fire of Life, move from one existence to another as butterflies burst from the husks of dead caterpillars. The butterfly does not remember its life crawling on the ground. It knows only the freedom of the air.

The warped Romans do not study nature; only the works of men. This leads them to make the incredible assumption that when a human body ceases to breathe, life ceases to exist. What arrogance!

Vercingetorix and I sometimes spoke of these things, when the rest of the camp was asleep and we were lying on our backs staring up into the sky. Rix loved the night sky more than anyone I ever knew. Together we wandered the pathless stars and explored the womb of worlds.

Rix contained a warrior spirit, and warriors are not inclined to philosophy—the word the Greeks use to describe the speculations of druids. But he also possessed a degree of curiosity not often found in fighting men. Warriors need to follow orders without asking questions. Thinking is for druids. Thinking, and curiosity.

As a small child I had asked my grandmother, who was the wisest person I knew, "Why do we fall down and not up?"

"No one knows," she replied. "It's magic."

That was the first time I heard of magic.

When Rix asked questions I did my best to answer them, and prayed to That Which Watches that I might always give him good advice. For the most part, I did.

Except, except . . . Briga says I dwell too much on the past. Perhaps she is right, though I shall never tell her so. A man who has three wives learns what not to admit.

On the day we stepped off the edge of the world and into this boat, Briga laughed. The sound shocked me, I had not heard it for so long.

Not since Alesia.

Shortly after that disastrous defeat we had heard rumors that Caesar, not content with waging war for Gaul, also had sent his troops to the land of the Britons, wherever that was. I trembled for them.

While the wheel of the seasons turned and winters followed one another in grim succession, my small band of survivors fled into the trackless forest. During what the vile Caesar called "the pacification of Hairy Gaul," the Romans spent summer after summer scarring our homeland with roads and military fortifications. They did not find us, however. We had buried ourselves so deep in the wilderness we never heard a word of Latin. For us, everything beyond the forest ceased to exist. We knew nothing of Rome and Romans, but lived an inward life whose boundaries were the trees. Still, we did not feel safe. We were as quiet as birds pressing themselves against the earth as the hawk flies over. We never laughed aloud.

Our children lost their childhood while Rome was raping Gaul.

When the land was sufficiently "cleansed" of rebellious natives, settlers began to arrive. They started cutting down the great forest that sheltered us.

Then Keryth dreamed a dream in which she spoke with the handful of other druids who still survived. They were able to confirm her prophecy: Vercingetorix had been murdered in Rome. They told her every grisly detail which she then related, with great pain, to me.

Druids know the truth when they hear it.

As far as I was concerned it signaled the end of the world.

Yet now my Briga could laugh. She spread her arms wide as if she would embrace the sea, and laughed aloud with joy. "We will begin a new life, Ainvar!" My Briga crinkles her nose when she laughs.

The Celtic figure of the Two-Faced One possesses one set of features looking in one direction and another set looking the opposite way. It is open to many interpretations: life and death, summer and winter, nobility and debasement. If men look toward death, women look toward life. How wise was the Source to create such balance.

It is a pity the Source did not create boats. Boats are not natural, but manmade, so I have misgivings. It is difficult for me to accept that a vessel filled with people can float on top of the water. A stone weighing much less than a boat would sink immediately. Sometimes my head ponders on this.

We obtained these boats in the land of Armorica, from a trader who belonged to the tribe of the Veneti. They inhabit the westernmost shores and claim to know what lies beyond the sunset. I hope they do. Our future may depend on it.

Paying for the boats and crew took what little remained of our gold. The owner of the vessels demanded the last valuables we possessed, the jewelry of our women. We had no choice but to comply. Briga gave up her gold bracelets and an amber brooch set in silver, with a rueful smile. Behind her hand, she whispered to me, "I'm thankful he's not asking for my bowls."

Through all our troubles, my senior wife had managed to retain a collection of enameled copper bowls. They were cunningly made: nine altogether, the largest no bigger than a woman's skull, the smallest the size of an infant's fist. They nested one inside another so the entire set could be carried in a single pair of hands. Briga deemed them too precious for domestic purposes.

The household gods of the Romans were their *lares* and *penates.* Briga's were her enameled bowls.

When the time came for Lakutu to surrender her jewelry, she merely shrugged her shoulders. She who had once been a slave had never expected to possess fine ornaments anyway. The only hint of emotion was a glimmer of moisture in her eyes as she handed over the girdle I had given her on our wedding day. A wide band of fabric woven in the red-and-blue plaid signifying the tribe of the Carnutes, the belt was fastened by two interlocking Celtic knots finely wrought in silver and embellished with bosses of gold. It was a tradition in our tribe to give a new wife a girdle representing the connubial embrace. Lakutu had worn hers every day since we married.

Her son, Glas, saw the tears she tried to hide. "I'll make a new belt for you," he vowed. "An even better one."

Onuava made a show of being grievously injured. She proclaimed in a loud voice that as the widow of the king of the Gauls she was entitled to the perquisites of her former rank: her bracelets and ear rings and hair ornaments, her finger rings set with gemstones, and lastly but by no means least the massive gold torc once worn around the neck of Vercingetorix.

I would grieve for that torc as much as Onuava did. Fortunately my memories were beyond barter, safe in my head. All that we are and know is stored in the sacred head.

"Very well," I told Onuava, "keep your jewelry. But that will mean we'll either have to stay here or return to Gaul. No matter which we do, the Romans will find us sooner or later. They'll have no respect for your rank. They'll tear your gold from your body, enslave your children, and rape you to death."

So here we are.

On our way.

Once the Celts traveled long distances on horseback or in carts drawn by oxen. Now our little band must rely on wind and muscle. Four of our men have joined the Armoricans at the oars. They are Cormiac Ru, otherwise known as the Red Wolf; my brawny and reliable friend Grannus, who can fell the tallest tree in a single morning; Teyrnon the ironsmith, who stretches himself to the utmost to provide the basic tools of existence; and last but not least the Goban Saor, our bronzesmith, the greatest craftsman the Carnutes have ever produced. His amazing hands can turn raw ore into an elaborately ornamented shield, or free the figure of an ancient deity from a lump of common rock.

In some ways the talents of Teyrnon and the Goban Saor are the equal of mine. But they are not druids. Theirs are gifts of the arm, not of the head.

Including myself, our clan has four druids; five if one counts Briga. The others are Keryth the seer, Sulis the healer, and Dian Cet the judge. Briga, however, has never been initiated into the Order of the Wise. She has her reasons.

Keryth and Sulis are elderly women, though both still appear fresh and fair. Dian Cet was already an old man when I was a boy and looks almost the same now as he did then. Druids do not necessarily age at the same rate as other people. We are not exempt from time, but some of us can manipulate it to a limited extent. Time is fluid.

The Order of the Wise held the balance between the chieftains who ruled and the warriors who served. We were the calm center. Rank within the Order differed from one tribe to another. The chief druid was always paramount, but one tribe might bestow more honors on its bards, and another on its sacrificers. All branches of druidry were indispensable, however. Under normal circumstances members of the Order were never required to do physical labor.

Since the abhorrent Caesar's victory in Gaul, circumstances had been far from normal. During the years spent hiding in the forest we druids had done many things we never expected to do. We learned to perform all the menial chores necessary for survival. Everyone did them; even the children.

The children are the reason we have flung ourselves off the edge of the Earth. The children embody our tomorrows.

Briga has given me a wiry, clever son called Dara, who has survived nine winters by now. A year younger than he is a sturdy boy we named Eoin, who is followed by a cheerful, curious lad called Ongus, and last but by no means least a little girl we named Gobnat to please the Goban Saor. The great craftsman fashioned a dainty bracelet of gold set with carnelians for her birth gift. Briga had been willing to sacrifice her own treasures to pay the Armoricans, but she did not let them have Gobnat's bracelet. Instead she hid it in the secret recesses of her own body.

All four of our children have their mother's wide blue eyes and my jutting cheekbones and brown hair. Perhaps one of them has inherited a druid gift as well. That would be a great relief to me; to all of us.

Yet even then I shall never forget my firstborn daughter. My beautiful, stolen Maia, with her dark baby ringlets and her tiny crumpled ears.

Onuava has three sons. The oldest, whom she calls Labraid, meaning "the Speaker," was sired by Vercingetorix. Labraid is an argumentative boy of ten winters who could be mistaken for much older. Indeed, thinks himself every bit as much a man as Cormiac Ru, who is almost twice his age. This is the source of growing friction between them.

Onuava's other sons, Cairbre and Senta, are mine; quiet little lads who cause no trouble. Yet I am mindful they carry their mother's blood, too. They will bear watching in future.

Lakutu has a son and daughter. Glas of the nimble fingers was sired by my friend Tarvos the Bull, who taught the Egyptian to speak our language. After Tarvos was killed I married Lakutu, who subsequently bore me a daughter she calls Niav. It is, I believe, an Egyptian name. With her huge dark eyes and pretty ways, Niav enchants every male who sees her. Including me.

Although Labraid is a king's son, I predict it is Cormiac Ru who will one day take over leadership of our clan. The Red Wolf simply has a better head on him. Quiet, intense, and endlessly resourceful, he takes his name from his hair, which is the exact shade of burnished copper. His eyes are as colorless as clear water.

Water is sacred.

Cormiac was born to farmers who grew barley near the fort of the Carnutes. He was a fearless little boy who once told me that he wanted to be a champion when he grew up, and ride in a chariot. Unfortunately he was of common rank, not of the noble class. Worse still, the child had been born blind. No one expected him to survive to adulthood.

When Briga came to us from the Sequani tribe she had wept with pity over the little fellow. Some of her tears fell onto his eyes.

Within a few days he could see.

Since then Cormiac has been Briga's shadow, closer to her than the children of her body. Long ago his voice changed from a childish treble to one so deep and resonant I would recognize it among thousands. The Red Wolf is now as tall as I am and has an exceptional gift for the sword. He need only touch a weapon to have it leap into his hand, ready to serve his bidding. I would not want him as an enemy.

Cormiac respects me because I am Briga's husband. My membership in the Order of the Wise does not impress him. I am impressed by Cormiac, however; by the proud unyielding core of him. Vercingetorix had that, too. Nobility is not in the blood, but in the spirit.

The Greeks describe the Celts, or Keltoi, as they call us, as one of the four peripheral nations of the known world, the others being the Scythians, the Indians, and the Ethiopians. The Scythians, who were nomads from the steppes, penetrated the heavily forested territory of the Celts at some time in antiquity and introduced our ancestors to the ridden horse. This new mobility enabled the Celts to explode outward from their homeland. Travelers tell of having encountered Celts as far east as the plains of Anatolia and as far south as the mountains of Iberia.

Celtic tribes may appear to differ greatly from one another, yet they share a similar culture and possess common characteristics. Celts tend to be poetic and lyrical, volatile and reckless, boastful, generous, impulsive, high-spirited, bellicose, and courageous. All of those qualities were found in Vercingetorix. When I look at his son, Labraid, I wonder how much of the father is in the boy.

A child is both a riddle and an answer.

Late at night in the forests of Gaul, when the fires burned low and memory seized my throat with both hands and threatened to choke me, I needed to talk about Maia. My stolen child. She was Briga's child too, but for me no pain was comparable to my own. So I could not reminisce about Maia with Briga.

I talked to Cormiac instead.

He listened in silence, the Red Wolf with his intense face.

Cormiac had not yet enjoyed a woman. Since he became a man we had lived a solitary existence. We even avoided the remnants of other tribes for fear of paid informers. The Romans had corrupted our people and taught them to betray one another.

If someone is willing to buy, someone else is always willing to sell.

I might have asked Sulis to initiate Cormiac in the mating mysteries as she once did me, but since she married Grannus she had accepted no other partners. Cormiac, although tall and muscular, a fully adult male in every sense of the word, was still waiting for that singular moment that teaches a man why there are two sexes.

Meanwhile, the waters ran deep behind his colorless eyes.

Cormiac remembered Maia as well as I did. Furthermore, he had conceived the notion that she was his destined wife, her spirit the sundered half of his own. He once confided to me that someday he would find her and bring her back. In spite of its impossibility, Cormiac's dream gave me comfort.

How fragile is hope! Yet it can withstand the cruel cudgels of circumstance.

## *chapter* II

WHILE THE CARNUTES WERE STILL AMONG THE FOREMOST TRIBES of Gaul we often traded with the Armoricans. They roved far and had seen much. After a hard day's bargaining they sat with us around the fire and related their adventures. Many of these were the sort of stories men tell when they have had too much to drink. I paid little attention to them; our own bards told better tales. Occasionally, however, the traders spoke of a nameless island somewhere to the west. They described it as being rich in everything a person could possibly want; a place of astounding beauty and mysterious happenstance.

We listened with fascination, we who never left dry land.

Greek travelers passing through Gaul also had mentioned the existence of some island far out in the Great Cold Sea. This gave a certain credibility to the tales of the Armoricans.

Then came Caesar—may he die roaring and his progeny wither on the stem like fruit that will not ripen.

During the years when we were hiding in the forest the mothers had made up simple little stories to entertain their children. One of their favorites involved a fabled island in the far west. The women embroidered the tale to suit themselves, endowing it with their most wistful dreams. "The trees are weighed down with sweet apples," they told their little ones. "Gold glitters in the streams and no one ever grows old."

My ears had heard this story a number of times before my head finally paid sufficient attention.

One morning, in a sunny clearing where wild berries grew, I took off my hooded cloak to use to carry the soft fruits back to my clan. I lingered longer than necessary, enjoying the heat of the Great Fire on the dome of my forehead.

And an idea came to me.

If the far-traveled Greeks said the wondrous islands existed, they must. The Hellenes had described them as lying at the very rim of the world, where the sun sets. Surely even the Romans had not journeyed to the ends of the Earth.

*We* could escape to the sunset islands!

From the perspective of a tranquil clearing sheltered by a palisade of pines, it seemed like a wonderful idea. By the time I explained the plan to the others, however, my enthusiasm had begun to wane. My confidence was not what it used to be.

But Briga had strengthened my spine. Clapping her hands together like a child, she cried, "Oh yes, Ainvar! Let's go!"

My Briga is an irresistible force.

Keryth had studied the auguries, consulted the wind and the stars, read the entrails of birds and the spatter of sacrificial blood. All of these agreed with my senior wife. We should undertake a journey to the edge of the Great Cold Sea—and beyond.

So began our journey of exile. We, the dispossessed.

Making our way to Armorica had been difficult; we traveled on foot and mostly by night, hugging the shadows, avoiding any area where we might encounter Romans—or Roman sympathizers. Like ants, they were everywhere. It took a brave man to stand up to the conquerors, and the brave men were dead.

When we reached Armorica our first task had been to obtain boats. There were several Armorican tribes, including the Osismi and two or three branches of the far-flung Belgae, but we sought the Veneti. They, I recalled, had a reputation for building and sailing everything from multi-oared traders to inshore fishing boats.

In their territory we had found an assortment of seagoing vessels drawn up on the beaches. Trying to look as if I were knowledgeable about such things, I concluded that two of the smaller trading boats would serve our purpose. Two would be better than one. If half of us were lost at sea at least the other half might survive.

The Veneti were understandably reluctant to rent their boats to strangers. After being repeatedly rebuffed, I finally came upon a trader called Goulvan who owned two vessels in rather poor repair. He was an unprepossessing fellow; his eyes were too close together and his teeth too far apart. His pores exuded the smell of fish. I was careful to stand upwind while talking with him.

When I asked if we might hire his boats, Goulvan's eyes lit with avarice. "Can you pay? In advance?"

"We can pay," I assured him. "If you can supply us with a crew, that is. We have no knowledge of boats ourselves, we are inlanders."

I explained our predicament by telling Goulvan, "Since the conquest of Gaul my clan has been hiding in the forests, but now settlers from Latium have cut down so much timber our sanctuary is disappearing. We have no choice but to migrate."

"Don't look to me for sympathy, we've had our own troubles," Goulvan retorted. "At about the same time as they invaded Gaul, the Romans attacked Armorica. At first we submitted, but when we realized they wanted control of the tin route, we rebelled. The tin trade was our most valuable asset and we were not willing to give it up. We applied to Albion, the source of the tin, for aid, and received help from a branch of the Belgae. They sent several boatloads of warriors to us but in the end we were defeated anyway. Many of my tribe fled. Those of us who remain eke out a precarious living, as you see." Goulvan extended his empty hands palm upward and arranged his features in the woeful expression of a destitute man.

I thought it best not to tell Goulvan that I had been chief druid of the Carnutes and advisor to Vercingetorix. A crafty spirit peered through the trader's eyes. If he believed I was a person of importance Goulvan might turn me over to the Romans in hopes of a reward. He was already suspicious because we were prepared to pay for boats and crew, but I explained this by intimating we had robbed the dead on the field of battle.

The trader believed me. One tribe is always willing to believe the worst of another.

"I can provide six crewmen for each boat, including myself," Goulvan finally announced.

"Twelve men to transport twenty passengers? Do we really need that many? How much is it going to cost us?"

Goulvan was not stupid; he realized that our funds were limited. Given the condition of his boats he was in the same position. He needed us; we needed him. It is the best situation for conducting negotiations.

"If some of your party can handle the oars you can cut your costs a little," Goulvan told me. "Not much, mind you. But a little."

So it was agreed. And our women gave up their jewelry.

When I questioned Goulvan about the sunset island he claimed to be well familiar with the place, and further informed me it was inhabited by Celtic tribes similar to those of Gaul.

"Are there no Romans, then?"

"Not a one," Goulvan asserted.

"Will the natives resent us?"

"They're quite prosperous, they have more than they need. A score of new people will make no difference to them. Aside from the welcome sight of some new women," Goulvan added with a leer in the direction of my wives.

Briga rewarded him with a look that would have frozen fire. "If the men are like you, I would rather eat dung with both hands than have anything to do with them."

"My senior wife is only making a joke," I said placatingly. "Or perhaps you don't understand our sense of humor?"

His eyebrows drew together like two bulls rushing to butt heads. "That didn't sound like a joke to me."

"It was, I assure you. Before Briga and I were married she said dreadful things about me, it was her way of hiding her true feelings."

Goulvan looked at Briga with renewed interest. "Is that a fact? I like a spirited woman."

My senior wife scowled at me. "Ainvar," she said in the low, deadly voice a husband learns to recognize. Her intonation told me that I would not be warming myself with her body that night.

IN THE NORMAL COURSE OF EVENTS, A MAN WITH THREE WIVES COULD seek comfort from one of the others. Unfortunately that option was not open to me. Sometimes I actually suspected—with no proof at all—that my three wives were in a gleeful conspiracy against me.

From the beginning Briga had undertaken to make allies of the other two. Because she and Lakutu shared an interest in herbalism she had led the Egyptian from one patch of weed to another. My eyes had observed my second wife solemnly nodding as Briga explained how chewing this green leaf could relieve toothache, or a paste made from those stems could be smeared on the lids of clouded eyes to improve sight. The exchange of information was not all one way, however. Briga once informed me that among Lakutu's people strange spices were used to preserve the bodies of the dead for all eternity.

How she learned this, when I could get almost no information about Egypt from Lakutu, I shall never know.

Briga had established a bond with Onuava through their shared nobility. Soon Rix's widow thought of Briga as a sister, while I was merely the husband. Whenever a dispute arose between myself and either of them, the pair looked down their noble noses at me in unison.

My three wives presented me with a united front in all domestic matters. It was enough to make me consider taking a fourth wife and keeping her well away from the others. But the only other adult females in our band were Keryth the seer, who had lost her husband and children in the war with the Romans and vowed she would never marry again; Sulis the healer, who was the sister of the Goban Saor and married to Grannus; and Damona, the only wife of Teyrnon.

While one may sleep with another man's wife if both parties agree, one cannot marry another man's wife if he is still able to protect her himself. Besides, we had seen too much of war already. I did not want to have one of my few remaining friends come after me with his knife in his hand.

Arrangements in the boats were determined by kinship. With Goulvan in the lead vessel was my family, consisting of myself, my wives, and their children. Except for the son of Vercingetorix. As a show of independence Labraid demanded to go in the second boat. Although he could not yet be counted as a man, he was big and burly and increasingly felt a need to prove himself.

He and Cormiac had begun eyeing each other in the way of hounds with raised hackles.

Goulvan told me our voyage would follow the route of migrating birds. "It's a good omen, Ainvar. Immense flocks set off from these shores to enjoy the fruits of Albion."

"Albion?"

"Your destination," he said firmly. "No doubt about it; Albion's the place for you. Wonderful climate, hospitable people, and the entire island is fertile. In one summer your clan will be fat."

The trader claimed to be on excellent terms with the tribes in the south of Albion, where we would go ashore. "Everyone who matters knows me," he boasted, sucking the stumps of his rotten teeth. "The great chieftains of the Catuvellauni, the Dumnonii, the Atrebates—they're all personal friends of mine."

My head warned me that he was lying; great chieftains would not bother with someone like Goulvan. I chose to ignore my head's wise counsel. We had been driven to the edge of the Earth and must jump off, even if we died for it.

Death is of little consequence. However, Celts have a visceral aversion to rigidity. Because the natural world is full of movement, the curve and the spiral are beautiful to us. Romans, on the other hand, are addicted to straight lines. The squares and boxes they construct imprison free-flowing spirit. Even a day spent in a Roman cell would cripple our children.

Vercingetorix had been imprisoned in Rome; left to slowly starve in a cramped cell, he whose roof had been the stars. He whom duplicitous Caesar had promised to treat as befitted an honorable opponent. In the end, Rix had been dragged through the streets in a final act of humiliation and publicly strangled.

For this alone my spirit would hunt that of Gaius Julius Caesar down all the roads of Time.

BOATS ON THE OPEN SEA HAVE A NASTY EFFECT ON THE BELLY. THE only person who did not vomit over the side at least once was Labraid. When the two boats were close enough together to make conversation between them possible, Labraid called to his mother, "I think I was born for the sea. From now on you can call me Labraid Loingseach; the Speaker Who Sails the Seas."

Youngsters are not given the privilege of naming themselves arbitrarily. I caught Onuava's eyes with a question in mine. She shrugged one shoulder to indicate she had no objection.

"Labraid Loingseach," I repeated, validating the new name. "Don't get too used to the title, though. We're not going to do this again."

The boy grinned and tossed his head exactly the way Rix used to do. "I might," he said. He began pestering Grannus to be allowed to take a turn with the oars.

Unfortunately Ainvar the druid did not have a warrior's belly. Members of the Order of the Wise pride themselves on their dignity, but mine came pouring out of me in ugly gobbets that floated on the surface of the waves as if to taunt me. When I tried to read the omens in them, they capriciously dissolved.

At sunset the Armoricans took down the heavy sails and let us drift with a current which, they swore, was going in the right direction. Some of my people slept, but I could not. I lay awake with my head pillowed on Briga's warm belly and gazed up at the stars. They had changed, those stars. Their configuration was not quite the one I knew.

Would their changed Pattern change ours?

When the sun rose, the sails were raised also and we continued our journey. There was no land to be seen in any direction. Even the seabirds that frequent the coast had deserted us. Yet on we went, until a misty headland rose before us. "Albion!" Goulvan announced happily.

The relief I felt was short-lived. Even as we were bumping through the pebbled shallows, I spied a settlement on a promontory. A square, sturdy, fortified settlement built in a style I recognized.

I rounded on Goulvan in a fury. "There *are* Romans here!"

He tried to look surprised. "Are there?"

"You know there are! What place is this again?"

"Why, Albion. I told you."

"By some terrible chance could Albion also be known as the land of the Britons?"

"I believe it is," the scoundrel conceded.

"Which means the Romans are here before us, you wretched pustule! What was your plan, Goulvan—to sell us to them like bags of wheat?"

The trader held out gnarled hands. "By the wind and the waves, I swear—"

"Swear nothing. Your words are brass posing as gold." I turned toward the second boat, which was following close behind us. "I need a sword!" I cried. We all carried personal knives but I wanted something more intimidating that could be clearly seen by the crews in both boats.

Although his beard had not begun to grow, young Labraid's body housed a fully fledged warrior spirit. His proudest possession was a shortsword modeled on the Roman gladus. Labraid had coaxed and bullied Teyrnon into forging the weapon for him shortly before we left Gaul.

In response to my cry Onuava's son drew his sword from its sheath. Holding it by the leather-covered grip, he brandished it in the air. "Here, Ainvar! Catch!"

"No!" I shouted. If either boat rolled at the wrong moment, a useful weapon would be lost to the sea.

I need not have worried.

While Labraid was waving his sword around, Cormiac Ru assessed the situation accurately and sprang from his boat to ours in one tremendous leap. He landed in a crouch at my feet. Straightening up, he drew his sword from its bronze-and-leather sheath. My father had carried that sword. Made in the ancient Gaulish design, longer and heavier than a shortsword, the weapon had fought in many battles. The iron blade was permanently discolored by old bloodstains.

On his fifteenth birthday, the age when Celtic boys traditionally took up arms and were counted as men, I had given my father's sword to the Red Wolf.

Now he offered it to me.

"It's still yours," I told him. "Show Goulvan how sharp your blade is."

The sword sprang forward to press against the trader's neck, delicately slicing the flesh until a thin red line appeared. A necklace of tiny ruby drops on a windburned throat.

Goulvan rolled his eyes like a panicked horse.

I asked him, "Is this the only island?"

"There's one farther west of here," he stammered, "but not nearly as big as Albion. And you wouldn't want to—"

"Have your men row away from the shore as fast as they can," I demanded, "and order your crew in the other boat to follow us."

"Where shall we go?" His voice was a hoarse croak.

"Toward the sunset."

"No!" Goulvan cried.

The very fact that he did not want to go in that direction was enough for me. "Yes!" I roared with all the power in my lungs. "We go west! What is the name of the next landfall?"

Goulvan muttered under his breath.

"What? I can't hear you."

"I said 'Hibernia.' If we're lucky. Or unlucky," he added cryptically.

By this time I had no faith in Goulvan's word. Perhaps there was no other island. Or if Hibernia existed, perhaps it too had been seized by the Romans. In that case I would force the crews to row on and on until we were swallowed by the endless sea, which might not be the worst fate for us.

At least we would be free.

Accepting the inevitable, I sat back down in the boat and surveyed the heaving sea with something akin to complacency.

The Armorican crewmen were not so sanguine. They dug their oars into the water so violently I feared we would overturn while they jabbered of boiling seas and monsters as big as mountains.

Onuava soon lost her temper. Onuava in a rage was like a huge male swan protecting his brood: terrifying and gorgeous. More the former than the latter, however. "You're frightening the children," she shouted at the crewmen, "and I won't have it! If you won't take us any farther I'll personally throw the lot of you over the side. We can row the rest of the way ourselves."

The Armoricans shuddered at the threat. Like most seamen, none of our crew could swim.

# *chapter* III

WHILE WE BATTLED HIGH WAVES AND ROUGH WEATHER, DAY DIED and was born anew. The color of the sea changed from sullen gray to a blue so dark it was like a well of night. The height of the waves lessened but my stomach was not mollified. There was nothing on, under, or above the earth that I wanted as much as I wanted to set my feet on dry land. Nothing except the knowledge that my children were beyond the reach of the insatiable brute called Caesar.

If only I could go to the Great Grove of the Carnutes; if only I could once again be alone in the sacred silence with That Which Watches! By drawing on the wisdom of the oaks my head would become wise again. Sadly, all that remained of the Great Grove were charred stumps. The affliction called Caesar had burned the ancient trees and sown the earth with salt.

The Romans, who are unwilling, or unable, to understand any society other than their own, described the druids as ignorant savages who worshipped trees. A Roman simplification for simple minds.

Trees are a visible representation of the sacred forces of wind and water and sun. Their shapes conform to the wind that swirls around them; their roots drink from the breast of Mother Earth; their arms are lifted in supplication to the Great Fire of Life. Therefore we worship *among* trees and *with* trees. Our reverence, like that of the trees themselves, is directed toward the Source of All Being.

The Source has many faces, each a living embodiment of its power. Sun and moon and fire and water are sacred to us as aspects of the Source. When we offer appropriate sacrifices to them the Source sees. And knows.

That Which Watches.

The Romans, on the other hand, adore statues. It is not the marble they worship, however, but human images hacked out of the stone. They bow down before gods and goddesses they have made for themselves—and can unmake just as easily.

Slumping down in the boat, I pulled up my hood and retired to the world inside my head. My imagination created a tree-covered island set like a jewel in the sea. A place where no one ever grew weary in his spirit. Druid magic, as strong as it ever had been, lay like stardust across the hills.

Time passed while I drowsed and dreamed. The sea heaved around us but I was secure on my island. There are times when the contents of our heads are all we have.

"Ainvar!" cried Briga from some great distance. "*Do* open your eyes and look!"

She sounded exasperated. I must have been asleep for a long time. Rubbing my eyes, I sat up and followed her pointing finger.

A band of richest green lay on the horizon. Never in my life had I seen such an intense color. I thought it was part of my dream until Goulvan said, "There it is, that's Hibernia."

In the language of Latium, my head reminded me, *hibernus* meant "wintry." Suddenly I was wide-awake. "The Romans named this place," I cried, "so they've been here after all! Cormiac, acquaint this man with your blade again and make him tell us the truth."

Druids may not always recognize lies, but they know the truth when they hear it.

Cold iron is persuasive. With the edge of Cormiac's sword pressing against his throat, Goulvan revised his story. "The Romans may have known about this land for, ah, quite some time. They purchase native goldwork and pay high prices for certain giant hounds that are bred here, the largest dogs in the world."

"Go on," I ordered through clenched teeth. "There's more to this than trade. How did the island come by its name?"

"A Roman expeditionary party came here a few years ago seeking a site for a garrison. They sailed from Albion in late autumn, or so I was told, and made landfall in terrible weather. Howling gales and icy rain. The Romans hated the island on sight. Albion was cold and wet; they weren't looking for more of the same."

"Cold and wet," I repeated. "Yet you described Albion to us as a paradise."

Goulvan rolled his eyes. "You have to expect a trader to exaggerate a little! Anyway, the small party of Romans ran into a large tribe of belligerent natives who called themselves the Iverni. To Roman ears this sounded like 'Hiberni.' The coincidence suited the scouts perfectly. They hurried back to Albion to report that the island to the west was called 'Hibernia' because winter lasted all year. They claimed the island would not support a garrison.

"The Roman commander, whose supply lines were stretched to the utmost already, was willing to take their word for it. So this island was spared invasion. There are no Romans here, Ainvar. I swear it."

Perhaps not. But we Gauls were.

Unlike the Roman expeditionary party, we reached Hibernia in late spring on a day of dazzling sunshine. As we drew near the shore, my eyes informed me that even Gaul had nothing to surpass the verdant luxuriance of the land the Romans had rejected. A warm, fragrant breeze blew toward us. It smelled . . . green.

I made my way rather gingerly to the prow of the boat and raised my arms in thanksgiving to That Which Watches.

"The Source *is,*" I chanted. "We *are.*" And my people chanted after me, "The Source *is.* We *are.*"

We made landfall on a beach as white as salt. There was no sign of life apart from the seabirds who still hovered around us, hoping for scraps of the fish we had caught earlier in the day.

Yet our crew was visibly nervous.

As head of my clan I was the first out of the boat. With some trepidation I stepped into thigh-deep water, and felt the foam of the surf curl around my legs. A few steps took me to dry land.

I was the first of the Carnutes to set foot on Hibernia.

The moment my foot touched down something inexplicable happened. It felt as if I had come home.

Treason! cried my head. Free Gaul is home. This is only a place of exile.

I stopped and looked back at Briga, who was leaning over the edge of the boat. "What are you waiting for, Ainvar? Go on!" she urged. She vaulted over the side as sprightly as a young girl and came splashing after me.

Both boats were drawn onto the sand above the tide level. The children began to race up and down the beach. Freedom went to their heads like wine. Hibernia rang with their happy voices and I remembered something I had almost forgotten. Once, we were a people who sang.

I nodded to Cormiac Ru, indicating that he—and his sword—were to stand close by me while I further interrogated Goulvan. "Tell me more about these natives you mentioned. You say they call themselves the Iverni?"

"Some of them do."

"Are there other tribes, then?"

Goulvan dug into the sand with his toe. "Other tribes with other names," he admitted reluctantly. Beneath his perpetual windburn he had grown very pale.

I know a frightened man when I see one. He had described the Iverni as well armed; were they also hostile?

"Are the Iverni members of the Celtic race?" I inquired.

"They must be," said Goulvan. "They had rather fight than eat. They're all like that on this island. They attack one another day after day, year after year, for any reason or none. These people are quite mad."

I, who had been born into the warrior aristocracy, was amused. "Men who fight for pleasure terrify you, do they?"

The contempt in my voice stiffened his spine. "Of course not. I just don't like this place. I find the natives too difficult to deal with. They can turn against you between one breath and the next and you never know why. Honor means more to these people than life. They're not afraid to die but they're terrified of being humiliated. One other odd thing about them: Any foreigner who lies to them is slain without hesitation."

I smiled to myself. No wonder Goulvan disliked Hibernia. A trader who dare not lie would be at a serious disadvantage. "Slain how?"

"Decapitated. They mount his head on top of a pole."

"The Celts have taken heads since before the before," I commented. "Of course, the heads didn't belong to liars. They were trophies of war taken from the most valiant as an expression of admiration. In the lifetime of my father's father we abandoned the practice, however."

Goulvan looked over his shoulder apprehensively. "I'm afraid that change of custom hasn't reached here."

Following his glance, my eyes reported nothing more ominous than a fox far down the beach. The animal emerged from a clump of salt grass, saw us, and vanished again.

I was surprised to be able to see such a small creature so far away. While we were in the boats the constant wind and the fierce glare off the water had strained my eyes. They itched and burned so badly I had to keep them closed most of the time. I had even begun to fear my vision was permanently impaired.

The light in Hibernia was singularly limpid. Soft and luminous yet amazingly clear, it bathed a landscape dominated by the color green. An omnipresence of green, a hundred different shades of green that soothed my scalded eyes.

They feasted on the vista before us.

The salt grass was the silvery hem of a mantle of meadowland thickly embroidered with wildflowers. In places the verdant expanse was interrupted by masses of golden-blossomed furze and billows of purple heather. Beyond the meadow a succession of low hills rolled in waves toward a wall of forest.

Trees! my spirit exulted.

A land with such broad meadows and vast forests would richly support a great number of people. So why would the natives need to fight? Upon reflection, my head concluded that the Armoricans, like the Romans, did not understand foreign customs. What they mistook for warfare was likely to be a form of sport. Celtic sports could be exceedingly rough, as befits a warrior race.

Goulvan might be reluctant to leave the beach, but I must. And I wanted Dian Cet with me; his snowy beard would assure respect if the natives really were Celtic. I told him, "We have to come to an amicable arrangement with the Hibernians, because we're in no position to fight them. You and I are going to take Cormiac Ru as an escort and go in search of the nearest local chieftain. We'll try to bargain with him for enough land to settle on."

"Bargain with what, Ainvar? You gave the last gold we had to those thieves." Dian Cet, who was old enough to have dispensed with diplomacy, indicated the Armoricans with a gesture of his thumb, the finger of insult.

Tapping my head with my forefinger, I reminded Dian Cet, "Our greatest treasure is here. We have four members of the Order of the Wise, with abilities worth more than gold."

Once my words would have been true. But no longer; at least not about myself. Not since Alesia.

Among the possessions we had carried with us to that fateful siege was a bodiless stone head as high as a man's thigh. The image—a representation of the Two-Faced One—consisted of two huge faces looking in opposite directions. One set of features was placid, icily remote. The other was sly and cruel. The avatar, which was mounted on a wheeled platform for ease of transport, had been carved by the Goban Saor. His talent had found within the stone a fearsome quiddity. To gaze upon it was to feel the cold breath of the Otherworld.

Fear is a tool of magic.

After Vercingetorix was captured I had made a desperate effort to save a remnant of my people. Placing my hand on the surface of the stone image, I had concentrated all the formidable force of an exceptionally gifted chief druid.

No mortal can make the unliving live. Yet I did, at Alesia.

An incredible heat had exploded within me, raced down my arm, and poured from my fingertips. I made myself stand firm. Long ago, Menua had taught me the defining tenet of true druidry: *You will enter the fire but never feel the flame.*

I stood transfixed in a bubble of scalding light. I did not dare look at the carved figure, though it was changing beneath my hand. Even as Caesar's Germanic allies were bearing down on us, intent on slaughtering every Gaul in their path, I felt mottled gray stone turn to scabrous flesh. Fevered, pulsating; loathsome to the touch.

As soon as they got a good look at the Two-Faced One, panic seized the Germans. They fled in all directions, trampling one another in their desperation to escape. I had never heard such howls as they uttered. Their mad screaming surely tore their throats apart.

The Germans sped away.

And I collapsed. Fortunately the Goban Saor caught me as I fell. Over his shoulder I had one glimpse of the horror I had brought to life.

Squatting on its wooden platform, the figure loomed as large as a man. Four baleful eyes rolled wildly; two sets of nostrils snorted fire; two pairs of lips writhed over gnashing teeth while a guttural gibbering polluted the air. The monstrosity belonged in no sane world. Yet for a brief time it was blazingly, undeniably *alive.* Even death will not extinguish that memory. I fear I shall revisit it in nightmare through many lives to come.

Later we buried the awful figure in a deep hole and raised a cairn of boulders over it. By that time the image of the Two-Faced One was merely stone again. Perhaps. I thought, briefly, of saying a prayer of thanksgiving beside the cairn and rejected the idea. The terror the thing engendered had enabled a few of my clan to escape, but at a terrible cost.

My druidic gift had been spent in its entirety.

Not the least of my wounds was the one to my pride. I, chief druid of the Carnutes, had been able to materially alter the form and function of objects through a deliberate act of will. That ability had set me apart from all my people.

Its loss left me a sadly diminished man.

I had said nothing about my personal tragedy to anyone. Yet Briga knew. The first time she touched me after Alesia, she realized the power that once flowed through me was gone. Like the force used by a fragile shoot to escape the hard acorn, such power is only given once. I could never summon it again. But Briga, my wise and loving Briga, had touched me anyway. She mercifully reawakened my sexual desire so I could lose myself in her flesh long enough to forget.

As her reward I had brought her to the end of the world.

Goulvan's fears I could discount, but had Briga been apprehensive I would have ordered my people back into the boats immediately. Instead, my senior wife stripped off her sandals so she could run barefoot with the children.

Briga, my Briga. Whatever else we may find in Hibernia, we have brought life with us.

When I told her what I intended to do next, she approved. "It's much more sensible to bargain for land than to try to seize any, Ainvar. We're not Romans after all. We'll wait for you right here, and spend the time looking for food and firewood."

"Don't let the Armoricans leave until I return," I warned. "If anything happens and we don't come back, wait for only one night, then have them take you somewhere else."

"Where?" Briga had a talent for asking difficult questions.

Druids answer only those questions they choose to answer. I gently touched her cheek with the back of my fingers. Flesh can speak for itself.

She reached up to me in response, pushing back my hood so she could see my face clearly. Her smile sent small wrinkles fanning out from the corners of her eyes. "When you return I'd better shave you, Ainvar. Your tonsure's growing out." Her fingers danced across my forehead. "Fuzzy dome," she said fondly.

The druid's tonsure kept the front of the head bared to the Great Fire of Life. When, I wondered, had I stopped maintaining mine? Trust a wife to notice.

Young Labraid resented being left behind. He stomped around in a bad temper, making a nuisance of himself. "If you're taking Cormiac you have to take me, Ainvar," he insisted. "I have a sword, too."

"That's why I need you to stay here. We only have two young men with warrior spirits. I'm relying on you to protect our people until I get back." To mollify him I added, "It's the most important task you could perform, Labraid."

The boy grinned and puffed out his chest exactly as Vercingetorix used to do.

It would be extremely foolhardy to entrust the security of my people to a mere child. The arrangement was, however, safer than taking Labraid with us. His brashness could be a liability in dealing with an unfamiliar tribe.

Besides, the real responsibility for keeping the clan safe would fall on the broad shoulders of Grannus, as well as Teyrnon and the Goban Saor. Maturity is the most dependable asset.

Our exploratory party set out at once. Menua had instructed me in the languages of Athens and Latium, taught me to write using Greek letters, as many druids could, and also taught me ogham, the druidic method of leaving simple messages by carving esoteric marks on trees or stones. By this method I left signs announcing that Ainvar had passed this way. If anything untoward happened and the rest of my clan disobeyed my injunction and came after us, the ogham would guide them. Keryth could read it as well as I.

After we had gone some little distance, Dian Cet said, "Are you sure this is a good idea, Ainvar?"

"I don't see that we have any option. Besides, I trust Briga's instincts. She would have discouraged me if it were a mistake."

"I'm surprised you take counsel from your senior wife on such a matter. I never listened to any of mine."

"If you had," I commented drily, "there might have been more harmony in your lodge. I recall you suffering from dreadful stomach pains."

"Oh, Sulis cured me of those long ago."

"Did she?" I could not resist a wry smile. "And was the treatment medicinal, or tactile?"

"A man at war with his wife is entitled to seek relief where he can find it," Dian Cet said with a sniff. He was prickly on the subject of women. Although a gifted arbiter in his druidic capacity, he was inept when it came to himself. Only one of his wives had died in childbirth. Four others during his long lifetime had left him.

We do not own our women. Celts are free persons.

As we walked, Dian Cet's question set me to speculating on our bargaining position. If druidic ability was our only wealth, our purse was far too light. Avaricious Caesar had impoverished us. Among the four surviving members of the Order of the Wise there was no student of the sky to interpret the patterns of the stars and align human effort accordingly; no tribal historian capable of memorizing a hundred generations to assure the inheritance of rank and property; no sacrificer to provide the most certain means of interceding with the Otherworld. No bardic poet to celebrate the past and record the present.

As for the few druids we did possess, what value would they have here? Dian Cet was thoroughly familiar with the laws of Gaul, but what laws pertained in Hibernia and how long would he need to learn them? Keryth had been chief of the vates, or prognosticators, whose gift was the ability to dream reality even if the occurrence itself was taking place at a great distance. But foretelling was not immediately impressive. One never knew the accuracy of it until later.

Sulis was an experienced healer, though not as extraordinarily gifted as my own Briga, and healers were always needed. But a large part of healing depends on trust. Unless the natives were willing to entrust their care to strangers, neither woman would have the opportunity to prove her worth.

In order to create the impression we needed it might be necessary to demonstrate powerful magic. The highest order of druid magic was the skillful manipulation of natural forces. This was the singular and defining gift of a chief druid. Like Ainvar of the Carnutes.

The true adept knows that magic does not work every time. Infallibility is a sure sign of fakery. I would never attempt to fake magic—yet I was painfully aware that I could not rely on my own abilities. Not after Alesia. I had been used up to the very last drop at Alesia.

I trudged on, anticipating disaster.

Independent of my somber mood, my eyes and ears and nose made the usual reports to my head. Hibernia was beautiful in every aspect. The clear, glimmering light fell on rounded hills like the breasts of women; on meadowlands rapturous with birdsong; on sparkling streams that tumbled over water-polished rocks into fern-fringed pools of incredible clarity.

The earth hummed. Actually hummed. The sound was too low for my ears to hear, but the vibrations came up through the well-worn leather of my shoes and entered my bones. The brown soil exhaled a fecund aroma that unexpectedly stirred my lust.

I thought of my wives.

As we drew near the forest my eyes were gratified by the sight of alder and willow and oak. Especially oak. The word *drui* means "oak." To be druid is to be a child of the oak, gifted with wisdom, long life, and the ability to create awe.

Once I was druid. Mine was the vast dark sky and the spaces between the stars; mine was the promise of magic.

No longer. No longer. That knowledge was like lead in my belly.

How good it felt to be among trees again! This was not the Great Grove of the Carnutes, but a vast assemblage of living spirits, just the same. The green shade was like a refreshing bath of cool water. The ground beneath the trees was carpeted with bluebells. Our footfalls were cushioned by moss in the shape of stars. I imagined myself laying Briga down upon the moss and . . .

"Wolf," said Cormiac Ru.

"Where?"

"Just there." He pointed toward empty space. "Gone now, but definitely a big wolf. Maybe two."

"Wolf fur makes a fine cloak," Dian Cet remarked.

Farther on we surprised a herd of enormous red deer resting in a glade filled with bracken. They bolted at our approach, but not before we saw that they were sleek and fat. "Hibernia is generous to her children," I remarked.

Dian Cet said, "Let us hope she'll be half as good to us."

We continued to travel through the forest until Cormiac Ru halted abruptly. "I smell smoke."

We sniffed the air. The day was cool and bright with no hint of Taranis the thunder god, whose white-hot javelins ignite the trees to create a new nursery for seedlings. The fire we smelled was man-made.

"The smoke's coming from that direction," said Dian Cet, pointing. "I can see light between the trees."

We had found them, whoever they were. Our future.

We walked out of the forest three abreast. Three is the number of fate.

# *chapter* IV

BESIDE A REED-FRINGED LAKE WAS A SETTLEMENT CONSISTING of five or six round lodges with thatched roofs. Instead of solid timber logs the Hibernian lodges were made of woven hazel rods, like the temporary shelters we had thrown together as we fled from the advancing Romans. A barrier of branches had been erected to protect the compound from trampling by some small black cattle grazing nearby. But there was a yawning gap in the fence.

An open gate is an invitation.

Three abreast, my companions and I walked forward. I threw back the hood of my cloak to reveal my deliberately serene features. We must appear as men with legitimate business, not troublemakers.

An iron-headed spear thudded into the earth at my feet.

"Don't," I hissed to Cormiac Ru before he could draw his sword. Raising my voice, I called in the traditional way, "We salute you as free persons!" My dialect was that of the Carnutes, but I trusted my words would be understood here. If these people really were Celts.

A second spear whistled through the air and lodged itself snugly against the first. Whoever he was, he had an accurate arm.

Dian Cet said, "We must retreat, Ainvar."

"We can't retreat," said Cormiac Ru on my other side.

I forced myself to a moment of absolute calm. Then my head agreed with Cormiac Ru. Turning our backs on such hostility would invite a spear between the shoulder blades.

My feet took one step forward.

The third spear was not thrown.

Beckoning to Cormiac and Dian Cet to follow me, I walked toward the nearest lodge. There I stopped abruptly.

In front of the lodge was a pole topped by a human head. The features were still recognizable. Not long ago, the head belonged to a man about my age. And he had . . . I rubbed my eyes, unwilling to believe them . . . he had a tonsure.

Dian Cet made a small sound of distress.

The spear-thrower stood in the open doorway with the third spear in his hand. At first glance I saw that he was as tall as I, and I am not a short man. His hands were huge. "We salute you as a free person," I repeated, with a mouth gone dry.

He looked me up and down like a cattle buyer. I did the same to him.

He was dressed in a well-worn garment of soft leather that had been cut like a tunic, leaving his arms and lower legs bare. There were no shoes on his feet, not even sandals. His jaws were shaved, but a flowing brown moustache extended almost to his collarbone, where it did not quite conceal the gleam of gold around his neck. The man was wearing a torc, the emblem of a Celtic chief.

Relief washed over me. "We are of the same race as yourselves," I announced.

He regarded me wordlessly.

"I am Ainvar, chief druid of the tribe of the Carnutes. This is our judge, Dian Cet, and—"

"Druid?" There was an edge to the way he said it; this man definitely did not like druids. His attitude reminded me of my senior wife.

As a child Briga had sworn to hate the druids forever. They had sacrificed her adored older brother, Bran, in order to stop a plague that was destroying the Sequani. The sacrifice had succeeded but Briga never forgave. After we met, I had worked tirelessly to persuade her to accept both me and my calling. I also discovered that she possessed remarkable gifts herself. Yet Briga was never willing to join the Order of the Wise. She would go to her grave with her gift unadmitted.

The man in the doorway was glowering at me. "Druid," he said again, making it sound like an insult. He looked from me to Dian Cet, then to Cormiac Ru. "Who is this?"

There could be no doubt now that he spoke a Celtic tongue, though heavily accented. It reminded me of the language of the Sequani.

Cormiac Ru understood him well enough. "I am the Red Wolf," he said proudly.

With a deep sigh, the spear-thrower leaned his weapon against the wall. "Two frauds and a wild animal," he muttered. "No use to me."

"That's not true," I assured him. "We've made a long journey across the sea bringing gifts of great value."

"Gifts?" When he rolled his eyes back toward me I noticed they were bloodshot. His complexion was pasty. The man was well nourished but not in the whole of his health. This was knowledge I could use.

All knowledge is useful.

"You know our names," I said, "but we have yet to learn yours."

"Cohern," he said shortly. Here was a man who gave nothing away if he could help it.

Every name must have a meaning, but I could not translate his. Noticing my quizzical expression, he said, "Battle Lord." This act of courtesy raised the man a notch in my estimation.

I made my voice sympathetic. "Are you alone here, Cohern?"

Grudgingly, he admitted, "The others are staying out of sight until it's safe."

"How many others are there?"

He narrowed his bloodshot eyes. "Why do you want to know?"

"Just curiosity."

Cohern's eyes narrowed to slits. He peered between his eyelids like a toad peering out from under a rock. "Druid curiosity? That gives you no rights here. Besides, if you're a druid, where's your tonsure? Whitebeard over there has a tonsure."

It seemed unwise to make any further reference to druidry. "Dian Cet's going bald," I said.

"Your Red Wolf has no tonsure, either. I've never seen a fuller head of hair."

"I'm a warrior," Cormiac Ru interjected.

Cohern lost all interest in me. "At last! Someone I can use. Come into my lodge and we'll talk."

His lodge consisted of a small round room made of woven branches cemented together with dried mud. The interior was dark and musty. Before my eyes could adjust to the dimness, I stumbled over a rock and stubbed my toe. Pain shot up my spine.

Toes are as tender as noses. My head distracted me by asking: Is there some connection between the two?

"You don't have a warrior's moustache," Cohern was saying to Cormiac. "You'll have to grow one. Let me feel your arms and legs. Is that your own sword? Can you handle a spear?" If this was a battle lord, he was a battle lord with problems. I had never known anyone to be so excited by a single warrior.

Thus far, the interview was not promising from our point of view. I cleared my throat. "Our party includes an exceptionally gifted healer," I told Cohern, hoping to distract him from Cormiac. I was gambling that he really was ill and would welcome a healer.

One did not necessarily signify the other, of course.

Ignoring me, Cohern continued his examination of Cormiac Ru. As he bent to feel the muscles in the young man's legs, Cormiac's eyes met mine. *Be still,* I mouthed silently.

Labraid would have argued, or refused to obey. Cormiac did as he was told.

When he had satisfied his curiosity, Cohern stood up. "I'll take this one. He's as hard as new rope."

The man thought we were selling slaves. I must disabuse him of the idea at once. "Cormiac's not for sale. None of my clan is for sale, we are free people."

"Yes yes, but I need warriors and this one looks promising. I'll give you . . ." Cohern gazed around his lodge in a vain search for valuables. There were only some cooking implements, a battered loom, and a stack of fleeces spread with a torn blanket of woven wool. Wind whistled through the gaps in the walls.

Except for his gold torc, Cohern was poor. I could not help feeling sorry for him. If this was what Hibernia was like, we had not improved our situation. "Are you the chief of your tribe?" I asked uncertainly.

"Chief of the tribe. Ha." He laughed mirthlessly. "I'm only the chief of my clan. This clan: these few old men hiding in their lodges with the women and leaving me to face strangers alone. If you attacked us they would stand behind me, though. Oh yes. As far behind me as they could get.

"Now, Ainvar, tell me what you'll accept for this fellow with the fiery hair. I have some good wool, raised in the mountains and as thick as curds."

"We don't need wool. What we need is a place to build a settlement."

Cohern's bloodshot eyes bulged alarmingly. "You expect me to surrender our clanland to you? I've killed men for suggesting less!"

"We don't want all of your land, of course not," I hastened to say. "Just let us live in peace on any small patch you're not using."

His attitude underwent another lightning change. "What can you pay? We don't rent clanland without payment."

Mindful of the head on the pole, I decided not to offer him the services of druids. "What payment do you ask, Cohern?"

"Warriors like this one. How many more do you have?"

"I told you, I can't sell Cormiac, because he owns himself. As we all do."

Cohern gave a doleful sigh. "You have nothing to offer, then. You might as well leave now."

I could not go back to my people empty-handed. "Perhaps we can make an arrangement to suit us both, Cohern. I can't sell Cormiac, but if he agrees I might offer his services to you for a period of time." My eyes caught Cormiac's eyes and silently commanded him to cooperate.

Labraid would have argued. Cormiac merely gave a terse nod.

Cohern rubbed his nose, ran his fingers through his hair, scratched himself in the armpit. Winning a little time to think. "All right, Ainvar. Will you exchange a dozen warriors for the holding of a piece of land for six years?"

Praise be to That Which Watches! Bargaining was a skill that required no druid talent. The man did not appear to be physically able for protracted negotiations. If I could wear him down with talk first, this might yet work out. "My people will insist on knowing something about you before we can do business, Cohern. They've been badly treated in the past and you are a stranger to us."

"My clan and I belong to the tribe of the Iverni, in the kingdom of the Deisi."

So Hibernia was divided into kingdoms! Without giving me time to consider the ramifications, Cohern said, "The Iverni are descended from Éber Finn, who, as everyone knows, was the finest warrior and the most noble of all the sons of Milesios."

I tried to look impressed, but it was difficult since I had no idea what he was talking about. "Who was Milesios?" I asked.

"A king of the Gael, a Celtic tribe that lived in northern Iberia twenty generations ago. Milesios claimed to have Scythian blood in his veins."

My head was intrigued. It wanted to explore the connection further but Cohern kept on talking. "In search of a new home, several of the sons of Milesios set sail for a richly endowed island that the sea traders told them about. This island. With them the Milesians brought their wives and children, Iberian cattle, and horses from Africa."

My head was being overwhelmed with questions. What shores had Celts not visited? What lands had not felt their feet?

Listen! my ears commanded.

Cohern said, "When the Milesians arrived here they found the island was controlled by a tribe called the Túatha Dé Danann. They were not many but they were everywhere. They'd even named the place for one of their queens, Eriu."

Eriu. A rippling, insubstantial sort of name.

Hibernia suited my tongue better.

"The sons of Milesios wanted this land and its resources for themselves," Cohern went on, "but the Dananns were unwilling to surrender it to them. A great battle was fought; a battle strange and terrible."

"Obviously your side won."

"Yes," he said in an odd voice. "They won."

"What happened to the Dananns afterward?"

"They disappeared."

"That's an odd choice of words," I said. "I assume you mean the Dananns stepped aside and left the Milesians as the undisputed rulers of Hibernia."

"Who calls this land Hibernia? I never heard that before."

"The traders who brought us here use the name. They thought it was Hibernia for the Iverni—or perhaps for Éber Finn?" I added shrewdly.

"Ah." Cohern was pleased. From that moment he warmed to me. It was easy to keep him talking. He overflowed with partial memories handed down from bygone generations; the sort of tales we had called "grandmother stories" in Gaul. The most interesting of these concerned the Túatha Dé Danann, for whom he made claims that hardly seemed credible. "They could cloud men's minds and make them see the impossible," Cohern said. "They could summon great mists to blanket the land, they could whistle up storms to churn the sea into foam. They could vanish while someone was looking at them and reappear moments later in another place entirely."

If even half of these things were true, the Danann had possessed magic of a very high degree. In defeating them the Gael had won an extraordinary victory.

"No sooner had the Gael settled here," said Cohern, "than the sons of Milesios began arguing over the division of territory."

"Battles between brothers are the most savage," I commented.

He agreed. "The quarrel fed on itself and grew, until it was passed down from one generation to the next. Eventually the Gael divided into a handful of tribes, each one tracing back to one of the sons of Milesios. And we continue the fight."

"Do you enjoy fighting?"

"It's what I do."

"That's not what I asked, Cohern."

He gave yet another sigh. This was an unhappy man. "I used to like to fight, but I've been doing it all my life and now I'm tired."

"Then why continue?"

"My clan's too weak to swim against the tide."

"What determines a clan's status within the tribe?" I wanted to know. My own clan had been foremost among the Carnutes because we had produced a number of druids, but under the circumstances I thought it might be wise not to mention this.

"Status depends on how many warriors the clan can provide to the chief of the tribe," Cohern told me.

The result, my head observed, was predictable. In Hibernia, battle had become the only means by which men defined themselves; male pride taken to a self-destructive extreme. Cohern's clan was a perfect example. With its young men lost to war, his family was on the verge of extinction.

By questioning Cohern further, I learned that the Gael had developed a clever stratagem to assure the survival of the tribe as a whole. When tribal numbers were in danger of becoming too depleted, each side in a war nominated a champion. The battle of champions decided the outcome.

If during the battle for Gaul we had challenged the Romans to a battle of champions, Vercingetorix would have defeated the scrawny Caesar without drawing a deep breath. But Caesar—may he be cursed from a height!—would never have agreed to single combat. His concept of warfare was dispatch wave upon wave of warriors to kill his opponents, then pursue their families and slaughter them to the last person.

Now the Romans had Gaul.

We had Hibernia.

I noticed that Cohern's voice was growing weak. Seizing the moment, I made an offer. "There is a woman with us who is a skilled healer, and we have two outstanding craftsmen. We would be happy to share their skills with you. Furthermore, if you allow us the use of some land, we'll keep your people supplied with venison."

"What about warriors?"

He was stubborn, I grant him that. "Cormiac Ru is the only warrior we have at present. But there is a lad called Labraid whose father was a mighty warrior and—"

"Done!" Cohern croaked.

It was agreed that Cormiac and Labraid would live with Cohern's clan and fight in his name whenever required. As recompense for their services, we would be allowed to build a few lodges on Cohern's clanland. For two milk cows, a young bullock, and six sheep, we would pay Cohern half of our butter and fleeces, plus any leather we subsequently harvested. In effect, we would be tenants occupying land at the mercy of the clan chief. We who had been freeholders in Gaul.

Even so, we were being treated better than invaders had any right to expect.

When the deal was concluded Cohern gave a shrill whistle. Several old men and half-grown boys appeared at the doorway of the lodge. The male members of his clan were as simply dressed as their chieftain, including bare feet. Cohern called their names in turn. Then he identified us to them, beginning with Cormiac Ru. Warriors had more rank in Hibernia than druids.

Once the men had made their appearance the women gradually came out into the open. They had fine eyes and fresh complexions but were not as ample as I like; even Cohern's wife. He had only the one. The man really was poor.

That night we were given fat mutton, thin oatmeal, and a few gritty chunks from a blackened loaf that resembled no bread I knew. There were none of the seasonings we had enjoyed in Gaul. No kinnamon or black pepper purchased from eastern traders, no olive oil from the south, so silky on the tongue.

These people badly needed the salt we had brought with us. But we had best keep it for ourselves; we had little to barter with otherwise.

The meal was washed down with a reddish ale known as "coirm," made of malted barley and too sweet for my taste. As an option I was offered an equally unpalatable drink of fermented bilberry juice, so insipid one might as well drink water. Wistfully, I recalled the robust Gaulish wine that made all women look beautiful and all men feel virile.

For the rest of Thislife, my head informed me, Ainvar will eat and drink like this.

For the rest of Thislife.

To distract myself from the unhappiness of my mouth, I listened to the conversations going on around me. I soon learned why Cohern had referred to Dian Cet and myself as "frauds." Shortly before our arrival a druid belonging to another clan had claimed he could cure Cohern of a persistent fever. The man had failed. His was the head on the pole.

A war between the two clans could be expected at any time.

I also discovered that Cohern's clan did not take part in the trade Goulvan had mentioned. They were too reduced to have anything of value to offer. The only item any of them possessed that would appeal to a foreign trader was the chieftain's torc, and Cohern would rather die than relinquish it.

Interestingly, the Order of the Wise was unknown in Hibernia. Separate branches of druidry were not recognized. Cohern flatly stated, "All druids are sorcerers, but even the best aren't as adept as the Túatha Dé Danann. My fever was a curse put upon me by the Dananns."

"I assumed they were all gone by now," I said.

"They are."

"Then how could they cause your fever, Cohern?"

"Magic," he replied with a ferocious scowl. "We slaughtered the lot of them, yet they still attack us through magic. Generation after generation. It's a terrible long time to carry a grudge."

As the survivor of a slaughtered race myself, I felt sympathy for the Túatha Dé Danann.

Was it they, rather than the Iverni, who frightened Goulvan so badly?

That night I slept on the floor of Cohern's lodge, wrapped in my cloak and dreaming confused dreams. Once or twice I sat up abruptly and wondered where I was. There is a moment between sleep and wakefulness when one is totally vulnerable. During that moment my spirit trembled within me.

At first light Dian Cet and I set out for the coast. We left Cormiac Ru with Cohern, and promised to deliver Labraid when we returned. I bade Cormiac farewell by saying, "You're still one of us and always will be."

The Red Wolf gave a terse nod.

I added, "I'm relying on you to uphold our side of the bargain."

His face was impassive. Only his colorless eyes flashed fire. "I always keep my promises, Ainvar. Always."

Cohern walked with us to the gateway. "That woman you mentioned, the healer? Will she be coming with you?"

"She will."

"If she's any good, I might be willing to buy her."

The distance back seemed much longer than the distance coming. Too much food and too little sleep weighed heavily on me, and Dian Cet was in worse shape. Several times he stopped and sat down. I joined him, ostensibly to be polite, but in reality with relief.

As we drew near the beach where we had left the boats, Briga came running to meet me with the sunlight on her face. My arms folded around her; I buried my face in her hair. It felt different, stiffer. Yet it was my Briga's hair, and that's all I needed to know. She was warm in my arms and soft in my arms and her softness summoned a most delicious hardness in myself. We must build lodges very soon.

Briga and I stood unmoving until our hearts began to beat with the same rhythm and we were one again. When I raised my head I saw that my clan was still gathered on the beach. But the boats were gone.

I stared at the space where they had been. Then looked to the sea. The empty, empty sea. I felt nothing. Since Caesar invaded Gaul I had received so many shocks, I could not absorb any more.

"Where did the boats go?" I asked faintly.

My wife's eyes sparked with anger. "As soon as you were out of sight, Goulvan ordered his men back into them and they all sailed away."

The others were crowding around us. I did not see Labraid among them. "Where is he?" I asked Onuava.

She knew exactly who I meant, and why. When she answered her words ran together too fast. "He tried to stop them, Ainvar, I swear he did. All the men tried to stop them, but the Armoricans were too strong."

Too strong for Teyrnon the ironsmith, and the sinewy arms of the Goban Saor, and stalwart Grannus who never took a step backward in his life? If I had left Cormiac Ru with them, things would have been different.

Looking around, I observed that the faces of my friends were battered and bruised. Even young Glas had a purple eye. At that moment, if I could have got Goulvan's neck in my hands I would have snapped it like a dead branch.

My ears reported that Onuava was still babbling. "Labraid's always been as fearless as his father was, you know. My brave little prince ran headlong into the sea and began beating the water with his arms and legs. I shouted after him but he ignored me. Ignored his own mother! His head stayed atop the water for a little while, but he never even got close to the boats. Then suddenly he disappeared."

My ability to feel returned in full measure. Agony shot through me. This latest disaster was one too many. If the son of Vercingetorix had drowned due to a bad decision of mine, my failure was complete.

Briga sneezed. "Labraid didn't drown, Ainvar," she said in her hoarse little voice. "I went after him."

"But you can't swim."

"No," she agreed.

My second wife took a step forward to get my attention. "Briga went out and Briga came back," Lakutu said simply. "With Labraid."

## *chapter* V

"BRIGA WADED INTO THE SEA BEFORE WE COULD STOP HER," THE Goban Saor elaborated. "I was sure they both would drown and tried to go after them myself, but Grannus and Teyrnon held me back."

"We couldn't afford to lose everybody," Grannus said reasonably.

"Just so. Anyway, while we watched, Briga kept going in the direction where we had last seen Labraid. She went a long way out, Ainvar. Her feet could not possibly have been touching the bottom. Besides, the surf was very strong. When we saw the waves break over her, we thought we'd lost her, too. Then she reappeared holding Labraid. While we stood and stared like a tree full of owls, she returned to us. They both returned to us."

This explained the texture of Briga's hair. It was stiff with salt.

Grannus took up the story. "Sulis stretched Labraid out on the sand and pummeled him until he coughed up the water he'd swallowed. He's all right now, though considerably quieter than he was yesterday, which is no bad thing. He's asleep over there under my cloak."

Fear snapped the thread of my temper. "Don't ever do anything like that again!" I shouted at Briga.

She gave my arm a little pat. "Oh, Ainvar, a bit of water won't hurt me."

"We're talking about the Great Sea!"

She just smiled at me.

Teyrnon thought he had seen Briga swimming, but his eyes were not young and sometimes deceived him. In Gaul, when we went bathing in the lake, Briga had always stayed in shallow water. When I offered to teach her to swim she demurred. "Why would I need to swim? I never go into deep water."

Yet here she had gone into deep water.

Lakutu had a different version. My second wife said flatly, "The water parted and let Briga pass through."

If this was true—and I had never known Lakutu to lie—it was magic of a very high order.

Briga laughed at the suggestion. "I didn't work any magic, Ainvar, I wouldn't know how. I just did what had to be done."

"What, exactly, did you do?"

She pleated her forehead for a moment, then gave a Gaulish shrug of dismissal. "It all happened so fast, I don't remember."

Because she was Briga I chose to believe her. Had she been Onuava, I would have demanded a pinch of valuable salt first. My third wife liked to embroider the truth or even stretch it completely out of shape. When Onuava tugged at my arm with her own version of the incident, I did not bother to listen. Much later I would wish I had.

When I regained my composure, I related our encounter with Cohern and the deal we had struck, including the promise of sheep and cattle. "They'll give us a small supply of food to begin with," I said, "but Goulvan was right about one thing: This land is teeming with game. We're in no danger of starving."

The Goban Saor spoke up. "While you were gone, Ainvar, I did some exploring. The tales we heard are true in one respect. There's gold in the streams flowing down from the mountains. I also found rocks containing iron and copper ore, so as soon as we get settled, Teyrnon and I will be able to forge metal. We even have an apprentice. Lakutu's son, Glas, is interested in craftsmanship and he's good with his hands."

"As soon as you make some shears for me and Grannus builds a loom," Damona chimed in, "I can weave the wool from our new sheep."

Already my people were planning new lives.

Fortunately the women had unloaded our supplies before the Armoricans deserted. I have no doubt that Briga's enameled bowls were the first items removed from our boat. They had been set to one side where no clumsy foot would stumble over them.

In addition to our clothing we had brought a few iron spearheads and axeheads, one iron cauldron, knives, flesh forks, emmer wheat for planting, smoked pigmeat, dried venison, hard cheese, a large bag of flour, and a small sack of salt. Salt had been the earliest wealth of the Celts, a scarce commodity that lured traders from the Amber Road to a village high in the Blue Mountains. A village called Hallstatt, the womb of our race.

Before the before, that was.

On the beach in Hibernia we distributed our belongings so that every person carried a share. Except for Labraid. Thanks to the overenergetic pounding our healer had given his back, the youth had a broken rib. An apologetic Sulis slathered his torso with unguents, then bound his body tightly so he could walk without much discomfort.

Grannus carried Briga's big iron cauldron strapped to his back. Her beloved bowls, wrapped in her favorite cloak, were tucked safely inside the cauldron. Instead of walking with me she paced along behind Grannus, keeping a watchful eye on her property.

Cohern's clanspeople gave us a better welcome this time. They came out of their lodges to greet us; their smallest children soon were playing with our smallest children. I sent Sulis to the chieftain straightaway. She disappeared into his lodge and did not reemerge until the following morning, looking exhausted but pleased with herself.

By the next sundown Cohern's health had begun to improve.

His people made us as comfortable as possible in their lodges. As I had surmised, the clan had been seriously reduced through warfare. The survivors lived primitive lives. Everything was pared down to the bone. Cohern's people grew a little barley for ale, and a few oats, but they subsisted primarily on mutton and cheese. Cattle were raised for their hides. Leather was the only valuable commodity the clan had to trade.

Without strong men to defend the herd from raiders, Cohern would be totally impoverished. Meanwhile his clan stood a very real chance of being captured by an enemy tribe and taken into bondage. The blood of Milesios would not save them.

Noble blood had not saved Vercingetorix, either.

The Order of the Wise teaches: We rule in one life and serve in the next.

I spoke privately with Cormiac because it was only fair to warn him. "If you are captured and taken into bondage we might never see you again."

The Red Wolf showed his teeth in a thin smile. "What makes you think I'd let myself be captured? Don't worry, Ainvar, I'll never be far from you and yours."

"Cohern and I have an agreement."

"I understand, and I'll honor it—unless it happens that your needs conflict with his."

"What will you do then?"

His smile widened by an infinitesimal degree. "Melt away as the wolf melts away into the forest."

When he began to feel better, Cohern summoned me. "I've decided where your people can live, Ainvar. At the far edge of our clanland is an uninhabited valley with plenty of good grass."

"Is there fresh water?"

"On . . . er, Hibernia? Don't make me laugh. Rivers, lakes, bogs, waterfalls . . . throw a stone in any direction and you'll have water splashing in your face."

I asked the obvious question. "If this valley's so good, why aren't some of your own people living there?"

"Ah, right now there aren't enough of us, Ainvar. You know how clans are. They wax and wane like the moon."

I accepted his explanation. My own family had waned severely. "Tell me more about the valley. How far is it from here?"

"Less than half a morning's walk. A morning in winter, that is, not high summer. In high summer we have almost no night at all."

A summer of nightless days. Magic.

Cohern cannily refused to let us leave for the valley until his recovery was complete. I thought of asking Briga to help speed the process, but discarded the idea. I was never certain of the exact dimensions of Briga's gift. If there was a serious illness in our family she always sent for Sulis. Was that to show respect for the older woman? Or was she afraid to treat her own children because she might fail? In our time together I had seen Briga do a number of things that could not be explained, yet none of them, aside from healing Cormiac's eyes, inspired awe. Until her rescue of Labraid.

Whether she belonged to the Order of the Wise or not, my senior wife was druid.

Fortunately Cohern's recovery was rapid. He sent us on our way with four cows, a bull calf that bawled continually, and a small flock of sheep. He presented Sulis with some domestic fowl as a gift of gratitude.

Labraid and Cormiac Ru he kept for himself.

Guided by an old man whose vocabulary was limited to grunting and pointing, we reached the valley long before high sun. Cohern's clanland was not very large; we would be living closer to him than I liked. I feared he would be peering over my shoulder and finding fault with our foreign ways. There was one compensation, however. Among his clanspeople were several young girls. Glas and my son Dara would soon be of an age to take wives.

Cormiac Ru was old enough already, but I had long since accepted his fantasy. The Red Wolf was destined for Maia.

His mission fulfilled, the old man left us without even a grunt of farewell. We stood together in a tight little knot of hopes and fears and looked around. What we saw was better than I could have hoped. The valley lay in the lap of low mountains that shielded it from the prevailing wind. A herd of red deer were napping in the tall grass. As we approached, they leaped to their feet and bounded away up the forested slopes. Their sheer grace made my heart sing.

"Meat," said Grannus.

"And good water!" Briga drew my attention to a river that emerged from a gorge at the head of the valley. A dancing little river that tumbled over its rocky bed and sparkled in the sunshine.

Here was all that was necessary for life.

A nearby stand of mountain ash and whitethorn provided enough dead wood for a ceremonial fire. Briga had a deft hand with flintstones; she could coax a living spark from the dampest timber. Standing around the blaze in solemn assembly, we chanted our thanks to the Source.

Then we got to work.

There is no energy like that of a woman setting up a new household. While we men watched bemused, our womenfolk brisked about, choosing sites for lodges. In the Gaul of my youth a man and his senior wife had occupied one lodge, with separate accommodations built for other wives as they came along. While hiding in the forest we had enjoyed no such luxury. Of necessity, we had thrown up communal shelters as quickly as we could because we had to move so often. In Hibernia we continued out of habit.

My three wives conferred at length, with many excited gestures, before deciding on a site for the lodge we would share. The doorway must face the rising sun. The ground should be high enough to avoid flooding. There had to be room inside for a central hearth with a cauldron and spit, a loom, a stone kneading trough and other necessary domestic furniture, and an adequate number of beds. When a man and woman lie together—or sit or stand or roll around in each other's arms—those who share their lodge neither see nor hear them. That applies to everyone from the toothless grandmother to the toothless infant. We had no toothless infants among us but there were plenty of children. My lodge had to be big.

I decreed that Grannus and Sulis share a lodge with her brother, the Goban Saor, and Keryth the seer. Dian Cet would live with Teyrnon and Damona, who were quiet in their ways. To avoid overcrowding in my own lodge—and give the boys the benefit of steady example—I assigned Dara and Glas to Teyrnon as well.

Once the lodge sites had been selected, the women drew a supply of water from the river and milked one of our new cows. Rather, they attempted to milk the cow. She was not cooperative.

"Perhaps she's too young," I remarked to Grannus, who was sitting on a stone in the sun. Grannus was a great believer in sitting whenever possible. He claimed it conserved his strength. Perhaps it did. Grannus had neither druid gifts nor a warrior spirit, but he was the strongest oak in the forest, a man of immeasurable value in circumstances such as ours.

"In my experience females take a lot of coaxing, Ainvar," he said to me.

"Are we talking about cattle, or women?"

"Females," Grannus replied succinctly.

Sulis had long refused to marry anyone. As she once explained to me, "Carrying children in my body could interfere with my ability to heal others, because I would be concentrating on the life within myself."

If my Briga had been willing to join the Order of the Wise she could have demonstrated the fallacy of that belief.

Grannus had waited until Sulis was past the age of childbearing, then pursued her as few women are ever pursued. Sober, serious Grannus had, for three full seasons, been charming and witty and endlessly attentive, and won himself a great prize.

Our conversation was interrupted by Damona, who announced that the work had proceeded to the stage where male strength was required. No druid exemption was allowed. So after conducting a ritual to placate the spirit of the trees, we began cutting oak and spruce to build our lodges. Only the oldest trees were used, those nearing the end of their lives. Nothing young was harmed. New life is sacred.

I enjoyed using my muscles instead of my head. The body is not as cruel as the mind.

Our work did not end with woodcutting. While hiding in the forests of Gaul we had deluded ourselves into thinking the situation was temporary, and had made do with temporary expedients. But Hibernia was not temporary. We would be here for the rest of our lives and the lives of our children's children, and our women wanted permanence. They provided us with an endless list of tasks. As long as there was light, we labored.

Once or twice during those early days I glimpsed Cormiac Ru on the mountainside. He did not come near, but it was reassuring to know he was keeping an eye on us. On Briga.

By the next change of the moon a lot of hard work had produced three sturdy timber lodges in the Gaulish style and a fenced enclosure for our livestock. We also built a roofed lean-to for Teyrnon, where he could set up a forge. Otherwise it might be difficult to keep the fire going. The Gaulish summer, which I recalled with a yearning heart, had been filled to the brim with sunlight. The Hibernian summer was cobwebbed with gentle rain.

My senior wife came to me with a handful of grain. "I don't think our wheat will sprout here, Ainvar."

"Why not? You can see for yourself how fertile the soil is. Vegetation is positively leaping out of the earth."

"Look up," she replied.

I looked up.

"Now look in that direction." Briga nodded toward the east. "And that." She gestured to the west. "Do you see any sunshine?"

"Not at this moment, no." I had to defend our newfound home; I was responsible for bringing us here in the first place. "But the sun does shine, Briga. I've seen it break through the clouds twenty times in a single day, and when it does, the land sparkles."

"Oh yes," she agreed, "the land sparkles, it's beautifully green. But the sun is not hot enough for long enough. Our wheat won't grow here."

"How can you be so sure?"

Assuming a listening expression, she held her hands close to her face and poured a few heads of wheat from one hand to the other. "It tells me so," she said.

I knew better than to doubt her. All sorts of things talked to Briga: flowers, grain, broken bones. . . .

"What do you expect me to do about it?" I asked reasonably.

"I don't know, you are the chief druid."

She said "are" instead of "were," although she knew better. Apart from myself she was the only one who did. Perhaps it was a slip of the tongue. "Planting crops is women's work," I reminded her. "Men only plow the fields, and a chief druid does not even do that."

"Then what good are you?"

Briga said it with a laugh, but I wished she had not asked me that question.

We would not go hungry. Grannus and young Glas kept us supplied with game. The river teemed with fish unfamiliar with the craftiness of man; laughably easy to catch. There also were edible roots and herbs, wild soft fruits, and delicious mushrooms. Yet we would have no more bread made from the sort of wheat I had eaten all my life. I never appreciated it until I knew I would not taste it again. At night I began dreaming of crusty loaves hot from a stone oven.

We wanted more than subsistence, however. We longed for what we had possessed in Gaul: our culture, our way of life. I began thinking of ways to restore a semblance of it to my little band. One way was through art; the art of the craftsman.

Perhaps I had been hasty in refusing to offer a prayer of thanksgiving to the Two-Faced One. Without him we would not be alive today. Perhaps, my head suggested, I should ask the Goban Saor to carve another when he had more time.

One of his first tasks was to make a churn for Briga. He was using only wood from the oaks. "Wise wood makes wise butter," my grandmother used to say.

As we re-created our community, many of those old sayings came back to me; came back to all of us. We think we build new lives for ourselves but we build on old foundations.

My senior wife was very particular about her butter. Churning was never done during the dark of the moon. The milk must be no more nor less than three days old. Cream was carefully skimmed from the top of the milk with a wooden spoon, poured into a cool stone bowl, then covered with a strip of clean linen to allow it to ripen. The result was a butter so delicious it could be eaten by itself. The children were fond of scooping a treat out of the churn when no one was looking.

So was I.

Halfway up the valley stood a solitary dead tree. Bees had colonized the rotten cavity, but whenever we tried to gather their honey the creatures went wild. Both Grannus and Damona were badly stung. Then one day my small daughter Gobnat walked up to the tree and casually thrust her arm into the cavity. Briga gave a shriek of alarm, but her fear was ill-founded. The bees were charmed by Gobnat. They would let her take a handful of honeycomb dripping with golden sweetness whenever she liked. We put honey onto almost everything until the novelty wore off. My clan was delighted.

I had another reason to rejoice: The druid gift had appeared anew.

Not everything was lost after all.

As the wheel of the seasons turned, we surveyed our handiwork with pride. Our roofs were snugly thatched with reeds from the stream. Firewood was stacked against the north wall of the lodges to break the wind. We had sufficient butter and soft cheese and salted meat to see us through the winter. For anything else we must apply to Cohern. That too had been part of our agreement.

As the autumn evenings drew in upon us, and in the darkness before dawn when only druids are awake, I brooded on our situation. We had a place to live but no real freedom. Cohern was adamant that we not wander beyond our allotted space. "That's all your clan's entitled to, Ainvar. If they stray outside its boundaries anything could happen."

"Would one of the other tribes attack us?"

"*Anyone* might attack you," Cohern had replied.

So here we were. Penned in by mountains, with no view of the far horizon. Penned in. Penned in.

I regretted having agreed so readily. A druid with a wise head would have made a better deal. But I was no longer a druid.

Fraud, Cohern had called me, as if he knew my deepest fears.

When Briga got out her shears and razors and offered to restore my tonsure, I declined. "I've decided to let my hair grow. If druidry is in bad odor here, it might be best not to proclaim ourselves so visibly."

"As you wish," said Briga. I think she was secretly pleased. In spite of all that had passed between us, and her own demonstrable gifts, she still had misgivings about the Order of the Wise.

Letting my tonsure grow out did not change my true self. Druids are always drawn to trees, which is one of the early indications of a druid spirit.

Superficially the Hibernian autumn differed little from summer. The days were shorter and cooler, but the trees stubbornly held on to their leaves for as long as they could. The grass stayed green. Change was revealed in small ways. The velvet covering the deers' horns was stripped away by repeated, ferocious assaults on the trees, until the branching antlers were transformed into a warrior's magnificent headgear. The bellow of rutting stags reverberated through the forest.

During our first autumn I set out to explore the slopes from which we took our timber. Trees are equally beautiful when clothed in leaves or standing bare, with their spirits naked to the sky. They feed the eyes.

The extended family of trees and shrubs consists of four ranks, ranging from the most noble to the most humble. Some of the trees I knew in Gaul did not grow in Hibernia. Either their gifts were not required in this climate, or others with similar abilities had been substituted for them.

Nature ever strives to maintain balance.

Among the noble trees, primacy was claimed by the oak, the wise and mighty chieftain. With my first sight of an oak in Hibernia something had eased inside of me. I had been like a child who lost its father and then found him again. The world, which had been tilted, came aright.

Other members of the Hibernian nobility included the yew, which kept its foliage throughout the year and therefore was the tree of death and rebirth. We druids would make our staff from yew wood. The red berries of the holly recalled the Great Fire of Life. Hazelnuts contained a wealth of hidden knowledge, while hazel twigs could find underground water. The prolific ash was the symbol of good health. The long cones of the native pine emulated the shape of the human phallus, thus embodying fertility. Last but not least among the nobility was the apple, whose freely given fruit was invaluable.

In the second rank were hawthorn and willow, birch and rowan, elm and alder and wild cherry. Although commoners, they were revered as hardworking and productive. The third rank comprised blackthorn, which is valued for its sloes, elder, aspen, juniper, spindle-tree, arbutus, and the shrubby white hazel. Lowest of all were the "slave trees," yet even they had value. Bracken was used for making soap and bleaching linen; likewise, brambles, heather, bog myrtle, furze, broom, and gooseberry all had contributions to make. The Source created them; we respect them.

As the days grew still shorter I began to spend more time inside my head. Briga's rescue of Labraid was haunting me. When I tried again to question her about the incident, she turned my words away with a laugh. "It isn't important, Ainvar, I don't even want to think about it. Please, let it go."

At day's end my little clan liked to gather around the hearth in my lodge before retiring to their own beds. The fire on our hearth never went out. Briga considered tending the fire to be a sacred rite, as it had been for our ancestors in a much colder climate. Fire was heat; fire was life. If the fire was allowed to die, calamity could follow.

Sometimes my people talked among themselves. Sometimes we were content just to be together while the stars wheeled in the cold sky and the friendly fire warmed our bones.

One evening Briga asked the seer, "Can you see far into the future?"

"How far? Tomorrow? Or next season?"

"How about . . . the future of my grandchildren's grandchildren. A hundred generations from now."

My senior wife was being fanciful, as she sometimes is, but Keryth took her seriously. "Give me your hand, Briga." Keryth ran her fingers up Briga's wrist and closed them tightly over the place where the blood pulsed most strongly beneath the skin. The seer gave a slow, thoughtful nod and closed her eyes. Her breathing gradually became deeper. She might almost have been asleep, but her grip on Briga's wrist remained firm.

Slowly, the atmosphere in the lodge changed. Tingled like the air before a thunderstorm. We sat very still, scarcely daring to breathe.

Keryth was working magic.

"One hundred generations," she murmured. We waited. The seer's eyes rolled beneath her eyelids. She drew a swift intake of breath. "They think they are rich. But, ah! They are poor."

"How poor?" Briga asked. Knowing my senior wife, I knew she would want to help; to find some way to alleviate poverty a hundred generations in the future.

"They have many possessions," Keryth told us. "I never saw so many *things.* Countless man-made objects whose purpose I cannot even imagine. Yet the people are starving."

Briga was alarmed. "Have they nothing to eat?"

"They have more food than they can ever hope to eat," Keryth said from that distant place where she was viewing through other eyes. "They build immense lodges to store the excess in, and still throw away enough to feed a hundred tribes. Their problem is not a want of food. The grandchildren's grandchildren are starved for what we have in abundance."

"I don't understand. We have nothing in abundance."

"We have time," Keryth replied. "We have space."

She said nothing more. After a while she opened her eyes, bade us goodnight, and went to her bed. But I lay awake long that night, trying to imagine a world starved of time and space. Surely there could be no worse fate.

I would prefer to be slaughtered by the Romans.

ONE MORNING BRIGA TOLD ME SHE NEEDED A STONE. "THERE ARE stones everywhere," I pointed out. "Help yourself to any of them."

"No, Ainvar, the stone must be of a certain size and shape. It has to be rough-surfaced, flat on the bottom, and larger than a newborn infant, but not quite so large as a newborn calf. Too big for me to carry anyway. If you will bring me a stone that answers to that description, the Goban Saor can carve a hollow in it to make a quern."

"Why do you need a quern? You told me yourself that we can't grow our wheat in this climate."

"No, Ainvar," she repeated, "but other grains do grow here. If Cohern will sell us some seed corn, we'll plant in the spring and harvest in the autumn, and make meal and flour. For that we'll need a quern."

I swear those wide blue eyes of hers could already see the grain standing tall in the field.

I went in search of a suitable stone.

The stones of Hibernia had unusual qualities. Some of the larger boulders hummed beneath my hands and made the hairs stand up on my forearms. Once or twice I drew back my hands as abruptly as if I had been stung by bees.

What strange force dwelt in this land? Was it benign—or malign? I still did not know, but for the sake of my people I worried. Lying beside Briga, who always slept soundly, I worried.

Night, do your simple duty, I thought. Close my eyes and extinguish the tiresome fire in my head.

COHERN'S CLAN DID HAVE A SMALL AMOUNT OF OATS AVAILABLE, which the clan chief regarded with surprising contempt. It was evident he thought meat the only proper food for a man. Even given its scarcity, the price he set on the grain was outrageous. He demanded we promise our entire first crop of lambs. "Plus, I'm going to need more warriors as soon as your young lads are ready," he said pointedly. "Arm them, teach them to fight. Make them practice every day."

I returned long-faced to Briga.

She was undeterred. "Didn't Cohern say that our valley was at the edge of his territory?"

"He did."

"Then we can assume that another clan's territory lies beyond those mountains. I suggest you visit them and ask if they will sell you seed corn."

"Cohern has forbidden us to leave here, Briga. He says it's dangerous."

"Do you believe everything he says? Did you encounter any danger when you set out to find him?"

"No," I admitted.

She folded her arms across her chest. "Well, then. There you are. Cohern's a poor man with a poor clan and no control over much of anything, so he's trying to control us. Don't let him."

"What if he's right?" I asked, recalling the Armoricans' nervousness on the beach.

"What if he's wrong?" she countered. "That's much more likely. No one has raised a hand to us so far. There's no good reason why you should not take a little journey and attempt to do a little trade."

"But I'm not a trader, I'm a—"

"You're a man who needs seed corn."

"I'm the chief druid of—"

"That was then and this is now," she said bluntly. "But you do have the highest rank of any man here, which makes you chief of our clan." She reached up—a long way up, for she is small and I am tall—and put her hands on my shoulders. "It's your responsibility to provide for us, Ainvar." A softer, gentler voice, but all the more powerful because of it.

I had been clinging to the old way of thinking about myself because it was comfortable, and familiar. Briga had survived the losses that unmanned me by being as stalwart as stone, as resilient as river. Which of us was the leader now?

Her blue eyes fixed on mine. "Go up the valley to the gorge, Ainvar. It's a pass through the mountains."

# *chapter* VI

THE SHORTNESS OF THE DAYS WARNED THAT WINTER WAS almost upon us. Yet the weather denied it. On the morning I set out in search of seed corn a gilded light slanted across meadows still vibrantly green. An exaltation of larks serenaded a cloudless azure sky. The breeze was almost as warm as fresh milk.

Having no adult warrior to be my guard of honor, I took my eldest son. It was unthinkable that I go alone. Not because I was afraid, but because of my rank. My first encounter with another tribe must demonstrate that I was a person of importance.

Dara had not yet shown any evidence of a warrior spirit. I hoped it would surface if needed. Teyrnon had given him a spear and made him promise to return the spearhead undamaged. "And don't let it drag on the ground!" the smith admonished.

As we left our little settlement I glanced over my shoulder. A shaft of brilliant sunlight illumined the cluster of lodges, turning their thatch to gold. In front of the largest lodge stood Briga. When she saw me looking back at her, she touched her fingers to her lips.

Sometimes the biggest words are said through the smallest gestures.

As we reached the head of the valley the sunshine faded. A cool wind, scented with rain, swept down from the mountains, making me glad of the woolen cloak Briga had insisted I wear. She was the only one of my wives who worried about such things.

No sooner had we entered the gorge than we were enveloped in a thick mist. We had to make our way forward step by step. I warned Dara not to fall into the river running through the bottom of the gorge. The water chuckled like a happy child, yet was deep enough and fast enough to drown someone.

Hibernia was a crystal with a cloudy heart. A radiant jewel that could turn dark and morose, reflecting the two sides of Celtic character.

I decided that I would not ask the Goban Saor to make a new image of the Two-Faced One. Instead I would request a carving of my senior wife. Briga rejected the Two-Faced One. Her totally integrated spirit chose to see only the radiance, and moved toward it instinctively. That, I told myself, was the image we should keep with us.

Briga was right; the gorge was a pass through the mountains. At the far end of the pass the mist lifted abruptly. We gazed out over densely forested foothills that gave way to a broad plain with a river glinting in the distance.

Walking downhill was pure pleasure.

From the toes of the foothills I observed that the plain ahead was criss-crossed by cattle trails. Well and good, I told myself. A large number of cattle is a reliable sign of prosperity, and a prosperous tribe is sure to have enough seed corn to sell some to us.

Dara and I walked on, occasionally speaking of this and that; a father does not always know what to say to his son.

"Over there!" Dara cried suddenly. He pointed toward a low hill to the north, divided from a spur of the mountains by a belt of forest. I squinted to sharpen my vision. A number of objects on the hill did not appear to be natural formations.

"That might be a large clanhold," I said. "Let's hope they're friendly."

Drawing nearer, we could see that the base of the hill was encircled by an earthwork embankment. A deep ditch, formed by the removal of soil to build the embankment, provided a protective barrier. The embankment itself was surmounted by a timber palisade.

"That," I told Dara, "is how a fort should be built. Eminently defensible, nothing like Cohern's ramshackle affair."

An earthwork causeway spanned the ditch, leading to a large gateway in the palisade. The gate was ajar.

"Hold your spear properly," I said to Dara, "and try to look like a guard of honor. We want to make a good impression."

My son fidgeted with the spear until I approved of the angle. Then we strode forward. An ambassadorial delegation of two.

The lookout's platform above the gate was unmanned. Apparently the occupants of the stronghold did not think anyone would be foolhardy enough to threaten them. When we passed through the gateway we discovered another ditch on the inner side of the embankment. The causeway extended across this second ditch as well, and from its farther end a muddy track, deeply churned by hooves and wheels, led up the hill.

Adjacent to the trackway was a pen holding seven or eight horses. They were smaller than Gaulish horses, but finely made, with elegant heads, and muzzles so small a woman could cup one in her hand. Large, liquid eyes watched as we passed by.

A number of lodges dotted the hillside, clustering around a larger lodge at the top like chicks around a mother hen. The doors were made of heavy oak planks hung on stout iron hinges. Abstract, curvilinear shapes formed of silver and copper wire had been inset in the timber door frames. They resembled the decorative designs used in Gaul, but these people were more ostentatious. Similar designs had been painted in bright colors on every possible surface.

"Look at the giant dogs!" Dara exclaimed in a voice filled with wonder.

Several huge, coarse-coated hounds were lounging beside the nearest lodge. They raised their heads to look at us but did not bother to get to their feet. To dogs of their size we posed no threat.

Meanwhile men and women of all ages were moving about the settlement, doing those important trivial things that people do every day. They seemed as unfazed as the hounds by our appearance. And why not? They had us greatly outnumbered.

The majority were fair and ruddy, the usual coloring of Celts. Only a few had brown hair like mine. In Gaul we had called that "a touch of the Scyth," referring to the strain of Scythian blood that ran through us.

The inhabitants of the stronghold were well nourished and better clothed than Cohern's clan. Both sexes wore woolen tunics that extended to the knee in the case of the men, and to the ankles of the women. The garments were dyed in an array of colors: blue and green and brown, yellow and crimson and gray. Some were also speckled in a pattern unique to their clan.

The men belted their tunics with wide bands of leather held by huge bronze buckles. The waists of the women were encircled with corsets set with polished stones or plaited from the tails of young foxes. Underneath their tunics the women wore linen gowns embroidered with blue and crimson knotwork along the sleeves. Several of the older women also wore short, hooded capes made of badger skins, so skillfully sewn that it was impossible to detect the seams.

Yet everyone was barefoot.

"Stay close by me," I muttered to Dara. "Stand tall, and no matter what happens, say nothing."

"Even if they kill you?"

"I don't think they'll kill me." Trusting that Briga was right, I headed toward the largest lodge.

As I approached, a man emerged and stood watching me. He had a big red face as ample as a full moon, and piercing blue eyes below a heavy thicket of sandy-colored eyebrows. His torc betokened his rank: a massive gold neck ring much wider and heavier than the torc Cohern wore. Gold fasteners at his shoulders secured an immense cloak of wolf fur that hung down his back almost to his ankles. His tunic was of crimson wool. Heavy gold bracelets adorned both of his muscular forearms. More gold gleamed from his earlobes in the form of twisted rings.

When the sun struck him, he blazed.

"We salute you as a free person," I called out, trying to match the tone of my voice to the dignity of his appearance. "I am Ainvar of the Carnutes, and this is my son Dara."

"Free person. That is a fine greeting, Ainvar of the Carnutes. I am Fíachu, chief of the Slea Leathan, the tribe of Broad Spears, and this is the kingdom of the Laigin. You have entered my stronghold without invitation, but you will observe that I bid you welcome. My clan is famed for its hospitality." He smiled, revealing large square teeth. "I myself am a direct descendant of Éremon, and as everyone knows, Éremon was the most gracious and the most noble of all the sons of Milesios."

That sounded familiar.

Having observed the formalities, Fíachu—whose name meant "Deerhound," though the dogs we had observed outside were too heavy of bone to be deerhounds—ushered us into his lodge. The interior was at least three spear lengths across. In the center of the room was a hearth made of carefully placed stones in the form of a spiral. The curvilinear design of the iron fire dogs was recognizably Celtic.

A sheaf of spears with iron heads was stacked just inside the doorway. Painted shields made of boiled leather attached to wooden frames hung on the walls. Even in daytime, beeswax candles burned extravagantly, revealing a packed earthen floor almost covered by carved timber boxes and wickerwork chests. Like his jewelry, the Deerhound's lodge testified to his status as the chief of a powerful tribe.

Once the Carnutes had been a powerful tribe. This place might almost have been the Gaul I knew before Caesar.

Fíachu invited Dara and me to seat ourselves on a bench padded with furs. Two very pretty women provided basins of heated water so we could bathe our hands and faces, then gave us silver cups brimming with golden liquid. The aroma of fermented apples flooded my nostrils; the richness of the fermented honey seduced my tongue. My head warned me to guard my speech, lest the mead make me foolish.

The warning was timely. We no sooner drained our cups than Fíachu began asking the sort of questions one asks of strangers.

"We've traveled across the Great Sea from our homeland in Gaul," I told him.

"Gaul? I don't know it."

"One of the Celtic lands," I said, verbally reclaiming our sacred earth from the loathsome grip of Caesar. "As I'm sure you're aware," I added to flatter him, "the territory of the Celts stretches from one sea to another."

"Of course, of course," he replied in the manner of a man who has no idea what you are talking about. "Gaul." He pronounced the name with a peculiar twist of the tongue. "Are you here to do trade? When are you going back?"

Going back? My testicles shriveled as if a cold wind blew over them. "We're staying, Fíachu. We intend to raise our children and their children here."

"Aha! You were either starving or driven out, then. It's an old story. But if you come as allies, not enemies—allies of mine," he stressed, "then you're welcome." He gave us a broad, if rather calculating, smile. "Did you bring any silk thread with you? My wives love silk thread. Or perhaps you brought a seed bull I could use on some of my cows?"

"I'm afraid not."

"Aha." A change of tone. "No silk. No bull." A moment's silence. "What is your rank in your homeland?"

His eyes were very sharp; the eyes of a man who can see through a dissembler. I decided I had better tell the truth. "In Gaul I was the chief druid of my tribe."

Those piercing eyes narrowed further than I liked. "And do you propose to be chief druid of a tribe here?"

I saw where this was going. "My tribe will not be coming to this land," I assured him. "The Carnutes don't even exist anymore. I brought the last living remnants with me: a very small clan indeed. There are barely a score of us and we're no threat to anyone. Women and children, mostly."

Fíachu's whole face brightened. "So! Where are you living?"

"On the clanland of Cohern."

He gave a disdainful sniff. "Too bad for you, then. Cohern's tribe is descended from an inferior son of Milesios. When the Slea Leathan go to war against the Iverni we always win."

His claim fell on my ears like seeds on stone. From long experience I knew that a warrior's boast is self-aggrandizement and not always to be believed.

"Cohern is a man of bad aspect," Fíachu confided. "He would never admit it, but I suspect one of his mother's mothers was Fír Bolg."

"Fír Bolg?"

"A tribe that was here before the Milesians," Fíachu said vaguely. Obviously the subject did not interest him, but it intrigued me. Who were they? And what of the Túatha Dé Danann?

Everything I learned in Hibernia led to more questions.

"Actually, I've been aware of you for some time, Ainvar," Fíachu said. "My scouts reported that Cohern had strangers as clients. It was only a matter of time before you learned how worthless he is and began looking for a more valuable protector."

Honor compelled me to say, "Cohern has treated us well enough. Our only quarrel with him is about seed corn, for which he asks an excessive price."

"Seed corn, is it?" Fíachu waved a hand weighed down with finger rings. Gold and silver and beautifully enameled copper the Goban Saor would appreciate. "We do no farming, we're cattle people. We trade for our grain. But you can take as much as you want from my stores. For nothing," he added, to my astonishment.

Women are naturally generous; the Source imbues them with that quality to prepare them for giving birth. But when men give something, they usually expect to get something in return.

I stood up, in order to put our dealings on a formal basis. "We'll pay for enough grain to plant," I said firmly, thinking of our precious salt. "We prefer a fair exchange to being in debt."

Thoughts flickered behind the chieftain's eyes like fish darting through shallow water. Before I could catch one and examine it more closely, he said, "Your dealings with Cohern have misled you as to the true character of the Gael, Ainvar. Allow me to make this gesture on behalf of the line of Éremon. You can have your seed corn, plus the free holding of a portion of our tribeland, so your women and children can feel secure. We refuse to accept payment for either. The Slea Leathan can afford to be generous."

A freehold on his land? That would make us at least nominally members of the Slea Leathan. But why not? They could give us a degree of protection we had not enjoyed in years.

"If you put it that way," I told Fíachu, "on behalf of my people I can hardly refuse."

He gave me a mighty slap on the back that nearly drove me to my knees. "Sit down, sit down, Ainvar, and we'll fill our cups again. A bargain must be sealed with good drink. And meat, no? We'll roast an ox for you tomorrow. Two, if you like!"

His inclination to expansive gestures boded well, I thought.

"Is there anything else we can do for you?" he asked.

I hesitated.

"Yes? What?" Fíachu leaned toward me, deliberately moving into my space. Breathing my air. But I could not draw back, for fear of insulting him.

"Well," I said, "I would like to know more about those people you mentioned earlier. The Fír Bolg."

The tangled eyebrows crawled upward toward his hairline. "Why?"

"Cohern never mentioned them, and I'm curious."

"Cohern doesn't know anything about anything," said Fíachu. "My bard can satisfy your curiosity."

"You have a bard?" Cohern never mentioned bards; I had supposed they were unknown in Hibernia.

"Oh yes, there are quite a few bards among the Slea Leathan. The best is one of my cousins, a man called Seanchán, who will entertain us tonight."

My spirit sang at the prospect of hearing a bard again.

In Gaul the bards were among the most highly regarded members of the Order of the Wise. They spent as much as twenty years on their studies. Some memorized the entire lineage of their clan to the thirty-third generation. Others learned the vast body of tribal history since before the before. Still others observed current events and committed them to memory so they would not be lost in the river of time. All of this was accomplished through the medium of poetry: a stern discipline. Every word and phrase had to be chanted without the slightest deviation.

Without having access to bards, people were cut adrift from their past. We know who we are by knowing what we have done.

Caesar the mendacious had justified genocide by inventing monstrous lies about the Gauls. Although many druids were familiar with Greek letters, we had no written account of our people with which to refute him. The Order of the Wise insisted that no matter of importance be committed to something as easily destroyed as parchment. Knowledge engraved on the brain and scrupulously passed down from generation to generation was immortal. Therefore we had stored everything within the bone vault of the skull.

A conqueror's most dangerous opponents are not the warriors, but the thinkers. Realizing this, Caesar had ordered his legions to hunt down the Order of the Wise and put all they found to the sword. With those murdered men and women had died much of our past.

No bard survived to enrich our small band of refugees. Perhaps in time some child of ours would demonstrate the gift, yet who was there to teach that child the true history of the Gauls?

My head does me no favors by asking questions I cannot answer.

That night Fíachu introduced us to Seanchán the bard. Seanchán was a big man, tall and wide, but his mouth was as tender as a woman's.

The lips of one who recites poetry must be supple.

I took for granted that Seanchán was a druid. To my surprise, he denied this. "I'm no sorcerer, Ainvar, I'm a storyteller."

"There is sorcery in storytelling," I assured him. "A good bard enchants his audience."

Seanchán frowned.

At that moment Fíachu caught me by the elbow. "Come with me, Ainvar. I want you to meet another of my cousins, Duach Dalta. *Our* chief druid."

"What are his duties here?" I asked out of professional curiosity.

"He conducts the rites of inauguration for chieftains and kings."

"What else does the chief druid do?"

Fíachu gave me a blank look. "What else is there?"

"Well, what are the functions of your other druids?"

"They interpret omens."

"Is that all?"

"What else is there?" he repeated.

What else indeed.

My thoughts ran back to Gaul. Druids whispering to seeds in the frozen earth so they would burst forth in the springing time. Druids lighting the fires that called back the sun from the kingdoms of ice. Druids recalling the past and foreseeing the future. Druids supervising birth and burial. Druids keeping the dead and the living in harmony with each other, with the Earth, with the Otherworld. The whole complex structure of druidry that had been so elaborately interwoven to cherish the creations of the Source.

Gone.

Duach Dalta was about my age, with the powerful body and elastic movements of a much younger man. Fíachu introduced us by saying, "Ainvar claims to have been a chief druid in his homeland." Duach Dalta's expression curdled like sour milk. I murmured his name, he murmured mine. His long, sharp nose twitched derisively. He quickly abandoned me to speak to someone he felt was more important.

I made my way back to Seanchán and tried to resume a conversation. "In the land where I was born," I told him, "bards were the equal of princes."

"Among the Gael there was a bard who was also a prince," he replied. "He was Amergin, a son of Milesios. But that was a very long time ago. And the Slea Leathan are not his tribe." His tone informed me that the descendants of Amergin were not allies of the descendants of Éremon.

I dropped the subject.

That night we were served a feast that put Cohern's to shame. With my first bite I realized these people did not need to buy our salt. They seasoned their food with seaweed. Watercress provided a delightfully peppery taste. In addition to the promised roast ox we were offered boiled mutton and wild pig; trout and salmon and eel; seven different cheeses; oatcakes glistening with butter, porridge drenched in cream; wild apples simmered in honey; buttermilk and mead and malted ale. Copious quantities of ale.

I ate until my belly hurt.

After the feast Seanchán rose to speak. His listeners made themselves comfortable as he smoothed his tunic and cleared his throat. I was sitting on a padded bench, for which my bones thanked me, while Dara flopped down cross-legged at my feet. Boys have no bones.

Seanchán carried a beautifully carved harp. It consisted of a triangular wooden frame fitted with brass strings, and was small enough to be held by one hand.

In my experience, the bardic harp was used to intensify the mood by replicating the sounds of nature. A ripple of water could soothe, a roll of thunder could excite. I looked forward to hearing the voices of Hibernia that Seanchán would summon from his instrument.

He allowed an expectant hush to build, then strummed the harp strings once or twice. After that the instrument lay idle in the crook of his arm.

Obviously he preferred the sound of his own voice.

"Before the before, this land belonged to the birds and the beasts," he began. "And the trees. This was the island of trees, with a dense forest that stretched from north to south and from east to west. Then an adventurer called Partholon arrived with a fleet of ships to establish a colony."

I recognized Partholon as a Greek name. My mouth opened with a question but Seanchán plowed on. I should have known better anyway; bards reject interruptions. "The colonists cleared enough land to build a few settlements," he was saying, "and planted the corn they had brought with them. They also began trading with others who were beginning to venture into these waters.

"But after several generations the Partholonians succumbed to a terrible plague. A few escaped in a single boat, living just long enough to tell their story. No more traders visited these shores.

"Then only the song of the wolf, the grunt of the boar, and the roar of the stag were heard here. Alone was the land, and content in her loneliness. She dwelt with the sea and the sky and needed nothing more."

Now, and at last, Seanchán spoke like a true bard. Young Dara sat spellbound.

The moment was too brief. Seanchán resumed his narrative in a commonplace tone. "When sufficient time had passed for the warning to be forgotten, another group of colonists arrived: surly, coarse-fibered folk who heard no music in poetry and saw no beauty in nature. They called themselves Fír Bolg, meaning men of the bag, because they were slaves whose masters forced them to carry heavy objects in leather bags.

"In spite of their low station in life the Fír Bolg possessed a certain cunning. Some of them mastered the skills of seafaring. Led by a man called Nemed, they watched for their opportunity and stole enough ships for their people to escape. When they reached these shores they thought they were safe at last. They lived on the fruits of the sea and the forest, and also established trade with Albion to obtain tin for making bronze. It is said of them that they were skilled craftsmen.

"But they were not as safe as they thought. All too soon, the Fír Bolg were being attacked by a race of marauding seafarers called the Fomorians. The Fomorians, who worshipped a terrible fire god they knew as Baal, landed here to capture sacrifices for their insatiable deity. In an attempt to repel them the Fír Bolg built great stone fortresses along the western coast."

I had assumed Hibernia was our secret sanctuary. I was wrong. Any number of people knew about this place.

The discovery brought Caesar chillingly close. I actually shuddered.

"At last the Fír Bolg succeeded in defeating the Fomorians and held this land uncontested," Seanchán related. "But only until another wave of invaders appeared. They called themselves the Túatha Dé Danann: the people of the goddess Danu. Although they cunningly disguised their origins, it was believed they came from the region of the Mid-Earth Sea.

"The Danann defied understanding; wizards and sorcerers, all of them. They could fly with the birds and swim with the fish. They talked to one another without words. Their wealth was incalculable. They possessed a cauldron that was never empty and a stone that could turn a man into a king." I longed to ask questions but Seanchán never paused for breath. "The Túatha Dé Danann loved this land, and the land loved the Danann. Love can end in grief, however."

To illustrate this the bard described the war that had ensued between the Fír Bolg and the Túatha Dé Danann. Curiously, he related the epic from the point of view of the defenders rather than the invaders. We were given a vivid picture of the descendants of Nemed being overwhelmed by a spectral magic they could neither understand nor counter. The Fír Bolg were commemorated as heroes, even as they went down in defeat, while the infinitely more fascinating Túatha Dé Danann were kept in the distance like figures in the clouds.

In Gaul the bards had not immortalized failures. They had concentrated on the high deeds of victors. Yet Seanchán did his best to exclude the Danann from their own story, as if he feared his very thoughts might summon them.

Once again I thought of Caesar. Then hastily slammed the doors in my head.

The climax of the bard's story was the arrival of the Milesians. In narrating this event Seanchán concentrated on the invaders. The Milesians had brought swords and spears of iron, as opposed to the bronze weapons of the Danann. Cold iron had proved to be a powerful weapon against magic. Defeated, almost exterminated, the Túatha Dé Danann were forced to surrender the bountiful land they called Eriu. Some of them fled into caves under the ground. Others simply melted into the hawthorn trees and became one with them.

"Now their land is ours, and shall be ours forever!" the bard concluded triumphantly. Rediscovering his harp, he strummed it once or twice before bowing his head in acknowledgment of the enthusiastic applause.

My head contemplated the tale he had told. Was it history? Or myth, as history so often becomes? The overlapping of myth and reality is like the twinning of spirit and flesh, a manifestation of the Two-Faced One.

I did not believe Seanchán had given us the whole story, however. Druids are sensitive to nuances. Whenever he mentioned the Túatha Dé Danann I detected a disturbing change in the bard's voice, an undertone of lingering fear.

Not fear. Terror.

## *chapter* VII

In my youth I once had happened upon the strange ritual the druids called the Crow Court. A solitary crow was encircled on the ground by a flock of his fellows. The unfortunate creature had transgressed some law of crow society. The others would not allow him to fly away, but forced him to stand waiting while they strutted around him, eyeing him in eerie, unnatural silence.

Then they all flew at him at once and pecked him to death.

On the occasion I witnessed, the slain crow's only crime had been that he was an albino. If he had resembled the other crows he would have been safe.

Nature is ever the teacher.

When the feast in Fíachu's lodge was over, Dara and I retired to bed. We were not invited to sleep in the chieftain's lodge but offered accommodation nearby, with a family of his cousins. They supplied us with sheets woven of linen and blankets of wool. They even put a pitcher of mead close to hand, in case we were thirsty in the night.

Fíachu had not overestimated his clan's hospitality.

I had a little talk with Dara before we slept. "As of this night," I said, "we must cease to be Gaulish."

The boy stared at me as if I had suggested we leap into the air and fly. "How can we, Father? How can we stop being what we are?"

"We have no choice. It's a matter of survival."

"What shall we become, then?"

"Were you not listening to the bard?"

"Oh yes," the boy murmured. "I was listening."

"Then you heard him say that in order to survive on their own terms after their defeat at the hands of the Milesians, the Túatha Dé Danann became something else. We must do the same."

"You're going to work magic again!" crowed the boy.

His faith in me, though misguided, was touching. "No, this is a magic the whole clan will have to work together. I propose to turn the last of the Carnutes into Gaels."

"I don't understand."

"I believe we share a common background with these people," I explained. "So it should be possible for us to blend in with them until Caesar himself could not tell us apart."

Yet even then, I knew I would still dream of Gaul.

I lay awake for most of the night, developing my plan in my head. I realized that Cohern could present a problem. He had been good to us in his way and was sure to resent our leaving. At the least he would think us ungrateful; at the most, treacherous. He might precipitate a fresh outbreak of hostilities between the Iverni and the Slea Leathan which would result in the final extinguishing of his clan. And the possible deaths of Cormiac Ru and Labraid.

Yet I must do what was best for my clan as a whole. Responsibility is a heavy stone to carry.

Dara and I spent a complete phase of the moon in Fíachu's clanhold, studying the people and developing ties of amity with them.

Hunting was a favorite pastime among the Slea Leathan. Their territory abounded with wild boar, wolf, red deer, and badger. In the early morning the glens resounded with the echo of horns and the cry of hounds. Cormiac would be in his element here, I thought. He too loved the chase.

The red deer of Hibernia was the giant of its species, as tall at the shoulder as a horse. They customarily were hunted with deerhounds but were almost too fleet for a man to follow. The deer sometimes escaped. Because a large clan required a lot of meat, a more satisfactory method had been devised. A spear, point upward, was firmly fixed in stocks at the bottom of a deep pit. A complicated wooden framework was erected along with the spear, so that even if a deer escaped the iron spearhead, its legs would be firmly caught and held. The mechanism was concealed beneath a light covering of branches. These traps were placed at random intervals throughout the forest and checked daily, almost always yielding at least one deer. Similar traps were also employed for wild boar, who were very dangerous if cornered, and occasionally for birds.

These people had good heads, my own observed. We could learn from them.

Dara became Seanchán's shadow. Revealing a prodigious memory for a lad so young, my son began to memorize the sagas of the Milesians. I was amazed by his eagerness to learn, because he had never seemed anxious to learn anything from me. But a parent is handicapped by being too familiar. Children are intrigued by the new and strange.

Dara informed me that a Gaelic bard composed his work under very particular circumstances. A special bed was prepared for him, using wattles of mountain ash covered with the hide of a bull. The bard's eyes were bound with a thick piece of cloth before he lay down on the bed. Then he was left alone in the darkness, with nothing to distract him but his thoughts.

"The bull's hide summons inspiration through the spirit of the animal," said Dara.

In Gaul we had no such custom. Yet I detected a distant echo of druidry in the use of tree branches, and there had been a time when Celtic shape-changers covered themselves with animal hides to lure game within range of the hunter.

Dara told me that he was going to ask the Goban Saor to make a harp for him.

I had no doubt that the great craftsman could fulfill the task; he could pattern the instrument on the one belonging to Seanchán. But there would be a problem. "Who will teach you to play it?" I asked my son.

"I'll teach myself," he said with the confidence of youth.

I was not sure I wanted the bardic life for my oldest son. A poet must be detached, almost remote, if he is to observe clearly and chronicle accurately.

Dara was a vital boy. I thought he should plunge into the center of the stream and live fully as I had done, rather than stand on the bank watching.

But that was not mine to say. It is always a mistake to force a child to follow the parent's Pattern.

Dara blended easily into the society of the Slea Leathan. I, being older, was less adaptable. In large ways and small I felt my differences. Going barefoot, for example, was painful. After only one day I had a distressing accumulation of cuts and bruises. I had never really looked at my feet before. Ugly things, feet. Yet they serve us so well; they are indispensable. This led me to consider my body as a whole, until I acquired an almost filial love not only for my feet, but for my hands, my limbs, all the outposts of my head, without which I would be left desolate. What is a head without a body?

But the body must make some sacrifices. Although wearing a Gaelic tunic beneath my druid robe added a welcome layer of warmth, the robe itself set me apart from the men of the Slea Leathan. So I discarded the robe.

Fíachu gave me a wide leather belt carved in the designs favored by his tribe. "This will hold your tunic close to your body and keep out cold drafts," he said, adding with a wink, "but take care not to outgrow it. A man who gets too fat to wear his belt loses status."

"That should be no problem for me. I've always been lean."

He studied me as if deciding how large a hole would be needed to bury me in. "Bony, I'd say. Anytime you feel hungry, ask one of my wives for something to eat. I'd recommend the porridge they make. It's something you can eat right- and left-handed until you've put a little padding on your ribs. We don't want you leaving here with gaunt cheeks, Ainvar; someone could accuse me of breaking the laws of hospitality." He threw back his head and laughed.

My new friends appeared to be as guileless as children. The expressive shrug so ubiquitous in Gaul was unknown among the Gael. Great talkers, they let their words speak for them. A man or woman would abandon the most urgent task to carry on a protracted conversation about trivial matters. They constantly complained to one another about the weather, though their climate was mild by our standards.

The Gael were more spontaneous than we, and more exuberant. Quicker to laugh, slower to cry. When one of them did weep it was a great flood of tears that carried all before it, then passed as swiftly as a Hibernian rainstorm and was replaced by a rainbow of smiles.

As I studied them I felt myself changing. Tight knots inside me that I had never even suspected began to dissolve. The dignified Ainvar was giving way to a man who might someday enjoy going barefoot.

By the end of our visit the Slea Leathan had fully accepted us. When he bade me farewell, Fíachu said, "What was that greeting you gave me on the first day, Ainvar? I salute you as a free person? You and your clan will be free persons on the Plain of Broad Spears. Your holding will be inherited by your children's children." He beamed at me and gave me another ferocious slap on the back.

Fíachu's beneficence proved that hospitality was one of the foundations of Gaelic society.

So was honor. Which meant I must deal honorably with Cohern.

As we headed southward Dara inquired, "Why are you frowning, Father? Haven't things turned out well for us?"

"I'm wondering what to say to Cohern. He forbade us to leave the valley for our own good, you know, and now we've disobeyed. He well may feel that we've betrayed him."

The boy grinned. "I can persuade him we haven't."

Young eyes see no hills too steep to climb. "This is a serious matter, Dara, not a game for children."

"Would you agree that Seanchán the bard is no child?"

"I fail to see what he has to do with this."

"I've been listening to him carefully, Father. There's a certain rhythm to his speech that gathers his listeners like fish in a net. When they're firmly caught they believe everything he says."

"That's an astute observation. However, I can hardly ask Seanchán to explain our situation to Cohern."

"You don't have to." Dara turned to face me. Standing with his feet firmly planted and his head thrown back, he closed his eyes. Haltingly at first, then with gathering confidence, he began to chant the story Seanchán had told. Instead of the words he put his emphasis on the rhythm. The magic inherent in the rhythm . . .

In spite of his youth his voice resonated in his chest. Resonated in my bones.

And I knew.

My eldest son would never be a warrior. Hibernia had presented us with another druid talent.

Briga welcomed us home with joyful abandon. She threw herself into my arms and pressed her body so tightly against mine that the pair of us barely made it into our lodge. "I'd begun to fear I might never see you again," she whispered. Just before we fell onto our bed in a tangle of arms and legs.

Later—much later—Briga turned her attention to my feet. Noticing their condition, she made the tut-tutting noise familiar to every man who has a wife. She rummaged through her collection of herbs, put several aside, and took a lump of butter from the churn. I watched as she kneaded herbs into the butter.

"Sit down by the fire, Ainvar, and put your feet on that stool."

Kneeling before me, my senior wife began rubbing the butter into my feet. She started with my toes, repeatedly caressing each one from the root to the toenail. Warmed by her hands, the fragrant grease sank into my flesh. Her fingers found every injury and soothed the hurt away. Slowly she worked her way up the arch of the foot. Rubbing, stroking, massaging. Bending over with her hair unbound, so that an occasional lock strayed across my bare ankles.

A glow of pleasure spread through my groin. Briga was making love to my feet. My poor, ugly, damaged feet.

In the morning there was not a cut or a bruise to be seen.

The following day I received a private welcome first from Lakutu, and then Onuava. Much time had passed since I last lay with Lakutu; I had almost forgotten her exotic arts. Even at her age she retained the ability to stir and surprise me. Afterward I held her tenderly in my arms and stroked her hair as she stroked mine, in mutual gratitude.

Onuava never wanted tenderness, only praise. Intensely competitive—what a match she had been for Rix!—she did her best to outdo the other two. She performed for herself, however, and not for me. Or perhaps for the shade of Vercingetorix, watching from the Otherworld.

It can be exhausting to have three wives.

"I've brought no seed corn with me because we're going to plant our grain elsewhere," I told my clan. "On the other side of those mountains is the territory of a powerful tribe. Their chieftain, Fíachu, has offered us land, not as tenants, but as equals."

"We can't shift to another place," wailed Damona, "we're barely settled in this one. I've just found a good puddle of clay for making pottery."

"Our roots are still shallow," I said. "Here we are ferns by the riverside. A flood would carry us away. On the other side of the mountains we can put down deep roots and grow strong."

The women might be uncertain but I could see that the men were interested. After a brief conference, the Goban Saor spoke for them all. "Do whatever you think best, Ainvar. You've got us this far, we'll go the rest of the way with you."

On the next bright morning I went to see Cohern. One should never attempt persuasion on a dark day. Dara went with me. He carried a spear but it was just for show. The real weapon was in his mouth.

Cohern greeted us by saying, "It's about time you came for that seed corn. I feared it would sprout before you collected it."

"We appreciate the offer," Dara replied courteously, "but we no longer need your grain. We have a gift for you, however."

The clan chief looked from me to my son and back again. "This mere boy speaks for you now, Ainvar?"

"He's growing fast and needs to learn the skills of a man. Negotiation is one of them."

"If you think using a child will soften my heart and make me lower my price, I warn you: It won't work."

"You need not lower your price," Dara said smoothly. "We have made other arrangements."

While Cohern was trying to adjust to this news, Dara told him, "Fíachu of the Slea Leathan has promised not to attack your clan again if our clan joins his tribe. That is our gift to you. A chance for peace."

Cohern's mouth fell open.

"Let me tell you how it will be." Dara's voice dropped into his chest, became a rhythmic chant as his words painted pictures on the air.

We returned in triumph to the valley. No longer a man and a boy, but a man and a much younger man who had done what his father could not do.

"Dara was amazing," I told his mother. She listened with the smug smile women wear when their children are being praised. A smile that says, I knew it all along, and most of the credit is down to me, though I'm too modest to say so.

"Dara's skills are not yet polished," I went on, "but he spoke with surprising authority. And his voice, Briga! It rolled and rippled, soared and sang. Within a dozen eyeblinks he captured Cohern by describing the benefits he would gain if we joined the Slea Leathan."

"Cohern accepted it?"

"He did indeed. Dara showed him a vision he couldn't resist."

Dara chanted, "Fat on the knife and fat under the skin. Boys live to sire children and become old men." He smiled at his mother. He was very pleased with himself. "Cohern's willing for us to go now, in fact he's eager. As soon as we arrange a truce with Fíachu, he'll release Labraid and Cormiac Ru from his service."

Briga looked toward me. "Are you sure you can arrange a truce?"

"Our son can," I replied with perfect confidence. I was still caught up in the spell of the bard myself.

That night in our bed I told Briga of my plan to merge our clan into the Slea Leathan. She accepted it without hesitation, and went one step further.

"Caesar is destroying Gaul, Ainvar. His people are planting Roman crops and building Roman villas and speaking the Roman tongue. The Gauls who survive are being forced to accept the Roman Pattern. That's the final extermination, the ultimate crime.

"We must reject the Roman Pattern entirely. This land took us in when we had nowhere else to go, so it is right and proper that we adapt ourselves to her. We'll worship among her trees; we'll do homage to her mountains. All the faces of the Source are sacred no matter what name one uses."

Briga was the first of us who truly became a Gael.

The accents of Hibernia came easily to her lips. Already she knew the name of every hill and hollow in our immediate vicinity, and if they did not have one, she gave one to them. "It's important, Ainvar," she stressed. "Being named consecrates a common clod of earth. This is our place now; this is our earth."

I fleetingly wondered if my Briga consecrated the earth simply by walking upon it.

Most women hate to abandon a nest once it is built. With the exception of Briga, the women of my clan were no different. So Dara painted word pictures for them, too. Larger lodges built of sturdier timber; cows who gave more freely of their milk; more children for their own to play with and grow with and marry. Best of all, the comfort of being part of a strong tribe again.

My son. Hardly more than a child himself, yet with the head of a man. The druid gift defies understanding.

We were warmly welcomed by Fíachu's clan and given land an easy walk from his fort, with loamy fields for planting. Our new lodges would stand at the edge of an immense forest which offered an unlimited supply of timber for building and deadfall for firewood.

When we awoke in the morning, the first breath we drew would be the exhalation of oaks.

On the other side of our new clanhold Briga discovered a grove of wild apple trees. She came running back to tell me, "We can make vinegar!"

My senior wife was a great believer in the efficacy of vinegar.

She was equally pleased to find an expanse of bog in the other direction. "Sphagnum moss, Ainvar!"

"We can't eat moss."

"No, but we can use it to keep the bottoms of infants dry, and to stanch the flow of blood from wounds. That particular moss will soak up many times its own weight in liquid."

I saluted Hibernia in my head. We had arrived as impoverished refugees; we were going to spend the rest of our lives in the midst of plenty.

With the help of Fíachu's men we began to build our lodges. It would be a race against time; the women wanted the roofs thatched before the worst of the winter. The chieftain himself strolled out to observe our progress. He seemed quietly amused. Eventually I asked why.

His bright blue eyes glittered. "Cohern put you on his border to use as a buffer against me. Now the obstacle is removed."

That possibility had never occurred to me.

The Gael were neither as simple nor as guileless as I assumed. I had to wonder if Dara would be able to affect a truce between Fíachu's powerful tribe and Cohern's enfeebled clan. Probably not.

Surely not.

We had betrayed Cohern after all.

"Poor Ainvar," Briga commiserated when I shared my thoughts with her that night. "Don't torture yourself about it. You had good intentions."

"Look what my good intentions accomplished! Cohern was clever to locate us where he did, and now I've removed his only shield. He's vulnerable to Fíachu again."

"We could always go back to him, you know."

"Then we'd be vulnerable to Fíachu, who would not thank us for refusing his hospitality. No, we'll have to stay here."

"You don't sound very happy about it, Ainvar."

"It's all the fault of my head. I should never use it to make plans anymore. The time we spent at sea addled my brains with all that rolling and heaving."

Briga laughed. I did not see anything funny.

At least we had left Cohern better-built lodges than his own. He would not occupy them while they were so close to his enemy. But Cohern expected us to change his enemies into friends.

Deep in my mind was a story I had heard long ago in Gaul, from one of our own bards. Among the early Celts there were shamans known as shape-changers who assumed the form of wild animals. Changing one thing into another seemed to be a Celtic specialty.

Like changing people into hawthorn trees . . .

Was it possible that the Túatha Dé Danann were Celts?

I spent a sleepless night on speculations. Outside the lodge where I lay—one which Fíachu had put at my disposal while our own were being built—was the usual complement of night noises. Sometime before dawn they changed. The rustle of trees in the wind became a chorus of sibilant voices.

Listen, I commanded my ears.

In addition to the voices there were other sounds, like the pattering of small bare feet. Moving carefully so as not to awaken Briga beside me, I got up and went to the door of the lodge. When I looked out I saw only the surrounding lodges. The bare earth was white with moonlight.

Yet I could hear whispering voices and running feet. Very, very close now.

The hairs rose on the back of my neck.

"What is it, Ainvar?" Briga called sleepily. Lakutu began to stir in her bed. Onuava coughed, and little Gobnat made querulous, about-to-wake-up sounds.

"I thought it might be raining," I said.

"And what would you do if it were? Stop the rain?"

That was cruel; probably because she had been awakened out of a sound sleep. Briga knew I could no longer stop the rain.

I continued staring into the empty moonlight. Wondering what had been summoned by my thoughts. At last I went back and lay down again, but I still could not sleep. Fear crept over my skin like a skulk of foxes.

Once I was brave. A long time ago. Warriors must be crazy-brave, able to face anything. My courage came from being self-controlled and thoughtful. For most of my life that had been sufficient. Until Caesar. As casually as the scythe cuts the mistletoe from the oak, the fiendish Caesar had stripped me of my courage.

Briga is the opposite. When we first met she was a frightened child who aroused my most protective feelings. That which has broken me has made her stronger. She is the brave one now, as fierce as lions if need be. It is Briga who protects Ainvar, who lifts my heart and stiffens my spine.

I should be grateful. I am grateful. Yet a small, mean part of me hates her for having the courage I lack.

Love and hate; the Two-Faced One. Can the faces ever be reconciled?

# *chapter* VIII

WITH THE HELP OF FÍACHU'S MEN OUR NEW LODGES WERE SOON built. They were even larger and more beautifully crafted than those we had abandoned. The Goban Saor carved our doors as Fíachu's tribe carved theirs, and Glas decorated the door frames with colorful Celtic designs. Teyrnon demonstrated his ironwork by making door hinges so intricately shaped that they attracted attention in their own right. While he was forging them I wandered over to watch.

"It's like magic," I said, paying him the ultimate compliment. "You make it look so easy."

Teyrnon grinned; flash of white teeth in a blackened face. "You have to work at the forge to feel the heat, Ainvar."

Soon Fíachu's clansmen were requesting new weapons from him. Their womenfolk asked him to fashion cauldrons and flesh forks. No one asked Teyrnon to forge a plow, though. The Slea Leathan were cattle people.

By talking with them while our new lodges were being built, I extended my knowledge considerably.

I learned that society in Hibernia was highly stratified and militarized. The island was roughly divided into a handful of kingdoms. Each was ruled by an overking who claimed the allegiance of the tribes in his territory and demanded tribute from them in the form of cattle and warriors. In return the king defended his kingdom against incursion by outsiders.

The kingdom of the Laigin extended south from a river called the Liffey. A vast stretch of bog in the midlands served as the western boundary. The major tribes of the Laigin were ruled by chieftains who claimed descent from Éremon. They and their related clans comprised the warrior elite. Below them in rank were freemen with less prestigious antecedents, and then the unfree: men and women in bondage who had been seized in warfare.

The king of the Laigin was elected from among the tribal chieftains. The current king was an elderly man long past his fighting prime. Although Fíachu hoped to succeed him, his fellow chieftains also coveted the title.

A similar situation pertained in the kingdom of the Deisi, southwest of us, and also among the Ulaid in the north, from whom the Laigin obtained woven linen when the two kingdoms were not at war. Which was not often. No wonder warriors were at a premium. All Hibernia was a battleground.

Ensconced within a strong tribe, at least my little clan would have a degree of security. "We were wise to accept Fíachu's offer," I told Briga. "For the first time in years, we stand with the winners."

My senior wife said smugly, "Aren't you glad I sent you for seed corn?"

In honor of our new homes, Fíachu's clan treated us to a celebratory banquet. The principal dish was roast swan. The bird, so rare in Gaul, was common on the lakes and rivers of Hibernia. The chieftain's wives had pillows stuffed with swansdown. The creatures were highly regarded, however, and rarely slain for meat.

Briga managed to get through the whole meal without taking a bite of swan. When I asked her why not, she said, "They're too beautiful to eat, Ainvar."

Suddenly I had no appetite for mine, either.

When our lodges were ready Briga made a little ceremony of unwrapping her set of enameled bowls, lining them up, admiring them, then rewrapping them in fresh linen and secreting them at the very bottom of the wooden chest that would hold her possessions. She never looked at them again but we knew they were there.

We knew we were home.

The first night we slept in our new lodge I had a troubling dream about the Crow Court. The crows taking part in the ritual were all female, though how I knew this I could not say, since male and female crows look alike. When I awoke in the morning I interpreted my dream to mean that our women were in danger of alienating the Gaelic women.

Which proved that I had no gift for prognostication.

The following morning the air was full of the crisp, white smell of winter. Stepping outside to do the necessary, I felt ice crunch under my poor bare feet.

Later in the day I went to call upon Fíachu. I found him wearing soft, low boots of untanned leather though his legs were still bare. The boots were formed of two pieces, with a separate sole, and were slightly pointed at the toe. The upper surface was decorated with elaborate stitching.

"I didn't know you wore shoes," I remarked.

"My people have better sense than to walk on ice barefoot, Ainvar. I'm surprised you don't."

As soon as I got back to my lodge I put my old shoes on.

Almost every day brought something new. Relentless in his search for materials with which to work, the Goban Saor reported, "This land is rich beyond measure, Ainvar. There's not only gold and iron but ample deposits of copper and lead. In fact, just about any sort of mineral one might want. Some can be ground into powder to use for enameling. Others can be polished and set as gemstones. And speaking of stone—I've found marble, granite, sandstone, limestone; an absolute plethora of building materials we could use if we wanted to emulate the Greeks. How clever you were to bring us here."

I responded with a modest smile as if I had known it all along.

Never refuse a compliment.

We were frequent visitors to the chieftain's stronghold that winter. At every opportunity, my Briga praised the beauty of the Slea Leathan women and admired their domestic skills. She made them feel good about themselves. Before spring my senior wife was the most popular woman in the whole area. Wives sought her advice about their husbands. Young girls asked her how to attract the men of their choice. More often than not, when I entered my lodge I would find Briga sitting cross-legged on the ground, plaiting some girl's bright locks while she chatted over her shoulder with a graying matron.

Many women were drawn to Briga, but aside from sharing communal tasks such as dyeing fabric, most of them had little to do with one another. Their lives were extremely circumscribed. Loyalty was limited to their immediate families; ties of blood were considered stronger than marriage.

It was not much better for the men. The Gael clung to the heritage of personal rivalries that had plagued them since their arrival in Hibernia. A man's "friends" were those who fought beside him or, more rarely, were willing to lend him something of value. Like love in a marriage, true friendship was considered a fortuitous adjunct to a much more important alliance.

Onuava was jealous of Briga's popularity. She reacted by flaunting herself in front of other men. Onuava of the tawny hair and opulent breasts could still draw men's eyes. Neither of Fíachu's wives liked Onuava. When my third wife stood near him a fine dew of perspiration beaded the chieftain's brow and his attention wandered.

Onuava also caused problems in another way. She kept urging me to bring Labraid back from Cohern.

"Cohern won't release him until there is a truce between himself and the Slea Leathan," I tried to explain to her.

"Then do it now, Ainvar. What are you waiting for?"

"It's not that easy. Fíachu's happy with the situation as it is."

"Well, I'm not. Do something!" She stamped her foot and tossed her hair; the lodge echoed with her strident voice. Briga ignored her. The children hurried outside.

Vercingetorix had been able to control Onuava. He had even enjoyed her tantrums, but she rubbed my nerves raw and made my head ache. A man must have peace in his own lodge, so I spoke to Dara. "We have to get Fíachu to proclaim a truce with Cohern as soon as possible. Have you mentioned it to him yet?"

The guilty expression in my son's eyes was my answer. "I thought maybe you would say something first, Father? Prepare the way for me?"

As chief advisor to Vercingetorix during the battle for Gaul I had been at the center of a giant spiderweb, with threads stretching in every direction. My task was to accumulate and assimilate information and determine the best way to use it. This required an understanding of our warriors and those of our allies; the Romans; their unpredictable German allies; their traitorous Gaulish allies . . . and foul Caesar himself.

Demanding though it was, and tragically though it turned out, I was gifted for that sort of work. My intuition about other people usually was sound. My own family was more difficult. I was never certain how to handle any of them.

"Dara, you wanted to do this, remember?"

He scuffled the earth with his toe. "Yes, Father."

"So you must have thought you could."

"I did at the time, but I'm not sure now. What if I make a fool of myself?"

The confidence of Vercingetorix had been contagious. It was almost enough to carry us to victory against overwhelming odds. I stood very still, reaching back into memory. Envisioning Rix at his most impressive. Then I hurled that image at my son. "You can do it, Dara," I said as convincingly as possible. "You can."

The following morning Dara went alone to the chieftain's lodge. I took myself into the forest to wait. Walking in large circles; nervously rubbing my elbows. Above my head the oaks knotted their limbs in sympathy.

It was a large responsibility to lay on the shoulders of a mere boy. Onuava was not the only one with a lot at stake. She wanted Labraid back; I wanted Cormiac Ru. The Red Wolf had become something more than a son to me. We need those people who fill in the missing parts of ourselves.

Which brought me back to Vercingetorix.

There was no denying the power of Hibernia to draw people to its shores. In Thislife I would never see Vercingetorix again, but we were soul friends; we would meet again. When we did, it would surely be here.

I tried to imagine what it would be like with both of us inhabiting very different bodies. Would our spirits recognize each other? And would Briga be there, too? Would I know her? Would—

Dara came running toward me. "It's all right, Father!" he shouted. "Everything's going to be all right."

Fíachu was going to meet with Cohern to discuss a truce.

It would not involve all of the Iverni, only a single clan, but would mean a radical improvement in Cohern's situation. A runner had been sent to invite him to meet Fíachu at a point halfway between their respective clan-holdings, and Cohern had agreed.

"Fíachu's asked me to accompany him to the meeting," Dara proudly informed me.

Not me, but my son. I was no longer at the center of the spiderweb. I thought I was glad. Yet when I saw Dara march off with Fíachu's retinue I felt a great longing for the old days with Vercingetorix.

We never fully appreciate today until tomorrow.

Onuava was ecstatic when Labraid returned. She paraded him around the clanhold, introducing him to everyone as the son of the greatest warrior who ever lived.

When Cormiac Ru rejoined us he looked older than I remembered. After the style of warriors, he now sported a flowing moustache and divided his fiery hair into seven plaits. But his eyes were the same, as deep and colorless as water.

I thought of the voices in the night and the little pattering footfalls. "I want you to sleep in our lodge," I told Cormiac.

His strange eyes looked into mine and straight through them to my hidden fears. "If you wish, Ainvar."

Onuava insisted on having Labraid with her, and the addition of two more men crowded our lodge considerably. The only solution was to build more lodges. Our little clan had not yet celebrated a new birth, but we were expanding all the same.

Life is good, I whispered to That Which Watches. It is well to give thanks whenever there is a reason to do so. The Otherworld rewards gratitude. And punishes ingratitude.

I hope Gaius Julius Caesar is ungrateful for the power he has achieved. I fondly imagine Taranis shriveling him with a bolt of white fire.

On a day of clouds and rain, Lakutu moved her children and her loom to a new lodge. Labraid carried Onuava's possessions to another one, while she trailed behind him, warning him not to drop anything in the mud. Cormiac went hunting with Dara and Echri, and little Gobnat fell asleep early.

Briga and I were alone. I had almost forgotten what that was like. She settled down beside the hearth and patted the ground, inviting me to join her.

Briga by firelight. Her fair hair turned to russet by the flame. Her complexion as luminous as a pearl moist from the sea.

Which is her element, I wonder. Fire? Or water?

My fingers tangle in Briga's hair. Does she know how I feel about her? I cannot tell her, I do not have the words.

Nor does she tell me. Yet once, when I looked back, she had touched her fingers to her lips.

THE ADDITIONAL LODGES DID NOT ASSURE ME OF A QUIET LIFE. Lakutu continued to spend much of the day in our lodge, returning to her own to sleep with her children. She even had her loom brought to our lodge so she could work there. If Briga resented the amount of floor space the loom took up, she was compensated by the beautiful fabrics my second wife wove.

Onuava was a less frequent visitor to our lodge. She preferred to be in her own place, where she was the center of attention. More and more women were coming to us, however, seeking Briga's help and advice. Her reputation as a wise woman spread beyond Fíachu's clanhold to the wider expanse of his tribe. Soon we had visitors—not all of them female—from as far away as a day's walk.

If they needed commonsense advice Briga gave it in full measure. Should they require healing for a physical complaint she sent them to Sulis. But when, as frequently happened, the remedies that had been efficacious for Sulis in Gaul failed to work in Hibernia, the sufferers returned to my senior wife. At Sulis's suggestion.

Briga did not always employ traditional methods. Her gift defied tradition. Perhaps every gift defies tradition, being unique to the recipient.

Using the druid intuition she would have denied, Briga scoured the countryside for bark and herbs and grasses. Many of those she found were unknown to her, yet she intuitively selected the ones that could help in healing.

In the same way, she sought out a number of springs in different locations and took water from each. "They have different properties," she explained to me as she poured the liquid into stone bottles. "This water is good for the eyes, this next one will heal sore throats, and that one over there will make wounds stop bleeding."

She did not test any of the liquids before making these claims. She *knew.*

She pounded yarrow and a pungent herb called finabawn into a thick paste, smeared it onto fresh grass with the dew still on it, and used this to poultice intractable boils. A plaster of cattle dung moistened with Briga's own urine was applied to painful insect stings. When a woman complained of an excessive flow of blood during her female season, Briga gave her a decoction of setfoil and furze blossom to drink.

When a child was brought to her with an excruciating, and unremitting, headache, Briga studied the child's head visually from every angle. Then she ran her fingers over the entire surface. Finally, she cradled the little skull in her hands and pressed gently, first on one area and then on another.

She treated an ulcerated leg by cutting her own leg and mixing some of her blood with sweet butter and the crushed flower of the cuckow weed, then spreading it on the limb. When an old woman came to my senior wife complaining of sadness and melancholy, she was given a drink made of borage, pure water, and wild honey, and a morning's cheerful conversation.

Briga's remedies worked. They worked every time.

With my senior wife so occupied, it fell to my other wives and Damona to provide us with clothing in the Gaelic style. I insisted that we resemble the Slea Leathan as much as possible. Lakutu did most of the weaving and sewing for my family, since Onuava considered both tasks beneath her. She did unbend enough to do a little embroidery with thread given to her by the local women. Silk, imported at great expense from the sea traders. "They call in from time to time at the mouth of the Liffey," Onuava informed me. She used all of the silk on her own clothing. Briga did not comment; I do not think she even noticed. Lakutu seemed to think it was right and fair.

To set an example, I made another try at going barefoot. With practice it became easier.

Druids know how to ignore pain.

Meanwhile Dara continued to shadow Seanchán and drink in every word that dropped from the bard's lips. When the Goban Saor agreed to make a harp for my son, I had a suggestion. "The yew is a tree of the first rank, and symbolizes rebirth. What wood could be more appropriate for the frame?"

So delicate an instrument could not be rushed. The wood must be carefully selected, slowly dried, and thoughtfully carved. Making the strings from brass wire and fastening them into the frame took more time. Dara's youthful impatience was strained, but the Goban Saor told him, "Never be in a hurry. When you hurry you are rushing to your grave."

During the long winter evenings while he waited for his harp, Dara entertained us with sagas of the sons of Milesios down the generations: the battles they broke against one another, the cattle they stole from one another, the mighty sons they sired who sired mighty sons in turn.

A man was not only named but described, such as Sirna the Beloved; or Ollum Fodla, Fierce in Valor. Every name was a story. Every story rang with high adventure. Or enduring love, or heartrending tragedy. Even small details were faithfully recalled. A person's life did not end with death. The men and women of the Gael lived on in the remembered history of their race, as vibrant as they had ever been. Truly, they were a people who loved words.

*We,* I reminded myself. *We are* a people who love words.

Following its own eternal pattern, eventually the long winter gave way to a radiant spring. My personal celebration of the new season began with throwing off my shoes. Barefoot in freedom, my feet rejoiced.

As the nights grew warmer Briga allowed the fire to burn very low on the hearth, but she never let it go out. Briga was our keeper of the flame.

One starry spring evening Fíachu came to my lodge. Mindful of the honor bestowed, I told Lakutu to offer him our best food and drink.

"I don't need feeding," Fíachu said. "What I need are sons. My wives give me nothing but girls."

"Yet your fort abounds with warriors," I pointed out.

"They're my cousins but they're not descended from my father; not in the direct line from Éremon, as he was. My brothers were in the direct line, but unfortunately they died in battle before they could sire children, and there must be something wrong with my sisters because they have borne only one male child between them. Your senior wife is gaining a reputation for wisdom, so I've come to seek her advice about siring sons."

Briga spoke up. "You have many lovely daughters, Fíachu, is that not enough? I'm sure the women who carried them in their bellies must think so."

"I have to have a son," Fíachu insisted.

"Why?"

"To lead the tribe after I die," he said bluntly. Usually he was more circumspect, but people open themselves to Briga. "Among the Gael the scramble for power begins before a chieftain draws his last breath. His tribe may fall into weaker hands and everything the dead man won for them can be lost. I've seen this happen time after time, but it's not going to happen to the Slea Leathan. I want to have a strong young man of my own choosing—someone closely bound to me by family ties—trained and ready to take my place. I'll name him while I'm still in the whole of my health, and demand on their word of honor that my people accept him."

In my experience, chieftains did not encourage successors. They did not want the tribe to think anyone else could lead them. Fíachu had a better head than most warlords; perhaps even better, in some respects, than Vercingetorix. The thought was disloyal but honest.

Briga said, "Why does this person you seek have to be a strong young man?"

"Because only a hero can lead the tribe, of course."

I could have warned Fíachu that his patronizing tone would annoy my wife.

Briga's voice remained soft. Deceptively so. I knew that deadly purr; it did not bode well for Fíachu. "You know all about heroism," she said, gazing up at him adoringly. "So tell me this. Does a man become a hero when he risks his life to kill other men?" she asked in her most innocent tone.

He nodded.

"A woman risks her life to produce new life, which, I assure you, is much more difficult than killing. Does that not make the woman heroic? According to your own way of thinking a strong woman could replace you, Fíachu."

Before he could frame a reply, Briga flashed a meltingly sweet smile. "However, if having a son is so important to you, perhaps I can help. Lakutu, please give the chief of the tribe a cup of water. With a drop of fermented honey in it, I think. We must not fail in hospitality."

Briga rummaged through her belongings until she found a small stone bottle wrapped in dried grass. She uncorked the bottle and sniffed the contents, then handed it to the chieftain. "This will do nicely, Fíachu. It's a potion to enable a woman to conceive a male child."

He squinted into the bottle. "There's not very much here. I have two wives, you know."

"This is intended for you."

"But the problem's with my wives."

"Of course it is," Briga agreed. "But this drink will make you even more virile than you already are. As we all know, a man who is tireless in bed begets sons." The melting smile returned; deepened. "Even if he must take another woman to do it."

My senior wife was a cunning and devious person.

"It was a good day's work when I welcomed your clan," Fíachu told me as he was leaving.

I waited until he was out of earshot before complaining, "You've never given me a potion to make me tireless in bed."

Briga laughed. "You don't need one, foolish man. It won't have that effect on the Deerhound's body, either; only on his mind. But if he beds enough women enough times, sooner or later one of them is bound to give birth to a boy."

"How do you know these things?"

"How does one know anything?"

"Don't answer me with riddles, Briga."

"I thought druids loved riddles." Briga could be maddening at times.

The following day Fíachu sent my senior wife a magnificent hooded mantle made of otter fur which reached almost to her bare ankles.

More and more people came to confer with her, and I grew accustomed to a lodge full of strangers. Their presence had a strange effect on Briga. When she arose from our bed at dawn each morning she looked like a young girl. By the time the day was half over and she had dealt with the problems of six or eight visitors, fine lines were gathering at the corners of her eyes. Her shoulders began to slump; she seemed shorter, thicker. Closer to the earth. By nightfall I would swear her hair was filled with gray threads and she had grown frail.

I had three wives but one of them was three women. I cannot explain this. I only know what I saw. We believe our eyes over any other authority. Why is that? I wonder.

Eyes can be deceived as easily as heads.

Cormiac Ru, who was never comfortable with crowds, spent most of his time out hunting. He loved to roam the mountains even if he found no game, but he always returned at sundown, smelling of clouds and pine trees.

I was thankful.

I did not hear them very often, the voices and the footfalls. But I still heard them.

# *chapter* IX

"WHEN THE SEA WAS MOUNTAINS AND THE SKY WAS FOREST, I was a young girl." This evasive remark was all the answer Briga gave to visitors who asked her age. The less she revealed about herself, the more impressed they were.

"They aren't really interested in me anyway," she told me. "They want me to be interested in them. And I am."

Her patience was inexhaustible, even with the most difficult individuals. When someone arrived at our lodge with an illness of the body or a cloud on mind or spirit, Briga welcomed them in and sat them down by the fire. First she gave them a cup of pure, sweet water to drink. Then she seated herself nearby and urged them to explain the problem.

Before they began to talk I usually left the lodge. But sometimes I lingered in the shadows, drawing no attention to myself. What druid could resist watching magic?

Briga was a wonderful listener. Her face mirrored the exact emotions the sufferer hoped to elicit, creating an impression of total sympathy. People told her things I doubt they would tell anyone else on earth. My senior wife had a gift for disarming others and getting them to open themselves to her. Perhaps it was her innocent blue eyes. I had once fallen into those eyes myself and never found my way out.

Sometimes just being able to talk about the problem was enough. Many ailments required more physical treatment, however. Briga would not undertake this unless she was assured that the local healer already had tried and failed. She prepared potions, or made up poultices, or suggested burning certain herbs and inhaling the smoke. Sometimes she manipulated aching muscles with her hands. In one memorable instance a man who was being driven mad by debilitating nightmares was told to put a knife under his bed to cut away bad dreams. After one cycle of the moon he returned looking ten years younger, and told Briga that the malady had disappeared completely.

On the rare occasions when she could not affect a cure, Briga would sit murmuring in a low voice to the sufferer and stroking the person's head and neck, until a great relief came over them. They went away to die in peace.

Her fame spread rapidly. Husbands brought wives, mothers brought children. No matter what the outcome of their visit, all left feeling better than when they arrived.

In this land that was not hers, among people who were strangers, my Briga had come into her own.

Meanwhile the truce between Fíachu and Cohern was holding. When I ventured through the mountains and down our old valley, Cohern made me welcome. "Our boys are growing into men," he said, "who will not die in battle. I may yet see my children's children." He sounded happier than I had ever heard him.

His clan had moved closer to the Slea Leathan by occupying our abandoned lodges. The boys who were growing into men were hunting in the mountains, where they occasionally encountered Cormiac Ru, and venturing down onto the Plain of Broad Spears to meet young women.

"It's not a bad thing," I remarked to Briga as she was mending a ripped seam in my best tunic. "Intermarriage could strengthen the truce."

"If both sides accept such marriages, yes."

"Why would they not?"

"Borders exist in the head, Ainvar. Either Fíachu or Cohern may have a border in his mind that he cannot bear to have crossed. Change can't be forced, it must grow at its own pace. I suggest you discourage Cohern's lads from their forays north, at least for a while."

As easy to stop the sun in its course! Hot-blooded youths do not take advice from someone they perceive as elderly, someone who could not possibly remember how it felt to be young. They listened politely to me, then did as they wanted.

At their age I would have done the same thing.

My Briga was exceptionally sensitive to the presence of water. In the forests of Gaul she had been the one to locate hidden springs where we could safely slake our thirst. In Hibernia she again searched for springs. "Do you recall the sacred wells of Gaul, Ainvar?" she asked.

"I do, of course."

"Hibernia must have her own sacred waters, places where the Source is very strong. If there are any near here I want to find them."

I could understand her feelings. After all, I had the trees.

The Gael divided their year into two equal parts, which were then divided again. Arragh was their name for spring, Sowra was summer, Fowar was autumn, and Gevray was winter.

In the solemn splendor of dawn on Imbolc, the first day of Arragh, Briga left our lodge. Impelled by the insatiable curiosity of a druid, I followed her. She knew I was there but never said anything. When we were out of sight of human habitation Briga began walking in a large spiral that took her ever outward. A murmuration of starlings descended from the sky and trooped along behind her on the ground.

Starlings are drawn to magic.

From time to time Briga stopped as a hound stops when it picks up the scent. "Here," she commented aloud. But not to me. And again, "Here."

In this manner she discovered not one but three hitherto unknown springs. She stood silently by each in turn, her brow furrowed in thought. At last she looked up. "It's here, Ainvar," she said softly. "The Source is as strong here as it ever was in Gaul. Stronger, even. Oh, my husband, we are truly home!"

Briga circled each spring nine times in a sunwise direction, absorbing the power inherent in the water. When she came back to me her face was radiant.

Druid, I thought. But did not say.

By the next change of the moon the women of Fíachu's clan were making pilgrimages to the sacred springs themselves. They also began keeping watch over their fires in the same way Briga did. Small rituals, transplanted. Putting down roots. Growing strong.

Among the tribes of Gaul, female druids had held the same rank as male. Otherwise a woman's rank had depended upon her father or husband. This was even more true of the Slea Leathan. The lodge was the only territory in which their women had any status at all. Until we arrived.

As Briga reached out to the Source, Fíachu's clanswomen stepped out of the shadows. Timidly at first, then with increasing enthusiasm, they joined her, finding within themselves a new devotion. Battle was not everything.

Life was.

The Source is.

We are.

In Hibernia, as in other Celtic lands, the end of summer was marked by a festival. On the grassy Plain of Broad Spears the people depended on cattle for their livelihood. They did not share the preoccupations of those who lived by the harvest, and so a cattle fair was the extent of their celebration.

But that was before we planted our grain.

From Fíachu's stores we had taken oats, barley, and a dense, dark grain that resembled Gaulish wheat but was subtly different. "This is the most highly prized of all cereals," we were told, "the food of kings and princes." Ground into flour, the Hibernian wheat produced a moist, chewy bread we learned to savor. I never did find out what Cohern's people used to make the gritty mess they called bread, but it was not the same.

My Briga took charge of planting of the grain. Adapting our old rituals to this new land, she and her women summoned an unprecedented fertility from the soil. Our first crop exceeded any we had grown in Gaul. In fact it was so abundant we had to enlist help with the harvest. Fíachu was astonished by the mountain of grain we produced. "In a hard winter," he said with a laugh, "I could feed all of the Broad Spears with this."

"Fortunately there are no hard winters in this land," I said.

Fíachu swallowed his laughter. "Oh, but there are, Ainvar. If a bitter wind blows on the thirtieth day of Gevray, the winter will be bitter."

"We've seen nothing like that since we've been here."

"You will," he promised.

"If that's true, Fíachu, I'm astonished the Laigin don't grow more grain. They could put aside enough to keep their herds fat until the sun returns."

Fíachu went away, looking thoughtful. The next morning he sent runners to summon the other chieftains of the Laigin to his clanland—with the exception of the two or three whom he considered his rivals for the kingship. For the first time we were to meet the wider family to which we now belonged.

Like many tributaries flowing into one river, cattle lords and their families began flowing onto the Plain of Broad Spears. Tall, strong Gaelic men and comely Gaelic women. Most were as fair and ruddy as Fíachu and his clan, though a sprinkling had darker hair, which might harken back to Iberia. Or even Scythia.

There were a few whom I surmised to be of Fír Bolg descent; low-built and swarthy, with surly dispositions. If I was right in my conclusions there was an explanation for their bad temper. Having endured misery in a prior life, they carried unforgotten anger like a bag full of stones.

I occasionally glimpsed others not shaped in the Gaelic mold. But I only saw them out of the corner of my eye. When I turned to look squarely at one, he was gone.

The first time this happened I told myself it was a trick of the light. Then it happened again. I had a fleeting impression of individuals shorter than the Fír Bolg, more fair than the Gael, so slim the wind might blow them away. Their skin was as luminous as moonlight.

When I mentioned them to the Goban Saor he said, "I think I've seen them too, but I'm not sure. The chieftains brought their own brews with them and I've been doing some sampling. By now I couldn't tell you what's real and what isn't."

I laughed. I was doing a bit of sampling myself.

When he was satisfied that everyone had arrived, Fíachu stood upon a boulder to address them. He was wearing all his gold and accompanied by six spear carriers and the chief druid. He began by saying, "I am ever mindful of the needs of the Laigin, not only my own tribe but all others, even the subject tribes."

The assembled chieftains exchanged glances. In their experience, altruism was not a feature of Gaelic kingship.

Fíachu ordered his men to bring forward the grain we had produced, bag after bag after bag of it, until the weary porters tottered under the strain. The grain sacks were piled into a huge pyramid. Fíachu again addressed the crowd. "This was grown in one summer, on the earth where you now stand. There is enough to feed us all if anything happened to our cattle. It is important to have a shield as well as a sword, and this could be our shield in the event of disaster. Next spring my tribe will plant as Ainvar's people have done. I suggest you do the same."

One chieftain began, "But we don't know how to—"

"That's why I've summoned you," said Fíachu, contriving to look benevolent. "Ainvar can tell you what to do."

He had not bothered to discuss this with me in advance, but I understood his intention. The demonstration was meant to gain the admiration and support of the other tribes, assuring Fíachu the kingship of the Laigin when the current king finally died.

Politics is the same everywhere. Among great chieftains and inside one's own lodge.

"There are some things women can do better than men," I told the crowd. "Men attack the Mother Earth, but women know how to coax her. My senior wife can explain far better than I can." I looked hopefully toward Briga.

She pressed her lips together and shook her head; she was no more prepared for this than I had been. I was asking a lot of her, but I knew Briga would never fail me. I gave her an encouraging smile. Keeping her eyes fixed on mine, she slowly came to stand at my side.

When she cleared her throat and raised her soft little, hoarse little voice, the crowd listened attentively. They could hardly do otherwise with Fíachu standing there, his arms folded across his chest and stern command etched in every line of his face.

"The Mother Earth must not be forced," Briga said. "She must not be raped."

There was a sharp intake of breath at her words.

"But if we ask with reverence, if we give as well as take, the mother will work with us and produce for us. Our task together begins on Imbolc, the first day of spring. . . ."

She went on to describe every step of the process. The gentle sacrifices of water and wine—mead, in Hibernia—to be made by the women; the solemn first breaking of the soil; the planting—done by the women again; the gifts to be given to the soil to help feed the seeds; the prayers to the Great Fire to ensure enough sun; and finally the harvest, followed by rituals of thanksgiving. Conducted by the women.

"As women assist one another in childbirth," Briga explained, "so they can assist the Mother Earth to give birth to a good harvest."

The tribal leaders were listening spellbound, as Dara had listened to Seanchán. Briga possessed more than one druid gift.

Perhaps she had them all.

When she finished speaking the men looked at their wives with new respect. The women gazed back. Behind their eyes they were thinking new thoughts.

At sunset my Briga lit a huge fire on the nearest mountaintop, where the children had picked bilberries only the day before. As my wife held a torch to the pile of wood, she turned her head and met my eyes. "This is for Lugh," she said softly, calling the name of the avatar of the sun whom we had worshipped in Gaul. I was deeply touched. She had not abandoned her roots, then; merely grafted new life onto them.

The people nearest to us heard what she said. "Lughnasa!" a woman shouted, throwing up her arms. "Lughnasa!" the others echoed.

The bonfire roared into life. In answer, the setting sun blazed crimson. Fire on the mountain and fire in the sky.

"Lughnasa!" The cry rang across the Plain of Broad Spears. "Lughnasa!"

The end of summer was commemorated with splendor that year. At my suggestion a runner was sent to Cohern to invite him to share in the festivities. He arrived with some trepidation, but stayed to the end and would have stayed longer with encouragement.

Nothing in my experience compared with the unrestrained joy of the exuberant Gael. Chieftains who, like Fíachu, owned horses, raced their mounts and wagered lavish amounts of gold on the outcome. Other men competed in contests of individual strength, or formed themselves into teams to play games that were as close to war as you could get without killing someone.

Caman was the most popular game. More familiarly known as a hurling match, caman was almost identical to a stick-and-ball sport I had enjoyed in Gaul. According to legend the early Celts had encased human skulls in wickerwork and hit them with tree branches. By the time I played the game it was less primitive; less reminiscent of our savage forebears. Skulls were no longer part of the equipment, but great stamina had been required. We had competed at the run with no pause for rest.

That was how the game was played in Hibernia, too.

The Gael had developed the hurling match into a test of skill bordering on an art form. Two teams, composed of a dozen or more to a side, met on a level playing field. Every man carried a "hurley," a long stick carved from ash wood with an outward bend near one end. The ball, or "sliotar," was about the size of a small woman's fist, and made of leather tied tightly around a wooden core. Goals were scored either by kicking the sliotar or striking it through the air. The most thrilling moments in the game occurred when a man raced down the field with the sliotar delicately, incredibly, balanced on his outthrust hurley, the other side in hot pursuit. At the ultimate moment the sliotar was literally hurled into the air by the stick, then hit with a mighty whack. A good player could send the sliotar through the goal from midfield.

While their menfolk played match after match, the women cooked and wove garlands and chased after the children, who busied themselves getting into all the mischief they could find. Meanwhile singers sang, drummers drummed, pipers played a sweet, wild music like the wail of the wind and the plaintive cry of the dying swan. Music filled the air like sunshine.

When the sun sank low in the sky the descendants of the Milesians came together to re-create ancient dances from faraway Iberia, their bodies weaving patterns that told age-old stories of love and loss and victory. I recognized the drums and the pipes; the patterns were not unlike those we had danced in Gaul.

The Goban Saor, whom I had never seen dance before, took a fair-haired partner from one of the other Laigin tribes and danced with her long after the rest of us were exhausted.

Over three nights and three days massive quantities of roast meat and blood pudding and summer cheeses were consumed. Cups overflowed with drink, children shouted with laughter, men and women nodded secretly to each other when no one was looking. People fell asleep on the ground where they had been dancing moments before, and awoke with the dawn to begin again.

By the third day Cormiac Ru was as adept at caman as any Gael. Glas had obtained several lengths of ash wood and was carving hurleys for my clan. Labraid was almost as good as the Red Wolf. Even my chubby Eoin showed some promise. He could not run fast enough to keep up with the action but when he had the opportunity to hit the sliotar he put plenty of power behind his blow.

Grown men willingly stepped aside to allow the little ones their chance to learn. Children were important to the Gael.

Meanwhile the flaming face of Lugh continued to beam down upon us. Not a drop of rain fell. Not a tear was shed. For once even Onuava could find nothing to complain about.

A highlight of the festival was a contest of bards. Most clans boasted a storyteller who called himself a bard. Each in turn delivered his best performance. His audience sat or sprawled on the ground around him, listening attentively. Many of the recitations were accompanied by grotesque expressions and frequent changes of voice to indicate different characters speaking. Some were highly amusing; others constituted biting satire. My head observed that while the assembled chieftains roared with laughter at humorous stories, they sat very tensely when a satirist began. Each man relaxed only when he realized the satire was not about him—this time.

Bards had some power in Hibernia after all.

When the speaker told of battles fought and won by the Laigin, battles in which every hero's name was remembered and every deed exaggerated, my clan cheered the Laigin's victories as enthusiastically as everyone else did.

An extraordinary shapechange was taking place. We, the dispossessed, were now an accepted part of a tribe far richer than the one we left behind. We were nascent Gael. And it was all my doing.

I drank quantities of mead and congratulated myself.

Indulging in what the Greeks call "hubris" is always a mistake. I should have known better.

The festival blew away with the last ashes of the Lughnasa fire, and I accompanied Cohern back to his clanhold. We were both still dazed with excitement. And drink.

I did not think to ask Cormiac Ru to accompany us.

By the time we entered the pass through the mountains, twilight had fallen. Although we carried torches we hardly needed them. We both knew the way. We sauntered along talking about cattle and crops and women. The night wind was warm and sweet. Cohern belched repeatedly. "A tribute to the feast," he said.

I bade my first friend in Hibernia a genuinely fond farewell at the door of his lodge, then I headed for home. Through the pass.

The distance was greater than I recalled. I walked and walked and walked and still the mountains rose beside me. My eyes searched in vain for a glimpse of the Plain of the Broad Spears. I began to walk faster.

Behind me a wind was rising with a strange sibilance, more like deliberate whistling than the simple movement of air. No sooner did I notice this than I realized I could feel no wind on my body. I stopped in my tracks.

The mist closed around me.

A strangely shining mist, damp but not cold as mist usually is, moving, swirling, thickening here, lifting there, but always obscuring. Shimmering like crystal; ringing like faraway bells.

My heart pounded in my chest.

The whistling turned into the sound of a rushing river. That was soon transformed into a cascade of laughter. Silvery laughter, coming from every direction and no direction. Mocking laughter with an undertone of cruelty.

"Who are you?" I cried. "Where are you? What do you want?"

The laugh multiplied until there must have been hundreds of them—whoever they were—hidden in the mist. They seemed to be circling around me like people dancing. There was not enough room in the narrow pass for hundreds of dancing people, or even a dozen, yet no one brushed against me.

I could feel them, though. A weightless weight like the weight of the wind pushed me forward again. Driving me as deerhounds drive deer toward the hunter. I tried to resist by catching hold of one of the rock outcroppings that lined the pass. My desperately reaching hands closed on mist.

The laughter grew louder.

My feet were moving faster, running.

"Please!" I cried, uselessly beseeching strange gods whose language I did not know. Nothing was solid but the earth beneath my feet. The firm, fertile flesh of Hibernia.

"Of Eriu," whispered a voice in my ear.

## *chapter* X

EVERYONE ELSE WAS LONG SINCE ASLEEP, BUT BRIGA HAD NOT gone to bed. When I stumbled into the lodge she caught me in her arms. Otherwise I would have fallen on my face.

She gave me a cup of water which I drank in one deep draft. Nothing had ever tasted so good. It soaked into me like rain falling on parched earth. Briga refilled the cup and I drained it again. Only then did I realize how loudly I was panting. How far had I run?

I tried to tell Briga what had happened, but words were inadequate. How does one describe invisibility, or convey the sound of disembodied voices? "I ran from the wind" sounded foolish, even to my own ears.

"There was something out there," I told her. "That's all I know. It was real, and it was there, and I can no more describe it than I can describe the bottom of the sea or the top of the sky."

"Don't try, Ainvar. Just come to bed and let me hold you."

I did.

The following morning I tried to recount my experience to Cormiac Ru, but with no more success. "I'll go back there with you," he offered. "Whoever assaulted you can't be allowed to get away with it."

"I wasn't assaulted," I said, "not in the way you mean."

"Were you threatened, then?"

"Yes. I mean no. I'm not sure."

He folded his arms across his chest. "Either you were or you weren't, Ainvar."

"I'm no old fool who can't tell dreams from daylight," I said indignantly.

"Then let's go back and confront them."

"There speaks the warrior whose only answer is the sword."

"Do you have a better idea?"

I did not.

Nor was I willing to give in to my fears. This was supposed to be a new life for all of us. So I agreed to go back with Cormiac, provided we went at night. I had a strong suspicion that nothing would happen in the daylight.

When Labraid heard what we were about, he insisted on coming with us. Having the son of Vercingetorix at my side would be a comfort, I thought. With the passing of seasons the boy had grown into a man who physically resembled his father in ways that sometimes made me catch my breath. He was big and bold and beautiful. There were moments when I could almost imagine Rix had returned to us.

Almost, though not quite. Labraid was still inclined to act before he thought, a quality he would carry to his grave.

Cormiac Ru was the better man.

The three of us set off as the sun was dying. Before leaving my lodge I drank several cups of mead to fortify myself against the cold of night. I also brought a blazing torch made of pine pitch.

My companions carried swords and spears. Iron weaponry to challenge mist and laughter. I had never felt more foolish. Nor been more frightened. At least the repulsive Caesar was flesh and blood. What I had encountered in the pass was not.

I had no intention of revealing my fear to Cormiac and Labraid. Sometimes pride can be an ally.

During their time with Cohern the two young men—I habitually thought of them as "the two young men," though Cormiac was much older than Labraid—had fought in several skirmishes together and thus shared the brotherhood of warriors. As the land tilted to meet the mountains they chatted amicably with each other. I paid only desultory attention to the conversation. My ears were listening for a certain whistle. Hoping it was there and hoping it was not.

Labraid claimed, "The Gael are the best warriors in the world."

"How can you say that?" asked Cormiac. "You never saw the Romans in battle. They defeated your own father."

"They did not. Vercingetorix was tricked into surrendering."

"I was there, Labraid, I know what happened."

"I was there, too."

"You were still in your mother's womb."

"But I knew things," Labraid insisted. "Can you prove I didn't?"

"I suppose not."

"Well then," said the other triumphantly. "And I'll tell you something else, too. If we had the Romans here right now we could beat them."

"Albion is infested with Romans," Cormiac replied, beginning to sound irritable. "Why don't we send for them and test your theory?"

"That's enough!" I snapped. I did not like the way the conversation was going. We walked on in silence for a while then, though my head was not silent.

Albion and Hibernia, I thought, two islands like sisters in the sea. If Albion was infested with Romans, what infested Hibernia?

The pass through the mountains yawned just ahead of us. The mountains were not very high compared to those I remembered from . . . No.

*We are truly home, Ainvar.*

The pass climbed gradually, narrowing as it went, until it was only a pathway on the lip of a deep defile. Water cascaded in sparkling streams from the rocks above and tumbled into the gorge below, where it became the little river I remembered so well. When the pass reached its narrowest we had to proceed single file. I led the way, holding my torch aloft. Brandishing it almost like a weapon. Behind me, Labraid and Cormiac began to talk again. Their voices echoing from the stone walls were the only sounds I heard.

Until the whistling began.

My torch sputtered and went out as if it had been doused in water. The mist—where had it come from?—closed around us.

I stopped so abruptly that Labraid bumped into me. "Look out!" I snapped.

"Look at what? What's going on?"

"It's started again. The mist. And the whistling."

"What whistling?"

"Don't you hear it?"

"No."

"Neither do I," said Cormiac.

"But you do see the mist?"

"I see low clouds sinking down onto the mountains. That often happens when I'm out hunting."

If I was the only one who could hear the whistling, then something was trying to communicate with me alone. Remembering the name that had been whispered in my ear once before, I called, "Eriu?"

"What?" said Labraid. "Who are you talking to, Ainvar? There's nobody here. Are you drunk?"

The exasperation Labraid engendered in me exploded. "By the rocks and the rivers! Cormiac, take him back the way we came."

"I won't leave you, Ainvar."

"I'm not asking you to leave me, just remove this fine fellow for a dozen spear lengths, will you? And keep him there."

In the all-enveloping mist I could not see the brief scuffle that ensued, but there was no doubt who won. I could hear Labraid being frog-marched back down the pass, protesting indignantly until a large hand was clamped over his mouth.

Then there was silence except for the whistling. It did not sound as if it came from human lips. A less sensitive person might have assumed he was hearing only a ringing in his own ears. But I knew better.

"Eriu?" I called again.

The whistling was replaced by a voice. A silvery, rippling voice, almost sexless; almost female. "Who seeks Eriu?"

"Ainvar," I replied as steadily as I could.

"Who is Ainvar?"

Old habit dictated my answer. "Chief druid of the Carnutes."

"Who are the Carnutes?"

I replied with a question of my own. "Where is Eriu?"

A nacreous light suffused the mist. It could not be moonlight, for the moon had not yet risen. When I held my hand close to my face, the moisture on my skin glistened like jewels. "I don't understand."

"There is nothing to understand, Ainvar of the Carnutes. I am here. I am in the Otherworld. I am Eriu."

At her words a jolt passed through my body as if I had been struck by one of the white-hot javelins of Taranis. The mist thinned, allowing me one tantalizing glimpse of a brilliant chaos where one color was all colors, where all shapes were one shape, where the sheer intensity of *being* surpassed mortal experience. I staggered, unable to cope with the overwhelming sensations flooding my senses.

The veil of mist descended again, protecting me from sights not meant for mortal eyes. With an effort I regained my balance. Then I felt myself . . . change. I could not see the walls of rock on either side of the pass but I could feel them through the pores of my skin. I could hear trees murmuring in the night wind on the far side of the mountains. I could taste the sweet pure water in the most distant rivers. I was part of all of these, and they of me.

Rapt, transported, I stood exulting.

Here was validation for one of the principal tenets of druidry: belief in the unseen. In the presence of mystery and terror I was not afraid.

"Ainvar."

"Yes."

"Do you understand?"

"No. But I accept."

"As we all must."

"Your people . . ." I hesitated to name them.

"Yes?"

"Do they mean my people any harm?"

"The Carnutes?"

"We are the Gael now," I told her.

The mist turned cold. Moisture began to freeze on my skin.

"Lads?" I called out uneasily. "Are you still there?"

There was no answer from Cormiac and Labraid.

"*I* am still here," said Eriu. "Before the Gael invaded I was here. When they have gone I will be here. Nothing they have done can drive me out." If the voice had come from a human throat, those words would have been spoken through clenched teeth.

Druids believe that existence is finely balanced between Chaos and Pattern. Both are necessary.

By her own admission Eriu spoke from the Otherworld.

Yet she was with me as well. When I drew in breath I inhaled Eriu. When I put down my foot I touched Eriu—who had every reason to hate the conquering Gael.

Fíachu had spoken of being "cursed with dark skies from morning to night. Infants are born dead and the limbs of children wither. Rain turns to sleet, snow turns to ice, grass freezes, and cattle starve."

Had he been describing one method by which the Túatha Dé Danann took revenge? With their mysterious powers could they do even more dreadful things?

Horrifying thought.

By joining a powerful tribe in order to protect my people, I had made them subject to Eriu's anger. A sacrificer might have been able to placate her, though I doubted it. Besides, I was no sacrificer. All I had was my head.

Think, head; think as you never thought before.

"The Carnutes were destroyed by a conqueror in a land far away," I said to Eriu. "In order to survive, my clan needed a place to hide. That's why we came here in the first place. Because we were hungry to belong to a tribe again, in all innocence we joined with the Gael. But we're not your enemies, Eriu. Believe me, we are not your enemies. We merely ask to be accepted by this land."

"Why?"

"Because it feels like home."

The mist swirled around me more thickly than ever while a judgment was being made far beyond my ken. I realized how truly I had spoken. My body was married to Briga—and Lakutu, and Onuava—but my spirit was wed to Eriu. I could not say when it had happened. That first moment on the beach? Perhaps.

"Eriu?"

"Yes."

"Are we accepted?" I held my breath. When she did not reply immediately I took a daring chance. "May we stay here under your protection?"

After a measureless moment the answer came. "You may, as long as you pay the price."

"What price do you ask?"

"Remember us," whispered the voice. *"Remember us."*

I bowed my head. "We will."

All at once the mist blew away on a warm wind and there stood Cormiac and Labraid, an exact twelve spear lengths from me.

"Whatever is the matter with you, Ainvar?" Labraid demanded to know. "Why are you staring at us like that?"

## *chapter* XI

THE CHOICE BETWEEN LIFE AND DEATH IS MERELY ANOTHER CONfrontation with the Two-Faced One. Neither victory nor defeat last forever. What matters is the style, the triumphant beauty of those who fight their best no matter what the outcome.

Alone in the mist I had fought a battle that no one else saw. The noblest warriors do not always win. Force of will is not enough. Success and failure are determined in the Otherworld.

On this Lughnasa night, Ainvar of the Gael had dealt with the Otherworld. And won.

I returned to Briga as proudly as if I carried an enemy's head on a pole.

This time I made no effort to explain what had happened. The wild and wonderful magic of Eriu was too personal to discuss with anyone. She had spoken to me and to me alone. The undeniable fact of her existence was my private treasure.

Cormiac and Labraid simply thought I had taken too much drink. I let their story stand.

Only two who were present that night would ever know the truth. And one of them was no longer human.

I had regretted our lack of a bard to recount the stories of Gaul. But that, I realized, was a working of the Pattern. Gaul was the past. Our future would take a different shape.

The following morning I said to Dara, "You've learned a lot from Seanchán. You know the sagas of the Milesians almost as well as he does, but you must do more. Reach beyond his limits."

Dara furrowed his forehead in the customary way. "How am I supposed to do that?"

"Travel the length and breadth of the Plain of Broad Spears. Sit at the feet of every bard. Listen closely and remember everything you hear."

He looked at me aghast. "Everything?!"

"Everything you hear about the Túatha Dé Danann," I specified, to his obvious relief. "When we were fighting the Romans, we tried to learn as much as we could about the enemy. I suspect the Fír Bolg did the same when they were fighting the Dananns. Some of that knowledge must survive, woven into the legends of any Gaelic clan the Fír Bolg married into."

"How can you be certain the Fír Bolg married Gaels?"

"Because life calls to life," I told my son. "Set out at sunrise tomorrow and don't come back until you've gleaned all there is to know about the Túatha Dé Danann. Listen, memorize, carry it within you like a brimming cup. Don't forget the smallest detail."

"Why are you asking this of me, Father?"

I set my features in stone so he would make no mistake. "I'm not asking. I'm demanding."

Never before had I used the word "demand" to one of my children. We are free people. We do not respond well to demands. Yet on that day I made a demand of Dara, and to his everlasting credit, he obeyed.

Briga was not entirely happy about seeing her firstborn son leave us again. That night she fed him all his favorite foods and made a fuss about arranging his bed just so, as if these small, womanly touches would hold him. She and I both knew better. Someday some other woman probably would try to hold him close in a similar way, but if a man has wings he must fly.

Dara left at the next sunrise. I waited until I was certain he would not turn around and come back prematurely; children can be unpredictable. Then after moonrise I went out under the vast bowl of the sky and walked among the whispering trees. Among the oaks. "Eriu," I said softly. "We will remember."

A lark began to sing nearby. Larks do not sing at night, but this one did; a paean so beautiful it made my throat ache.

I became acutely aware of every leaf and branch. Even the tiny insects scurrying underneath the bark were known to me. It was as if I were part of the earth herself.

Menua had told me, "Druidry is inclusion, not exclusion. To be druid means to be part of, not apart from."

I was druid. In spite of everything, I was still druid. That was my personal gift from Eriu.

However, Duach Dalta, chief druid of the Laigin, had made it plain that he needed no assistance from me. Briga was gaining renown as a Wise Woman, but none of the druids from Gaul had any official position in our new tribe. We were what the Romans called "supernumeraries." Like so many words in the Latin tongue it had a flat, final sound. Like the lid of a stone sarcophagus slamming down.

A professional class composed of specialists in the druidic arts was unknown in Hibernia, where the druids exerted little control over everyday life. The Gael were not amenable to discipline anyway. Teaching was left to mothers—and, as the saying went, "whatever a child might lick up off the ground."

The study of the sky and its influence upon the Earth was totally neglected. When I asked the reason for this, Duach Dalta told me, "Before the before, there was a race that built great ritual centers patterned on the tracks of the sun and moon. They are gone now and the stones they raised have tumbled down. They would have been better served raising cattle." He laughed at his own wit.

"What were those people called?"

"I have no idea," said Duach Dalta. "If they are gone they do not matter." I did not contradict him. He was the chief druid. Now.

In the ceremony that elevated a chieftain to the rank of king, the throat of a white mare representing the land was cut by the chief druid. The candidate for kingship then bathed in the mare's blood. On other occasions the chief druid might sacrifice an animal or animals, but there was no separate sacrificer among the Gaels. And human sacrifice was not practiced.

When I asked Duach Dalta why not, his answer surprised me. "Only inferiors sacrifice their own kind."

"What do you mean by 'inferiors'? Slaves?"

Leaning toward me, he lowered his voice. "Former slaves, one might say."

"Are you talking about the Fír Bolg?"

He nodded. "The Men of the Bag sacrificed their firstborn infants. Held them by their heels and bashed their brains out against a stone idol they called 'Crom Cruach,' " he elaborated, flaring his nostrils in distaste. "Fortunately there are no Fír Bolg anymore, only the Gael."

Foolishly, I went a step too far. "And the Túatha Dé Danann?"

Duach Dalta blanched visibly.

I was intrigued. Apparently the bards could speak of the Dananns, but the merest mention of them upset the chief druid. There were layers upon layers of mystery here. I comforted myself with the thought that my clan need not fear the Túatha Dé Danann. I had made a pact with Eriu.

That night in my bed I pondered the differences between Gaulish druids and the druids of Hibernia. Was human sacrifice something we were meant to leave behind? Would there be benefits to us? Or would we merely escape some unguessed retribution in the Otherworld?

The unfolding of the Pattern is endlessly fascinating.

The women of the Laigin sought Briga's help in increasing numbers, until she was so occupied with them that Eoin and Ongus and Gobnat began coming to me if they needed anything.

I already had acquired a number of non-druidic skills. Caring for children was another new accomplishment. When Niav joined the group, I discovered that children know things that adults have forgotten. If a little girl sits crouched on her haunches, prattling in a language all her own, is she merely playing? Or is she, perhaps, communicating with the unseen? A communication that seems as normal to her as everyday conversation is to us.

I enlarged the group further by inviting Onuava's two younger boys, Cairbre and Senta, to join us. All my children together.

The language of the Athenians contains a word, *patriarchos,* that means "head of the family." It is not the same as chief of the clan, but describes more precisely how I felt with the young ones around me.

As chief druid of the Carnutes I had been, in many ways, alone. The responsibility for an entire tribe was a heavy burden and one I could not share, any more than Duach Dalta could. But the nature of our burdens was different. In Hibernia the chief druid conducted those rituals that were of tribal significance. He did not, in spite of Cohern's contention that druids were sorcerers, attempt the manipulation of natural forces.

I had.

And on a few memorable occasions, I had succeeded.

I could not explain how it was done, any more than Gobnat could explain how she charmed bees. True magic does not depend upon tricks, nor even upon rituals, which only serve to concentrate the mind. True magic . . . happens. In the moment before it happens there is a great gathering inside of one, a stillness more total than death and more intense than birth. Nothing else, even lying with a woman, produces the same rapture. Until they put my emptied husk into my grave I will hunger to experience that rapture one more time. Just one more.

No Gaelic druid could possibly understand. They were still at the beginning place. They had not been exposed to the influences that affected Gaul. For many generations travelers from distant lands had crisscrossed our territory, bringing with them new ideas and new ways of thinking. From the East in particular we druids had acquired much esoteric wisdom, which we added to the simple forest lore handed down from our ancestors.

To be druid is to learn.

In Gaul we had lived as fugitives. There had been little time to educate the children in anything other than the basic necessities for survival. Now there was time. Another gift of Hibernia.

I took my children into the forest to observe nature's lessons as Menua had taken me. We found a glade carpeted with moss and fragrant with the sweet smell of damp soil. I invited my young companions to sit down and took my place in front of them.

"The most important thing in life is to learn," I intoned. "To learn continually. People exist to learn—and to procreate, though we are not studying that now."

Ongus, who found it almost impossible to sit still for any length of time, said peevishly, "*Why* do we have to learn? There's lots of things to do that are more fun."

"We learn so that each of us can add his unique knowledge and experience to the Source of All Being. That is our gift in return for life."

"What source?" Eoin wanted to know.

"Each person must find the answer to that for himself."

"But where shall we look?"

"Everywhere. The Source is in you and above you and beneath you. The Source permeates all of creation."

The youngsters nodded in unison like a tree full of young owls. They did not understand, of course; but they would. In time.

"Every aspect of the Source, and there are many," I told them, "should be respected."

Cairbre, a golden-haired scamp, asked, "What's an aspect? Will it jump out and bite us?" He elbowed his brother Senta, who grinned and elbowed him back.

"Whatever was not made by the hands of man is an aspect of the Source. The sacred is all around you. Look. And see."

They turned this way and that, gazing without comprehension at the surrounding landscape. I stood quietly, waiting.

Awareness takes time.

Understanding slowly dawned on their faces. They began *seeing.* Seeing the sentient trees with their roots buried in the heart of the Mother. Seeing drops of life-giving moisture glinting like tiny pearls upon the moss. Seeing insects scurrying about with the busyness of their own lives and their own sense of purpose. Seeing the pale, luminous flesh of mushrooms; neither fish nor fowl, sprung from decay yet abundantly alive.

"The world is full of wonders," I said.

My tree full of young owls nodded solemnly.

"The Earth herself is one of the greatest wonders. She is alive. Part of you has always known this. Through the food we take from her, her life flows into us. She makes us one with all creation, linked in the great dance of Becoming. Honor the Earth. Treat her with the love and reverence due your own mothers, for without them both you would not, could not, exist.

"Everything created by the Source has its purpose. Our bodies not only provide housing for our spirits, but also can instruct us. We are born equipped with everything we need to learn how to count. Ten fingers and ten toes comprise a score. Add to that one head and four limbs and you have a generation.

"Look down at your hands. Four fingers and a thumb, each with a slightly different function, yet all able to work together. Should one be missing, the ability of the entire hand would diminish. Now consider your toes. Only the largest has much strength, but if you lost any one of them, even the smallest, your balance would be compromised. The most insignificant part of your body is needed. The most insignificant person has a place in the tribe."

I gave them a few moments to digest this. Even the smallest child needs to know he has value.

"No part of your body is as important as your head," I said. "You can lose a finger, an arm, even a leg, and still be yourself. But that which is *you* is contained in your head. Take care of your head and every part of it. Without eyes to watch, ears to report, a nose to smell, and a tongue to taste, the spirit that dwells in your skull would be alone in total darkness."

Little Senta, who had a vivid imagination, shuddered.

Glancing up, I saw Cormiac Ru half-hidden among the trees, watching us. It was the habit of the Red Wolf to appear and disappear, always silently. There was something comfortable about his presence, though I never told him so. One did not need to tell Cormiac Ru things. He simply knew.

"Which of your head's servants do you value the most?" I asked my listeners. Niav, who loved music, chose her ears. Chubby Eoin preferred his tongue. Cairbre inhaled a great deep breath, unfortunately laden with pollen, and sneezed so loudly he frightened the birds.

We all laughed.

Standing between trees, Cormiac Ru touched his fingertips to his eyelids. I beckoned to him to come and sit with the children, and after a moment's hesitation, he did.

Soon the lessons in the glade were a daily occurrence. Sharing topics of interest with receptive listeners provided me with unexpected pleasure. What had begun as a chore became the height of my day.

As always happens when one teaches, one learns as well. I learned that the way to gain the attention of a noisy, energetic audience is not by outshouting them. The more quietly I spoke, the quieter they became. It was the only way they could hear me.

I made sure that what I had to say was worth hearing. Even the most prosaic subject can be invested with magic.

Dara, filled to the brim with discoveries, returned from his travels among the Slea Leathan. He was disappointed to find that the promised harp was not yet ready, but decided to come to my little school in the forest glade while he waited. There he spent his days listening to me. At night in our lodge Briga and I listened to his stories of the Túatha Dé Danann. Wondrous tales of a vanished race whose magic was as mysterious as the birth of the wind.

And, perhaps, as natural. All true magic has its roots in nature.

In the Source.

I went out under the stars and whispered, "You are not forgotten, Eriu. You are not forgotten."

Soon quite a few young ones from Fíachu's clan were among my students, too. Drawn by curiosity, retained by interest.

Even Labraid joined us in the forest glade. I did not flatter myself that the son of Vercingetorix came on my account. Labraid simply wanted to do whatever Cormiac did. He was intensely competitive with the older man, yet loved him too, in his way. The Red Wolf occupied more than one space at the same time. He was almost my son. He was almost Labraid's father.

When my students had finished exploring the cosmos of their bodies, I introduced them to the cosmos overhead. On clear summer nights we lay on the grass and read the glittering face of the Source. In Gaul, druid healers had aligned a sick person's body with the stars that were present at his birth, thus helping return him to the state of newborn health.

Sadly, we had no druid who had dedicated his life to studying the stars. Yet as a chief druid I had learned something of every discipline, so I pointed out the pinpricks of light I recognized, and we discussed the pictures they formed.

The young people enjoyed our exploration of the sky. Labraid in particular wanted to know how to find one's way by the stars. He, who usually took an opposing view to whatever was said, listened avidly to my every word. It pleased me to think I was finally getting through to him.

To my surprise, one morning Fíachu's firstborn daughter came to the school in the forest glade. Aislinn, whose name was the Gaelic word for dream, was a slim reed of a girl who arrived unobtrusively and seated herself at the back of the gathering. Taking my lead from her diffidence, I did not call undue attention to her. But I was glad that she joined us.

I had long since observed that like my Niav, Aislinn could twist her father around her finger.

She soon became an accepted part of the group. No mere dreamer in spite of her name, she asked intelligent questions. But my eyes noticed that she paid a great deal more attention to Labraid than she did to me.

I encouraged the members of my clan to share their skills with my students. "Everyone has something to teach," I told them, "and everyone has something to learn." The girls were intrigued when Lakutu demonstrated how to fold a simple length of cloth into a flattering garment. The boys watched attentively as Teyrnon showed them how to build a forge.

As was our custom, on the first night of the full moon the Order of the Wise gathered to discuss those things that only interest druids. Dian Cet commented, "You've become a fine teacher, Ainvar. You're opening doors in those young minds."

I began a self-deprecatory shrug. My head reminded me that the gesture was not Gaelic. My shoulders froze in midlift.

Keryth the seer saw my thoughts. "Don't be so hard on yourself, Ainvar. None of us find it easy to become different people."

"Briga does."

"Briga's different. She was meant to be here from the beginning, it's her Pattern. The rest of us are simply caught up in it."

"Let me remind you that coming to Hibernia was my idea, not hers," I said rather testily.

"And what gave you the idea, Ainvar? Did you drink it in wine, or eat it in bread? I think not. The Great Fire shone on your forehead and drew Briga's Pattern in your mind."

"I don't believe you."

"Why not? Did you think you were the center of everything?"

Sulis gave a wry little smile. "If that's not just like a man."

One autumn evening I returned to our lodge on shaky legs. The youngsters with their boundless energy had prolonged our discussions until I was exhausted. For some time I had been bothered by a slight cough, not uncommon in a damp climate that encouraged coughs and sneezes. I tried to hide it from Briga because she would fuss over me and give me some vile-tasting potion to drink.

My senior wife was scrubbing one of her iron pots with sand when I entered the lodge. She glanced up and twinkled her eyes at me. My head ached;

my bones ached. I felt every one of my years, but squared my weary shoulders and gave her my brightest smile. Perhaps a little too bright.

Briga put down the cooking pot. "What's wrong, Ainvar?"

"Nothing's wrong."

"Are you hiding something from me?"

"I'm not hiding anything."

Briga knew when I was lying. She might not know what the lie was about but she could smell its existence as a cat smells a rat. So she made a guess. "Have you been talking about Gaul to those children and making them unhappy?"

That was unfair; I never discussed Gaul with the children. "What if I have?" I snapped.

"Oh, Ainvar, I'm disappointed in you. Gaul doesn't exist for us anymore. Everything we cared about there is gone. You have to forget."

Angrily, I cried, "Can you forget our Maia so easily?" I was irritable because I did not feel well—but there is no excuse for making excuses.

Briga's face crumpled; her eyes filled with tears. At that moment Cormiac Ru entered the lodge. He took in the scene in one scorching glance.

The Red Wolf turned on me with his teeth bared. Actually bared. I thought he would kill me where I stood.

So did Briga, who threw herself between us. "Don't, Cormiac!"

"I won't let anyone make you cry." His fingers twitched dangerously close to the hilt of the knife in his belt.

Briga put her palm against Cormiac's chest and pushed him back. "Ainvar didn't mean to hurt me. Sometimes he speaks without thinking."

That was not fair, either.

Laying his hand over Briga's, Cormiac said, in the gentlest voice I had ever heard him use, "You still weep for Maia."

"Of course I do, she was my child. I'll always grieve for her. But she's gone and nothing will bring her back."

Over Briga's head, Cormiac looked at me. "Is that what you believe, Ainvar? Is Maia truly lost to us? Is she . . ." He forced the next words out. "Is she dead?"

By this time my skull was pounding like a goatskin drum. Ba-da-*boom,* ba-da-*boom.* "I don't know, Cormiac. My cousin Crom Daral hated me because he had wanted Briga for himself. Crom had a bad head. As an act of revenge against me, he stole our daughter to sell to the Romans. That was a long time ago, though. Anything might have happened since then."

The last words came out in a croak. My mouth and throat were parched, yet I felt as if I were drowning. It was impossible to draw a deep breath.

Ba-da-*boom,* ba-da-*boom.*

Helplessly, I looked around for my bed. I could barely see it because the interior of the lodge was fading away in the mist.

The mist. The Túatha Dé . . .

I tumbled down into sleep.

The night lasted much longer than a night should. I knew it had passed when I could hear, as if far away, the sound of people talking. Then hands touched me. Someone started to bathe my face but I flinched away. "No," I think I said. When I opened my eyes the light hurt them, so I screwed them tightly shut again and lay listening to the buzzing in my ears.

After a time my nose reported that food was simmering in the pot. My only reaction was nausea.

I tried to sleep but it was impossible. Something with claws began tearing my chest apart from the inside out. Soon I was gasping for breath. Then breathing became torture. The skin of my throat felt as if it were being flayed. Meanwhile the clawed thing redoubled its efforts in my chest. The pain went on and on, like waves washing onto a shore.

When I thought I could not stand any more, the waves of agony mounted higher and crashed over me.

My head observed that I was burning with heat and freezing with cold. Yet this phenomenon did not interest me. Nothing interested me except the possibility that I might escape my torment by dying. Ainvar of the Carnutes might die.

I have no fear of bodily death. My spirit is a permanent part of the immortal Source, creator of stones and stars and spiderwebs.

As are we all.

Initiation into the Order of the Wise included Deathteaching, the most secret of druidic rituals. A prospective druid must experience dying in order to understand the true nature of death; what it is, and what it is not. Such knowledge—personal and firsthand knowledge—eliminates fear.

Before being accepted into the Order, I had been stripped as bare as an infant emerging from the womb. Dying is the reverse of being born. If we survive injury or illness for long enough we grow feeble and infantile. This is as it should be; in old age we are prepared to return to the unborn state. Death is the condition of being unborn. Death washes memory clean of burdens that are too painful to carry. Death rests and refreshes the immortal spirit, until it is ready to begin a new life in a new body woven from the strands of creation.

Every person's experience of dying is different, shaped by the Pattern that has governed his life. When Menua and his fellow druids initiated my dying I had found myself in a place of lurid red light. There I had confronted the Two-Faced One. When I could have gone either way, I had chosen the face that looked toward life.

Much had happened to me since those long-ago days. I had accumulated a number of memories too painful to bear, and Ainvar's body was exhausted with pain. Now I longed to be unborn. My spirit would rest in a quiet backwater of the Otherworld and wait for a new future to unfold.

Would I meet Rix there? And what of Briga?

At the thought of Briga a gentle light shone behind my closed eyelids and I could see again, though not with the eyes of my body. My spirit saw Briga as a young girl, with eyes the color of bluebells. Why had I never realized that her eyes were the color of bluebells?

Dizziness overcame me and I spun away. Or she spun away. Into the mist.

I was choking; drowning. Someone was piling boulders on my chest. Yet in spite of my agony I struggled to hold on to the essential Ainvar. It is important to pass through dying intact. The more of our selves we can retain, the more of our gifts we can take with us into the next life.

Ainvar's mortal body was on fire inside.

After a measureless time the pain receded slightly and Briga appeared to me again. A mature Briga, woman and mother. How ripe her figure was. Every lush curve was known to me, memorized by my hands and eyes and tongue as a bard memorizes the history of his people. Briga was my people, she was my whole world.

Spinning away, away.

I did not want to die after all! No matter how savage the pain, I wanted to be alive in Thisworld with Briga. Had I made that discovery too late?

Regret has fangs and claws.

Even after he was brutally tortured and publicly humiliated, Vercingetorix had fought to live. Accursed Caesar threw him into a dungeon to starve to death, but his courage had so impressed the noble matrons of Rome that they smuggled food to him. At last it had been necessary to strangle Rix in order to kill him.

How could I face my soul friend in some future life if I had willingly surrendered what he strove so valiantly to keep?

I made a mighty effort to push death away as my mouth filled with the coppery taste of blood. For the first time I fully understood why the head was sacred. If I could keep Ainvar's head alive and thinking, I might stand a chance.

The tide of darkness rose inexorably. Lapping around my trembling knees. Climbing toward my laboring heart.

She appeared to me one more time. Briga as an old woman. A crown of silver hair; a tiny body that had folded in upon itself. Yet the same bluebell eyes. Nothing could dim the spirit that looked out through them. It was the same spirit I had recognized so long ago, and loved from the first moment. But the love I had felt then was nothing compared to the love I felt now. The tracks of time had inscribed her face with a beauty so great it shook me to the core.

Youth is the bud; age is the blossom.

I reached out toward my Briga. She was life itself.

And she spun away, away.

"Bring her back!" I screamed.

The final darkness closed over me.

# *chapter* XII

LIKE BIRTH, DYING IS NOT A SIMPLE PROCESS—EVEN WHEN IT appears instantaneous. The newborn encounter a bewildering array of fleshly experiences as they enter this life. The newdead have to traverse the mysterious landscape that separates Thisworld from the Other.

Frequent adjustments need to be made along the way.

Influenced by the arcane East, the Order of the Wise had been as concerned with afterlife as with living. Our sacrificers had conducted rites of passage to ease the young into life and the old out of it.

The druids of Hibernia had developed along different lines. No sacrificer was available to guide me to the gates of the Otherworld and see me safely through.

If I had no choice but to die alone, I was determined to do it well.

Meanwhile, my insatiable curiosity explored the condition of dying. There was a sensation of lightness, a promise of weightlessness that was very tempting. At least death would have its compensations. When I entered the Otherworld I would throw off the leaden bonds of flesh. With them would go not only pain, but volition. I could drift wherever the Pattern took me.

My spirit would be free.

Still partially anchored to my body, I yearned outward. Almost immediately I was met by a sound that was not music but greater than music, a harmonic emanating from the Source of All Being. The darkness took on texture and formed itself into a spiral, the most sacred configuration in the cosmos, the dance of the sun and the stars. I was carried on the surface of the spiral like a leaf on a whirlpool. Darkness above and below and around me. One deep note ringing through me. Ecstasy!

Movement ceased; I floated. The darkness turned crimson. The experience was strangely familiar. Was it something I once dreamed? Or something I remembered?

I must not let myself be afraid. Rix was never afraid.

Rix. Briga. Ainvar.

*Think, head!*

Three is the number of fate.

With a sickening swoop I dropped toward a lake of light. Toward, not into. Beings swam upward from the light. They moved; I moved. Yet in opposite directions. We did not communicate with one another.

They passed me and were gone.

The light was no longer below me but ahead of me, glimpsed through the thinnest of membranes. The light was warm and soft, pulsing in rhythm with that singular continuous note. If I could reach it my fractured self would be whole again.

While I struggled forward the light melted into a shimmer of rainbow colors. Surely the great gates lay just ahead. One bold stride would carry me through.

I was confused. Was Briga on the other side? Or was she still in the place I was about to leave?

As a druid I had been taught that each life contains one test to pass, one task to complete, and one lesson to learn. Which was this?

Think, I commanded my head.

I had last seen Briga as an old woman. She must be waiting for me in the Otherworld by now. One bold stride and . . .

A furious female voice—not Briga's—shouted from somewhere behind me, "This is your fault, Ainvar! I could kill you!"

You can't kill me, I thought smugly, if I am already dead.

I gathered myself, relieved that the moment had finally come. Now all the mysteries would be solved and all the questions answered.

Yet something was holding me back. Invisible hands clutched me and pulled me. How dare they! I fought as hard as I could, but to no avail. If this was my test, I was failing. Despair was added to my agony.

The pain was a ferocious beast that gnawed and tore at my vitals. I would not be allowed to escape. Grimly, I set myself to endure the worst that living had to offer. At the final extremity there is nothing else to be done. Perhaps this itself was the test.

Drawing on the strength my spirit had accrued in a hundred forgotten lifetimes, I waged my solitary battle.

A voice that sounded like Briga's murmured in my ear.

The pain flared in a final burst of excruciating agony. Then it faded.

I was alone in a vast silence.

The Two-Faced One. The three faces of Briga. Three, not two, is the number of fate.

"Briga?" I whispered. And opened my eyes.

She was sitting beside me.

For a moment I could see all three Brigas, the young, the mature, and the old. Then they melted into one and there she was, the living breathing woman.

"I'm here, Ainvar," she said.

My face felt as if I was smiling at her. I hope I was. But before we could speak, my eyes closed of their own accord and I fell into sleep. An easy, healing sleep, as warm as Briga's arms around me.

When I awoke again I realized that the wheel of the seasons had turned. I had fallen ill during a golden autumn. Now a cold, blue light filtered in through the open doorway, heralding the onset of winter.

Briga bent over me, tucking blankets around my shoulders. "How do you feel, Ainvar?"

"Better." My voice was weak and my chest was still sore, but there was no pain.

Had I left it behind at the gates? I tried to remember the gates but they were fading from my memory. The entire experience was vanishing like a pattern etched in the sand, then deliberately rubbed out.

Rubbed out by whom?

My senior wife's voice interrupted my musings. "You have visitors," she said. "They wouldn't wait any longer, they want to see for themselves that you're getting well."

Looking past Briga, I saw that the lodge was crowded with people. All three of my wives and most of our children were there, together with Sulis, Keryth, Grannus, Teyrnon, and Damona, the Goban Saor. Everyone I loved.

Except . . . "Where's Cormiac?"

"You should be asking 'Where's Labraid?' " cried an angry voice. Brushing past Briga, Onuava bent over me. Her face was crimson, her breasts were heaving with emotion.

Briga said, "Not now, Onuava, Ainvar's not strong enough yet. I said you could see him only if you behaved yourself."

"Would that make any difference tomorrow or the next day? Labraid will still be lost to me." Onuava's voice skittered on the brink of the condition the Greeks called "hysteria." "I've been robbed of a king's son!" she shouted at Briga. "You couldn't possibly understand what that meant to me! I'm no one now, not even the wife of a chief druid because that wretched Ainvar isn't the chief druid anymore."

The Goban Saor caught my third wife by the elbows. It took all his considerable strength to turn the big woman around and march her out the door. Over her shoulder she screamed, "You shouldn't have done what you did, Briga! This is Ainvar's fault. You should have let him die!"

As the Goban Saor led her away, her cries increased in volume until they were diminished by distance.

"I'm sorry about that," Briga said to me.

"Obviously something's very wrong. What's this about Labraid and where's Cormiac Ru?"

Lakutu tugged at the sleeve of Briga's gown. "We do not know the worst," she said, "but Ainvar will imagine the worst unless you tell him."

"You must, Briga," Sulis chimed in. "He won't be able to rest otherwise."

Keryth added, "None of it is your fault, Ainvar. You have to believe that." Her words were enough to make me feel guilty even before I heard the whole story.

Briga gave me a wooden cup containing cool water, then sat down beside me. "Drink this slowly, Ainvar. It will do you good."

Keeping my eyes on her face, I sipped obediently.

"After you collapsed," she said, "I could not wake you up again. I tried everything I knew but it was no use."

"Briga sent for me, of course," Sulis interjected. "Yet even I could not restore you. We finally decided it would be best just to let you sleep and hope the illness would wear itself out."

Briga said, "Lakutu and Onuava took turns sitting with you, but I was here all the time."

"I knew," I told her.

"We women were not strong enough to tend you by ourselves, so I asked Cormiac Ru to help us lift you and keep you clean."

"I'm surprised he was willing, under the circumstances."

"Oh, Ainvar, you know how he is. He was angry because you made me cry, but when he realized how ill you were he was very upset. Like me, he never left your side—until the day you cried out, 'Bring her back!' Cormiac thought you were calling for Maia. He convinced himself that seeing her again would save you, so he's gone for her."

"He *what*?"

"He went to bring Maia back, and Labraid went with him."

I could not take this in. "Labraid? He's just a child."

"He's facing into his fifteenth winter, when he must be counted a man—as he reminded his mother when she shouted at him and tried to stop him. But no one ever stops Labraid from anything he wants to do, you know that. I'm only surprised Cormiac was willing to take him along."

## *chapter* XIII

I WAS NOT STRONG ENOUGH TO WORRY ABOUT THE TWO OF THEM simultaneously. My spinning thoughts concentrated on the Red Wolf. "Cormiac can't be gone, Briga! It's not possible." He had become a fixture of our lives, as certain as the sun. Whatever else might happen to us Cormiac was always there.

"Well, he is. Look around." Jumping to her feet, my senior wife circled the lodge, pretending to seek the Red Wolf in one ridiculous place after another. "Is he in the hen's box? He is not. Is he hanging from the cloak peg? He is not." My Briga could be playful, it was one of her most endearing qualities. She might almost have been playing a joke on me. But when she turned back to me and reiterated, "He's gone, I tell you," there was no mistaking the pain in her voice.

"This makes no sense, Briga. Cormiac would never leave you, not for anything."

Her shoulders slumped. "That's where you're wrong, Ainvar. No one is ours to keep forever. Not in this life."

I spent long days and nights lying on my bed while Briga fussed over me and made me drink vile-tasting potions. When I held my hand in front of my face, the skin was so thin as to be translucent. If I turned over on my side my bony knees pressed painfully against each other. But at least I was alive.

We could not be so sure about the Red Wolf and Labraid Loingseach.

They had set out together with their swords in their belts and their faces resolutely turned toward the east. Briga had done her best to dissuade them but it was no use. I was not surprised; when the Red Wolf made a decision he never turned back. But the problems were insurmountable. To begin with, how and where would they acquire a boat? The Plain of Broad Spears was well inland; Maia, wherever she might be, was on the other side of the sea.

Recalling that vast expanse of turbulent water made my stomach churn.

Labraid's arrogance was such that he might truly believe he could challenge the sea and win. Cormiac Ru had a wiser head, but he was impelled by his heart. By the time I knew they were gone, they probably both had drowned.

To grieve is to surrender to death. I knew death was not final, but still the loss of the Red Wolf was heart-wrenching. Briga felt the same, though she kept her pain to herself and put on a hopeful smile for my sake.

As for Onuava, every few days she came storming into my lodge to upbraid me further. I tried to defend myself by saying, "I never told either of them to undertake this madness, Onuava. If I had been in my right mind I would have stopped them."

"You speak to me of madness? You're the mad one, Ainvar, to think that child of yours could still be alive after all this time. Even if she were, how could they hope to find her?"

"I never asked anyone to bring Maia back. Cormiac jumped to that conclusion on his own."

Onuava said bitterly, "He's paid for his foolishness. You haven't. You've cost Vercingetorix his son."

If she had stabbed me through the heart she could have hurt me no worse.

The next time she came Briga tried to keep her out, but Onuava simply brushed my senior wife aside and renewed her vituperative attack on me. No amount of protestations on Briga's part could deter her. Like Vercingetorix—or Labraid, for that matter—Onuava recognized no obstacles to her will.

Help came from an unexpected source. Of her own volition, my second wife stationed herself outside the door of my lodge. Lakutu slept curled up in a ball at night and sat on a little three-legged stool during the day, steadfastly refusing Onuava admittance. She was half the size of my third wife, yet when the Egyptian narrowed her dark eyes and hissed through her teeth, Onuava backed off.

She did not have to be present to cause trouble. Hatred becomes a ball of poison that lingers in the atmosphere, feeding on itself and constantly growing until it damages everyone in its vicinity. My clan, shaken by the violence of Onuava's emotion, began snapping and growling at one another.

What I wanted to do was stay in bed indefinitely, while Briga stroked my forehead and little Gobnat fed me bits of honeycomb. What I did was drag myself off the bed as soon as I was strong enough, and go to see Fíachu. "You've heard about Cormiac and Labraid, I suppose?"

"Everyone's heard about them, Ainvar. When she was refused admittance to you, that big handsome wife of yours came down here wailing and moaning. There's no ignoring her. One of my own wives," he said with a careless laugh, "has even suggested I take her into my bed to keep her quiet for a while."

I looked surprised, but I was not. That was a mask of convenience. Damona spent much of her time in Fíachu's fort gossiping with the older women, a pastime that I encouraged because it does no harm to have extra ears working for you. Teyrnon's wife had already passed this tidbit on to me, and I had been mulling it over.

"Do you want to bed Onuava?" I asked Fíachu.

"Would that keep her quiet?"

"In my experience, no." You should always be honest with someone from whom you seek a favor.

Fíachu still had no sons. Onuava had just lost the son of a king, for which she blamed me. If she had a son by the king of the Laigin, under Gaelic law the child would inherit his father's rank and Onuava could once again boast of being a prince's mother. Besides, Onuava was a woman of considerable appetites. Even if she forgave me, in my present condition I would not be able to satisfy those appetites for quite some time.

Selfishness serves no one. By being unselfish with Onuava I could benefit a number of people.

"You might not be able to keep Onuava quiet," I told Fíachu, "but if you wish to take her to your bed I can promise you a most remarkable experience."

"Are you serious? You wouldn't mind?"

"It's an honor to serve the king," I replied solemnly.

Afterward Briga congratulated me on my cleverness. She was as eager to see the back of Onuava as I was, and Lakutu would be glad to spend her nights in her own lodge again.

But Cormiac Ru was gone. All my cleverness could not change that.

If I had expected Fíachu to be diplomatic about his bedding arrangements, I was mistaken. He was a chieftain. He simply took Onuava into his fort and installed her in a lodge near his own. He could not marry her because she was married to me, but he treated her at least as well as he treated his wives.

His wives were not favorably impressed. Even the one who had suggested the arrangement was disgruntled. "I meant it as a jest!" she protested. Which only demonstrates that women have a different sense of humor from men.

I did not visit the fort again during my convalescence, but members of my clan reported back to me. "Fíachu looks absolutely drained," said the Goban Saor, sniggering. "His women are at one another's throats and even a chieftain can't control a situation like that."

Rescue was at hand. By the time the meadows were drowsy and blowsy with summer, a new war—or rather, a renewal of an old war—broke out between the Laigin and the Ulaid. The king of the Laigin summoned the warriors bound to him by their tribal chieftains. Led by Fíachu, the men of the Slea Leathan rushed off to enjoy a good fight far away from home.

And Onuava had returned to us. Even the tough shell of her spirit was not proof against the barbs of Fíachu's other wives when the chieftain was not around.

My third wife no longer stormed into my lodge to berate me. Instead she moved around our little settlement with the dreamy, abstracted expression women get when they carry new life.

"A male child," Keryth announced after reading the omens.

Perhaps that would mollify Onuava, though it could never replace the son

Vercingetorix had lost. In some future life I must face him. The Source demands that balance must be achieved in all things, no matter how long it takes. Would I be given a chance to replace Rix's loss with something of equal value? Or would he mete out a punishment to even the scales?

We still did not know the fate of Labraid and Cormiac Ru. I even sent Dara to Cohern, with a request that he ask his tribesmen along the southern coast if any bodies had washed up on shore. None had. They were simply . . . gone. Swallowed up in immensity; swallowed up by the sea.

Such a death would be appropriate for Onuava's son, who had foolishly called himself Labraid Loingseach. The Speaker Who Sails the Seas had nearly drowned once before due to his rashness. That Which Watches must have decided it was time to close the circle.

But I could find nothing in the Pattern of Cormiac Ru that would have led him to such an end. Against all the odds, I was forced to conclude the Red Wolf must still be alive.

I paid a professional visit to Keryth.

"What you suggest is not possible, Ainvar," she told me.

"Why not? We made the voyage successfully."

"Yes, but we had two boats and an experienced crew."

"Cormiac may have acted impulsively, Keryth, but he knows how to take care of himself; he's a survivor by nature. Examine the omens and see if he lives."

She looked dubious. "If you're right, they might even be in Latium by now. I don't think my abilities reach that far."

"The same stars shine over both sides of the sea," I pointed out. "Their positions may have changed, but they're the same stars."

"For this divining I'll need more than stars, Ainvar. Can you bring me a wolf? A live wolf?"

"A dead wolf is one thing, a live wolf is quite another. Wolves are strong and quick and clever. I'd need someone like Cormiac to . . ."

"Exactly," said Keryth. "We need a wolf to find a wolf."

I am no hunter; the requisite skills were more the province of Grannus. When I asked him, and explained the reason, he agreed to try. "It's going to take more than one man to capture a wolf alive and bring him back unharmed," he told me. "You'd better come with me, Ainvar."

We planned to set out on the following morning.

When I awoke my nose reported damp air and cooking smells before I opened my eyes. I had slept later than was my habit. Briga had already left on some woman's business and Lakutu was preparing a meal for me.

I stood up and stretched. Slowly, thoroughly. Another valuable lesson learned from observing nature. A man who stretches himself first thing in the morning will spend the day in a more comfortable body.

"It's starting to rain," I observed through the open doorway. "Again."

Lakutu, who rarely ventured an unsolicited comment, said, "At home the sun always shines."

"It rains a lot in Gaul. You've forgotten."

She responded softly, "I was not talking about Gaul."

When I met Grannus outside his lodge he assured me the weather was in our favor. "Rain will intensify the scent, Ainvar."

"Not enough to enable me to smell a wolf."

"The wolfhounds will do that. I've borrowed a dog and a bitch from a friend of mine in the fort. They're right over there; have a look at them. Wolves often den up in the daytime and we might never see them, but they can't hide from a hound's nose."

"I'm not certain that's a good idea, Grannus. Those animals are trained to kill wolves, not capture them."

"Don't worry, I can control them." Like most strong men, Grannus was full of confidence. "They're wearing stout collars and I have two leashes of plaited leather. They can't possibly get away from me."

Yet when I looked into the eyes of the great shaggy hounds I was not so sure. They had the same eyes as the wolves we were seeking.

As we set out for the mountains the morning grew darker rather than lighter. Briga had insisted that I wear her otter fur mantle. "You were ill not so long ago," she reminded me, "and this garment will turn rain."

I was reluctant. Men of every tribe like to pretend they are impervious to weather. But Briga was Briga and so I left the lodge wearing my wife's mantle—which barely reached my knees.

Over my shoulder I carried a net fashioned of twisted rope. We hoped it would be strong enough to contain a wolf. The Goban Saor had also fashioned a device consisting of a noose affixed to a long hollow pole, and attached to a leather thong that ran up through the middle of the pole. In theory, we would slip the noose over the wolf's neck, pull it tight using the thong, and thus incapacitate him while we bundled him into the net.

In theory.

Strapped to his back Grannus carried five spears capable of bringing down a wolf if necessary. Two more were thrust through my belt.

I had invited the Goban Saor to come with us and demonstrate his contraption personally, but he declined. "Wolves are shy creatures, Ainvar. The more people you take with you the less likely you are to find any."

"You're right, of course," I replied. "It would be a mistake for you to come with us, so stay here and build a pen for our wolf when we bring him back."

"I'll model it on the trap in the deerpits, nothing ever escapes one of those." The Goban Saor was trying hard not to look relieved. But druids can see with more than their eyes. Our master craftsman was deathly afraid of wolves.

In Gaul, where wolves abound, it is well known that a wolf will not attack a healthy man. Such stories are used to frighten small children and make them behave, but bear no resemblance to the truth. However, lies have long legs.

Everyone is afraid of something. In his heart, which I knew better than anyone, Vercingetorix had been terrified of losing. My Briga was afraid of remembering.

And I was afraid of forgetting.

By the time Grannus and I reached the foothills the rain was hammering down. The shaggy hounds frequently paused to shake themselves, which only made Grannus wetter. Briga's cloak gave my head and body welcome protection, while the deepening mud proved the practicality of the Gaelic custom of going barefoot. Shoes would have been an impediment. It is far easier to pull a bare foot out of mud, and if the surface is slippery, bare toes can grip almost like fingers.

Before long the hounds picked up a scent. Grannus ran with them while I trotted along behind. My illness had left me with a shortness of breath, which I tried to ignore, concentrating instead on watching the wolfhounds. The dog was the color of the clouds above us. The bitch, slightly smaller and narrower through the loins, had a white coat splotched with glossy red. The pair loped along like horses with their heads up, reading the messages the wind brought them. Clearly they knew what they were about. In a land where wolves were plentiful, they were specialists.

Our path grew steeper, taking us through a stand of pines toward a tumble of granite boulders. If the wolves of Hibernia were anything like the wolves of Gaul, they would have a den in this vicinity. The hounds agreed with me. They halted as if by mutual agreement, with the bitch slightly in the lead.

She froze. Her whole body seemed to vibrate. Both hounds visibly gathered themselves. "Hold on to them, Grannus!" I cried.

It is painful to see a man discover that he is not as strong as he thought he was. When the wolfhounds leaped forward in unison they dragged the hapless Grannus after them as if he were a child. The trio sped up the slope. Grannus was shouting commands at the dogs but they ignored him. Instinct spoke to them more strongly than any human voice. For a moment I was lost in admiration as I watched the powerful hindquarters of the hounds gathering, bunching, propelling the animals forward in huge bounds.

Then I began to run, too.

All too soon, my throat was aching and my chest hurt. I could not possibly keep up the pace—nor prevent what was sure to happen. Silently cursing my failure to anticipate this, I scrambled up the trail as best I could.

The name of Eriu crossed my mind. For no particular reason.

As silently as a cloud forms, a wolf appeared on a ledge above us. A very large wolf, silver gray in color, with black legs and mask. He stood without any sign of fear; without any obvious emotion. His calm yellow eyes took in the approaching hounds, and Grannus, and then looked straight at me.

The wolf gave me his eyes.

The world tilted around me, and I knew I was in the presence of great magic.

There is a unique feel to great magic. A sense of dislocation; an intense focus that precludes any outside awareness. This was the moment I had longed for, yet feared would never come again. This time, however, it was not I who was creating magic.

It is the wolf.

I am looking out through his eyes. I am thinking his thoughts.

I see myself below him, staring upward. Contempt floods through me. *Puny two-legged, bad-smelling male creature.*

*I am aware of the den hidden far back among the rocks, where my mate lies with her newborn cubs. We have had other litters. Some are still with us, others have gone to join other packs. But my mate and I will be together for life.*

*The rest of our pack is watching from concealment nearby. I can summon them with a twitch of my neck. They are subject to my authority. Outsiders may be allowed to join us if they are sufficiently subservient to me, but as the dominant pair, my mate and I are the only ones permitted to breed. The future of the pack depends upon our having and raising cubs. We all join in caring for them.*

*Life is good. We eat and sleep and play with one another. When we hunt we take down the old and the weak and leave the strong to breed. On clear nights we throw back our heads and share the ecstasy of singing to the sky.*

*Among our number is a formerly dominant male who abused his power. He was attacked by the pack, males and females alike, and defeated but not killed. Instead he was made the lowest of the low. This is not uncommon in the wolf tribe. We allow him to follow the rest of us at a distance and feed from our scraps. If he comes too close the others drive him away. If he cringes and tries to hold his ground, the males urinate on him. The outcast will spend his life on the fringes. He understands and accepts this, knowing that as long as we have food he will not starve. Eventually he will wander away to die alone. Wolves prefer to die alone.*

*Today the two-legs have come to kill us. To kill the cubs. I have seen it before. I have seen helpless little ones dragged from their den and clubbed to death.*

*This time it will not be allowed. We do not attack two-legs, they are not our prey. But we will attack them now. Our pack has grown large enough to bring its enemies down.*

As the wolf thought these thoughts, I gave him my eyes.

He entered my head. He thought my thoughts, becoming aware of my own mates, and of the youngsters I cherished as he cherished his cubs. He learned that I had not come to kill him but to seek his help. For the sake of the Red Wolf.

Time stopped.

As part of my training with the Order of the Wise, I had striven to develop an intensity of imaginative will capable of altering natural reality. I had believed that power was unique to druidry; to the chief druid in particular. I was wrong. While the wolf and I looked at each other time stopped, but it was not my doing.

Man and wolf gazed across an abyss wider than the physical distance between them; wider even than the distance that separated their species. Yet in that moment of magic they were one and the same.

## *chapter* XIV

UNTIL I FACED THE WOLF IN THE MOUNTAINS OF HIBERNIA, I HAD thought of animals as . . . animals.

They are not. They are spirits who in Thislife inhabit bodies very different from our own.

I had more in common with the wolf on the ledge above me than with many humans. The beast was loyal and sagacious; a tender father and devoted mate. Unlike the malevolent Caesar, the wolf did not engage in genocide. He killed only to eat and feed his family, as should we all.

I would break my spears over my knee rather than throw one at the wolf.

He knew my thought as soon as it entered my head. His eyes remained locked on mine for a heartbeat longer, then he turned and vanished like smoke among the rocks.

Time started again.

Grannus was still plunging up the mountainside after the hounds, who were baying now in spite of the constriction of the collars on their throats. My own throat was on fire but I ignored the pain in order to shout, "Kill those dogs if you can't stop them! The wolves are not to be harmed!"

Grannus was a man of action, rather than thought, but in an emergency his head worked well enough. Since he could not stop the hounds by pulling back on their leashes, he wrapped the leashes around his arms and threw himself to the ground. In spite of their strength the hounds could not drag his dead weight up the steep incline. They halted in confusion. Grannus sat up, looking equally confused. And extremely muddy. "What do we do now?" he asked when I reached him.

"I'm not sure."

"Do you mean you've brought us all this way, Ainvar, and don't know what to—" His eyes slid past me. His jaw dropped.

I whirled around. The wolf was standing not a spear's throw from us, but he was not alone. Beside him stood another male wolf, an animal that was more tan than gray and had a slightly crouched posture. It did not look at us but kept its eyes fixed on the silver wolf.

Our hounds were going mad.

"Take them away from here," I told Grannus.

"But those are wolves! You don't want me to leave you alone with two wolves."

Locking eyes with the big silver male, I said over my shoulder, "That's the very thing I do want. Go now, Grannus. Not all the way back; just a little way down the mountain. Wait for me there."

"But—"

"If I need you I'll shout," I said firmly.

Never had I known my old friend to be so close to revolt. However, after a few moments he did as he was told. He was so busy trying to control the hounds and make them go with him that he did not see what happened next.

As soon as he had gone the silver wolf took another step toward me. The tan wolf stayed where he was, flattening himself until his belly almost touched the ground. Keeping his eyes on mine, the silver wolf came so close I could have stretched out my hand and touched him. I could smell him, a unique scent compounded of clean fur and bloody meat and fragrant pine trees and sheer wildness.

For one heartbeat I longed to throw off my human form and join him. I could do it. I knew I could. The air between us tingled with the magic of potential.

With a great effort I recovered my self-control. I could not act for myself alone; I was responsible, as was the silver wolf, for a whole pack.

He looked from me to the cringing tan wolf and back again. His long, full tail wagged slowly.

"Yes," I whispered, not quite sure what I was agreeing to.

The silver wolf looked at his comrade once more. Still on his belly, the tan wolf crept toward me. He flattened his ears tightly against his skull as he passed the dominant male, but did not stop until he was right at my feet.

He looked as if he might die on the spot. I have never seen an animal so frightened in my life.

The silver wolf gave a short, sharp bark, almost like a dog. Then he trotted away and disappeared among the boulders.

The tan wolf stayed where he was. The poor creature was trembling all over. Slowly, carefully, I removed the belt from my waist. Bending down, I encircled his neck with it, using the extra length as a lead. When I gave a gentle tug he stood up and came with me.

On our way home I sent Grannus ahead of us. The tan wolf was obedient to me, but I could not be certain he would remain so if the hounds were allowed to get behind him.

We must have been an odd procession as we approached the lodges. Grannus first, alternately dragging and cajoling two big wolfhounds who were almost insane with rage, having seen all the laws by which they lived overturned. Followed by me, with a fully grown wolf beside me, pressing his shivering body against my leg as if I were his only protection in the world.

The children saw us coming and started to run forward, but with my free hand I waved them back. "Keep your distance," I called. "I don't know what he'll do if you come too close."

They stopped where they were and stood staring.

I made my way to our lodge, where Briga met me at the doorway. For once her eyes did not light on me with joy. They locked on the wolf with an expression of horror. "You've gone mad, Ainvar," she said in a barely audible voice.

I was in no mood to argue. "Where's Keryth?"

"I'm not sure. What does she have to do with this?"

"Send Lakutu to look for her."

My senior wife backed into the lodge, too frightened to take her eyes from the wolf, and Lakutu took her place at the doorway. She too gave the wolf a long look, but she did not seem frightened. Quite the opposite. "May I touch?" she asked.

Lakutu is an endless amazement.

"I don't know," I told her. "Hold out your hand and see what he does."

She moved forward one tiny step at a time, and held out her hand. The wolf trembled more violently than ever but showed no other reaction.

My second wife bunched the fingers of her left hand together and brought them toward his nose. "Kss," she said softly. Then again, "Kss. Kss."

The wolf's ears stirred. Pricked. He stretched his neck and took the tiniest sniff of her fingers.

Lakutu raised smiling eyes to mine. "Nice," she said.

She was reluctant to leave her new friend long enough to fetch Keryth, but like the tan wolf, she was obedient to me. While we waited, the wolf and I sat down outside the lodge. On close inspection I saw that he was an old animal, with worn, broken teeth and a lot of gray hairs around his eyes. He had begun panting heavily and I was beginning to worry about him.

To give her credit, Briga brought out a bowl of water for the wolf. She set it down a great distance away from us and scurried back into the lodge. I led him over to the bowl and urged him to drink. Vessel and water smelled of humans, however, and he would not touch it.

When she arrived, Keryth echoed my concerns. By that time most of my clan had gathered to see the wolf—with the exception of the Goban Saor, who had remembered urgent business elsewhere. "Perhaps you should put the animal in that pen the Goban Saor made," Dian Cet suggested, "and leave him alone for a while. Give him time to calm down."

I shook my head. "I can't explain, but he's acting under orders and doing his best in what must be, for him, a terrifying situation. I doubt if any of us would have his courage. For his sake, the sooner he's back with the pack the better. So do what you have to do with him now, Keryth."

With the seer leading the way, the wolf and I left the vicinity of the lodges. The others started to follow us but I waved them back. "Druid business," I said sternly.

That was enough.

We crossed the patch of stony ground where we customarily went to relieve ourselves, and struck out across the grassland. I saw nothing that might provide an appropriate ritual site but Keryth seemed to know where she was going. Eventually she came to an abrupt halt, just as the hound bitch had halted when she located the wolves.

"Here," said Keryth. "Do you not feel it?"

I did. The humming of the earth beneath my feet. The sense of being held in a bubble. The old wolf felt it, too. He sat down on his haunches and looked up at me with what I can only describe as an expectant expression.

From the bosom of her gown Keryth produced a worn leather sandal that had belonged to Cormiac Ru. She held it out toward the wolf, but he shrank back against my leg and would not even look at her. "Let me give it to him," I suggested.

When I took the sandal into my hand I could almost feel Cormiac's foot within it. The leather still retained his shape. I slowly lowered it to the wolf.

He smelled it all over, missing not the tiniest part. I wondered what messages the scent conveyed, but I would never know. The Source gives wondrous gifts to the animals that we humans are not allowed. Do the animals dwell in a richer world than ours? What have we done to be denied such privileges?

"Ainvar!" Keryth said sharply, calling me back from my druid musings.

The wolf had finished his minute examination of the sandal. He stood up. For the first time he abandoned his abject posture and I could see the wolf he must have been in his youth. Strong and sure, with a proud, unyielding core . . .

*"Yes!"* Keryth extended her arms until her hands were over the wolf's head, palm down. This time he did not flinch away. "Touch him," the seer told me.

I stooped—I am a tall man—and gently rested my hand on the wolf's head between the pricked ears. When he accepted it, Keryth took my other hand into one of hers. Then, closing her eyes, she began to hum. As the earth was humming.

As my bones were humming. As the wolf was humming. Singing the music of the great circle of power that flowed through the three of us.

Three is the number of fate.

Never had I felt more attuned to all that is life and living. Earth and animal and human, parts of one whole. How pure and simple, yet more complex than even a druid could understand.

Time did not stop; it did not even slow. It simply ceased to exist. We are. The Source is.

I bowed my head in worship.

When it was over I took the wolf back to the mountains. He was like a different animal, cheerful and revitalized, his tail awag with confidence. I should have liked to keep him with me. What druid would not be proud of such a companion? But I would no more enslave his wild spirit than I would chain a king and drag him behind my chariot as Caesar had done to Vercingetorix.

So we set out together, he and I, to take him home. Halfway there I slipped the collar off his neck. He continued to trot along beside me and I found myself talking aloud to him as to an equal. Looking up at me, he wagged his tail harder.

"You've done me a great service," I told him. "Through you Keryth touched the spirit of the Red Wolf and found it still encased in living flesh. I'm convinced he will come back to us someday. What do you think?" I asked this question as seriously as I would have asked another man.

The old wolf gazed at me as if he understood. No, that is not correct. He gazed at me. He understood. Not through spoken language, but through the deeper levels of communication that exist in the animal kingdom. Did we once possess them, too?

As we walked on I continued to talk to him and he continued to listen. I told him things I had never told a living human being. He took them into himself and eased my burden.

We had a long distance to go and I was not as young as I used to be. Neither was the wolf. We stopped several times and sat down, me upon a boulder or a fallen tree, he upon his haunches. When we stood up again we were both a little stiff. Once, when I winced, he gave me a look of sympathy.

I had never thought to see a wolf express sympathy for a man. The truth is, I had never thought. The arrogance of humans had made me blind. My eyes were open now.

As we approached his home territory my companion's subservient demeanor returned. He lowered his head and appeared to shrink within himself. I could not see the pack but he knew exactly where they were. He knew exactly what the future held for him.

"You don't have to stay here," I told him. "If you want, you can come with me. I promise you no man will raise his hand to you. You can sleep outside my lodge and my women will keep you fed, and when winter arrives you can come in and sit by the fire."

He lifted his head and looked at me. There was no fear in his yellow eyes, only calm resignation. He was at peace with himself. Wiser than man, the wolf did not argue with nature.

I longed to pat him good-bye but that would be cruel. He was practically an outcast already; it would only make matters worse if he approached the pack freshly reeking of human scent. I contented myself with one last look.

See him, eyes, I commanded. Take your time. See and appreciate all of him.

His unique self. His pale golden eyes, the ruff of tan fur at his neck, the long forelegs and slender, delicate toes, as lovely as a woman's. A magnificent creature perfectly designed for the life he led.

"I salute you as a free person," I said to the wolf. And turned and walked away. I could feel his eyes upon me but he did not follow.

I had not expected him to.

# *chapter* XV

I TRIED TO TELL BRIGA ABOUT MY EXPERIENCE WITH THE WOLVES, but she, who could work a very high order of magic herself, paid little attention. She had no hesitation about using her extraordinary gifts to benefit anyone who needed them, yet steadfastly refused to acknowledge the magical. In all our time together I had not managed to convince her otherwise.

To Briga, the Source of All Being was a tangible entity. Its works were tangible, too: the shining of the sun, the falling of the rain, the upthrust of the mountain. I knew that what we called magic was also a manifestation of the Source but I could never convince my senior wife.

Lakutu was different. When I told her about the wolves she was fascinated. "In Egypt we consider animals the equal of humans," she said. "The earth is meant for man and beast to share equally. We worship the hawk, the snake, the crocodile, and most particularly the cat as gods."

"Why?"

Her dark eyes were opaque. "Why? Because they *are.*"

After meeting the silver wolf I was fully willing to accept that there were animals who possessed extraordinary powers. I longed to know specific details about the beliefs of the Egyptians, but Lakutu's unquestioning assertion offered me only a blank wall. She had a simple, straightforward mind. She believed what she believed and that was that.

When I told Onuava I was convinced that Cormiac was still alive, which meant that Labraid might well be alive too, she was pitifully eager to believe me. Even the hardest tree has a soft heart. Her credulity did not come from faith in the druids, for when Gaul fell Onuava lost all faith in the powers of druidry. But there is something beyond faith: a certainty that seeps into the bones.

I *knew* that Cormiac was alive. Through me, so did Onuava.

Her expression softened. "Perhaps I've been too harsh with you, Ainvar. You were very ill; I suppose you had no way of knowing what Labraid and Cormiac would do."

"I would have prevented them if I could."

"I'm sure you would, Ainvar."

"Does this mean you don't hate me anymore?"

She gave a little laugh. "I never hated you, not really."

"Oh yes, you did. Women can hate and love and hate again in a single breath."

"There's some truth in that," she agreed. "Men are more sluggish. Their emotions take a bit of time to rise and fall. Rather like their lances of flesh," she added with a wicked sparkle in her eyes.

I was not accustomed to having such a conversation with my third wife. I had always thought of her as a gorgeous animal, rather than the possessor of a thinking head.

But lately I had been rethinking my opinion of animals.

Perhaps this was the right time to ask Onuava an important question. "When I was waking up after my illness, I overheard you tell Briga that she shouldn't have done what she did. You told her she should have let me die. Just what did Briga do?"

Onuava turned her head so I could not see her eyes. "That's all in the past. Let's speak of something else, Ainvar. Is your health fully returned? Your color is quite good."

Onuava had many skills, but subtlety was not one of them. "What did Briga do?" I repeated in a firmer tone.

Still not looking at me, she began pleating the fabric of her gown with nervous fingers. "Perhaps I was mistaken."

I recalled an earlier, even more mysterious incident: the day Briga pulled Labraid out of the sea. Onuava had been a witness to that, too. She had told a story to which I had paid little attention at the time. Now my head saw a connection. "When Briga rescued Labraid," I said, "Lakutu claimed that the water parted and let Briga pass through. Exactly what did you see that day, Onuava? I demand to know."

"Thinking about it still gives me a strange feeling in the pit of my stomach, Ainvar. Are you certain you want to hear?"

"I'm certain."

She took a deep breath and met my eyes. "Briga walked to the edge of the sea and kept walking until the crest of a wave broke over her head. I was sure she was going to be drowned, but a ridge of sand rose out of the sea in front of her. It formed a narrow causeway between her and Labraid. When she ran toward him she left footprints in the damp sand." There was no mistaking the awe in Onuava's voice.

"Briga bent down and lifted my son in her arms—and he bigger than herself!—then turned and started back toward us. Even as she walked, the water flowed over her footprints and washed them away. By the time she stepped back onto the beach the ridge of sand had disappeared entirely. There was only the empty sea."

I tried to envision the scene. Bizarre though it was, I found I could clearly picture it in my mind.

Menua once told me that anything a man could picture in his head was possible. Not necessarily probable, but possible. The head contains the mind which contains the spirit which is a spark of the Great Fire which is the Source of All Being.

"Very well, Onuava. Now tell me what Briga did when she thought I was dying."

The normally florid roses in my third wife's cheeks faded away. "She went after you like she went after Labraid. There was no sea and no sand. Just you, lying on the bed, and Briga and me sitting on a bench beside you. Lakutu was exhausted, she'd fallen asleep on the floor at your feet.

"Your breathing had been ghastly for a long time, Ainvar. At last it stopped. We waited and waited but there was nothing more, no sound, not the slightest movement of your chest. I admit, I was glad for your sake. You had been suffering so much it hurt me to watch. It hurt me to see your pale dead face too, so I stood up, meaning to pull the blanket over it.

"Just then, the candles in the lodge . . . dimmed . . . and smoked . . . and the smoke formed itself into a sort of wreath around you. I couldn't even see you anymore, Ainvar. But I saw the light from the candles shine out of Briga's eyes."

Onuava fell silent, staring at me from a shadowed place where candles dimmed and smoke formed a wreath.

"Go on," I whispered.

"Without a moment's hesitation Briga stretched her arms into the smoke. I heard her say, 'He's almost gone but I think I can still reach him.' Her arms vanished in the smoke up to the elbow. Just vanished. I was very frightened, I can tell you. But then they vanished almost to the shoulder, and she flexed her back and groaned like someone lifting a great weight. She fell back onto the bench and sat there panting, with her head hanging down. I was too scared to move. She stood up and reached into the smoke again. And again. And . . ."

"And?"

"And at last she backed out of the smoke holding you. And you were breathing."

This time I believed Onuava. Believed her completely.

Druids recognize the truth when they hear it.

When I returned to my lodge I did not mention my conversation with Onuava. If Briga wanted me to know what happened she would have told me herself.

The private territory in one's head should not be invaded.

My own head was fully occupied. In fact, there were too many thoughts demanding attention. To help clear the clutter, I resumed teaching.

Following the lead of Aislinn, more members of Fíachu's clan joined my original band of students. Aislinn herself was silent and downcast, a girl in mourning, yet she missed very few lessons in the forest glade. Neither did the others. Perhaps their interest went to my head. Perhaps my head let its guard down, just a little.

In spite of what Briga thought, from the beginning I had restricted our lessons to subjects that were appropriate to Hibernia. But with so many eager faces looking up at me I began to wander farther afield. It was hard not to make a fleeting reference, and then a more detailed excursion, into the realms of Gaulish lore. When I outlined the druid hierarchy as it had existed in Gaul, my listeners were fascinated. They wanted to know about the various specialties: how the gift was discovered, how it was developed, and how it was practiced. Each young one began looking into himself to discover what hidden treasures might lie there. They were eager and excited; how could I deny them?

Inevitably, one of my students mentioned the content of our lessons to the chief druid.

One morning Duach Dalta appeared at the door of my lodge. He was swathed from head to foot in a cloak dyed the color of blood and painted with Celtic designs. I must remember to tell my students that druids in Gaul shunned ostentation, I thought to myself as I ushered my visitor inside.

Dara was there, waiting to go to the forest with me. When the chief druid entered, my son gave him a respectful nod and surrendered his place by the hearth. The older man sat down, hawked, spat, and looked around for something to drink.

Briga offered him water.

"Is this what you give a guest, Ainvar?" he asked icily. "Your wife is badly trained in the art of hospitality."

Duach Dalta might be a venerable member of Fíachu's clan, but I would allow no one to say such things about Briga. Particularly not in her own home.

"My senior wife pleases me very well as she is," I said.

The chief druid's expression was turning more sour with every heartbeat. "I should have expected no better. You are strangers here who have taken it upon yourselves to mislead our youngsters. That must cease. Your ways are not our ways. I insist that—"

"We were born in another land," I interrupted, "but now we belong to the Slea Leathan tribe. We've adopted your customs, we're even acquiring your accent."

"Speaking like a Milesian will not make you one, Ainvar."

"Admittedly, I'm not of the Milesian race. I understand that Milesios claimed to have Scythian blood, however?"

Duach Dalta gave a reluctant nod. "What of it?"

"The Celts of Gaul," I replied, "are descended from the Celts of the Blue Mountains, whom the Scythians taught to ride horses and take the heads of their enemies. Inevitably the blood of Celt and Scyth was mingled. I'm not as far removed from you as you think."

His nostrils flared. "How dare you presume—"

Dara's voice cut in. "As for being descended from Milesios," he drawled, "I have memorized the complete lineage of Éremon and your name is not included, Duach Dalta. Your father's fathers were among the servants the Milesians brought with them."

For a moment I feared the chief druid was having a fit. His long nose twitched violently; his eyes bulged from his head. He rose to his feet with a clenched fist and advanced on my son as if to hit him.

Dara held his ground. He was no warrior, but he had knowledge on his side and knowledge can make a man brave.

Before it could come to blows between them, I said, "Are you so afraid of the truth, Duach Dalta? Real druids never fear the truth."

It was a calculated insult, but my own temper was dangerously close to being out of control.

He whirled toward me. "I knew you were trouble from the very first night," he hissed, "when you asked all those questions. Fíachu never should have taken you in."

"Did you tell him so?"

"If you were really one of us, you would know that chieftains don't take advice from druids."

I fought to remain calm. "Things were very different in Gaul," I said. "Druids there had stature. The great Vercingetorix himself, who was called 'King of the World,' took advice from me."

Duach Dalta curled his lip in contempt. "That's a transparent lie. Why would any king listen to you, Ainvar?"

"Because I've spent my life training my head to think."

"I can think!"

"How do you do it?" I asked.

"What do you mean, 'how'? I . . . that is . . . thoughts come to me, of course."

"On their own?"

"Certainly."

"Do you mean they flit through your head uninvited, like deer running through a forest?"

Duach Dalta blinked. "I suppose so."

"Then you're not really thinking," I told him. "A well-trained head continually examines the information provided by eyes and ears and nose and skin. At the same time it reflects on past experiences and considers future possibilities. All of this requires deliberate *thought.* A thorough knowledge of one's current situation is imperative. So is a keen understanding of human nature, without which one cannot anticipate future behavior. Intuition plays no small part. And of course one must always consider the Otherworld. In the act of thinking, all of these elements are deliberately brought together, sorted through, and consulted. That is how my head functions, Duach Dalta. What about yours?"

"I . . ." A thread of spittle formed on his lips; thin, withered lips that refuted the evidence of his youthful body. His mouth trembled with an old man's confusion. "I mean . . ."

Before he could decide just what he did mean I glimpsed a movement at the open doorway. Several youngsters peered in at us. When I was not waiting for my students at the accustomed place, they had come looking for me.

I would not humiliate the chief druid in front of them.

"It was kind of you to pay a visit to us, Duach Dalta," I said with all the warmth I could muster. "I have enjoyed our discussion. Perhaps we may continue it another day? I am expected elsewhere now. Briga, will you give our guest some mead and make sure he is comfortable for as long as he wishes to stay?"

I took my cloak from its peg by the door and hurried outside. Dara trotted along in my wake, chuckling to himself like a stream running over stones.

"It isn't funny," I said, pitching my voice low so the others would not hear. "A person can't be blamed for what they don't know."

"Unless they refuse to learn. That old man won't learn anything from you, he despises you. I think he's jealous of you."

"He has no reason to be jealous of me, Dara." The boy was correct, though, and I knew it. I had begun to trespass on the chief druid's territory. Worse than that, I had made him aware of his shortcomings.

People will forgive you for many things. But not for being right.

Trusting Briga to smooth Duach Dalta's ruffled feathers, I began the day's lessons in the glade. On one level my head was thinking about my students, while on a deeper level I reexamined the conversation with the chief druid. I began to regret flaunting my cleverness.

But I am allowed to have pride. I too had been a chief druid.

Returning from the glade that evening, I surprised a red deer on the path. An immense stag with a spectacular, wide-branching rack of antlers. He halted, facing me, with one foreleg delicately raised. There were only a couple of strides between us, yet his huge liquid eyes surveyed me from a vast distance, as a mighty chieftain might look at the lowest of the low. Was he hiding his fear out of a sense of pride? Or was his confidence in his strength and speed so great that he could afford to give in to a momentary curiosity?

Our eyes locked and held.

For a moment I was terribly tempted. A single thought stopped me. If I saw through the eyes of the deer would I ever be able to eat venison again?

I waved my hand. The great stag bounded from the path and vanished, leaving not a leaf disturbed to mark his trail.

On the following day our lessons concerned the nature of thought. "Thinking is a creative process," I explained. "When we think we perform an action, rather than being acted upon by someone else. Thought is infinite. It has power that we can use for ourselves or pass on. Thought is imperishable. If I give you a thought of mine, when I die that thought continues to live in you and can affect your life and the lives of others. Therefore what is more valuable than thought, and what is worth more than a head?"

"Is every head precious?" asked Niav.

"Every one. The head of a dog or a bird is as precious to that creature as yours is to you. Obviously, however, a wise head is a special treasure."

Eoin said, "A wise human head, you mean."

"Not necessarily," I told him. Thinking of the red deer. And of the silver wolf, who was tangled in my thoughts like a burr in a woman's hair. His physical intelligence was greater than all the acquired wisdom in my head.

What might we not learn from animals, I wondered, if we did not war against them?

I believed my horizons had shrunk when I ceased to be chief druid of a powerful Gaulish tribe. But they had only been altered, forcing me to look more closely at what was right in front of me. Perhaps that was a necessary part of my Pattern. If so, where would it lead me next?

More questions; always questions.

I forced myself back to the task at hand. From discussing thought it was but a short journey to the topic of magic. "Magic begins in the mind," I told my listeners. "The first step is to imagine. What you can imagine can be made real."

The son of one of Fíachu's many cousins gave a delighted gasp. "Everything?" As clearly as if I could see into his head, I knew its thoughts. They were concentrated on a plump girl with plump breasts and a plump mouth.

"Magic is rarely necessary," I said. "Thought and patience can accomplish a lot on their own. Especially patience; it's a quality women appreciate."

His face flamed with embarrassment. His comrades laughed.

"Is that magic?" asked Cairbre. "Knowing what he was thinking about?"

"No, it's remembering. I was remembering my own youth. Never forget yours. Memory is a key that will unlock many doors. No matter how different someone seems, that person has a lot in common with you. Finding the common ground will give you better understanding."

My younger students did not yet comprehend, but I saw a dawning wisdom on the face of the older ones.

We spent several days discussing the simpler permutations of magic. "Every creation of the Source contains its own magic," I explained. I would have liked to tell them about the wolf but they were not ready.

I am not sure that I was ready for the wolf.

Instead, as a first exemplar I chose the trees. I explained their ranking, beginning with the oak, then moved on to discuss the particular magic properties of each. "Through close association with the oak one can slowly acquire some of its wisdom, which is the result of great strength as well as a long life. The oak is an observer. Its roots go deep into the earth, its head rises high into the sky. It provides nourishment and shelter for multitudes, and something of the multitudinous wisdoms of bird and insect and animal are absorbed into the great tree. Because it stays in one place it cannot act upon what it knows, but only store the knowledge. Be with the oaks. Sit beneath them, lean your head against them . . . and be patient," I added for the benefit of the boy who wanted a certain plump girl.

I explained that objects made of yew wood should be given to the dying to encourage their rebirth. "The yew appears to die in its center, but the outermost branches bow down and take root, and the yew's life begins all over again."

"But is that magic?" I was asked.

I smiled. "All of life is magic. If you learn nothing else, learn this from me.

"The rowan is not one of the noble trees but it can work great magic. Rowan has the ability to protect. Tomorrow I want you to bring me rowan berries and rowan bark—taken gently, without endangering the tree—and we will fashion some simple protections."

How excited they were! Looking back, I could recall my own excitement when I first began to study magic.

During the days that followed my students studied meditation with the ash tree and erected defenses with the holly. With each new lesson our numbers grew. Children told their parents, parents told their friends; soon a small crowd was waiting for me each morning in the forest.

Something else was waiting for me, too. I could sense the chief druid's growing enmity like a stain on the air, though he did not pay me another visit. Our confrontation had left him bruised.

If Duach Dalta complained about me to Fíachu when he returned from war, I felt confident the chieftain would take my side. I had proven myself in the matter of growing grain and increased his support among the other tribes. There was now every expectation that Fíachu would be elected king of the Laigin when the time came. What had Duach Dalta done to compare?

To be certain I was safeguarded against any malice on the part of the chief druid, I gathered rowan and holly and worked a little private magic on my own. After that I stopped worrying about Duach Dalta. His abilities were no match for mine.

Arrogance was another quality I seemed to be acquiring from the Gaels.

The wheel of the seasons turned.

The Goban Saor set off on a mysterious journey and returned with a wife: his fair-haired partner from the Lughnasa festival. She was young and nimble and good-natured, with broad hips that promised easy childbearing.

"The Goban Saor will soon enrich us in more ways than one," Keryth said with a mischievous twinkle in her eye.

"That," I told her, "is not a prediction but an inevitability."

The seer threw back her head and laughed.

The number of my students was increasing. So was the complexity of their lessons, determined by their interest. When I outlined the various aspects of Gaulish druidry they wanted to know more about divination and judgment, so I asked my fellow druids to address them.

Keryth described some of the techniques she employed, such as chewing the raw flesh of a wild boar before a divination. "The boar is fearless," she explained, "and one must be fearless when asking the Source for a glimpse of the future. In my sleep afterward, the knowledge I sought was revealed."

Of course she did not tell them everything she did. At the heart of every branch of druidry there is a secret known only to the initiated.

My Briga did not tell even her closest friends every item she put in the cooking pot.

Sulis talked at length about the abilities of healers and the way to diagnose illness. "One of the surest methods is to taste the urine of the ill person," she explained.

Several of the girls grimaced. One nodded.

At first Dian Cet was reluctant to discuss the duties of a judge. "In Hibernia all judgments are made by the chieftains," he said. "What would Fíachu do if I usurped his privilege?"

"You'll be doing no such thing. You'll simply be telling them how it was done in Gaul. We were fortunate to be there and see the Order of the Wise at its peak. Knowledge should never be lost."

"No," Dian Cet agreed. "Knowledge should never be lost."

So he did as I asked and told my students how he came to be a judge. He described the arduous tests he had been given by the Order of the Wise, to be certain he was capable of being impartial in the most difficult circumstances. "Unlike chieftain or king," said Dian Cet, "a druid must make decisions based upon a higher imperative than self-interest."

A boy from the fort spoke up; a lad called Morand, who was inclined to be disputatious. "That may be your way but it's wrong. Our chieftain makes all our important decisions."

"Suppose there was a quarrel between Fíachu and another member of the Slea Leathan. Whose side would your chieftain take in rendering judgment?"

The young fellow stared at me in consternation. I responded with a bland smile. "Every tribe has its own customs, Morand. One leaf is not superior to another, merely different. The more different leaves we examine, the more we learn about the nature of all leaves."

Trying to beat an idea into someone's mind only breaks the skull. Far better to allow the intended recipient to discover it for himself. I displayed druid wisdom as a merchant displays his wares, stood back, and watched my students stumble across treasures.

In time Morand became an avid student of the laws governing tribal behavior.

Another lad could not resist laying hands on wounded creatures and helping them to heal. One of the girls had demonstrably prophetic dreams. And there was my own son Dara, with the tongue of a bard.

Those of my clan who possessed gifts of the arm were proving themselves as well. Young Glas made a number of bracelets out of bone and carved flowing Gaelic designs into them. After staining them with ocher to resemble old ivory, he gave Damona her choice of the collection in return for a wide band of finely woven wool. Glas took the rest of the bracelets to the fort and bartered them for two unworked lumps of silver. Gold, being found in so many rivers and streams, was easier to acquire. Glas fashioned the silver into two interlocking knots of Gaelic design and set them with gold bosses. When the girdle was complete he presented it to his mother.

Lakutu promptly brought it to me. "Fasten this around me, please."

I did.

# *chapter* XVI

When we first came to Hibernia I had thought myself a failure. A man can bear many things, but a sense of failure is not one of them. Discovering that I loved teaching raised my spirits. The Pattern had brought me where I never thought to be, but that is the magic of the Pattern. I was content.

Contentment is more to be desired than happiness. It can last longer.

All people want security and respect. Unfortunately there are men who believe they acquire these things by taking them away from others. Something is very wrong with a head that thinks such thoughts.

I was not taking anything away from Duach Dalta. By introducing an expanded concept of druidry I was enriching his tribe. He would have his moment of personal glory when the time came to inaugurate Fíachu as king of the Laigin. Contentment is more desirable than glory, in my opinion. But then, I am not a warrior.

On a night of stars, Onuava gave birth to a son.

The child's father returned to the Plain of Broad Spears with all the glory any warrior could want. Fíachu had won a number of battles and taken many cattle from the Ulaid, as well as valuable plunder and several healthy young women. The plunder included a Ulidian chariot. When I saw it I could not help thinking of Cormiac Ru, who as a small boy had aspired to ride in a chariot.

Once Gaulish chieftains went to battle in chariots, but that practice had largely died out by the time of the Roman invasion. Vercingetorix had ridden a splendid black stallion with a great fall of mane that extended almost to its knees, and a tail that touched the earth. Rix loved that horse more than he loved any of his women. Caesar—may his teeth rot and fill his mouth with pus—had murdered the black horse as he murdered Vercingetorix.

Romans have no respect for nobility, human or animal. But the Source brings all things into balance. Sooner or later, the Romans will be crushed beneath the heel of those they call barbarians.

A Gaulish chariot, or battle cart, was made of timber with four large wooden wheels. It had to be large enough to carry the warlord and his weaponry, his personal shield-bearer, and a driver to manage the horses. A slow, clumsy vehicle, the chariot was merely a means of transport, allowing a chieftain to save his strength for his enemies. Once he reached the battlefield he fought on foot.

The chariot Fíachu had captured from a chief of the Ulaid was neither slow nor clumsy. The body was skillfully woven of wickerwork and mounted over a single axle between two wheels. The flexible wicker absorbed most of the jolting that had made Gaulish carts so uncomfortable. There was only room for one warrior and—if the man were thin enough—a charioteer. Extremely light in weight, the chariot traveled as fast as its team of horses could gallop.

With typical Gaelic fondness for decoration, the Ulidians had covered the outer surface of the chariot with gorgeous plumes and painted the hubs of the wheels in brilliant colors. The wheels were inset with bands of iron and copper. Iron for strength, copper for gleam.

Fíachu gleamed, too. Standing in the chariot he looked taller than ever, and broader, filling the cart until there was no room for a charioteer. He held the reins himself, driving a pair of horses who matched each other stride for stride, galloping with astonishing speed. The feathered chariot skimmed over the earth like a swallow. Behind it ran the warriors of the Slea Leathan, drunk with victory.

My head was pleased to observe that Fíachu, who had never been in a chariot before, was open to new ideas. I remarked on this but Briga just looked at me. When my senior wife looks at me in a certain way without saying anything, I feel uneasy.

Following Fíachu's return an immense feast was held at his stronghold. Every member of the Slea Leathan who could run, walk, or crawl made an effort to attend. The ostensible reason was to celebrate the chieftain's newborn son, but the real reason was to be present when he divided up the loot from the north.

It was to be expected that Fíachu's favorites would be given the best cattle and their choice of the women. A woman taken in battle became a bondwoman. Thus the daughter of a chieftain might find herself a servant in her captor's household.

The Source brings all things into balance.

No matter what their original rank in society, however, those in bondage were treated with dignity. They might be servants but they were not slaves; not like the slaves of the Romans. Their captor numbered them among his possessions but never abused or humiliated them. Such actions would bring dishonor upon himself.

Even in defeat, bondmen and -women were counted among the Gael, and the Gael were a free people. *A free people.* You could see it in their faces, in the way they walked and talked and stood.

I had not known a genuinely free person in a long time. The last, I suppose, was Vercingetorix. Now my entire clan was free. We had joined the Gael.

Dressed in their best, my clan made its way to Fíachu's celebratory feast. My three wives walked with me. Briga at my side; Lakutu and Onuava, with her tiny son in her arms, a step behind. As we passed through the gate of the fort, Onuava strove forward to walk on my other side. Had she not been carrying Fíachu's child I would have sent her back where she belonged. The ranking of wives must be strictly observed or marriage breaks down in a welter of resentment.

"Perhaps Fíachu will give us a few more cattle," I said to Briga.

"I suppose a lot depends on how well Dara performs."

"What has Dara to do with it?"

"Oh, Ainvar, don't you ever pay attention? Our son's going to recite at the feast. He mentioned it just this morning, weren't you listening?"

My well-trained ears hear everything. But they only report on the things that claim my interest. These are not necessarily the same ones that Briga notices.

We caught sight of Dara in a crowd of young men near Fíachu's lodge. Our son was wearing a new tunic that I had assumed Briga was making for me. Before I could ask her about it, she turned aside to speak to some of the women. Onuava and Lakutu joined her and I found myself alone.

The head is always alone.

I worked my way through the crowd to Dara's side. "Congratulations!" I said. "It's rare for an apprentice bard to help entertain the chief of the tribe. Seanchán must be very pleased with you."

"Seanchán didn't invite me. Fíachu did."

"Are you sure?"

"Absolutely. Yesterday I was standing right where you are now, admiring the new chariot, when Fíachu walked by and asked if I could compose a praise-poem about his victory and recite it tonight."

"But you've had no time to compose a poem!"

Dara smiled. "Ah, but I have. I've been working on it since the day Fíachu and his army set out for Ulidia."

There could be no doubt that Dara was druid. His head worked on many levels.

"What about the harp? I know the Goban Saor finished making one for you, but have you had time to familiarize yourself with it?"

He shook his head. "The harp is wonderful but I can't do everything I want to with it, not yet. And I must not hurry. Tonight I'll rely upon the composition alone."

I left him with his friends and went looking for his mother, so she and I could bask in the glow of our son's success. For a parent there is no happier fire. Briga's reaction was not what I expected. She gave me one of her looks; the one meaning "I know more than you do."

My excitement seeped away. "What's wrong?"

"Dara and Seanchán, you and Duach Dalta. I'm not a seer, Ainvar, but even I can see trouble brewing. We're newcomers here and newcomers are always suspect, no matter how warmly they are welcomed. You and Dara are slipping into the shoes of men long-established and they're sure to resent it. Duach Dalta's already given you a warning. Will Dara be next?"

"You can't expect us to go on tiptoe for the rest of our lives for fear of offending. We're part of this tribe now, Briga, and we have a right to seek our own level. You've made a place for yourself; would you deny that right to your husband and son?"

"Just be careful, Ainvar. That's all I'm asking."

I gave her the reassuring smile women like to receive from their men. But her apprehension worried me. At the feast my eyes and ears must be vigilant.

At first it seemed we had nothing to worry about. Seanchán and Duach Dalta were both present; they were among the select guests who would join the chieftain in his lodge while the rest of us celebrated outside. Duach Dalta saw me before he entered and gave a nod by way of greeting. I nodded back as if we were the best of friends.

Then we followed our noses to the feast.

Two great firepits had been dug in the center of the fort and lined with stones. Whole bullocks were roasting on iron spits. As melting fat dripped from the meat, the flames snapped and crackled. My stomach gurgled approval. One of Fíachu's women circulated through the crowd, handing out cups. She was followed by other women, carrying pitchers of mead.

By now I could drink as much honey wine as any Gael. Since I had not been raised on the stuff this feat did not come naturally to me. After several unfortunate experiences and a miserable day after, I had been forced to resort to a little magic.

Magic begins in the head.

I had told my head that the liquid in my cup was the purest, sweetest spring water. With every swallow I repeated this message. When the cup was empty I spent time reflecting upon how delicious the water had been, and recalling my exact feelings on other occasions when I had quenched my thirst with water.

Mead went into my mouth. But it was water that entered my belly.

Therefore my head was clear when Dara was summoned to the chieftain's lodge to recite. He held out his hand to me. "Come with me, Father."

"I wasn't invited."

"I invite you," said my son.

The eyes of the crowd followed me until I entered Fíachu's lodge. Inside I was met by the eyes of his guests, including those of Seanchán and Duach Dalta.

Fíachu greeted me as warmly as if he had invited me himself, and gestured me to one of the benches. This necessitated some crowding over on the part of those already seated. I offered a placating smile. After a moment, the man nearest me smiled back.

I whispered, "My son's reciting a composition of his own tonight. It's the first time he's been asked to entertain publicly." Then I settled myself to bask in Dara's success—if success it was to be.

I need not have worried.

The highest level of bardic poetry strives to express that which is beyond expression, striking responsive chords in the unplumbed depths of the spirit. True bardic recitation does not follow the everyday rhythms of sowing and reaping and breathing. Alternately fluid and fiery, it adapts to the dreams of the listeners.

No sooner had Dara begun to speak than his gift became apparent. He recounted the old tales of the Milesians in a grand saga that was fresh and new. On the surface the tale glittered like a sunlit river; in its depths lurked dark mysteries. The darkness yielded to the magic of the bard as Dara gathered up his listeners and swept them irresistibly along from one crest of excitement to the next.

Dara was better than Seanchán. He was better than any bard I ever heard. I wished Briga could be with me to share this moment, but the only women allowed inside the chieftain's lodge were his wives.

Perhaps in time that custom could be changed.

When my son stopped speaking Fíachu leaped to his feet. "Did you not hear the roar of the ocean and the rhythm of the oarsmen? Did you not see this land rising out of the mist? Did you not feel the clash of battle and the joy of victory? This young man has brought our ancestors back to life before our very eyes!"

Holding his cup in one hand, the chieftain wrapped his other arm around Dara's shoulders. "Drink, all of you," he cried, "to the new bard of the Slea Leathan! Abu Dara!" Dara Forever!

As we drained our cups I sneaked a glance at Seanchán. He was staring fixedly at my son. When a person tries too hard to keep his expression impassive, strong emotion forced to the surface by inward pressure can seep through the cracks and crevices.

Seanchán was rancid with bitterness.

Yet the old tree must fall in order for sunlight to reach the young tree.

Fíachu had not finished speaking. Turning toward me, he said, "As for the man called Ainvar, he brought his clan to us with little more than the clothes they wore. One might think it was a mistake to take in such impoverished people. But no. Looking back, I can see a change in our fortunes from that very moment. Ainvar's people have enriched our lives with their skills and craftsmanship. They have taught us how to plant and harvest enough grain to protect ourselves from hunger no matter what the weather brings. This in turn has greatly raised my esteem among the tribes of the Laigin."

His listeners exchanged meaningful glances. They supported his ambition to become king because it would greatly benefit the clan.

"Last but by no means least, Ainvar has been very generous to me personally," Fíachu said with a grin. We all knew exactly what he meant. "In addition, I have been informed by a woman who is, ah, very close to him, that he is a skilled practitioner of magic. If the son is an exceptional bard, then the father is a great druid. We need more like him."

This time they raised their cups to me. "Abu Ainvar!" they cried. Except for Duach Dalta, who now wore the same expression as Seanchán.

Honor bestowed on one is often perceived to be stolen from another.

For the rest of the night I kept my head down. When someone spoke to me I made a point of being modest about my abilities. The more diffident I became, the more people swarmed around me, eager to absorb whatever special qualities I might possess.

Magic is not contagious.

As soon as I could slip out of the lodge without attracting too much attention, I went in search of Briga. I told her of Dara's success but said nothing of my misgivings about the evening. Perhaps I thought I was sparing her any worry. Perhaps I was just saving myself the pain of admitting to her that she was right.

Later—much later, when even the stars had closed their eyes in sleep—I found an opportunity to speak with Dara out of anyone else's hearing. "Your composition in praise of the Milesians was splendid, but it hardly mentioned the Túatha Dé Danann except as 'the enemy.' "

"That's what they were, Father."

"They were much more. I want you to commemorate the Dananns. I thought you understood that."

"I do. But if I celebrated the people his ancestors slaughtered, would Fíachu thank me? I think not. Tonight I followed the wise path just as you would have done, and limited my accolades to the Milesians."

The wise path. Had I been so wise after all? Dara was right; Fíachu would not want to hear the Dananns praised.

For several nights and days the Slea Leathan feasted on victory, talking of little else. The chieftain's fort was aswirl with people, food, drink, shouting, laughing, boasting. The jubilant atmosphere was irresistible. Yet life has a way of creeping in like grass breaking through paving stones. Eventually we had to address ourselves to the tasks of every day.

Tragically, some of the Slea Leathan could not. A man who goes to battle puts on a warrior face which he must set aside when he returns to his women and children. But if the fighting is too savage and goes on for too long, a few cross a line they cannot cross back. They come home with the blood still boiling in their veins. The scars on their bodies will heal; the scars inside their heads will last a lifetime. Bal Derg, Fíachu's nephew, had been an affable young man before the war in Ulidia. He came home surly and belligerent.

My head wondered: What effect would battle have on Labraid, if he was still alive?

# *chapter* XVII

THE PHYSICAL ENERGY OF MY YOUNG STUDENTS EXCEEDED MY own. At close of day they often left me and went off to play games or run races. I watched them go rather wistfully, but the comfort of a fire on the hearth and a hot meal in the belly were more appealing.

One evening as I returned from the forest I noticed a stillness in the air; an abnormal hush that alerted my senses. Before I reached our lodges Briga came running to meet me. Her face was the color of milk with the cream skimmed away. "Oh, Ainvar! Something terrible's happened!"

"What?"

"It's Onuava."

"Is she hurt?"

"She's been killed. She and the baby both."

Not just dead. Killed. "Onuava?" Sudden shock can numb the head. While I could ask questions, I could not comprehend answers. "What happened?"

"The bodies were discovered just a little while ago. It looks as if they were beaten to death."

"Beaten to death," I repeated. Trying without success to take it in.

"Onuava and Lakutu were supposed to dye wool together today. When she didn't appear Lakutu began work alone, assuming—and you can't blame her—that Onuava was simply ignoring an unpleasant task. Dyes smell bad and she's always complained about them. But when the day grew old and there was no sign of her, Lakutu was worried. So she went to Onuava's lodge and found her . . . found her and the baby. . . ."

"Found them how?"

"Lying on the ground in a pool of blood, with their skulls smashed." Briga stared up at me with stricken eyes.

The sacred head.

Rage ripped through me. If at that moment Onuava's killer had stood before me, I would have torn him to pieces with my bare hands.

I fought to regain control. "Are you certain they're dead? Could you not . . ."

"There was nothing I could do," Briga said in a defeated voice. "The bodies were already growing stiff."

"And no one heard anything? I don't understand how that could happen."

"I heard the baby crying early this morning, but he's a fretful little lad and cries . . . cried . . . a lot anyway. When he stopped I paid no more attention."

The disaster was beginning to seem real to me. "Have you seen them?"

Briga nodded. "I sent Grannus to the village to tell Fíachu about the killings. Are Cairbre and Senta with you?"

Until that moment I had not thought of Onuava's other sons. My sons as well. Motherless now. Like a stone dropped into a pool, a single death creates concentric circles of loss.

"I want to see Onuava, Briga."

She shuddered. "No you don't. It's horrible."

"I've seen more awful things." We had all seen more awful things.

The sight of Onuava's corpse was bad enough, though. That big, tawny woman, always so proud of her appearance, was nearly unrecognizable in death. Stooping down, I lifted the blood-matted hair away from her face. One savage blow to the side of her skull had been enough to kill her; surely it had not been necessary to beat her face to a pulp as well.

Among Celtic tribes it is a breach of honor to brutalize a slain enemy.

As for the baby . . . I could not imagine who would do such a thing. After one swift look I had to turn away.

I went back to Onuava with the regret that death engenders flooding into my throat like vomit. I should have paid more attention to her. Should have praised her more often. Should have . . . I bent down to plant a last caress on her ruined face.

As my fingers touched her skin they detected the lingering essence of her killer. The hairs rose on the back of my neck.

Fíachu arrived at the run, bringing a dozen well-armed warriors with him. "Who did this awful thing?" he demanded when he emerged from Onuava's lodge.

"We don't know," said Briga, "but we've asked Keryth to read the signs."

"She wasn't a witness to the killings, was she?"

"No, but she's a seer. Telling the unknown is her gift."

Fíachu glanced at me. I nodded. "Keryth was the best in Gaul," I assured him.

"Very well, then. Let her try."

At Keryth's request, everyone except me moved away from the lodge. "Stand at the doorway, Ainvar," she directed. "Make sure I'm not disturbed."

While the two bodies lay on the ground like the discarded husks they were, Keryth built a fire on the hearth. From leather pouches tied to her girdle she took an assortment of dried herbs and powders. One at a time, she sprinkled them on the flame. Some were as pungent as ripe fruit. Others had the bittersweet fragrance of half-forgotten memories. One, as foul as burning hair, made me cough.

I watched Keryth's fingers weave the cloud of smoke into grotesquely writhing shapes. It appeared as if she were dancing with the fire. Three times she paused and turned to look at the dead woman. The third time, she spoke to the corpse in words too low for my ears to report.

Keryth used three buckets of water to kill the fire and then sank down on her haunches beside the drowned ashes. She remained there for a long time, immobile, staring into the shadows of here and now with eyes that saw otherwhen.

I have always been fascinated by the way Keryth practices divination. She does it in a variety of ways. Once I saw her spin around and around with arms outstretched until she fell down from dizziness. When her head cleared and she was able to get to her feet without staggering, she related a wondrous vision from the Otherworld. Someone else might try the same technique and get no more than an upset stomach.

The method by which a druid, any druid, achieves a result is intuited according to the circumstance. Exceptional intuition is a large part of the druidic gift.

The first druid had no teacher. Druidry cannot be taught, only encouraged. The gift itself is innate.

Long before the time of our fathers' fathers, someone whose name we do not even know became aware of a unique quality in himself—or herself—that set him apart from his fellows. Fortunately he possessed enough curiosity to follow the newly discovered internal path and see where it led. Thus the first druid stumbled upon the unseen world that envelops our own.

Imagine his astonishment! What my colleagues and I consider natural must have struck him like a bolt of fire from the sky. Did he tell anyone? We can never know. But as the wheel of the seasons turned, a few others discovered similar gifts. The first of anything is never the last.

When they began using their special abilities to benefit their people, the Order of the Wise was born.

Realistically, all I can teach my students is how to search within themselves. This is akin to standing in the forest listening to the multitude of birdsong and trying to pick out a single voice. With intense concentration, a born druid can recognize that voice.

There is no druid but a born druid.

For every one who is genuine, there are many who want to be. They may even pretend to have the gift. When asked to prove themselves they must rely on trickery and the gullibility of others.

Keryth had no need for trickery. She was genuine. Her gift lay in being able to trace the invisible pathways that join all the elements of creation. Sometimes, though not always, she could find the point where individual Patterns connected.

Alone in the lodge with the dead woman and child, Keryth sought their murderer. I did not envy her the task.

After a timeless time she called my name. "Ainvar? Are you still out there?"

"Of course I am."

"Then you'd better come in and help me up. My old knees are locked."

When we emerged from the lodge Fíachu and his men, as well as my own clan, crowded around us. By torchlight it was obvious that Keryth was exhausted. Her hair hung in wet strings and her skin was deathly pale. Fíachu was not concerned about her condition; only one thing mattered at that moment. "Do you know who did this thing?" he demanded of her. "Was it a member of the Deisi or one of the—"

"The killer belongs to your tribe, Fíachu."

"The Slea Leathan? That's not possible."

"I'm afraid it is. More than that, he's a member of your own clan."

"In living memory no descendant of Éremon has slain a woman, never mind a child! Tell her, Ainvar; tell this woman she's wrong."

"I cannot," I said sadly. "I'm no seer, but when I touched the dead woman I found a lingering shadow of her killer. The members of a family share a certain . . . smell, for want of a better word, though it is not detected by the nose. Onuava's killer smelled of your clan."

Fíachu spread his feet wide apart, bracing himself. It was obvious why he was chief of his tribe. The big man had the spirit of an oak tree. He was badly shocked, but already his head was beginning to work again.

I read his thoughts in his eyes and confirmed them. "If one of your own clan has committed this crime," I said, "you'll have to decide where your loyalties lie."

Fíachu turned toward Keryth. "Are you absolutely certain of what you claim?"

"I saw the event as clearly as I see you now. Before he struck Onuava the first time her attacker threw off his cloak. He was wearing the speckled tunic of your clan. No one else wears that design. I can tell you his every move, Fíachu. I can even describe the efforts Onuava made to defend her child, if you wish to hear."

"Just give me the killer's name. That's all I want from you."

For the first time I sensed a hesitancy in my old friend. "In my vision his back was turned toward me most of the time, and the fire was out, so the light in the lodge was dim."

"But you did see him?"

"Yes."

Fíachu deliberately moved closer until he towered over her. "Then, who was he?"

If she had been a younger woman Keryth might have been able to resist the intimidation of Fíachu's physicality. The weight of many seasons pinned her down while he skewered her with his eyes. She said in a faint voice, "He was very strong and agile. A young warrior, I think."

"That's not good enough. I have to have his name."

Keryth shrank into herself. She glanced to one side and then to the other, but we could not intervene. Fíachu was the chieftain. "Tell me, woman!" he thundered.

"I'm afraid it was Bal Derg," Keryth said in a whisper.

Fíachu stiffened. "Bal Derg?"

"Your nephew."

"Bal Derg," the chieftain repeated through lips gone numb.

She said with obvious reluctance, "He killed Onuava and her infant in a mad rage and ran away. He's hiding somewhere."

On the battlefield I have seen strong men absorb terrible blows. To give Fíachu credit he did not flinch now. He blinked several times in swift succession, but that was all. "His mother was my oldest sister. She raised me on her knee after our mother died. Until Onuava's child was born Bal Derg was the nearest thing I had to a son. How can I . . ." Fíachu stared at me helplessly.

I pitied him. "You should not have to. Ask someone else to judge the man."

"Will you do it, Ainvar?"

"Not I, it's not my gift. But our Dian Cet was a brehon judge before I was born. He's been trained to be impartial."

"Training is all well and good, but was Onuava his blood kin?"

"She was not, Fíachu. She was an Arvernian."

"I see." The chieftain swallowed. Hard. Clenched and unclenched his big fists. Men of action have to do something while they are thinking. "The situation could hardly be worse than it is now," he said. "Bring Dian Cet to my lodge tomorrow at sundown. In the meantime, Ainvar . . ."

"Yes?"

"Will your women care for Onuava?"

"They will, of course. And the—"

"Not the infant," Fíachu interrupted. "I'll take my son with me now, and return him to his mother at her funeral. I leave it to you to arrange the ritual."

In my life I have seen many sad sights, but one of the saddest was that big strong man walking away from our lodges with a tiny bundle in his arms. He stopped once to uncover the little battered face, and pressed his lips to it. Then he went on.

Keryth said, "That was the only son he'll ever have."

"Are you certain?"

"Yes. Very certain."

"And about the other? Bal Derg?"

"Are you challenging my gift, Ainvar?"

The people nearest us pricked up their ears, as people always do when they sense a quarrel brewing. "No," I said firmly. "Of course not."

My clan slowly dispersed. I doubt if anyone felt like eating a meal that night.

Dara came to my lodge long enough to collect a leather hide, then went off somewhere alone. He reappeared late the following morning to announce that he had composed a lament for Onuava and her child. "Do you think Fíachu would like to hear it?"

"I'm sure he will. Come with us this evening."

The three of us—Dara, Dian Cet, and I—made our way to the stronghold of the chieftain together. In the crook of his arm Dara cradled his new harp.

We saw Bal Derg as soon as we entered the fort. He was bound hand and foot and tied to a strong post. Four armed warriors stood guard while the captive alternately roared with anger and sobbed with anguish. There was blood on his clothing. Fíachu's nephew had not surrendered easily.

His clan was gathered around him. I kept my eyes straight ahead as I walked past, but ordered my ears to listen.

"I don't understand how this could happen," a man remarked.

"Neither do I," said one of Bal Derg's sisters. "He was such a quiet lad when he was little. I can't believe he would do such a thing."

Her husband interjected, "If he did do it, Onuava provoked him to it. You know how she was, she rolled her eyes at every man who looked her way. She probably teased him until he could stand it no longer and he bashed her."

"What about the baby?" a woman asked. "What harm could an infant at the breast have done him?"

An old man pointed out, "When that child was born Bal Derg ceased to be Fíachu's favorite."

"If he killed a child we should cut off his head!"

"But no one saw him commit the crime. We have to let him go."

"Do you want a murderer running around loose?"

"I don't want the blood of a kinsman on my hands."

"We'll all have blood on our hands if we let him get away with this."

Discussions were becoming arguments. Violent acts engender violent reactions.

We found the chieftain alone in his lodge. He had sent his wives away; I suppose they took the infant's body with them. Fíachu looked up when we entered. "Do you hear what's going on out there? Any decision I make will turn half the clan against me."

"That's why I'm here," Dian Cet reminded him. "I can take that burden from you so you remain blameless. But first you must ask your people if they are willing to abide by my judgment."

Fíachu bridled. "I'm a chieftain, I don't ask permission."

"Very well, then. May I speak with the accused man?"

"Go ahead, but take a couple of warriors with you."

"Bal Derg is well guarded and securely tied. He can't hurt me, Fíachu."

"Perhaps not, but feelings are running high. Anything could happen."

My head agreed with Fíachu. These were Celts and Celts were volatile. I made a suggestion. "My son Dara has composed a lament for Onuava. Perhaps if he recites now, while Dian Cet has a word with Bal Derg, the poem will distract people as well as having a calming influence."

Fíachu looked dubious. "It had better be good."

Unbidden, an image of the harp came into my mind. The harp made of wood grown from Eriu's earth. "It will be," I predicted.

We left the lodge and approached the muttering crowd. The chieftain raised his arms for silence. "Dara the son of Ainvar knew the dead woman well, and has asked to sing her lament."

These were Celts and Celts love to be entertained. All faces turned toward my son.

Dara waited for total silence. He spun out their patience like a spider's thread, judging the exact time when one moment more would cause it to break.

Then he lifted the harp.

From seven brass strings like threads of gold Dara summoned a feminine murmur. It might have been a woman's voice, humming to herself as Dara chanted:

*"Twice she came among strangers, Onuava the Arvernian*
*Big-limbed and stout-hearted, the fair Onuava*
*Came while in mourning for one slain by the Romans*
*Came with her head up and her grief hidden in her bosom*
*To join the Carnutes for a new beginning."*

The voice of the harp turned into the voice of the wind, filling us with a sense of far horizons.

*"To the land of the oak and the yew, the noble Onuava*
*With a king's young son, and the sons of a druid,*
*Came without fear and without looking backward*
*Came with her passion for life undiminished*
*To begin yet again with the tribe of Broad Spears."*

The sound of the harp was mellow and smooth. Creamy, like Onuava's skin. How long had it been since I last told her she was beautiful? I could not remember.

*"Three lives had the woman called Onuava*
*She faced each in turn with unflinching courage*
*She who loved life lived to the fullest*
*She who loved children, killed no mother's son*
*Weep for Onuava who never wept for herself."*

Under Dara's hand the harp cried like a child, a sound so painful I could hardly bear it.

Only then did I realize the full extent of my son's gift.

*"Lament her sadly, lament her sweetly*
*Lament her kindly, all who knew her*
*Commemorate Onuava not with anger, but justice*
*For she was no stranger*
*She was one of your own."*

Dara summoned one last sound from the harp: a soft falling away, like earth dropping onto a grave.

Throughout the fort there was absolute silence. Even Bal Derg was quiet.

Dara lowered his harp and stood with bowed head.

Fíachu had to clear his throat twice before he was able to speak. "This young bard sang of justice. A wise judge is a just judge, but in this matter I am pulled into too many directions to identify the just path. Therefore I have appointed Dian Cet to make the determination for me." As the first startled exclamations arose, Fíachu said firmly, "You will abide by his decision. On my honor, so will I."

He beckoned Dian Cet to step forward.

# *chapter* XVIII

IT HAD BEEN A LONG TIME SINCE THE OLD MAN FUNCTIONED IN A judicial capacity, yet he still radiated authority. His hair was whiter than a cloud; his spine was straighter than a birch tree. When he spoke the words came slow and clear, so that he seemed to be responding to an inner voice, drawing on a wellspring of inspiration.

"The killing of Onuava and her son is an unthinkable crime," said Dian Cet. "Our race does not war on women and children.

"We know only three things for certain. Bal Derg was caught hiding like a guilty man but denies any guilt. Killing him will not bring his victims back. Letting him go unpunished will outrage the entire tribe.

"Therefore this is my judgment. I decree no violence for Bal Derg. His official punishment will be to have a large notch cut from his ears. Then he will be released."

"What does that accomplish?" someone asked.

"From this day forward, notched ears will mark a person as an outlaw. That means the individual is *outside the law.*" Dian Cet stressed the phrase deliberately. "Being outside the law means a person cannot call upon the law to protect him from the actions of others. Anyone who wishes to harm him may do so with impunity. An outlaw can be killed for the clothes on his back or the cup in his hand and no action will be taken."

An excited buzz arose among the people, like the sound of a hive of disturbed bees.

Dian Cet went on, "Onuava was the daughter of a prince and the widow of a king. A man desiring to marry a woman of her rank would have had to pay her nearest male kin at least forty cows. If her infant had lived to weaning age his head price would have been higher, because he was the son of a chieftain. Under the circumstances, however, compensation is due only for his mother.

"Therefore I decree that Bal Derg or his nearest kin—his sisters, in this case—must pay the dead woman's husband forty cows."

Bal Derg's sisters uttered shocked exclamations.

Dian Cet continued, "This payment will be considered redress in full. Upon its receipt, the matter will be closed. No grudge may be carried forward. The restoration of amity must be the aim of any judgment. That is vital to the maintenance of law.

"Should Bal Derg or his sisters fail to pay compensation, I decree that the dead woman's husband is entitled to go and sit in front of their lodge. They must provide a bench for the purpose."

The baffled crowd gaped at the brehon.

"Ainvar will refuse any food or drink until the payment is made. Among the Gael, hospitality is paramount, and a failure of hospitality is as great a crime as murder. Should Ainvar starve to death while waiting for redress, the penalty will be as follows:

"The names of Bal Derg, his sisters, and their husbands will be forgotten. The assets of the tribe will no longer be shared with them. Nor will their offspring be included in the history of the tribe, which means they can inherit nothing."

In my life I had heard a number of brehons render judgments, but never had I been present when a whole new law sprang into being. Dian Cet's pronouncement was so innovative, yet so just, that I could find no fault with it.

Neither could anyone else. Except for Bal Derg, who appeared dazed, and his sisters and their husbands, who were dismayed.

Fíachu had been listening with his arms folded and his eyes half-closed like a man in pain. When Dian Cet finished speaking he stepped forward.

"As chief of the clan I accept this ruling on behalf of my kin," he intoned. He had no choice; he already had agreed on his honor. "As chief of the Slea Leathan I accept this ruling on behalf of my tribe. From this day forward it will be in the interest of every family to assure that its members commit no crime." He pointed toward the men guarding the prisoner. "Notch that man's ears and turn him loose."

Bal Derg fought with all his strength to resist, but it was no use. Two large triangles were cut from the upper portion of his ears while he squealed like a pig. Blood ran down both sides of his neck, staining his clothes afresh.

His bonds were released.

The clan moved back until he stood alone in the center of a huge circle.

I was reminded of the Crow Court.

Breathing hard, Bal Derg held out his hands in a plea to someone, anyone. A man with a bushy beard shifted weight from one foot to the other and drawled, "You hit me the other day for no reason. I've always fancied those gold arm rings of yours." He casually reached for the knife he wore in his belt.

With a cry of horror, Bal Derg broke and ran.

Bushy-beard winked at the others and sauntered after him.

I had to stand in line to congratulate Dian Cet. He had not attracted much attention before, but now everyone wanted to talk to him. "No chieftain ever made so wise a judgment," one of his new admirers claimed.

After I returned to my lodge, I repeated the remark to Briga.

Her eyebrows stitched a frown. "Fíachu will be angry if people think Dian Cet is a better judge than he is."

"They were just praising the old man. Fíachu didn't hear them."

"Did he not? A word spoken is like a bird released into the air, Ainvar. Sooner or later it may fly his way."

"We acted in good faith. Fíachu was glad to accept our help at the time."

"I'm sure he was. But if it costs him a loss in stature he may change his mind."

"Fíachu's a Gael and the Gaels prize honor."

Briga pursed her lips. "He's a *man,* Ainvar. You must avoid doing anything that would diminish him in his own eyes."

"Why didn't you say this to me before?"

"You didn't ask me before."

My senior wife is most exasperating when she is right. Yet without her I would be diminished. Male and female are equal, two halves of the whole. Without that balance humankind staggers.

In warrior societies men are dominant and women are relegated to hearth and home, their other talents ignored. This, I believe, is why such societies are doomed to disaster. I saw it demonstrated with the Gauls. I hope it proves equally true for the Romans—may their urine run red.

In the Order of the Wise, male and female are equal.

I began to plan an appropriate funeral for Onuava. Although she would be buried among the Gael, the accompanying ritual must also reflect the traditions of the Arverni and the Carnutes.

Since first we learned to ride horses, we of the Celtic race had been great travelers. My third wife had made one of the greatest leaps of all, from the kingdom of the Arverni to Eriu's land.

Eriu.

The name reverberated through me. As clearly as if she had called to me aloud, I heard her.

Eriu.

Whom I could touch through her trees, her grass, her sweet soft earth. Eriu, who was a huge part of my Pattern. Perhaps the center that held it all together.

My surviving wives insisted upon being left alone while they washed and prepared Onuava's body for burial. I suspect that Lakutu performed certain services for the dead that were unique to her people, but neither woman confirmed this. Briga did tell me that they had applied ocher to the bloodless cheeks and lips, and carefully arranged the abundant hair to hide the damaged face. They wrapped the body in a winding sheet of undyed cloth for its return to the earth.

Eriu's earth.

On the third day after Onuava's murder a solemn convening was held at the fort, involving every member of Fíachu's clan and my own. Only Bal Derg was absent. He was never seen again, but Bushy-beard was wearing his gold arm rings.

We greeted the dawn by joining hands in a huge circle to mimic the flaming orb rising above the horizon. With one voice we repeatedly chanted the names of Onuava and her son. Sparks of the Great Fire.

Afterward we made our way to a level field where the Slea Leathan often raced horses. At either end of the racecourse stood a pair of pillar stones, delineating the arc of the turns. Under my direction the Goban Saor had carved the name of Onuava on one of each pair, in ogham.

Borrowing from the traditions of Gaul, I had organized funeral games. We had taken the concept from the Greeks and found it very sensible. Engaging in strenuous physical activity beforehand helped men remain calm for the more sober aspects of the ritual.

The games began with foot races. Fíachu and I stood together, watching. "My son would have been a fine runner when he grew up," he remarked.

I nodded.

"My son would have been a great warrior, too."

I nodded again.

"But I'll have other sons."

I said nothing.

Fíachu fixed his piercing gaze on me. "Your senior wife told me I could have sons."

"To be precise, Fíachu, she said the potion she gave you to drink would enable a woman to conceive a male child. Which Onuava did."

"Then have Briga make up another potion for me. I'll take more women, as many as needs be." He must have seen the truth in my face. Anxiously, he asked, "I will have more sons, won't I?"

I had to be honest with him. "Keryth says not."

"Keryth says? Ah." He could have chosen to disbelieve, but Fíachu did not become chief of his tribe by refusing to accept the Pattern. I watched him absorb this new information as stoically as he had absorbed the circumstances of Onuava's death.

His eyes swung back to the foot racers skimming over the grass. "When I had no sons, at least I had my sister's son. Bal Derg was fleet of foot and mighty of arm. He would have made a worthy chieftain."

"There was a flaw in him," I pointed out.

"There is a flaw in everyone, Ainvar." Fíachu turned his back on me and walked away.

Wrapped in an outer covering of green, bushy branches, the bodies of mother and child were laid in the grave together. Atop the leaves I placed Onuava's ivory hairpin, an Arvernian trinket she had worn for as long as I knew her. The honor of presenting the second grave-gift should have gone to her eldest son. Instead it was Cairbre who proffered a girdle woven in the Carnutian style. Senta's gift was a bowl made of Hibernian clay. Thus the three phases of the dead woman's life were represented.

Fíachu gave his only son a massive gold ring as big as the baby's fist.

A great mound of soft soil had been piled nearby. Following my lead, all of those present, down to the smallest knee-child, took a double handful to drop into the grave. This continued until the yawning mouth in the earth was filled.

As the last clods fell, the women of the Gael unexpectedly uttered the most hair-raising cry I had ever heard in my life. Somewhere between a shriek and a wail, it was filled with despair. The nearest thing to it was the sound of a man being disemboweled on the battlefield.

"What in the name of all the stars is that?" I gasped.

"Keening," said a man standing near me. "Our women always keen the dead; it's a sign of respect."

I doubt if Onuava had ever been so respected in life.

The keening was horrific, yet there was a curious rightness about it. The men had spent their burden of emotion in games; this lamentation belonged to the women. It was purely Gaelic.

The keening continued while we raised a cairn of stones over the grave. Somewhere beyond our vision Onuava and her child were moving farther and farther away from us. In the privacy of my head, I bade them farewell.

The day was to conclude with a funeral feast. Before we ate, and at Fíachu's request, Dara repeated his lament for Onuava. Everyone applauded except for Seanchán, who kept his arms folded.

During the feast Fíachu's senior wife proclaimed in a loud voice, "When I die I want the sort of funeral Onuava had."

Bit by bit, our influence was seeping into the Gael. Shapechanging them as they were shapechanging us.

The following evening, my clan gathered to remember Onuava among ourselves. "For her sake I hope she did not see her baby die," Sulis remarked.

*Keep quiet,* I warned Keryth with my eyes. *Don't tell us all you know.*

Ignorance can be kinder than knowledge.

Briga gave a sad smile. "Those who die as small children never grow up. I still dream of little Maia as I saw her last. I actually feel her in my arms; her warmth, her weight. She comes to comfort me."

"When I was a boy," said Dian Cet, "the chief druid of the Carnutes was my father's mother. She too was called Maia."

I straightened in surprise. "What? I never heard that before."

The old brehon turned toward me. "Do you not recall my suggesting her name for your daughter?"

"I don't remember," I said honestly. Yet within me was a vibration like the plucking of a single harp string; the recognition of another element of the Pattern.

As soon as possible, I must tell my students about the Pattern.

In the following days I noticed a disturbing change in Fíachu's attitude toward me. At first there was half a heartbeat before the smile on his lips reached his eyes. Then there was not even a smile on the lips. I had never deluded myself that we were friends, but if he had turned against me my clan could suffer.

The more I thought about the matter, the more certain I became. Druid intuition.

During our last years in Gaul all I had to worry about was survival. How clear and simple that seemed to me now, when I went from one worry to the next without respite.

At night when I longed for rest my head trudged on relentlessly, asking questions, formulating possibilities, turning over rocks to see what lay beneath. Beside me Briga slept untroubled. I wondered where she went in her dreams.

As if the change in Fíachu was not problem enough, Cormiac and Labraid were much on my mind. I had not the slightest hope that they could find Maia, but if they searched for her long enough they were bound to encounter the Romans. Under torture—and Caesar's agents were skilled at torture—I was confident that Cormiac would never reveal anything about us. Labraid might.

It was the policy of Gaius Julius Caesar to pursue his enemies and eliminate them to the last man. Even after all this time, Caesar would consider the chief advisor of Vercingetorix a trophy worth hunting down, no matter how far he had to go.

Once again I was confronted with the Two-Faced One. One face expressed joy because I was convinced that Cormiac Ru survived. The other face was horrified because if he was alive, the mission he had undertaken could lead the Romans to us after all.

AFTER NINE DAYS' MOURNING FOR ONUAVA, I RESUMED TEACHING IN the forest glade. Aislinn, Fíachu's daughter, attended with the others. Apparently her father's feelings had not turned her against me.

I wondered how often she thought of Labraid.

I began the new lessons by explaining what lay at the heart of druidry. "The Source of All Being does not work at random, though to our eyes it may appear so. Always remember: There are no coincidences, just unexpected glimpses of a hidden Pattern.

"To begin to understand about the Pattern, you must learn to see with more than your eyes." Stooping, I scraped up a little soil and let it trickle through my fingers. "Observe," I said.

I stretched up to pluck a leaf from a tree and displayed it to them. "Observe," I repeated. "The Earth is the leaf is you is me. What do I mean? It is my way of telling you that an unvarying building block forms the mote of dust and the tallest mountain. Both conform to the same Pattern. The Source resonates equally through all creation.

"The Pattern affects us, too. Our mortal bodies conform because they have no choice, but our spirits, as sparks of the Great Fire of Life, have more freedom. A spirit that ignores the Pattern can suffer dire consequences. The study of druidry will help you recognize the Pattern. Only by following it as it applies to each separate one of you can you live in harmony with Thisworld."

Senta asked, "How can the Pattern be the same for everybody?"

*"As it applies to each separate one of you,"* I reiterated sternly. "Senta, you were daydreaming again. Pay attention. As I was about to say, all elements of the Pattern are linked. Stars and stones, humans and animals—"

"I can see where they meet!" Aislinn cried. Everyone turned to look at her.

"What do you mean?" I asked the girl, trying to ignore my excitement at her words.

"My father's favorite mare likes to rub her head against me. When you mentioned animals I thought about her and then . . . she was touching me again, Ainvar. I can't describe it, but the horse and I melted into each other. As if she was a line drawn on the ground and I was another line on the ground and the two lines came together. I could see them as plainly as I see you."

Her eyes pleaded with me to understand.

I did. "Aislinn, you have just seen one of the invisible threads that connect all creation."

And as simply as that, we had found our next druid.

# *chapter* XIX

My senior wife noticed the speculative looks I was slanting in her direction. "What is it, Ainvar?"

"Nothing."

"I know you too well; you're absolutely unable to think of nothing. Some can, but not you. Tell me what you're thinking about."

"You might not like it."

"All the more reason to tell me, then." She put her little fists on her hips and stood waiting. She would stand like that until I answered, no matter how long it took.

"I was just wondering. Both Dara and Gobnat have revealed unexpected gifts since we came to Hibernia. If we had been able to stay in Gaul, would you have become the wise woman you are today?"

"I always was a wise woman."

"I'm glad to hear you say so."

She was instantly suspicious. "Are you still trying to persuade me to join the Order of the Wise?"

I could reply in all honesty, "There is no Order of the Wise in Hibernia."

On the previous day I had discussed this very subject with Sulis, Keryth, and Dian Cet. We had decided to replace "the Order of the Wise" with a Gaelic term. After much discussion we chose *filídh,* meaning "poets": repositories of wisdom.

By admitting to being a wise woman—in other words, a repository of wisdom—Briga unwittingly became one of the filídh. Out of consideration for her feelings I might never tell her, but the rightness of it pleased me. As did my own cleverness.

"Why are you smiling, Ainvar?"

"I, ah . . . you were right, as usual."

"Of course I was," she happily agreed. "What about?"

"The resentments we've incurred. I have to repair the damage if I can."

"How?"

"I'll begin with Fíachu. We can't afford to lose his support."

"What makes you think we have?"

"A lot of little things, Briga, but mostly druid intuition. Like me, Fíachu tends to trace a situation backward, step by step, to its beginning. He's concluded that the loss of his nephew can be traced to my arrival here."

"That's ridiculous. It's not your fault that Bal Derg attacked Onuava."

"No, but the murders were the last link in a chain of circumstance that does lead back to me. If I had never brought my people here, Fíachu reasons that his nephew would still be alive."

"Bal Derg would have gone mad anyway, Ainvar. His head was unhealthy."

"At least Fíachu could not blame me."

"Why would he want to?"

"Because chieftains take credit for themselves and apportion blame to others. It's one of the ways they hold on to power."

"Power." Briga looked through me and past me. "The only real power comes from the Source."

Recently there had been times when I felt I was losing her. She shared her body with me, but her spirit was moving into a different realm. Had it begun when she brought me back from the Otherworld? Or even earlier, when she rescued Labraid from the sea?

She laid a gentle hand on my arm. "Stop brooding about Bal Derg, Ainvar, you'll make yourself ill again. You can't change the past."

Wives are quick to tell a man what he cannot do.

"No, but perhaps I can change the future if I give Fíachu what he desires."

"Another son? Keryth claims he will have no more sons."

"Onuava had more than one son," I said.

"Not sired by Fíachu."

I had spent most of the night preparing the proposition I was about to put to Briga. "If a man lies with a woman, is there not a connection between him and the children of her body? They've shared the same intimate passageway."

Her nose crinkled with laughter. "Now you're the one who's being ridiculous."

"I don't think so. Fíachu will accept any line of reasoning that gives him what he wants most. The king of the Laigin is an old man who's expected to die soon, and there's little doubt that Fíachu will be chosen as the new king. Remember what he said about appointing his successor as chief of the tribe? That will be doubly important to him once he's the king. If Bal Derg were still alive the honor would go to him, but—"

Briga clapped her hands in delight. "You propose to suggest Cairbre! Or Senta. Onuava would be so pleased."

"Neither of them carries the blood of a chieftain," I reminded her. "The tribes would never accept a man of lesser rank as king."

Her eyes widened. "You're talking about Labraid!"

"He fullfils the requirements."

"But he's dead."

"No," I said, hoping I spoke the truth. "I don't believe he is."

At twilight I found Keryth in the forest. Throughout the day a chill wind had been blowing from the north, and the seer was swathed in a heavy fur cloak. In unguarded moments her posture revealed her true age. Stooped shoulders and a shuffling gait were reminders that every mortal life must come to an end. The old making way for the new.

"Keryth?"

She made a conscious effort to straighten her back before turning in my direction. "Were you looking for me, Ainvar? Or did you come here to be alone?"

"I need something from you. Can you call Labraid and Cormiac Ru back to us?"

"I'm a seer, Ainvar, but I can't affect what I see, nor can I be heard. My role is strictly that of observer. Besides, I don't even know if Labraid is alive. I didn't see him."

"He has to be," I said through gritted teeth. "I need him."

She squinted at me in the dusk. "More than the Red Wolf? I thought he was the object of your concern."

"Things have changed. I still want Cormiac to come back, but it's imperative that he bring Labraid with him. Are you sure you can't contact them?"

"You of all people should know the limitations of the various branches of the Order, Ainvar." She sounded slightly exasperated. "The only way to reach Labraid or Cormiac would be through the Otherworld, and for that we require a sacrificer. We have none."

Through the Otherworld! I had been overlooking the obvious. Had the passage of time changed me so much, then? Must we inevitably lose part of ourselves to gain something else?

Druid speculations. For which I had no time.

I gave Keryth an apologetic smile. "I would like to be alone, if you don't mind. Alone with the trees."

"As you wish." Keryth gathered her cloak more snugly about her body and walked away. With every step she took her shoulders drooped more. Dear Keryth. A human life is like a summer day; we do not fully appreciate it until the chill winds of winter begin to blow.

I waited until the invisible turbulence created by another person's presence ceased. Then I waited some more. The wind died with the sun. As night closed in the cold intensified. Nearby, a stand of birch saplings still glimmered with the pale promise of youth. The oaks, invisible in the darkness, sighed with the burden of their longevity. Some of those oaks were growing here when the first ships carrying the Milesians arrived. What had they not seen during their long reign as chieftains of the forest?

As I was tucking my hands into my armpits to keep them warm, a faint stirring in the air caught my attention.

"Eriu?" I said tentatively.

The trees were very quiet. Watching.

"Eriu."

Silence. Waiting.

With the massive effort of gathering myself into myself, I called for a third time, "Eriu!"

My ears heard no answer yet it came. The atmosphere enveloping me was as articulate as a voice. Eriu was there. Always. There for me.

With that knowledge I experienced the rarest of all sensations: the blessed inner silence that eludes humans throughout their lives. In that silence I slowly raised my hands, palm upward, until they were as high as my shoulders.

Power flowed outward from my body. Power that came of being totally one with the natural world and able to bend its components to my will.

The sound rose from the ground, following my hands. A muted roar like the distant ocean.

Saplings began to sway without any wind. The night air shimmered with a strange luminosity.

"I am here," said a voice.

All that lives is connected. Eriu was alive. I could feel her as surely as I could feel Briga when she lay beside me in our bed.

"We remember you," I said in a voice thick with awe. "Our young bard tells your story again and again."

"Does he say we were beautiful?"

"He does not know what you looked like."

"We were small and slender and as pale as the moon. We did not walk, we danced. No willow was more graceful. No flower more fair. We danced and sang and laughed. Oh, how we laughed!"

Her words were the chime of distant bells.

The bells faded away.

The shimmer in the air faded away.

In a tone as flat as dried blood, Eriu said, "We were different so they killed us. We were small and they were tall so they killed us. We were gentle and they were aggressive so they killed us."

She laughed a laugh that was not human. The coldest north wind was warmer than that laugh. "Now they are afraid of us," said Eriu.

At that moment, so was I. "Do you ever harm them?"

"There is no need. They harm themselves."

"They believe you control the weather."

"Is that what you believe?"

"I believe you are able to do things beyond mortal ability."

"That much is true, Ainvar of the Carnutes."

"Ainvar of the Gaels," I corrected.

"Oh yes. I forgot."

She had not forgotten. It was a test of my honesty, my honor. I was beginning to know Eriu. What a remarkable woman she must have been in Thisworld.

How thankful I was for the immortality of the spirit.

Eriu said, "You want something of me."

"I do."

"Is there any reason why I should give it to you?"

"None at all."

The forest was quiet again. Anyone would have thought I was alone. I was not. I was less lonely than I had ever been in my life. She was in me and through me and all around me, an intense, aching sweetness.

"Tell me what you want, Ainvar of the Gaels."

"First I must ask a question. Are there boundaries in the Otherworld, or can you go where you will?"

"Movement is limited only by the strength of one's spirit."

I had no doubts as to the strength of Eriu's spirit. "The first time you spoke to me," I said, "I was in a mountain pass with two young men."

"I was aware of them."

"Are you aware of them now?"

"Do you want me to be?"

My heart began to pound uncontrollably. "Can you?"

"Of course."

"They left this island more than a year ago, in the late autumn."

"Time means nothing here." To my alarm her voice began to fade, drifting away like smoke across the hills.

"Please, Eriu!" I beseeched before she was gone entirely. "Please find them and bring them home!"

When she spoke again it sounded as if her lips were beside my ear. I could feel her breath on my cheek. "Home to *me*?"

"Yes!" I cried.

In an eyeblink she was gone.

But I was warm.

Afterward—and why is it that we think of such things when it is too late?—I realized that if Eriu could find Labraid and Cormiac Ru, she could find Maia. Yet I had not asked. I had buried Maia in my heart long ago. When I ceased to believe my daughter was alive, had something vital been irretrievably destroyed?

Menua, I thought to myself, would have handled this better. Within the capacious head of my teacher and mentor had been more knowledge than I ever attempted to mine. It is always so. We do not want to follow in our elders' footprints but insist on breaking new trails—often to our cost.

I did not tell anyone of my encounter in the forest. What transpired between Eriu and me was too precious to be shared.

"Eriu," I whispered to the wind from time to time. "Eriu."

And the wheel of the seasons turned.

With one eye on Aislinn, my oldest son began composing poems of love and singing them to his harp. Aislinn had Labraid in both her eyes and never noticed Dara.

I longed to be able to tell the girl that Labraid would come home again. How hard it is to keep good news to oneself. I silently nurtured it within my bosom as a bird nurtures her egg, knowing that magic must ripen in its own time.

At the change of the moon I had an unpleasant encounter with Duach Dalta. He found me skinning a hare behind my lodge. Grannus spurned such small game, but my wives had a taste for the meat and my son Ongus was adept at setting snares.

"How appropriate," sneered a voice behind me, "to find Ainvar up to his wrists in blood."

I whirled around to meet Duach Dalta's flinty-eyed gaze. "Why are you creeping up on me?" I asked as I got to my feet.

"In the territory of the Slea Leathan I can go anywhere I want."

I endeavored to remain polite. "This holding belongs to my clan, and we did not invite you here today."

"Have your pompous judge explain the Gaelic laws concerning land to you, Ainvar. Tribeland belongs to all of the tribe in common. A holding is an allotment, not sole ownership. You're only here on sufferance and we want you to leave. Leave the Plain of Broad Spears for good!" Taking a step toward me, Duach Dalta shook his fist in the air.

He thought to intimidate me with his fiery outburst, but water can extinguish fire. I concentrated on water; calm and cool. I became water. A spring, a river, a whole sea of water that no fire could harm.

Allowing the chief druid to simmer, I crouched down and thoroughly wiped the blade of my skinning knife on the grass. Deliberately ripped up more grass to clean the blood from my arms. Carefully spread the hare's skin over the meat to keep it from drying out.

Then I stood up. "Fíachu hasn't said anything to me about our leaving, Duach Dalta."

"He feels as I do."

"Let him tell me himself."

"Don't you believe me? I'm the chief druid!"

I waited for three heartbeats before replying, "I've been a chief druid for most of my adult life. Would you care to pit your magic against mine?"

"Magic." There were no snakes in Hibernia, yet Duach Dalta invested that single word with enough venom to kill a score of men. "Your foreign magic has no power here."

Making assumptions is a serious mistake. I would teach Duach Dalta that valuable lesson; I would perform an act of magic perfectly suited to Hibernia. With my most disingenuous smile, I said, "If I'm powerless, why object to a contest between us?"

"I have no objection, Ainvar, provided you go first. You're the one who issued the challenge."

"Name the time and the place, then."

"Right here," said Duach Dalta. "Right now."

The well-trampled area behind my lodge was not the ideal setting for magic, but at least we were alone. What I intended to do was private.

Standing very straight, I filled my lungs with the breath of the distant trees. Perhaps I inhaled too deeply; perhaps my chest had been permanently damaged by my illness. I was seized with a fit of coughing and had to begin again.

Duach Dalta watched with a cynical expression. You'll change that expression soon enough, I thought to myself.

The body of the hare lay on the ground near my feet. With my bare toes I touched the small corpse to indicate that the creature was being offered as a sacrifice to Eriu. Invoking her name, I raised my hands, palm upward, in perfect confidence that the roar would follow them up from the earth.

Nothing happened.

The ground, which was littered with domestic debris, did not roar. Nor did the saplings sway. There were no saplings. We were surrounded by lodges.

"Eriu!" I called again in a louder voice.

There was no response.

Lowering my arms to my sides, I took another deep breath. Be steady now, I told myself. You can do this; you have done this.

Once more I lifted my arms. Concentrated on Eriu with a fierce intensity, envisioning her as she must have been in life; in human form. Small and slim and beautiful, a girl who danced instead of walking. A silvery slip of a girl who wore flowers in her hair. A girl whom I loved with a passion unlike any I had felt before. She was not a woman for mating. She was a dream for cherishing.

Eriu! I pleaded silently. Come to me now. Show this unbeliever what true magic is.

"Eriu!"

She did not come.

There were only the two of us. Me with my hands in the air, and Duach Dalta, beginning to laugh at me.

"So that's your idea of magic, Ainvar? I can do it too, watch me." He flapped his arms like a fledgling vulture attempting to fly. "Ayr yoo," he called. "Oh, Ayr yoo!"

Never in my life had I been mocked.

Still laughing, Duach Dalta sauntered away. He paused once, though, to look back at me. "Oh yes, Ainvar; about your leaving us? The sooner the better. Take your relatives with you. They're a burden on the tribe."

When Duach Dalta was out of sight I fled to the trees. Menua had taught me many things, but never how to deal with humiliation. Like a gravely injured animal, I chose the solitude of the forest in which to lick my wounds.

I was a broken man when we came to Hibernia. Since then my confidence had been restored. The broken man was whole again. More than whole; I had achieved a shining triumph that outweighed all my failures. I had been in direct, personal contact with a being from the Otherworld. My gift had proven itself more extravagantly than I ever dreamed.

So why had it failed me now?

Running, panting, stumbling over exposed roots and dodging branches, I went farther and farther into the forest until a terrible stitch in my side forced me to stop. I stood for a while with my head down, listening to the ragged sound of my own breathing. When at last I raised my head, nothing I saw was familiar.

Every tree has its own individual character, expressed in its outward appearance and as unique to that tree as a man's face is to him. There were trees all around me, hundreds of them stretching into the green gloom of infinity, yet not a single one was an old friend.

But at least they were trees. Sanctuary.

Duach Dalta had watched me and laughed. The trees watched me uncritically. To a tree, simply being alive constitutes success. A dying leaf returns to the earth to feed future generations and continue its life through them. Shame and ridicule mean nothing to trees.

Slumping against a sturdy tree trunk, I tried to come to terms with my abruptly changed situation.

Think, head.

Druid ability is a rare gift, and a gift can be taken away. There was no chance it would be granted to me twice.

If the manipulation of natural forces now was beyond me I could no longer pretend, even to myself, that I was a chief druid. Druids were supported by their people in return for the use of their unique abilities. I was not entitled to eat my clan's food or share their shelter if I had nothing to offer in return. I could not be a seer, or a tribal historian, or a . . . Thoughts were running around inside my head like trapped mice. Then one stopped running. Stood alone for me to examine.

A sacrificer.

That was a gift I could give. I could sacrifice myself for my clan.

I could lie down on the ground and command my spirit to slip away. My will was still strong enough for that. By the time my body was discovered everything would be over. My family would grieve for me; Briga and Lakutu might even keen. But more important, Fíachu, who was a good man in many ways, would take pity on my people and let them remain with his. By dying I could give my clan the security I had jeopardized. A newly dead person is forgiven everything.

Yet if I were dead, who would organize my funeral ritual?

There were certain things I would want done that were not done for Onuava. No one knew of these plans; they were inside my head. Besides, a chief druid, even a discredited one, deserved the perquisites of his rank. The only person who could conduct the funeral was another chief druid, and we could expect no cooperation from Duach Dalta.

I had better live.

Yet how could I? Once, mine was the vast dark sky and the spaces between the stars; once, mine was the promise of magic.

No more.

With a groan, I lay down upon the ground, turned on one side for comfort's sake, and closed my eyes. Tightly. Concentrate on the gates of the Otherworld, I told my head.

Heads are not always obedient. My nose sniffed the dusty aroma of the dead leaves around me. My ears listened to rustlings in the undergrowth. My skin developed a maddening itch in the center of my back, out of reach.

The gates of the Otherworld were being obscured by the Here and Now.

I wanted no part of the Here and Now. Telling Briga of my humiliation would be unbearable. Escape to the Otherworld was the only solution. I gathered my will and tried again. But I still could not concentrate.

Near my head, something was breathing.

I opened my eyes.

Two round, black, exceedingly brilliant eyes looked back at me. They were set in a triangular face with conspicuous ears. The little animal had an elongated body and short legs and resembled a weasel, but its tail was bushy. A creamy patch on the throat contrasted with glossy brown fur elsewhere.

The Gael called these usually shy creatures pine martens. They were hunted for their fur, though one skin furnished only enough to make an arm ring. I had never seen a living pine marten up close before.

Dying could wait for a while longer.

Without moving his feet, the impudent little creature stretched his sinuous body forward until his nose was almost touching my face. I held very still. He took half a dozen short breaths in rapid succession. His bristly black whiskers vibrated with excitement. His eyes, almost all pupil, were those of a nocturnal animal, yet here he was in the daylight, daring to investigate a being that could easily kill him.

My visitor was not anticipating his mortality. He was living fully in the Here and Now.

Nature, instructor in all things, was making a point.

There was a sound in the forest like a dead branch falling, and with a whisk of his luxurious tail, the pine marten vanished. But he did not go far. Within moments he peeped out of a fringe of ferns and twitched his whiskers at me.

Step by cautious step, he returned. I breathed as shallowly as I could while he circumnavigated my body. His whiskers tickled my bare ankles. He sniffed up my spine to the nape of my neck. His small feet pattered around my head in a veritable dance of inquiry. Once again he stared into my face. I wondered if he could see my spirit in my eyes, as I could see his: bright little spark of the Great Fire of Life.

For that brief moment, our concentration on each other was total.

Magic.

When the pine marten had seen all he wanted to see of Ainvar, he bounded away in search of other adventures.

How, I asked myself, could I contemplate fleeing to the Otherworld when Thisworld had such wonders to offer?

Stiffly, I got to my feet. Brushed off my clothes. Squinted at the sunlight slanting through the trees to determine the direction of home.

Do your best, Duach Dalta. The pine marten and I are not afraid of the likes of you.

# *chapter* XX

I must have been smiling when I entered the lodge, because Briga remarked, "You're in a good mood for someone who ran off and left his wife to finish dressing the hare for the pot."

"I didn't run off. I was called away."

"By whom?"

"Life," I replied cryptically. "Is the hare cooked yet?"

"Cooked and eaten, no thanks to you. Lakutu helped me with both."

My senior wife has an independent streak, which has become more pronounced since we came to Hibernia.

Lakutu, who was sitting by my hearth while digesting my hare, did not move over to make room for me. I fear my formerly docile second wife is now emulating my first. While the women chatted about women's interests I sat in the shadows and brooded. They paid no attention to me. They had each other.

Three wives could be too many, I told myself, but two were not enough. My nature craved a unique companion: one who could illuminate the darkest caves within me.

No one but me had heard Eriu's voice. I had never mentioned her to anyone else. She had been my selfishly hoarded treasure; proof that I was a chief druid even after the debacle in Gaul. And now she had failed me.

Or I had failed.

Either way, how dare I go on pretending to be the leader of my clan? Briga knew of my lost powers and had never said anything to the others, but that was only because she loved me. Sooner or later—particularly if Fíachu threw us out of the tribe—they would all know the awful truth.

Who would lead them in my place? The only man I considered capable was Cormiac Ru. And he was gone.

How much can a man lose and remain a man?

My feet took me out under the sky. Although the sky was lit with a rose-and-gold sunset, a bank of dark cloud was looming in the north. The evening was cold, and as empty as the hollow under my breastbone. The hollow where I had cherished the secret of Eriu.

I went back into the lodge.

Menua used to say, "It is foolish to bleed before the knife cuts." I decided not to tell my wives about the threat of expulsion hanging over us. They could do nothing about it anyway. As for leadership of the clan . . . I had no strength left. All I could do was wait for the Pattern to work itself out, as I knew it would.

Sometimes that is all any of us can do.

When I woke up in the morning my first thought was: Will Fíachu come today? My last thought before I fell asleep at night was: Will Fíachu come tomorrow?

How long would it take for Duach Dalta to persuade the chieftain to send us away? And where would we go? Ulidia? Or perhaps the kingdom of the Deisi? Would Cohern be willing to take us in again, or would that jeopardize his truce with the Laigin? Was there some small corner of Hibernia where no tribe held sway and we might burrow in and be forgotten?

In my head I imagined a dozen fresh starts. Exhausted myself with futile mental excursions. Dreamed wild dreams that offered impossible solutions that faded with the coming of the light.

Briga began asking, "What's wrong, Ainvar? What are you thinking about?" Women always do that. If we wanted them to know we would tell them.

Eventually I lost my temper and snapped at her, which only confirmed her fears that something was amiss. When I refused to confide in her she looked hurt. "I don't understand, Ainvar. You always tell me everything."

"Where did you get that idea?" As soon as the words were out of my mouth I regretted them, but it was too late.

"You mean you *don't* tell me everything you think?"

No matter how honest a man wants to be, marriage forces him to lie. "Of course I tell you everything that's important, Briga. But ten thousand thoughts flit through my head in a single day like a giant cloud of gnats. Do you want to hear every one of them? Or perhaps . . . just those that involve you?"

Placing the tip of my little finger on the center of her chin, I slowly traced along the curve of her jawbone until I was stroking the soft flesh just behind her earlobe. This was an old signal between us.

Against her will, Briga's eyes grew misty. She wanted to go on arguing but the rose between her thighs had begun to bloom. The language of the body is older than the spoken word.

I took my wife in my arms. While waiting for the worst to happen, I made the most of Here and Now.

On the day following the full moon Fíachu's clan challenged another clan to a hurling match. Caman was serious business; war in miniature. The match would be played on Fíachu's racecourse. The pillar stones inscribed with Onuava's name would serve as goalposts.

A rousing game was just the distraction I craved. Although many summers had passed since I took an active part in sport, I still enjoyed watching. In my head I would again run with the young men; in my head I would strike the winning goal.

The lives we live in our heads can be the most vivid of all.

If Fíachu was going to banish me I felt confident he would not do it publicly; he was stern but not cruel. To be safe, however, I embedded myself deep among the spectators on the far side of the field.

It was an exceptionally hard-fought match. The action swept up and down the field without the slightest pause. Most of the players were young men who had survived no more than twenty winters. A few were older: the cunning ones, the heads who plotted every move in advance. Caman had few rules but strategy was all-important.

As I watched, my legs remembered how good it felt to run with an excited team. My feet remembered the sensation of skimming over the earth with wings on my heels.

Before I fully realized what I was doing, I had seized a stick from the spare hurleys stacked at the end of the field. Heedless of the fact that my presence would make the sides uneven, I ran out onto the field of play.

Another spectator quickly redressed the balance. Duach Dalta came running toward me from the opposite side. For a fleeting instant I thought he intended to beat me to death with his hurley, but that was only my imagination. He threw himself into the game as I had done, revealing an exceptional speed and agility for a man of his years.

Every sport has its rhythm. This is doubly true of caman. At its best, the members of a team appear to be following one drumbeat. If one side can disrupt the rhythm of the other it gives them a great advantage. The unexpected arrival of Duach Dalta and myself on the scene threw both sides off their timing. The game sputtered to a near halt.

We did not notice. In the center of the playing field, surrounded by other men, we saw only each other.

Duach Dalta got possession of the sliotar. On his face was an expression compounded of hatred and jealousy and grim determination. As he ran toward me with the sliotar perfectly balanced on his hurley, I realized he was better at the game than I was. At exactly the right moment he checked his forward rush and hurled the sliotar upward with his stick. Step, bend knees, twist, and a mighty swing sent the ball flying. Straight at me.

Men sometimes lost their front teeth during a match. I did not think Duach Dalta would be satisfied with knocking out my teeth. He wanted to break my head.

My sporting reflexes might not be as quick as his, but my head was quicker. By the time the missile reached me I was already throwing myself to the ground. I felt the wind of the sliotar's passing.

Duach Dalta hid his disappointment well. "Ainvar the useless!" he crowed. Some of the other men laughed.

I lay on the ground while I regained my composure, then stood up, wearing a good-humored smile. "I never was good at games," I lied. "It doesn't take much effort to best me at any of them."

The chief druid, his triumph diluted, glared at me.

I carried my hurley back to the end of the field and returned it to the stack. "Try to get along without me, lads!" I shouted. Some of the men who had just been laughing at me, laughed with me. One of them called, "Anytime you want a little practice I'll help you, Ainvar. I need some, too."

I replied with a cheerful nod and headed off toward my lodge.

To a tree, simply being alive constitutes success. I must remember that.

Although I expected Fíachu every day, he did not come. If Duach Dalta was buzzing in his ear it was having little effect—so far. The wheel of the seasons turned and we were still part of the Slea Leathan.

I threw myself totally into teaching. Those of my students who had found no druidic talent in themselves drifted away. Others took their place. Almost a score of young people were studying the disciplines I thought we had left behind us in Gaul.

The most gifted of my students was the chieftain's daughter. Aislinn needed little instruction. Her mind was as nimble as a young deer. While I was formulating one thought she leaped ahead to the next with perfect comprehension. As I told Keryth, "Sometimes the Pattern is as clear to her as if it had been drawn on a stone with a burnt stick."

"I was like that at her age," Keryth said. "Everything was wonderfully clear to me. Old people—or what I thought of as old people, meaning my parents' age—were slow and stupid and I lost patience with them."

"It was the same with me. Was our vision flawed, Keryth?"

She shook her head. "Our vision was fine, we just couldn't see the dust."

"What dust?"

"The motes in the air. The obstacles. They were there all the time, but our young eyes were so clear we couldn't see them."

"Now the clarity's gone and the obstacles are still there, Keryth."

"I'm not even sure I can see the obstacles anymore. I'm losing my vision."

"If you're going blind, remember that one of Briga's springs has great curative powers for the eyes. I'm sure she could—"

"It isn't my eyes, Ainvar; it's much worse than that. My druid gift is fading. I can rarely *see* anymore, and even when I do I'm mistaken. My prognostications are no longer genuine."

"Oh, Keryth." I, above all people, could appreciate what she was feeling. I wondered if I should tell her of my own loss. But the habit of secrecy had become too ingrained. When we might have comforted each other, I could not bring myself to share.

Within a single cycle of the moon Keryth aged five years. The rapid change shocked me. Was it the result of losing her gift? Had a similar fate befallen me?

Surely not. Briga would have told me if I became an old man overnight. Or would she?

If the same thing happened to her would I tell her? Would I even notice? Probably not. To my eyes, Briga would always be the same.

When no one was around I visited a deep forest pool to seek my reflection. The visage that stared back from the fern-fringed water was a stranger. How long had it been since I looked upon Ainvar? Yet it was he, beyond a doubt. Same jutting cheekbones and dark eyes. Because I no longer shaved a tonsure, my hair had grown back above my forehead, and was still thick and abundant.

The Ainvar of the pool and I regarded each other with identical grave expressions. "You haven't aged," I told him.

Could that be construed to mean that I had not lost my gift after all?

I straightened up. Trying to ignore the sudden flutter in the pit of my stomach, I shaped Eriu's name with my lips and slowly raised my hands. Never in my life had I poured more effort into an act of magic.

Nothing happened.

Nothing.

*Nothing.*

I felt totally drained, knowing that I would never try again. There was no point.

Eriu had been more than real to me; she had been the proof of all I believed about the immortality of the spirit. How could she have disappeared so completely? It was almost as if she had never been.

My head took a step backward; surveyed the situation with a wider view.

Was it possible that Eriu had been a product of my own imagination?

The question shuddered through me. Had I been so desperate to believe there was a power greater than Caesar that I had shapechanged this bountiful, hospitable land into a goddess? Had I carved her body from random flickers of light at the corner of my eye? Had I spun her voice from the meaningless wailings of the wind? Was everything concerned with her a dream I had dreamed in the daylight?

Yes, I admitted to myself, it was possible. More than possible.

Druids are trained to deal with things as they are, not as they would wish them to be.

Think, head!

My cowardly head offered an array of distractions. I rejected all of them.

Druids are trained to concentrate.

My head's reluctance to examine the only topic of any real importance confirmed my worst fears.

*I could not summon Eriu because she did not exist.*

Somehow I made my way back to the lodge without being aware of a single step I took.

# *chapter* XXI

THE MOON CHANGED AGAIN, AND AGAIN. SINCE I NEITHER PLANTED nor harvested I was indifferent to the passage of time. I was indifferent to everything; all of the juice had drained out of me. When other members of my clan spoke to me I tried to pay attention but my thoughts wandered. Even when Dian Cet gave me the particulars of a very long and singularly detailed judgment he had made recently, I at first found it hard to concentrate. When I learned that Morand had taken part in the deliberations I forced my ears to listen harder and my head to commit the judgment to memory.

My students were going on to lives of their own. Without me. Which was as it should be, and yet . . .

The lessons I taught in the glade became mere mouthings because I no longer believed in them myself. It did not take long for the young people to start falling away. Dara was the last to give up on me. Day after day he patiently sat at my feet, listening to me prattle on about matters I now knew to be inconsequential. Then one day I saw pity in his eyes.

The following morning I did not go to the glade. Instead I continued to sit by the hearth, whittling on a bit of stick with one of Briga's cooking knives. After a while Dara took his cloak and went out by himself.

"Aren't you going?" asked Briga.

"Not today. It's raining."

She laughed, thinking I was making a joke.

I continued whittling.

Briga said, "Rain never stopped you before."

"Maybe I'll go tomorrow."

I did not go to the glade the next morning, either.

Yet I could not continue to sit in the lodge day after day. Without saying a word, both of my wives let me know that a man who spent his day under their feet was as welcome as mud.

If I had felt more comfortable at the fort I would have gone there and spent some time with Fíachu, whose bluff good humor had a way of raising spirits. That good humor was not available to me anymore.

The same interdiction did not extend to my clan, who remained unaware that we had been threatened with dispossession. Indeed, they were becoming more and more interwoven with the tribe.

Dian Cet was frequently approached to make one of his wise judgments. When a man died without repaying the debt he owed another, a debt that would impoverish his widow, Dian Cet considered the matter at length. He then pronounced: "Even a dead body has a right to a cow, a horse, a cloak, and the coverings of its bed. None of these shall be used in payment of the debts of the deceased, because they are the special property of his body."

This welcome innovation was added to tribal law.

Damona wove wool into original patterns that were quickly adopted by the women of the Slea Leathan. Teyrnon's ironwork was requested faster than he could turn it out, there now being a great demand for scythes and sickles and plows. Meanwhile the complex designs of the Goban Saor were exerting a powerful influence on tribal jewelry.

Ever since Dara eulogized Onuava in poetry his reputation had grown. He was invited to compose praise poems for other clan chiefs and to entertain at their feasts. How Seanchán felt about this I cannot say, but I suspect he was furious when a new title was bestowed upon my oldest son. Dara was being called an *ollamh,* meaning "master-poet."

The boys and girls who had been my students in the forest were making positive contributions to the tribe.

The Goban Saor and his wife had just enriched it with lusty twin sons.

Yet I had nothing left to give. When I was ill Briga should have let me die.

But oh, I did not want to go into the dark! Not while the meadows were buttered with every shade of yellow from furze to primrose; not while the thundering wings of a swan could stir up a matching thunder in my heart.

Not while Hibernia still beguiled me with a thousand beauties.

Not while Briga was warm in my bed at night, offering me sanctuary from my thoughts.

However, even my senior wife could not shield me for long. Druids are trained to think; we are not trained to stop thinking. In spite of instructions from me to the contrary, my voluble head babbled on and on, asking questions I did not want to hear; questions for which I had no answer.

If there was no Eriu, was there such a thing as an Otherworld? Or had we created it ourselves because we were afraid of the dark?

Stop, head! I forbid you to proceed any farther along this road. It will lead to the destruction of the pillars upon which my life is built.

Searching for something else to think about, one morning I ambled over to the forge to watch Teyrnon and the Goban Saor making a new sword. A chieftain's sword had been ordered by Fíachu, who was still willing to do business with my people. It appeared that only I was in bad odor with the leader of the Slea Leathan.

The forge was a scene of strenuous but highly organized activity. Each man had his particular work to do. Each in his own way was an artist.

In a time before the before, some distant ancestor had been attracted to a bright glitter in a lump of rock. Perhaps it was gold, perhaps it was copper. Moved by curiosity, the man had chipped the shiny substance free with a flint axe so he could examine it more closely. Eventually he—or one of his descendants—discovered that the ore would melt if held too close to a fire.

Metalworking was born.

At first its use was limited to the creation of ornaments to designate status. In time someone else used his imagination to combine several melted ores into a material strong enough to make tools. And weapons. First of bronze, then of iron.

Imagination is yet another manifestation of the Two-Faced One. Used creatively, it produces great benefit. Used destructively, it can destroy worlds.

The Goban Saor already had carved the sword's grip from oak to resemble the upper body of a Celtic warrior, inset with a face of polished bone. As I watched, the great craftsman began shaping the torso to fit Fíachu's hand exactly. He had taken an impression of the hand in beeswax to use as a model. When the fit was perfect he would cover the grip with beaten silver. The weight of the entire piece must be carefully calculated to balance the blade.

Teyrnon was forging the blade to his own design, an improved version of Labraid's weapon. Experience with the Romans had shown us the advantages of the gladus. The longer Gaulish sword, while terrifying when wielded by a man on horseback, was cumbersome in close quarters. When two men were fighting eye to eye and knee to knee, a leaf-shaped shortsword, with two cutting edges and a sharp point, could drive in under the breastbone or skewer a man through the throat. Either way was fatal.

Glas operated the leather bellows to keep the fire at the specific heat required for each step of the forging. By now Lakutu's son knew just when the fire must be cherry red, when it must be angry orange, when it must be as white as ice. A mistake on his part could have destroyed days of labor.

As they worked the men spoke to one another from time to time, but not about what they were doing. Their hands were so perfectly attuned to the task that their heads were free to think of other things.

Back in Gaul, I remembered, swords had been forged in what was called "pattern welding." The blades were so malleable they could be twisted into a spiral of three or four turns without breaking. This very malleability proved their downfall. They were quickly deformed in battle and had to be beaten back into shape with the nearest handy rock, which ultimately made them too brittle for further use.

Teyrnon was forging Fíachu's new sword out of successive layers of iron, each beaten very thin, then hammered into the next to build up a blade whose total was stronger than its individual parts. After every additional layer he pounded out the shape he wanted, then plunged the blade into cold water until it hissed like an angry snake. Then it was thrust back into the fire and hammered again, and quenched again. And on, and on . . .

So is man burned and chilled by the events of his life, my head observed. If he survives them he is stronger than ever before.

What if he does not survive?

I watched the making of the sword for a while longer, then wandered away, captured again by thoughts I did not want to have.

Without the Otherworld, where could our spirits go between lives? They had to await rebirth somewhere. Rebirth allowed the immortal part of us to learn and grow. Rebirth enabled us to resume interrupted friendships and rediscover lost loves. I could not make sense of rebirth without the existence of an Otherworld.

And I had lost faith in the Otherworld.

I was drowning in murky depths of disbelief. How could I save myself? Who could throw me a lifeline?

No one.

Those who might have helped me regain my faith were gone. The great Menua had been dead for over two generations. Gone into the dark from which there is no returning, as were the other druids who had studied the lessons of nature for countless lifetimes. So much wisdom.

Lost forever, I thought bitterly.

My head, my cruel head; always tormenting me. Perhaps when my ancestors relieved their enemies of their heads they did them a greater favor than they knew.

A man with no meaningful work to do is less than a man. As I wandered around our clanhold I thought I saw pity in the eyes of my family, and I turned my head away. The old Ainvar would have known what to do; would have performed some spectacular magic that would have restored him to his rightful place.

The new Ainvar was bereft of magic.

Yet magic was real; at least I was certain of that much. My own eyes had witnessed great magic being done. I had even done it myself. Through some failing of my own, great magic was now denied to me. Even the small magic of teaching was lost.

The greatest of all teachers still existed. Nature, once again making a point, was heralding the approach of another winter. The meadows flowered no longer. The swans deserted our rivers and lakes and flew off to their secret shelterings in the west. The days grew short and dull, while at night the stars blazed from the sky with a crystalline malevolence.

The dark side of the Two-Faced One was coming to the fore.

Throughout the Plain of Broad Spears people were preoccupied by the preparations for winter. In my own clanhold Briga was overwhelmed with requests for her help, while Lakutu was smoking meat and making warmer clothes and stacking up firewood on the north side of the lodges and grinding more flour and . . . There was no end to the busyness of women.

When I put my arms around one of my wives in her bed, I usually found her already asleep.

The cold of the approaching death of the sun seeped into the very marrow of my bones.

And all the while my head tormented me. The next question it asked came like a knife through my heart.

If there was no Otherworld, was rebirth just another comforting myth?

I could not stay in the lodge. Day by day, while the sun was visibly dying, I paced through the forest like a creature demented. The trees were dying, too; their annual death from which they would be reborn when the sun was reborn. If the sun was reborn.

What guarantee did we have for that? The age-old rituals of our people? Were those not conducted more in hope than in certainty?

My head observed that the wise oaks were the last to surrender to the coming winter. They held their browning leaves with a courage the lesser trees did not possess. Hold on to your courage too, Ainvar, they whispered to me when the wind stirred them.

Courage is a fine thing but one cannot see it with one's eyes. One cannot see pride, or honor, or hope. Or faith. Perhaps none of them exist. There was a time when I thought I glimpsed Eriu and the Otherworld and they were real to me, but I was wrong.

Do not hide from the truth, Ainvar, I admonished myself. Reject the illusion your imagination created.

We come out of the dark and we return to the dark. There is nothing else. Just the dark.

I wanted to scream. I wanted to cry. I wanted to pound my fists against the sky in raging denial. I did none of those things. They would have made no difference.

When I looked to the west I saw a dull red sun sinking into a pool of its own blood. Who could say if it would ever rise again?

Containing nothing immortal, my body turned and began its slow, sad walk home.

# *chapter* XXII

FOLLOWING A WINTER'S STORM, GRANNUS AND THE BOYS OF OUR clan spent several days collecting windfall from the forest to augment our firewood supply. Since I had nothing better to do, I joined them. It was a pleasant enough task. Mindless.

Late one day I returned to my lodge to find half a dozen men I had never seen before. They were gathered in a circle around my senior wife. While Briga talked, the strangers were chewing frantically.

My second wife still sat by her loom, patiently working the shuttle back and forth. I caught her eye and indicated the strangers with a nod of my head. "They're from the tribe that lives at the mouth of the Liffey," Lakutu said. "They've come all this way to ask for Briga's help."

Of course they had. Unlike mine, Briga's gift was still valuable.

One by one, the men held out their hands for my senior wife to examine. Fisherman's hands, red and callused and permanently chapped, with ropy tendons and ridged, broken nails. Hands that plunged into icy water and hauled heavy nets. Hands like feet; indispensable. In the course of their labors they had accrued serious injuries. Broken fingers that knit badly had shapechanged into useless claws; a tendon in the back of a hand was severed; gaping wounds that refused to heal were filled with maggots and pus.

I retired into the shadows and sat nursing my own pain.

Briga cleansed the suppurating wounds with apple vinegar and salt, and rinsed them thoroughly with quantities of pure water. She chewed sorrel leaves until her mouth was filled with a green liquid that she spat into each wound in turn, then applied poultices of ragwort and plantain leaves.

Using a sliver of deer's shinbone for a needle, she stitched the severed tendon back together with a single strand of badger's gut, working as deftly as Onuava had once embroidered with silk. The seepage of blood was stanched with cobwebs before the layers of cut skin were sewn closed. The hand was bound in cloth Briga had woven herself, from the wool of a virgin ewe.

She rebroke the misshapen fingers with a stone polished smooth and round by a rushing river. For this operation I thought she might need me to hold the man still, but like his companions, he appeared to be impervious to pain. He just kept chewing. Briga manipulated the bones into the correct configuration, coated them with another of her herbal pastes, wrapped each finger separately in unbleached linen, and strapped them together on a plank of ash wood.

When my senior wife had finished her ministrations, Lakutu fetched a wooden bowl and carried it from man to man. Each in turn spat out the contents of his mouth: sodden wads of herb and fungus and tiny hazel twigs.

Briga urged her visitors to sit around the fire and rest themselves. "You must spend the night with us and have a good meal to fill your bellies for the journey back." Soon the strangers were laughing and talking with my wives as if they were old friends. I stayed quietly in the shadows and listened. No one paid much attention to me, but that was what I wanted.

To listen is to learn.

I learned that the tribes who lived around the estuary of the Liffey did not rely solely upon fishing. They had a thriving export trade in furs and skins, salted fish, and leather. Albion and Scotia were their principal markets, but they also did business with the Armoricans. They even were visited by traders from the lands surrounding the Mid-Earth Sea. The man with the broken fingers said he could make himself understood in five languages.

How little we know of the way others make a living! A man sees no farther than his own horizon, so his troubles may appear larger than they really are.

What did it matter if I could no longer work magic? What did it matter if Eriu did not exist and our spirits were not immortal? Food still tasted good in my mouth. My women still felt good in my arms—when they had time for me.

My eyes turned toward my senior wife. How serene she was within herself! The light loved Briga. Even in the dim interior of the lodge a tiny ray found and illumined her hair, encircling her head with gold. From what wellspring, I wondered, did she draw her strength?

While Briga and Lakutu were preparing additional beds for our guests, I heard one of the men say something that caught my attention. I stood up. "Did you say 'Labraid'?"

"Do you know him?" asked the man with the broken hand.

"I know *a* Labraid. It's not a common name."

"The Labraid I know is an uncommon sort of fellow," the fisherman replied. "A very tough man. He calls himself the Speaker Who Sails the Seas."

Briga straightened up and turned toward me with a quizzical expression.

"When did you meet this Labraid?" I asked.

The fingers of the man's uninjured hand spidered across his head, scratching. "A few days ago. More or less."

"Oh, Ainvar!" Briga ran to me. Her eyes were huge.

"Where is Labraid now?" I demanded to know. "Why didn't he come with you?"

"They weren't able for it."

*"They?"* Briga and I exclaimed in unison.

"Three of them, all sick and injured."

*Three?*

Three is the number of fate.

I heard Briga gasp.

My next words were forced through dry lips. "Is one of the three a woman?"

"Couldn't tell you. They were the only survivors in a wrecked boat that washed ashore during the last winter storm. My tribe found them. By the time I saw them, two were wrapped from head to foot in blankets. This fellow Labraid was the only one who was able to talk. That's how I learned he calls himself the Speaker of the—"

"Did he identify the others?"

"Not exactly. All I heard him say about that was . . ." The fisherman paused and gazed up at the smoky underside of the thatch, trying to find a memory. "What I heard him say was, 'Only Briga of the Slea Leathan could save the Red Wolf. She can heal anything.' So I told a few of my friends about you and here we are!"

I wanted to smash his smug face with my fist. Yet without his unthinkingly selfish act, we might never have known about—

"Maia," Briga whispered hoarsely. "They've found our Maia and brought her home."

"Don't get your hopes up," I cautioned.

"It's Maia. It *has* to be." She tugged at my arm. "We must go to them immediately, Ainvar."

"How far is it to your tribe?" I asked the fishermen.

"Two or three days' walk. More or less."

Briga said, "Horses would get us there much faster."

"What do you mean by 'us'?"

"You heard him, they're badly hurt. They need me now and I'm going!"

The only horses in the area belonged to Fíachu, whom I had been avoiding for a long time. But if a trouble is meant for you, you cannot avoid it. I must do as Vercingetorix had done: take up the sword and meet it. For Maia and Cormiac Ru.

Strange, my head observed, how quickly I accepted that the third member of the group was Maia. Was faith transferable? Had Briga given hers to me?

"Very well," I told her, "I'll ask Fíachu for horses. But you don't know how to ride."

"I'll learn," she said flatly. "Go ask for them."

Vercingetorix had taught me a number of lessons. Perhaps the most valuable was the fact that there are occasions when one can think too much. If Rix was certain he must do something he did not want to do, he wasted no energy thinking about it. He just plunged in and did it.

Without allowing my head to think about the possible consequences, I set out at once for Fíachu's stronghold. Night already had fallen but my feet knew the way. As I walked I envisioned Teyrnon working at the forge, making a sword. Mentally I followed him through every step of the process. Fierce concentration was required, but druids are trained to concentrate.

I was surprised when I found myself at the door of Fíachu's lodge.

Only his second wife was inside, sweeping the earthen floor with a broom of hazel twigs before the family retired for the night. A plump, pretty woman who had everything a wife could possibly want except perhaps a third wife to do the chores for her. I had sometimes wondered why Fíachu, with all his wealth, did not marry more women. At least two clan chiefs of the Slea Leathan had three wives, and the old king himself was said to have five.

She looked up as I entered. "Ainvar? We haven't seen you here for a long time. Shall I heat some water so you can wash your hands and feet?"

"I thank you for your hospitality," I replied formally. She poured water from a large pottery jar into a bronze basin, which she set on the hearth, close to the flame. On winter nights the fire in the chieftain's lodge was kept well fed. When the water was warm enough, Fíachu's second wife brought the basin to me and placed it at my feet.

By now I was fully familiar with Gaelic custom. Because the owner of the lodge was absent, to show the extent of my trust I crouched down with my back to the doorway through which he would enter when he returned. After washing my hands I slipped off my winter footgear, then stood—back still to the door—and eased my right foot into the warm water. Five cold toes wriggled with delight. As soon as they began to tingle I removed them and gave the same treat to my left foot. Ah, the kindness of water! No wonder my Briga treated it with such reverence.

If Fíachu came home at that moment he could kill me with no effort at all.

My left foot was still luxuriating in the basin when I heard a sound at the doorway. All my willpower was required to keep me from turning around.

"See who's here, husband!" Fíachu's second wife called out. She handed me a square of linen to wipe my feet dry. "Ainvar's come to visit us at last."

Slowly, I turned around.

Fíachu was not smiling but at least he had no weapon in his hand. So the message of my exposed back had not been lost on him. "Ainvar," he said. Just that, with no inflection.

Searching the eyes of Fíachu with my own eyes, I found no malice, only a guarded watchfulness.

Duach Dalta had been talking to him, all right. Intimating, insinuating. Using all his skill to manipulate the chief of the tribe.

I knew something about manipulation. "Fíachu," I acknowledged in a tone as coldly formal as his.

"What brings you here? We thought you had forgotten us."

"Have you forgotten me?" I asked.

"No." Nothing else, just no. But that was enough to tell me this was not going to be easy.

The thoughts I had been trying not to think roiled in my head. If I was exiled my clan would go with me out of loyalty. Leaving behind those fine, solid lodges. The forge. The little shed where the women milked the cows. Perhaps even the cows themselves, the gentle cows who marched into the shed on their own every morning and evening.

We had lost too much already; there had to be an end to it. Resolve strengthened my voice. "Fíachu, I've come to ask a favor."

Up went the tangled eyebrows. "From me? You dare to ask a favor from me?"

Think, head! Think fast now. Once you dared Caesar himself.

My head had not let me down then, and it did not let me down now. Instead it reminded me of something I had foolishly buried beneath my worries.

I threw back my shoulders and assumed the confident voice of a chief druid who has nothing to fear. "You have horses and I need three."

Fíachu's eyebrows did the impossible: They crawled still higher. "You want my horses?" he asked as if he could not believe the evidence of his ears.

"I need horses if I am to bring back your son."

He looked bewildered. "But my son is dead, Ainvar. And buried."

"One of your sons is dead. You have another."

"What are you talking about?"

"Labraid."

Fíachu gave a snort and lowered his eyebrows. "Don't be ridiculous, you know he's dead, too. Has to be, by now. Anyway, he was sired by some man in Gaul, not me."

"Labraid was sired by the great chieftain Vercingetorix, who was known throughout Gaul as the King of the World. But the boy was carried in the belly of Onuava."

"What has that to do with me?"

"I have very good reason to believe that Labraid is still alive."

"So?"

I knew Fíachu; already he was searching for some piece of advantage to himself in this conversation.

"If Onuava had been your wife, Fíachu, you could claim her son as your son. Which means you could now be father to the son of the King of the World. Would you not agree that having such a son would vastly enhance your status among the tribes?"

"There's no point in speculating," he said brusquely. "I never married Onuava."

I smiled. "Did you not? Perhaps I have good news. Let me tell you about a judgment Dian Cet recently rendered to another clan of the Slea Leathan.

"A prosperous cattle lord had died; a man who had sired a number of children on his wife and also on a favorite bondwoman. At the man's death the children of both women demanded to inherit his property. The sons of the man's wife insisted that because the other children were not born of marriage they had no right to the dead man's possessions. The claim of the bondwoman's children was supported by their friends, who felt they were just as deserving as the wife's sons. The quarrel threatened to disintegrate into a full-blown war. This was to be avoided at all costs because this particular clan possessed many bondservants. In fact, they outnumbered their masters two to one.

"To resolve the situation the chief of the clan sent for Dian Cet and his apprentice, Morand. The two men deliberated the matter for a full cycle of the moon. Then Dian Cet pronounced the following judgment: 'Any sexual act capable of resulting in a child is deemed to be a marriage, whether a child was actually born or not.' "

Fíachu scowled at me. "How could there be a marriage if no ritual took place?"

"Ah, this is the genius of Dian Cet's judgment, don't you see? The ritual was the act of coupling itself!

"Furthermore—and I am told this was actually Morand's idea—Dian Cet suggested that marriage be divided into degrees. The first three degrees would be determined by the possession of property."

"I still don't understand."

"It's quite straightforward, Fíachu. The chief of the clan understood at once. And approved. Marriages in which one or both partners own valuable property such as cattle or bondservants or the freehold of land are now to be known as contract marriages, and agreed to in front of witnesses. In a union of the first degree both partners are equal in rank and property. In a marriage of the second degree the man owns the most property and supports the woman. The woman in a marriage of the third degree owns the most property, but supports the man as long as he agrees to work on her land.

"In addition . . ." I paused, relishing the moment. Here was the point I had been working toward, the inspiration for which I forgave my head its many failings. "In addition there is to be a fourth degree, known as 'the marriage of a loved one.' This has no contract based on property ownership, but transpires whenever a man takes a woman unto himself with her full consent and she lives in the manner of a wife."

A light came into Fíachu's eyes.

At that moment the chieftain's senior wife entered the lodge. She gave her husband a quizzical glance, but his full attention was fixed on me. I could have stopped right there, but the trained memory of a druid should never be cut off in the middle.

"A marriage of the fifth degree is one in which two people lie together from time to time but continue to live separately, and one does not support the other. This is the new law adopted by the second largest clan of the Slea Leathan," I concluded.

"Five degrees of marriage," Fíachu murmured. "An exceedingly clever concept."

"Do you approve, then?"

"Totally, Ainvar. And let me say, I am astonished at such wisdom on the part of—"

"Two members of the Slea Leathan," I hastily interposed. "Dian Cet belongs to your tribe now, and his apprentice, Morand, is a member of your own clan. If anyone is to be congratulated it is yourself, Fíachu."

Fíachu swelled with pride the way a toad swells when it finds water after a long drought.

I prudently took a half step sideways in case he tried to clap me on the back. It was best to avoid the chieftain's more ebullient gestures.

"Apprentice." Fíachu rolled the word across his tongue, then spat it out. "That's far too puny a title for such a fine young man. By what title is Dian Cet known among your people, Ainvar?"

"He's a brehon judge. Brehon is our highest designation for a long head."

Fíachu lit up the lodge with his grin. "I decree that from this moment, Morand is a brehon as well. And I further decree that the judgment of the brehons will be the new marriage law of the entire tribe of the Slea Leathan.

"Now, what was the favor you sought of me, Ainvar?" he asked ingenuously. But he had not forgotten; he promptly answered his own question. "Oh yes, horses. You want to go looking for my son, Labraid, I believe?"

His senior wife gave a gasp and put her hand over her mouth. His second wife protested, "But Labraid's not your son, Fíachu."

"Be quiet, woman! Did you not hear the law? Labraid's mother was joined with me in a marriage of the fourth degree so I'm entitled to call him my son. Ainvar, if you think there's the smallest chance that he's alive, take the fastest horses I have and go and bring him back to me!"

He reached out and clapped me on the back after all.

# *chapter* XXIII

EVEN BEFORE A PALLID SUN ROSE THE NEXT MORNING, I WAS ON my way back to the fort to select mounts for our journey. I found Aislinn already at the horse pen. Seeing me appear out of the gloom, she said apologetically, "I'm sorry I haven't been coming to the glade, Ainvar. But I'm kept so busy caring for the horses. I do all of the feeding and tending myself, you know.

"Make no excuses," I told the girl. "I haven't been there myself lately, though I'll be resuming the classes in the future. Your father wants more brehons; more judges."

"I don't have that gift."

"You don't need it, Aislinn; your own talents are quite sufficient. I'm here this morning because Fíachu is lending me three horses to ride for a journey we must make."

I heard, rather than saw, her swift intake of breath. "You're going to find Labraid!"

"Did Fíachu tell you?"

"He said nothing to me about it. I just woke up this morning . . . knowing," she replied. Her voice shook with repressed excitement.

In this girl the druid gift was strong indeed. "I want to ask your advice," I said. "Which of these animals is the fastest?"

She opened the gate and led me into the enclosure. The horses eagerly crowded around her. She gently stroked the most importunate muzzle. In the growing light I could see that the animal had an elegant, wedge-shaped head and a reddish coat. "This chestnut mare is probably the fastest," Aislinn said, "but she's hot-tempered and hard to ride."

"I'll need two more who can keep up with her."

"Two? Well, this big, dark brown horse is nearly as fast. And so is the gray over there."

The gray horse she indicated was the only animal in the pen who was still lying down. When I walked over to take a closer look the gray made no effort to get to its feet. I bent over the recumbent head. The gray opened one eye and looked at me, then closed the eye again. "I think this one's sick," I called to Aislinn.

She laughed. "Don't worry, he'll get up as soon as I start feeding them. He spends all his time either resting or eating, but he can run like the wind."

If appearances were any indication, the gray horse was not capable of stirring up a light breeze. He seemed tame enough for a woman to ride; I would choose between the other two. The third horse would go to Grannus, who was going to act as our guard. He was not a warrior by nature but I thought we might have need of his strength.

As far as I knew, neither Briga nor Grannus knew how to ride.

As for me . . . here was another example of the Two-Faced One. While I was overjoyed at the prospect of seeing Cormiac again, and possibly Maia as well, I was not at all happy about entrusting myself to the vagaries of a horse. Warriors ride, druids walk.

The only time I had ridden horses was during the war with Caesar, when it was imperative that I keep up with Vercingetorix. The experience had not been a happy one for me. Nor, I suspect, for the horses. Rix blended so totally with his black stallion that it was impossible to tell where one left off and the other began. Not me. The first time my mount trotted I bounced. When it galloped I fell off.

Rix had laughed at me. I had laughed too, rather ruefully, and silently promised myself that when the war was over I would never get on another horse.

For Maia and Cormiac Ru I would break that promise.

Memories of Rix decided me to take the big brown horse, who was so dark he almost looked black, and had a reassuringly calm eye. The fiery chestnut mare would go to Grannus. He should be strong enough to manage her, I told myself.

Rank has some privileges.

I was reluctant to attempt to mount with Aislinn watching, so I asked her to bridle the horses for me, then find her father and tell him which ones I was taking. She led the animals from the enclosure and tied them to the fence outside. As soon as the girl was gone I untied the dark horse and availed myself of the gate to clamber onto his back. In the process I accidentally kneed him in the ribs. He turned his head and looked at me.

"I am Ainvar," I told him in my most reassuring voice—though I wanted some reassuring myself—"and I'm not very good at this. If you're gentle with me I'll try to be gentle with you."

The horse flared his nostrils and made a little huffing sound. Bending his neck farther, he explored my foot with his soft muzzle. Through the worn leather of my shoe I felt the warmth of his breath.

I gathered up the reins of the other two and turned our collective heads for home.

By the time I reached my lodge Grannus was already there, with a sword in the sheath fastened to his belt. Briga had made up two leather packs. One held bread and cheese and a large assortment of medicaments; the other contained blankets. Grannus and I strapped the packs onto our backs before donning our warmest cloaks. Then we went to the waiting horses.

Thinking ahead, I had tied the dark horse beside a fallen log we used as a chopping block. I simply stepped up and onto my horse's back. Grannus lifted my senior wife onto the gray. Before I could warn him, he took a running start and vaulted over the rump of the chestnut mare.

Who bolted.

Not to be outdone, the other two horses followed. They were eager to join the race. To my surprise I did not fall off. More surprisingly, neither did Briga. She clung to the reins with one hand and wrapped her other hand in the mare's flaxen mane. I clung to the brown horse in the same way. Grannus was so far ahead of us I could not tell how he was retaining his seat, but I heard him give a shout that spurred the mare on to greater speed.

I suspect that was unintentional on Grannus's part.

When I was certain my seat was secure enough, I risked a glance at the wintry sun. By a fortunate coincidence we were galloping in the direction I had meant to take anyway.

Except there are no coincidences. Just unexpected glimpses of the hidden Pattern.

As the horses continued to run, my body remembered to relax and sit upright. Briga emulated me. She hardly needed a model, though. She had excellent balance right from the start.

Ahead of us Grannus was making a heroic effort to bring the chestnut mare under control. From the motions of his shoulders I could tell that he was sawing the reins, pulling the bit back and forth in her mouth.

If I were a horse I would hate that.

"Ease up on the reins, Grannus!" I shouted to him.

His voice came back to me in gasps. "That'll make her run faster, you fool!"

Grannus must be very frightened to forget himself so far as to call me a fool. "Trust me!" I cried.

To my relief, the frantic motions of his arms and shoulders slowed; stopped. After a few moments the mare slowed; stopped. He turned her around with little difficulty and rode back to us. She was soaking wet with sweat beneath her shaggy coat, as I was beneath my clothes.

"Whew," said Grannus.

"There was no need to go racing off like that."

"Tell the horse, not me. Why do you keep getting me into these situations, Ainvar?"

"You can hardly blame the mare for running when you gave her such a fright."

"*I* gave *her* a fright?"

"You leaped onto her back like a lion dropping onto a horse from a tree," Briga interjected.

There were no lions in Hibernia. There were not any in Gaul, either. The only lions I knew anything about were those the Romans had brought from Africa. Yet my senior wife could envision the interactions of prey and predator in a land she had never seen, and use these to understand the emotions of a horse in Hibernia.

Briga was an astonishing person.

No category adequately embraced the wide range of her gifts. She was like a newly created spirit appearing for the first time in Thisworld. Yet she accommodated herself so quickly, so easily, to the gray horse, one might think she had learned to ride in a prior life.

*No,* I told myself sternly. Do not be fooled into believing in past lives or future lives. That is just wishful thinking.

We soon caught up with the fishermen, who had set out on foot before us. I offered to let three of them ride behind us on our horses, but the man with the broken fingers demurred. "No point in getting ourselves hurt worse than we already were," he said cheerfully.

The remark did not cheer me, since at that moment my mount began to prance and snatch at the bit in a most unsettling way. The horses were fresh and unwilling to stand still for long.

The fishermen suggested we ride across country in a northerly direction until we came to the river Liffey, which rose somewhere in the mountains to the southeast and meandered in a large loop across the Plain of Broad Spears before turning toward the great bay on the coast. "Once you reach the river, just follow it to our settlement," said the man with the broken fingers.

"Mind the footing, though," another man added. "The Liffey's tidal; there's a powerful inflow from the sea when the tide turns. Beware of the marshes. You could drown before you know what's happened."

We thanked the fishermen for their advice. As we rode away from them Briga remarked, "I've been to the source of the Liffey, Ainvar."

"You have? You never told me."

Her nose crinkled in the way I loved. "Oh, Ainvar," she laughed, "I don't tell you everything."

I could hardly reproach her, since I did not tell her everything, either.

The kingdom of the Laigin spread out before us, a tapestry of meadowland occasionally lifting into low, rolling hills. Like Fíachu, the other chieftains had built their strongholds on the high ground so they could watch for aggressors. Their lookouts must have seen us ride by, but no one hailed us.

We kept the horses at a gallop. My big dark horse stood me in good stead. As long as we were on open ground the chestnut surged ahead of him. When we came to seas of bracken and nettles he unhesitatingly breasted through while the other horses hesitated.

He was a chieftainly horse.

We were crossing a part of our tribeland I had not visited before. I observed with interest that the range of heavily forested mountains that separated us from Cohern's clan also guarded the Plain of Broad Spears from the sea. Seen from a distance, it looked like an impenetrable barrier. From what others had told me, most of Hibernia was either heavily forested or mountainous or both, with plains only in the central region. The topography was designed by nature to keep the various kingdoms isolated from one another. Given the warlike nature of the Gaels, this was a good thing.

As we galloped on, my muscles began to ache. I knew my bones would protest in the morning—whatever the morning might bring. But we had no time to lose; the winter's day would be short. Briga kept calling to me, "Hurry, Ainvar. Hurry!"

Long before we reached the river we felt its influence. The horses' hooves sank into softer soil. They were breathing hard from their long run, so in spite of Briga I drew rein and slowed to a walk to allow them to recover.

To allow us to recover.

The air smelled rank. And damp, in spite of the cold. Listen! I commanded my ears.

In Gaul I had known the great rivers; the sacred rivers. Their voices had been as familiar to me as those of my friends. The Loire whispered, the Seine murmured.

The Liffey was different.

She sang to herself with a hundred different voices. She laughed and wept and giggled and threatened and shouted and hummed. The Liffey was a capricious creature. Kissed by the dim winter sun, she sparkled flirtatiously. Moments later she turned sullen, nursing secrets in her dark heart. She meandered this way and that, sometimes rushing forward, sometimes sauntering along as if she had no place special to go. But she did; she was irreversibly destined for the sea. That was her Pattern.

"We're all right now," I told Briga and Grannus. "From here on, the river will guide us."

The songs of the Liffey were accompanied by the cry of the curlew and the warbling of the thrush. Unseen frogs croaked counterpoint. As the river swung toward the east seagulls appeared, alighting on the riverbank to squabble over anything edible. Farther on we surprised a pair of fully grown otters frisking in the river like children. To avoid disturbing them, I turned my horse aside and led my companions a short distance inland.

The terrain changed. A detritus of waterworn gravel was piled in long ridges that extended like fingers into areas of low-lying marsh. "We had best be careful along here," I told the others. "Remember what the fishermen said?"

Briga spoke up. "Trust the horses, they know what's safe and what isn't." She stroked the neck of the gray. "Trust the horses," she repeated softly.

We rejoined the Liffey downstream at another bend in the river. We had been riding for a long time; I was thirsty and the sight and sound of water made it worse. I longed to drink. But if I dismounted I would have to get back on. My eyes searched in both directions for a useful log or boulder. They found only reeds.

The dark horse stretched his neck and yearned toward the water. The chestnut mare was fighting for her head. Grannus struggled valiantly, but when she got the bit in her teeth a single bound took her to water's edge. She plunged her muzzle greedily into the water. The other horses followed. We could no more stop them than stop the flow of the Liffey.

Briga flung one leg across the gray horse's neck and slid down. Gathering up her clothing in both hands, she waded into the river. The bitterly cold water did not seem to bother her any more than it had bothered the otters.

"Beware of the current!" I called. Briga merely shook her head. While I watched anxiously, she bent over and touched her lips to the surface of the river; more of a caress than a drink. She looked up smiling. "It's so sweet, Ainvar. Do come and have a taste."

The sound of the horses sucking in great mouthfuls of water was hard enough to resist, but it was impossible to resist Briga. I slid to the ground. My feet stung from the shock; my knees almost buckled. Instead of wading out into the river I rather painfully squatted down at water's edge and made a cup of my two hands. Grannus did the same.

Briga splashed back to join us. Wringing water from her skirts, she said, "The river isn't cold, Ainvar, once you get used to it."

I doubt if any river would dare to chill my Briga.

Humans and horses together, we drank as if the Liffey flowed with wine.

Afterward we relieved ourselves, then walked back and forth for a little while, easing our limbs. When it was time to remount, the dark horse seemed taller than I remembered. It was a long way up to his back. I could grasp his mane with both hands and pull myself up like climbing a rope . . . but no sooner did the thought cross my mind than he laid his ears back and stepped sideways. As clearly as if he spoke in words, my horse was telling me he did not like the idea.

Fortunately there is more than one way to mount a horse.

Once again, Grannus lifted Briga onto the gray. When he turned to the chestnut mare I warned, "Don't try to get on the way you did last time. She'll never stand for it. "

"Have you a better suggestion, Ainvar?"

"Actually, I do. I'll even demonstrate." I led my horse into the shallows and then downriver to a point where the bank rose straight up from water's edge. The Liffey was liquid ice. When the water came almost to my horse's chest and the current was tugging at us both, I clambered up onto the bank above him. From there it was a simple matter to ease myself down onto his back.

"See how easy that was, Grannus? Now you do it."

The chestnut mare danced and fretted, but the water impeded her. Grannus managed to get on without a repetition of the last time.

We resumed our journey along the Liffey's erratic course. Eventually the river grew broader, spilling out onto the floodplain. The sun was low in the sky when we came upon a large midden of empty shells, evidence of a nearby tribe that made shellfish a staple of their diet. Grannus's stomach growled. "Can't we halt for a while and eat that bread and cheese?"

"Not yet," I told him. "The mouth of the river can't be far ahead."

When the last rays of the winter sun were smothered by a mottled twilight, Grannus grumbled, "It's almost dark, Ainvar, and I've got used to having a layer of thatch over my head at night. We'd better get there soon."

"You sound like an old woman," I scoffed.

Then we heard the scream.

# *chapter* XXIV

THE CRY SHATTERED THE TWILIGHT INTO A THOUSAND ICY slivers. It might have been the ghastly shriek of a man being torn in half. Anyone familiar with Caesar knew the sound of agony.

Our horses shied violently. Grannus hit the ground with a thud. Briga and I brought our mounts under control, though they stood with their ears stiffly pricked in the direction of the scream. The direction in which we were traveling.

Cursing under his breath, Grannus got to his feet. He snatched at the mare's dangling reins. She snorted and danced out of reach. "Let me," said Briga.

She urged the gray horse forward, reached out, and caught hold of the mare's reins. "Take off your sword, Grannus," Briga said softly. Quietly. "Now give it to Ainvar."

The sword was heavy in my hand. Alien. My fingers did not know the shape of the hilt.

"All right," Briga told Grannus, "get back on your horse."

He looked around but saw nothing he could use as a mounting block. "How?"

Briga sighed. In just such a way, women must have sighed over the inadequacies of their menfolk since before the before. "Lean your chest against your horse's ribs," she directed, "and reach across her back. Gently, Grannus! Stroke her opposite side a time or two. That's fine. Now jump as high as you can and use your arms to pull yourself up and over."

As long as Briga was holding her reins, the skittish mare was willing to stand. When Grannus was seated on her back I handed him his sword. Carefully. He replaced it in the sheath. Carefully.

Only then did Briga relinquish the mare's reins to him.

I did not ask her how—or when—she had learned the trick of mounting a horse. I doubt if she knew.

My more immediate consideration was the scream. Were we riding into terrible trouble? My head thought we were, but my heart was in charge now. *Maia. Cormiac Ru.* Labraid, for that matter. I gave the dark horse a kick in the ribs and sent him cantering forward.

"How fast can you draw that sword if you have to?" I called to Grannus.

"Fast enough," he called back.

I told Briga to stay close to me, though the admonition was unnecessary. The horses bunched together of their own accord. The gray and the chestnut hung back just enough to let my dark horse take the lead, which he did unhesitatingly. Sitting astride his warm back, feeling his muscles flex and gather beneath me, I felt like part of him. Stronger than I really was.

My head wondered: If I had not been born with the druid's gift, might I have become a chieftain of the Carnutes and ridden into battle on a horse like this one?

Then I recalled how heavy the sword had felt in my hand. How alien.

Our destination was the tribe of Dubh Linn, the people of the Black Pool. Their chieftain was Rígan, whom I once met at the Lughnasa festival. Fíachu disliked Rígan. Given his own ambitions, Fíachu would resent anyone whose name meant "little king."

If Rígan was taking good care of my people I was prepared to love him like a brother.

The fishermen had boasted of the size of their tribe. Their territory extended from well above the Black Pool to the southernmost shore of the bay. "All of it prosperous and peaceful," they had assured us.

But we had heard that scream.

In an edgy voice, Grannus inquired, "Are you sure we're going the right way?"

A man on a horse is much taller than he would be on foot. And I rode the tallest horse. Glittering through the twilight like malevolent red eyes, I could see fires ahead. "I'm sure," I told Grannus.

All around us and behind us was darkness. Somewhere in that darkness was the thing that had screamed and the thing that had caused the scream. Ahead lay a settlement with fires and shelter. At that moment I did not care if the inhabitants were friendly or not.

I urged my horse to a gallop.

Presently we reached the first fire. It was, I later learned, at the western perimeter of Rígan's clanland. Two armed warriors huddled beside the fire, blowing on their hands to keep them warm. When we rode up they grabbed their weapons. "What do you want?" one demanded. There was a faint quaver in his voice that made me suspect he had heard the scream, too.

I drew rein. "We seek Rígan's stronghold. His people have given shelter to members of our tribe who were injured at sea, and we've come to take them home."

The warriors beckoned us closer so they could study our faces in the firelight. They looked longest at Briga. Oddly, the fact that there were three of us seemed to reassure them. "Go on, then," they told us. "Straight ahead, it's not very far."

Before we rode away I could not resist asking, "Did either of you hear a scream a little while ago?"

The men exchanged glances. One muttered a Gaelic phrase I had not heard before; it sounded like *bawn shee.* The other insisted, far too hastily, "We didn't hear a thing."

When we were out of earshot Grannus told me, "I don't like any part of this." Neither did I, but I kept my thoughts to myself.

Presently we passed an outcropping of rock on the south bank of the river. Beyond lay Rígan's stronghold. The fort differed substantially from that of Fíachu, having neither a protective ditch nor an earthwork embankment, only a palisade of woven wattles—interlaced rods of willow and hazel. There was a pervasive smell from the nearby mudflats.

At the palisade gate two more guards challenged us. Again I explained our mission; again they looked at us searchingly; again we were, with some reluctance, passed through.

There were enough fires within the compound to provide adequate light for my eyes to make their report to my head. I concluded that timber must be in short supply along the coast. The lodges were made of wattles plastered with mud from the river, and devoid of any ornamentation. The chieftain's lodge was identifiable only by its size. We rode toward it at a walk.

A man mantled in a magnificent sealskin cloak was standing in the doorway. He wore an exceedingly grim expression; his figure was rigid with tension. When he got a good look at us he visibly relaxed. "I am Rígan," he announced, "chief of the tribe of Dubh Linn, and this is the kingdom of—"

Interrupting him was a serious breach of tradition, but I could not wait while he recited his lineage. "You know me, Rígan, I'm Ainvar of the Slea Leathan. We've come for our people."

He peered up at me. "Ainvar?"

"It is."

He had a quick head. "Then you must mean the three from the boat. How did you know they were here?"

"Some fishermen from your tribe came to ask my wife to heal their injuries. They told us."

He gave a terse nod. "You'd best come inside, then." From his tone I could not tell if he had bad news for us or not.

I asked, "Will someone look after our horses?"

Rígan gave a shout and a boy came running from another lodge. I stiffly dismounted and surrendered the reins of the dark horse. Briga told the lad, "Rub these animals all over with dry blankets. Then give them just a few mouthfuls of water. Don't let them drink deeply yet, not until they've had some rest."

How did she know how to care for exhausted horses?

The inside of Rígan's lodge was already overfilled when we arrived. Crammed with weapons and lobster pots and chests and cooking utensils, plus a loom, a hen box, an untidy pile of rescued driftwood to use in making repairs, several women who could be either wives or bondwomen, and a swarm of small children. Whatever else he might be, the little king was prolific.

At his signal, a harried-looking female of indeterminate age edged her way toward us through the crowd. One could not help but admire the way she skillfully avoided spilling the brimming basin she was carrying. As I was washing my hands I asked Rígan, "Are they alive?"

He knew who I meant. "They're alive."

Briga gave an audible sigh of relief.

"But they're in bad shape," Rígan went on. "They're emaciated, and the one called 'the Speaker' told us they'd been attacked a number of times."

At that moment the details were unimportant; I just wanted to see them. To see Maia again. "We can talk later, Rígan. First, please take my wife and me to our children."

Our children.

"They're in another lodge," he said, "and may be asleep by now."

"You weren't."

"I . . . ah . . . thought I heard something."

I was torn between my desire to see Maia and Cormiac again and an almost equally compelling desire to solve the mystery of the scream. "We heard something too, Rígan; a terrible cry that frightened our horses. Do you know what it was?"

Instead of answering, he took me by the elbow and steered me toward the door.

The chieftain led us to a lodge almost at the edge of the river. The smell of mud and fish and water was stronger there. A fire within the lodge was burning low, creating more shadows than light. An old man and woman sat huddled together on a bench by the hearth. When we entered they got to their feet.

"This is Ainvar of the Slea Leathan," Rígan told them. "Let him see the people you're caring for."

The old man thrust a bundle of rushes dipped in pitch into the fire. The rushlight flared. Holding the torch aloft, he led us to a pallet of woven wattles upon which lay a figure wrapped in a blanket. In the smoky light from the torch it was hard to make out details, but the figure looked long. Tall. "Cormiac?" I said tentatively.

My voice startled the sleeper, who awoke with a grunt. He threw aside the blanket and sat up. It was Labraid Loingseach.

"Ainvar?" he asked groggily. "Is it really you?"

"Ainvar and Briga," I replied, squatting on my heels beside his bed. I tried not to show how appalled I was by his appearance. Onuava's big strong son had been reduced to skin and bone. "We've come to take you home," I said.

He threw both scrawny arms around me. Then he winced; the result, I learned later, of a festering wound in his shoulder.

Briga went on to the next pallet. I heard her say "Maia?" in a hopeful-fearful voice. Gently disengaging from Labraid's clutches, I joined her. She called Maia's name again. There was a stirring under the blanket. A faint yet deep male voice said, "Cormiac Ru."

And so it was.

I snatched the rushlight from the old man and held it up so we could get a good look at the Red Wolf. He was even thinner than Labraid and his features were contorted with pain. My nose detected the odor of putrid flesh. A lesser man might already have been dead.

The fire in Cormiac's eyes was not a reflection of the torch, but of his iron will to survive.

"I salute you as a free person, Ainvar," he whispered.

I wanted to emulate Labraid; grab Cormiac and hug him with all my might. He was too badly hurt for that, so I contented myself with grasping his hand. It was a bundle of bones loosely held together by flesh no thicker than a fish skin. "I was afraid we'd never see you again."

The gray eyes looked past me, seeking Briga. When they found her his pain-wracked features relaxed. "You shouldn't worry," he said in a slightly stronger voice. "I'll never be far from you and yours."

She bent down and pressed her lips against his forehead.

We turned to the third bed. I raised the rushlight higher. With trembling hands, Briga folded back the blanket, waking the sleeper beneath.

Who stared up at us.

We stared down.

At the long face, the high-bridged nose. The curly black stubble sprouting on jaw and chin. I did not recognize that particular face but I recognized the race from which it sprang.

I almost dropped the torch.

## *chapter* XXV

On rare occasions surprise can transcend shock, and so it was with me. When I discovered a male Roman where I expected to find my beautifully remembered daughter my brain did not freeze, it raced, offering me a dozen fantastic explanations. None of them remotely feasible.

"Who are you?" I demanded in Latin.

Briga was shouting at me, shouting at him, frantic with distress. "Where's Maia, what's he done with her? What have you done with her! I want my daughter!" Her sublime serenity was a thing of the past.

The Roman gaped at us.

Labraid was struggling to his feet. "We don't have her, Ainvar."

I lost control of my own emotions then. "You went to get her, didn't you?" I yelled at him. "What happened? Where is she? Who's this Roman maggot and what's he done with her? Tell me!" I grabbed Labraid by the shoulders; he winced for the second time.

From Cormiac's bed a faint voice said, "Don't blame them, Ainvar. It couldn't be helped. We never found Maia."

Briga began to cry. Little silent sobs, with her hands over her mouth.

"All right." I made myself take a slow, deep breath. "All right. Tell us everything. Not you, Labraid. Cormiac."

Before the Red Wolf could summon breath to speak, Briga lowered her hands. Her voice was shaky but resolute. "Not now, Ainvar. We're exhausted and these lads are ill. What matters now is that they've come back to us; explanations can wait. I'll do what I can to make them more comfortable and then we should let them sleep."

It was a brave and a compassionate decision on her part. Briga has always been both.

The old couple who were caring for the three injured men offered us their hospitality as well, which was fortunate because there was no room left in the chieftain's lodge. The old woman was as thin as her shadow. Her husband was so deaf he did not speak, he shouted. Neither seemed to mind having more mouths to feed. We were given a generous meal of gray mullet, bass, and a boiled seaweed called "bladderwrack." When we finished eating I lay down on a pallet made of rushes piled with blankets and invited my wife into my arms. Tired as we were, neither of us slept much. Briga was making preparations for tomorrow in her head, while in mine I was puzzling over a new mystery.

When he first saw us, Rígan had looked relieved even before we identified ourselves. Which meant we were not what he was expecting.

What had he been expecting?

And what had made that fearful cry?

At some time I must have fallen asleep, because I awoke in the morning so stiff I could hardly move. My body was a log with no give in it. I ached in places I never knew existed. Getting to my feet was prolonged torture, with new discoveries of pain every time I moved.

If anyone needed Briga's ministrations at that moment, I did. She, however, was totally occupied with caring for the invalids. I saw her bending over Cormiac's bed. Moving like a thousand-year-old man, I creaked across the lodge to her side. "How are they this morning?"

"Better, now that you're here," the Red Wolf replied with his eyes fixed on my senior wife. His voice was minimally stronger, and as deep as ever. He was still lying down, though both Labraid and the Roman were up. They sat on either side of the hearth, eating a fish stew redolent of the sea.

Daylight streaming through the doorway gave me a clearer view of the Roman. In my time I had seen far too many of his race; to me they were simply The Enemy; faceless, shapeless, characterless. Repellent.

But on his own, the Roman became an individual. I guessed him to be about ten years younger than my true age. More or less. All Romans looked alike to me so I could not be sure.

Naturally bony, but far less thin than our young men, he appeared quite fit. His sleeveless tunic revealed overdeveloped musculature in his shoulders and arms—especially the right one, the sword arm. A jagged white scar on his forehead and a crooked jaw that had been broken some time in the past confirmed my suspicion that he was a warrior.

When our eyes met he said, in the language of Latium, "I am Probus Seggo, son of Justinius, magistrate of Genova." In spite of his battered appearance the Latin he spoke was clear and precise, unlike the slurred gutturals of ordinary Roman foot soldiers.

"Your family means nothing to me," I said. "What are you doing with Cormiac and Labraid?"

Careful not to twist his upper body, Probus set his bowl to one side. "I grew up in Genova, and—"

I raised one hand to stop him. "I don't want your personal history. Just an answer to my question."

"But Genova is part of the answer. The city is a seaport on the Mediterranean"—he gave the Mid-Earth Sea its Latin name—"and—"

"I'm familiar with the place," I snapped, and stopped there. You should never tell the enemy more than he needs to know.

When Caesar's campaign in Gaul was just getting under way I had traveled through Latium with Vercingetorix. Disguised as merchants, we had crossed the land of the Ligurians and ventured southward along the coast toward Rome. Our intention had been to assess the forces arrayed against us. How long ago that seemed!

And how woefully we had underestimated the intentions of the abominable Caesar.

To Cormiac I said, "It's hard to believe you two went all the way to Genova."

"We didn't. On our own, we got only as far as the channel between Albion and Gaul."

"Where did you get a boat?"

Labraid answered; indicating, with an airy wave of his hand, the precincts of Dubh Linn. "Oh, that was easy, Ainvar. With my skills of persuasion we acquired a seaworthy fishing vessel and several experienced boatmen so we didn't have to do all the work ourselves."

"That's not what happened," Cormiac interjected.

"Ssssh," said Briga. "Lie still while I clean your wounds."

"And close your mouth to keep your teeth warm," Labraid added. The old animosity had surfaced between them, then; I was hardly surprised. Many days spent together in close quarters will make lifelong friends or lifelong enemies.

"Then you'd best tell me what did happen, Labraid."

My firm tone dampened his bravado. Slightly. "Well, Ainvar, we didn't exactly get our boat here. Rígan's people offered us hospitality when we arrived, but they claimed they had no boats to spare."

"Because you demanded one instead of requesting it," said the voice from the bed.

Labraid ignored him. "Anyway, we crossed the Liffey at the Ford of the Hurdles and—"

"Ford of the Hurdles?"

"The locals have made a sort of causeway to provide safe footing for their sheep when they drive them across the Liffey. It's made of layers of woven panels they call 'hurdles.' It works well; we went from one bank to the other without getting wet. The tribe on the north side of the Liffey were far more generous than Rígan's."

"Generous after we paid them," the Red Wolf commented.

"Keep still," said Briga. "Or must I tie you down?"

"You can put him out in the cold for all I care," Labraid said. "That'll quiet him down."

I ignored the remark. "Tell me how you paid for the boat, Labraid."

He rolled his eyes in my senior wife's direction. "We, ah, took a few valuables with us when we left the clanhold."

"Not we; you," said the voice from the bed. "He took your bowls."

There was a sharp intake of breath from Briga. "My enameled bowls!"

"It was none of my doing," Cormiac assured her. "Labraid insisted on doing all the negotiating. I didn't know we had the bowls with us until he pulled them out of his pack to display."

"I'd cleverly held them back," said Labraid, "to use as a final bargaining tool. It worked too, just as I thought it would. The tribe on the north bank of the Liffey had never seen anything like those bowls. They thought they were beautiful."

"They *were* beautiful," mourned Briga. "How could you steal them from me?"

"I didn't think you'd give them to me if I asked for them," he replied, unabashed.

It was time to move the conversation on. "So, Labraid, you traded my wife's bowls for a boat and crew?"

"The bowls, and some other things. You know." Another vague wave of the hand.

This was not the time to ask what else he had stolen, or from whom. The matter would be dealt with later and restitution made. I could not condone dishonorable behavior; we were Slea Leathan.

"Go on, Labraid. You acquired a boat. What happened next?"

"We set sail for the east."

"Did you make landfall on Albion?"

"We didn't need to. We took fresh water aboard at Mona," said the voice from the bed.

*Mona!* The name evoked a memory long buried beneath the wreckage of our lives. Menua, my teacher, had trained at the great druidical college on Mona. In my youth I heard him speak of the dark groves of that island, the "sacred gloom" in which extraordinary sacrifices were offered and unparalleled transactions with the Otherworld concluded.

Foolishly, I had never asked Menua the location of the island. I suppose I was too eager to get on with magic of my own. Our lives are shaped by the questions we ask. And even more important, by the questions we fail to ask.

When my clan fled Gaul the sacred island of the druids might have given us refuge, yet by that time I had forgotten about it entirely.

Years of constant anxiety can erode the mind.

"Mona lies to the west of Albion," Labraid said, "and almost in a direct line from here. It was my idea to go ashore. We obtained enough water to avoid landing on Albion at all. Wasn't that clever? I'm not just a warrior, Ainvar, I can make plans as well as any—"

I cut across Labraid's self-congratulatory spate to ask Cormiac if there were still druids on Mona.

Before he could reply, Probus said in Latin, "They are the only permanent inhabitants of the island."

I was startled to realize the Roman understood my language. "What do you know of Mona?" I asked him in Latin.

"Probus went there to spy on the druids," intoned the voice from the bed.

My head was concentrating on the ramifications of the Roman's revelation. If he was familiar with the basic tongue of the Celts I would no longer have to struggle along in my half-forgotten Latin. Using the dialect of the Slea Leathan, I asked, "Can you understand what I'm saying now?"

He nodded assent.

"And were you a spy?"

"I was an officer in the army of Rome," he replied with dignity, effortlessly switching between languages. His accent was exotic but comprehensible. "Our purpose was to extend the benefits of our civilization to the rest of the world."

"Pompous ass," Labraid remarked. He said it with a smile, though, as if this were an old joke between them.

Probus grinned back at him. "Barbarian savage," he retorted amiably.

Not the least of my surprises that day was the discovery that Labraid had made a friend. Apparently not everyone found him as obnoxious as I did. Of course, the friend was a Roman, and they have no judgment when it comes to a man's character.

While Briga completed her examination of Cormiac I asked Probus, "How is it that you can speak our language?"

"As I tried to explain before, my father was the magistrate of Genova."

My head tardily realized that Probus might not be a Roman after all; not a citizen of Rome, that is. But there was no doubt he belonged to the Latin race. As far as I was concerned, they were all Romans and equally guilty. Maggots swarming over the corpse of Gaul.

Probus said, "Growing up in and around a major seaport, I met many foreigners. I had been born with a gift for languages, so by the time I could walk I was chattering away with the barbarian traders. I can understand most of the Gaulish tribes, in fact, though a few sound like stones rattling in my ear."

This was the second time he had referred to our people as barbarians. Labraid did not seem to mind; in fact, he thought it funny. I was deeply insulted. "Barbarian" is a term the Hellenes apply without prejudice to any who do not speak Greek, but the Romans use the word as a pejorative. I clenched my teeth and remained silent, determined to follow this mystery to its unraveling.

"When I became a man," Probus continued, "I refused to enter my father's profession. I was too fond of adventure to sit on a bench all day adjudicating petty quarrels. My father was furious with me, but my mother persuaded him to purchase a commission for me in one of the Roman legions—which conferred automatic Roman citizenship."

So Probus was a Roman after all.

"I was posted to Gaul," he said, "where I served under Lieutenant-General Antistius Reginus."

Sometimes the body reacts before the head. My fingers scrabbled for the knife in my belt. Reginus had led the most brutal of the legions involved in the siege of Alesia.

Probus was indeed a warrior. His sharp eyes observed the gesture before my head was aware of it. "That will not be necessary, Ainvar. I am a deserter from the army of Rome, as your kinsmen will testify."

"But you were at Alesia!"

"I was, though I regret it now. There is no excuse for what was done at Alesia."

My ears could not believe what they were hearing. "You *regret*?"

"Caesar claimed all things are justified in time of war, but I disagree. The prolonged siege of Alesia, the deliberate starvation of all the women and children . . . in my opinion that was a step too far. No one was meant to survive."

"My clan survived," said Cormiac, "thanks to Ainvar. I told you about it, Probus."

Probus raked my face with his eyes. Realization was dawning in those eyes. "Are you *the* Ainvar? The man who brought the statue to life?"

"I am Ainvar, yes."

The Roman's swarthy skin paled. "Then I knew of you long before I met these two; knew of you by deed if not by name. My cohort was sent to retrieve a band of German cavalry who fled from the battle. They had been so badly frightened they soiled themselves. By the time we caught up with them they had half killed their horses and were almost incoherent. They claimed to have been attacked by a man who breathed fire and a stone god as tall as a tree."

I bit the inside of my cheek to keep from smiling. I refused to smile at any Roman. Bared teeth I would offer them, but never a smile. "Breathing fire is not within my gift, Probus. As for the stone figure, it did not come to my shoulder. Neither of us physically attacked anyone."

"Perhaps not, but you attacked their minds. That is where the damage was done."

The Roman was smarter than he looked.

A sharp elbow dug into my ribs. "Ask him about Maia."

"I was just getting around to it," I assured Briga.

"You were not. You were talking about any and every other thing and coming nowhere near the point. Probus, do you know what happened to my daughter? Please tell me, I can't stand this any longer."

"I wish I could help you," he said. "But I understand she was sold as an infant? Probably through a slave market?"

"She was." Briga's soft voice was almost inaudible. "We could never prove it, but everyone knew."

"Then all I have to offer is my sympathy." Probus sounded sincerely regretful. "Small children rarely survive that experience."

I thought of Lakutu, as resilient as the willow tree; but she had been an adult when the Romans captured and enslaved her. Maia had been a tiny little creature with dimpled knees and . . . I fought back the pain, lest it swallow me.

"Maia died a long time ago," announced the voice from the bed. It rang with absolute certainty.

Until that moment I had still nurtured a spark of hope. But a druid recognizes truth when he hears it.

With the extinction of hope came a strange relief. The spark ceased to scorch my heart; shapechanged into tender memories, as rain makes flowers bloom in a desert.

I put both arms around Briga and drew her tight against my chest. "Let Maia go now," I whispered into my wife's hair. "Let our little girl go."

Over her head I met the sloe-black eyes of Probus.

They glittered with tears.

# *chapter* XXVI

"WE ARE NOT ALL AS BAD AS YOU IMAGINE," PROBUS SAID TO ME later that day. "Frankly, I should be much more frightened of you than you are of me."

The two of us were walking beside the Liffey. The atmosphere in the lodge had become so foul with the smell of pus and burning herbs that the stinking mudflats along the river were infinitely preferable. The Roman was suffering from an injury to his back, but Briga said the damage was to the muscles rather than the spine. "A little gentle exercise would be good for you," she had told him. "And for you, too," she added to Grannus and me.

Grannus left the lodge with us, but as soon as we came to an overturned fishing boat he sat down. Planted his big feet wide, rested his forearms on his thick thighs. "This is as far as I go," he announced.

So Probus and I sauntered on together.

The winter's day was overcast; no hint of sunlight in any direction. We might have been walking beneath an overturned gray bowl. The wind was out of the northeast, bringing a sporadic pelting of sleet.

The curse of the Túatha Dé Danann, I said to myself.

I observed that the south bank of the river included a long ridge of stone and gravel, an extension of the outcropping we had passed on our approach. The ridge was mantled with hazel and hemmed by willow scrub. Below the ridge was a natural ford where a causeway had been constructed: Labraid's "Ford of the Hurdles." The permeable quality of interwoven rods of hazel and willow allowed water to flow through so the river did not wash the man-made path away, making it safe for beasts and men.

While my eyes examined the ford's ingenious construction, my head worked out the reasons behind it, predicated upon the nature of the place and the nature of its inhabitants.

From our hosts I had learned there were no horses in Dubh Linn except our own. The natives considered boats the superior form of transportation. This affected their lives in a number of ways. An oak forest lay south of the settlement, but harvesting its timber would require a large number of men to drag heavily laden sledges overland. They chose to build with local materials such as hazel and willow instead.

When Rígan's people traveled inland they had to walk. They rarely ventured beyond their own territory, however—and why should they? The largest portion of their needs was met by river and sea. In all seasons they feasted on fresh- and saltwater fish, oysters, mussels, cockles, lobsters, prawns, and the meat and eggs of seabirds. Edible seaweeds were boiled, chewed, or used as flavoring. Seals, which provided both skins to wear and oil for lamps, were common in the estuary. In addition to this bounty the people of Dubh Linn raised sheep and a small herd of cattle, and exchanged their surplus with the tribe north of the river for grain. Hence the ford.

The wind was dying down. Probus and I walked slowly, shoulder to shoulder. Talking with him was difficult for me. Conversation between us was bound to be colored by spilled blood.

"I'm not frightened of you in the slightest," I told the Roman in response to his remark. "But after what Caesar did to us, you can understand my aversion to your race."

"Sometimes I have an aversion to them myself. In particular but not in general, you understand. Taken all in all, the tribes of Latium are as good and as bad as any other."

"My senior wife might believe you."

"Meaning you do not, Ainvar?"

"I've had more experience than Briga. She tries to see the best in everyone. She wanted to forgive Crom Daral for stealing our child because he had a sickness in his head."

The Roman said, "I do not understand how she could ever forgive him."

"On that at least we are agreed, then. If I'd caught up with the man I would have killed him on the spot. But my Briga is unique."

"I can well believe you. She knows what I am, yet she is as kind to me as to her own kinsmen."

I turned to face him. "And what are you, Probus? You called yourself a deserter. Cormiac called you a spy. You admit you're a citizen of Rome, which means I have no reason to trust you. So what should I call you?"

"How about 'friend'?"

My harsh laugh sounded more like a dog's bark. "That's impossible." I resumed walking.

Undeterred, he kept pace with me. "Ainvar, I have done my best to be a friend to Labraid and Cormiac. Without me they would not be alive today."

"What do you mean?"

"It is a long story, and complicated."

"I have time. And I'm used to complications."

"Did you ever hear of a Celtic warlord called Commius?"

"Of course I did. Caesar had no legitimate authority in Gaul, but that didn't stop him from proclaiming Commius king of the Atrebates. King indeed! Commius was a traitor to his race."

"He was," Probus agreed. "Caesar installed Commius for one purpose only: to convince other Gaulish leaders of the wisdom of allying themselves with Rome. Commius, whom Caesar made a great show of befriending, was to be his emissary, singing his praises and making the path smoother for him. That was only one element in Caesar's overall plan, however.

"Accompanied by one legion and his favorite tribune, he made a brief visit to Albion a couple of years before the fall of Alesia. It was to be a reconnaissance rather than an invasion, but things went badly from the beginning. At first Caesar's troops were mauled by the natives. Ultimately they beat them back, a truce was hastily proclaimed, and Caesar withdrew. He did not intend to leave it at that, though. Not Caesar."

Here at last was another part of the story. If one is patient enough, most things are revealed in time. "What was there for him in Albion?" I inquired. "Aside from tin, that is."

"Albion has other resources, but they were not what drew Caesar. He wanted Albion for the same reason he wanted Gaul: as trophies he could brandish in the Roman Senate to consolidate his drive for political power."

"So hundreds of thousands of people had to be sacrificed to place a laurel wreath on his bald head." The words were bitter as bile in my mouth.

"Surely, Ainvar, you have lived long enough to know that men who seek power do not see things that way. They invariably claim the most noble reasons. They want to redress injustice or help the common people." Probus accompanied this last with a sardonic smile.

"The following summer Caesar sailed back to Albion with five legions and two thousand cavalry. A large army spearheaded by the tribe of the Catuvellauni was waiting for them. A summer of battles followed, with victory going sometimes to one side, sometimes to the other. Meanwhile, the situation in Gaul was growing critical, with new revolts breaking out, so in early autumn Caesar left Albion and returned to Gaul. The siege of Alesia followed soon after.

"I had arrived in Gaul as hot to fight as any man. Young blood boils easily." Probus gave an unexpected chuckle. "Your friend back there would have a hard time in the legions. Sitting down was not an option. Legionaries were primarily infantry, which meant they had to be able to carry all of their equipment and three days' supplies on their backs while marching double-time for ten miles, then fighting a battle. As an officer I was given a horse but that was the only concession to my rank. I still had to prove myself, and I did. By the siege of Alesia I was inured to the cries of the dying and the stench of bowels opening in death.

"After the fortress fell, Reginus took his legion back to Rome to participate in the triumphal celebrations. I did not go with them. Having revealed my familiarity with Gaulish languages, I was seconded to serve as an interpreter in the surrender negotiations with the surviving allies of Vercingetorix. In truth there was little negotiating done. We won; they lost. They lost everything.

"Subsequently I was reassigned to the legion led by Titus Labienus. They were fighting the Bellovaci, the last major tribe holding out against Caesar. Shortly after I arrived Labienus sent me with a band of centurions under the command of Volusenus Quadratus to have a parley with Commius of the Atrebates. With the exception of Volusenus, we did not know that Commius had gone back on his word to Caesar and was actively involved in a conspiracy against him. The parley was a ruse. The real intent was to seize Commius and kill him on the spot. We were not told this ahead of time so that nothing in our demeanor might warn the traitor.

"When Commius and his followers arrived at the arranged meeting place, Volusenus caught him by the hand and shouted at one of the centurions to kill him. Still believing Commius to be a friend of Caesar's, I thought we must have misunderstood the order and put out my arm to stop the centurion. I quickly realized the mistake was mine and urged the centurion forward again, but by that time the followers of Commius had rushed forward to rescue him. In the skirmish that followed Commius received a severe blow to the head. He gave a great cry and fell to the ground. His eyes rolled back in his head and quantities of blood poured from his ears and mouth. Volusenus believed he had suffered a mortal wound and allowed his followers to carry his body away."

Volusenus *believed,* Probus said. Which meant Commius had survived. I was beginning to appreciate the precision with which the Roman chose his words.

"Without the aid of Commius and his Atrebates, the Bellovaci were at last subdued," Probus continued. "Caesar then divided his forces and ordered the obliteration of any remaining pockets of resistance. I saw cruelty on a scale I had never imagined. Terror was the Roman weapon and they wielded it well.

"For a while I feared there might be a black mark against me because of Commius, so I made every effort to prove myself a second time. I did things I do not want to remember now." The Roman's voice was thick in his throat.

My imagination threatened to show me what he might have done. Shuddering, I fought back the impulse.

By this time the two of us had reached what was, obviously, the Black Pool: a large pond formed by the convergence of two smaller rivers flowing from the south and west into the Liffey. The pool was a major resource for

Rígan's people, providing not only fresh drinking water—the tidal Liffey was salt by this point, and undrinkable—but also a secure mooring for boats in need of repair. The Black Pool took its name from the mud on which it was bedded, a clay so dark it denied light to the water. Oddly, the pond did not stink like the mudflats elsewhere. The water here had a clean, sweet smell.

Part of my mind wondered what Briga would make of this place.

Probus was saying, "Apparently my actions during the mopping-up operations in Gaul were sufficient to cancel out any earlier error on my part. I even received a raise in pay and sixty days' leave. I spent them both trying to forget. It takes a lot of wine and women to make a man forget war. But Rome was not through with me. Upon reporting back to the legion I learned I was being reassigned to Albion. Another reward for services rendered," he added in a sarcastic tone.

My attention kept wandering.

Black water, black as death. Yet so sweet. Like little Maia's curls. Staring down at the water, I tried to envision my child dead. Dead. I who had seen so much death was familiar with all the stages. Bloating, decomposition, liquefaction, disintegration. In my bleakest moments I had never before surrendered to this terminal pain, but it was true. And truth must be acknowledged.

"Ainvar?" Probus touched my shoulder, calling me back. "Are you all right?"

"Of course I am. I was just thinking."

"About what?"

How could I explain the inside of my head to a Roman warrior, no matter how clever? "My little girl," I said. "Do you have children?"

"None that I know of."

"It changes everything."

"I am sure it does, Ainvar. Someday I hope to find out."

"You'll go back to Latium, then?"

"No chance of that. I am persona non grata. I will live out my years here."

"It's not a bad place, Hibernia." At least that is what I meant to tell him. Instead I heard myself say, "Eriu."

The ebon surface of the pool rippled as if a wind danced across it. Yet the wind had abated completely. I gave myself a little shake. "Go on, Probus; finish telling me how you got involved with Cormiac and Labraid. Distract me."

"Very well. During his time in Albion Caesar had established several frontier garrisons. A century of veterans from the campaign in Gaul, including myself, were assigned to an outpost on a southern headland. Ostensibly the garrison was a trading post; its actual purpose was to collect intelligence about the native tribes. I was admirably suited for this, since I not only understood Celtic languages but was familiar with their style of trade."

"Did you ever have any business with a man called Goulvan, from Armorica?"

Probus narrowed his eyes. "Let me think; the name sounds vaguely familiar. Was he . . . a gap-toothed fellow with eyes like a fish?"

"The very man," I affirmed.

"Once he tried to sell us spoiled grain and old rope hidden in the coils of new. Anywhere in Latium he would have been hauled up before a magistrate and tried for fraud. We let him go with a stern warning and a promise not to show his face in Albion again unless he had legitimate goods to offer. That did not really matter, of course. Trade was not our true purpose."

"No," I said. Fully aware that my clan may well have been the "legitimate goods" Goulvan hoped to sell to the Romans in order to put himself back in their good graces.

"We learned that the political situation among the tribes of Albion was highly complicated," Probus continued. "The Catuvellauni were the most prominent, but alliances were constantly shifting. Friends today were enemies tomorrow. Chieftains were far less concerned about any threat from Rome than they were about guarding their backs from one another.

"Meanwhile Caesar was going from strength to strength, conquering new territory and overcoming old rivals. We followed the news avidly, basking in Caesar's reflected glory.

"Then we learned that far from being dead, Commius secretly had escaped to Albion, where he had been given sanctuary by the Catuvellauni. When he married a daughter of their king he felt confident enough to surface. As well he might; he had been given enough land to establish a small kingdom of his own and had summoned the surviving Atrebates to join him. United with the Catuvellauni, they made a formidable army indeed. It began to look as if the conquest of Albion might be as difficult as the conquest of Gaul.

"Messages went to Rome asking what Caesar wanted us to do. The reply came back: Send an emissary to Commius. I was the obvious choice."

"Yes," I said.

"I was ordered to convince Commius that Caesar held no grudge against him and had no intention of interfering with his new life. He and his people need not fear any further Roman aggression."

"I assume that was a lie?"

"Not a word of the truth," the Roman affirmed. "The purpose was merely to mollify Commius until Caesar was ready to mount the long-promised full-scale invasion.

"Now I shall tell you an odd thing, Ainvar. In Gaul I had been part of the most successful military campaign since the days of Alexander of Macedon, yet I could not reconcile what I had seen with the grand vision of a Roman empire that Caesar's adherents were positing. I began asking myself questions no soldier should ask."

I pricked up my ears. This was the first time I ever heard a Roman allude to self-doubt. Was it possible they—or at least Probus—were as human as I was?

"I had no difficulty finding Commius," Probus went on, "and almost none in gaining access to him. He remembered as clearly as I did the details of our last meeting. To my embarrassment, he even thanked me for the part I had played in his survival. He listened attentively while I recited my little speech. I could tell he wanted to believe me; it is the nature of Celts to be credulous. One of the men in our garrison—a hard-bitten fellow named Anicius Bellator—used to laugh about it. He claimed their eagerness to be deceived was what made them ripe for the picking."

"Yes," I said.

"But in the end, Ainvar, I could not do it. Is human nature not peculiar? I, who had killed more men than I could remember, balked at being turned into a liar. Perhaps I had spent too much time with the Celts, to whom a man's honor is sacred.

"For whatever reason, I told Commius the truth as I am telling it to you now. He heard me through without comment, thanked me, fed me, and sent me back to the garrison with an escort to make sure no harm came to me on the way. I do not think we would have acted with the same courtesy if the situation were reversed.

"I dutifully reported the first half of my conversation with Commius to my commanding officer. But I never mentioned the second half; the part where I told him the real situation."

"Of course not," I said. Mindful that treachery comes easily to a Roman.

# *chapter* XXVII

AS I LISTENED TO HIS NARRATIVE PROBUS AND I HAD BEEN STROLLING around the rim of the Black Pool. Darkness was rapidly overtaking us. "Briga will be worried if we don't go back soon," I remarked.

"Your wife is a good woman, I would not like to cause her worry."

We began to retrace our steps. I took one last glance at the dark water—and halted without warning.

The sky above us was sagging with clouds yet I could see stars in the water. Stars without number. They were not all white. Some were crimson, some were cobalt, and some glowed with a sulphurous hue I found unsettling. The sky in which they hung was not clear; it was polluted by a sullen reddish glow akin to, but not as clean as, the glow from Teyrnon's forge.

"Do you see that, Probus?"

"See what?"

"Just there; in the water."

"All I see is water."

I rubbed my eyes and looked again. The surface of the pool was an unrelieved, gleaming black.

I was disinclined to question Probus any further that evening. A man's head can absorb only so much at any one time, and I had enough thoughts to be thinking for a while.

We found Labraid with more color in his cheeks and a froth of boasting on his lips. Briga praised Cormiac's improved appetite. "I've never known anyone to be so responsive to my healing," she told me. But that night the Red Wolf did not sleep well. He tossed and turned, muttering feverishly. Sometimes I could pick out a word or two; for the most part he was unintelligible.

"He's been injured in almost every part of his body," Briga told me, "and in spite of all I can do, he's going to be in pain for a long time."

"He is going to live, though?"

"Of course he's going to live," she said brusquely. "I won't allow any other outcome. But I don't think we should try to move him until the next change of the moon, at the very least."

I agreed with her. It might take that long to make the necessary arrangements anyway. When we set out for Dubh Linn I had assumed we would be able to acquire a cart and team here for the transport of our wounded men, but that was impossible. If worse came to worst—as it so often does—Cormiac, and Labraid if necessary, would have to sit on our horses while Grannus and I walked.

But what of Probus?

The following morning, while Briga was busy with Cormiac Ru, I asked the Roman about his plans.

"I have no plans, Ainvar. In the legions a man makes no plans, he simply follows orders."

"But you were an officer; surely that's different."

"Not really. There is always a higher officer."

"Why would any man willingly give up his freedom for such a life?"

"I was free," Probus answered with some asperity.

"You forget that I've seen the army of Rome. Every man in identical uniform, all step together, right left right, spears tilted at the same angle, eyes looking in one direction only, ears deaf to anything but the next command, heads empty, no doubt, of anything but obedience . . . you call that freedom? In Hibernia the slaves are more free than that."

"Don't bully him, Ainvar," said the voice from the bed.

"You're still alive, then?" I teased.

"I'm hard to kill. If you or anyone else abuses Probus they'll find out how hard."

The idea of Cormiac threatening anyone was laughable. He could hardly raise his head from the bed.

But he did raise his head.

Through the smoky interior of the lodge the eyes of the Red Wolf met mine. Colorless eyes, but deeper than the Black Pool.

"I apologize," I said to Probus.

He smiled; a flash of white teeth in a swarthy face. I was beginning to wonder if his ready smile was actually a ploy to disarm. "You have nothing to apologize for, Ainvar. There is truth in what you say. Perhaps the first free act I have committed in many years was deserting the army."

"Ah yes; you were going to tell me about that."

Briga turned from Cormiac's bedside and made brushing motions with her hands, the way a woman does when she is chasing hens out of the lodge. "Outside, both of you! Healing requires peace and quiet, and the old people would only be disturbed by your talk."

At that moment, any information Probus might impart to me was not nearly as important to my senior wife as the work of healing. Much later, of course, when our two heads were together on one pillow, she would extract every drop of the story from me. And reward me sweetly.

Sweetly, my Briga.

Grannus was sitting on the packed earth close to the fire. His raised knees were spread wide apart so the heat could reach his groin. Grannus took his pleasures where he found them.

I waggled my eyebrows at him, indicating he was invited to join us.

"It's cold out there," he said without moving. "And it's warm in here."

Labraid struggled to his feet. "I'm going with you, Probus, I'm strong enough now."

"You are not," Briga contradicted.

Labraid took a cloak from the peg and followed us out.

The weather was more than cold; it was bitter. Tiny particles of sleet bombarded my face. When I took a deep breath to clear my lungs of the stale air from the lodge, icy knives stabbed the inside of my chest.

If Probus felt the cold he gave no sign. Roman warriors were trained to be stoic. An interesting word: "stoic." It derives from an Athenian philosophy extolling the total control of passion and emotion.

There is no word in the Celtic tongue for stoic.

Labraid and I turned our backs on the wind as we trudged away from the lodge. Probus walked on my left. My head wondered if he put his sword arm between himself and others out of force of habit.

So I asked him.

"No, Ainvar. But if I considered you an enemy I would walk to your right, so I could pivot toward you and drive my sword into your belly in one smooth motion." He spoke with no more emotion than Teyrnon would use describing the forging of a door hinge.

"You're not carrying a sword now," Labraid commented. "Even if you were, Ainvar could melt the blade before it ever touched him."

Probus gave me a wary glance. "Could you?"

I was amused to observe that the Celts had no monopoly on credulity. "Labraid's having a joke at your expense, Probus."

"But you can work magic," the Roman insisted. "The statue at Alesia . . ."

"We've already discussed that. Today I want to hear how you came to be with Cormiac and Labraid, and why you claim to have saved their lives."

"He did save our lives!" Labraid cried. "This man is a great general who commanded a Roman garrison in Albion."

Probus cleared his throat. "I was never a general, Ainvar." He sounded slightly embarrassed. "And I was only in command of the garrison at the very end.

"For a long time before that, our commanding officer kept assuring us we soon would receive reinforcements and the assault on Albion would begin in earnest. But it never happened. Then we learned of Caesar's death and—"

"What?!"

Turned upside down, the world spun around me.

"Caesar was assassinated on the Ides of March," Probus said as if clarifying something I should already know.

My tongue had cleaved to the roof of my mouth, but finally I managed to mumble, "When?"

"Eight years ago."

*Eight years!*

I think I staggered. I know I gazed wildly around and passed my hand across my forehead as if brushing away cobwebs. Had time contracted for us while expanding elsewhere? Or was it the other way around? Druid questions.

Probus was looking at me curiously. "Can it be that you were unaware of Caesar's death?"

Think, head!

In the forests of Gaul we had avoided all contact with the Romans—or with anyone who might be in contact with them. Soon we would welcome our seventh spring in Hibernia, where the fate of a far-distant tyrant called Caesar was of no consequence. As far as the Gael were concerned the machinations of Rome might as well have taken place on the moon.

"We're . . . a bit out of the way here," I replied.

"Well, I know all about it," Labraid babbled. "Caesar's enemies cornered him in the Senate and hundreds of them pounced on him all at once and cut him into little pieces and—"

"It was not quite that dramatic, Labraid," the Roman corrected. "However, several members of the Senate did conspire to kill him; they stabbed him to death in front of Pompey's statue. On an earlier occasion Caesar had refused the crown of king but the conspirators were convinced he now meant to accept it. Rome is a republic; the concept of monarchy is anathema. Great Caesar had overreached himself at last and his ambition brought him down."

Caesar. Gone. How was that possible? Did the sun rise in the west now? Had the stars changed their patterns? The object of the hatred that had fueled most of my adult life was dead. Not just dead, but dead for almost a decade.

"My garrison did not learn of Caesar's death for several months," Probus told me, "and then only by rumor. Officially we were still under the command of Julius Caesar; realistically our little corner of Albion was forgotten in the turmoil. Other garrisons were recalled but no summons came for us, and without written orders our commanding officer was reluctant to return to Rome.

"After Caesar's death, Rome was ruled for a while by a triumvirate composed of Caesar's nephew Octavian, Marc Antony, and Marcus Lepidus, but then there was a power struggle and civil war broke out. Legionaries who had followed one standard all their lives felt the earth shift beneath their feet. Some changed sides, while others deserted altogether. It was a very confusing time. Our aging commandant, who had been anticipating a pleasant retirement in a villa in Tuscany, felt the wisest course was to stay where he was and keep his head down.

"Time passed; far too much time. Can you imagine what it was like to occupy a forgotten outpost in hostile territory? Occasionally we snarled at one of the tribes in our vicinity and they snarled back at us, but few battles took place. We did a little trading and a lot of foraging. We drilled on the parade ground until we were heartily sick of drilling. Our head carpenter amused himself by building miniature models of Roman forts. The rest of us mostly sat around and drank bad wine and talked about bad women. Our famous discipline grew very lax, Ainvar."

"I can well imagine. A warrior without a war to fight needs cattle to tend or fields to plow."

"I cannot tend cattle or plow a field, though I do think I would make a good trader," said Probus. "Eventually some bureaucrat buried in the bowels of Rome discovered us in the military records, and we were recalled. A skeleton force was picked to stay behind for maintenance of the garrison. Both of my parents were dead by then and I had no one waiting for me, so I volunteered to remain. The commandant put me in charge of a handful of other volunteers—including Anicius, whom I mentioned before—and went home to enjoy a well-earned retirement.

"Little was required of those who stayed behind: mending roofs, keeping the wells clean, that sort of thing. Conflict with the natives was avoided because our numbers were so small. Boredom became a major problem. We were all veterans of hard campaigns and accustomed to activity. Anicius in particular was going very sour.

"Deputations from the tribes of Albion visited Mona to seek the aid of the druids, whose 'holy island' it was, so I organized a fact-finding expedition to the place. The expedition was not just to relieve the tedium; I hoped it would provide information that might be useful when Rome resumed the conquest of Albion."

Labraid had begun fidgeting. Kicking pebbles. Whistling through his teeth. The Speaker was interested only in conversations that revolved around himself.

Aware of his impatience, Probus said, "I apologize for taking so long to explain, Ainvar, but I wanted you to understand my background."

"I believe I do."

"What I tell you next may be more difficult to understand. I am not a fanciful man, and you may laugh at me if you like; but the moment I set foot on the druids' island something strange occurred."

Intuition prompted my response. "You felt as if you had come home."

The Roman's jaw dropped. "How could you know?"

"What nonsense," Labraid said peevishly. "I never felt anything like that on Mona."

Probus gave him the glance an older brother might give an impudent sibling, understanding him but loving him anyway. "Different people react in different ways, Labraid. That was mine.

"We carried weapons concealed beneath our garments, but I had given orders not to use them unless absolutely necessary. Without any knowledge of the number of inhabitants on the island I did not want trouble. The first person we came upon was a man gathering nuts. Speaking to him in his own language, I said, 'We mean you no harm. We are only in search of knowledge. Mysterious tales are told of this island and we would like to know the truth.'

" 'Truth is everything,' the man told me. 'If you seek it you have come to the right place.' He led us into the darkest woodland imaginable, following trails so convoluted I doubted if we could make our way back to our landing site unaided. Anicius, who was walking behind me, said we were making a mistake. But I pressed on. This was my first occasion of real leadership and I could not let the men see me back down.

"At last we came out of the trees. In the center of a huge clearing we found a structure somewhat resembling a temple. As we drew closer I could see that it had been shaped by human hands, though it appeared to grow out of the underlying rock. The design was oval in shape and had no roof. Our guide explained that it was open to the sky so the movements of certain stars could be observed and their paths calculated.

"This was the heart, he said, of a druid 'college' called Tan Ben y Cefn.

The place defied classification, being neither city, town, nor fortress. In fact, the man-made aspect was kept to a minimum. Spread around the temple were various small houses that might almost have been random piles of stone, and domestic offices built of timber so they looked like clumps of trees. The buildings were enclosed within roughly rectangular earthworks, whose dimensions had been determined by the druids according to a formula of their own. There was no palisade, no gates. No armed guards.

"At first I thought the place deserted, but as we walked forward people appeared. Men and women but no children. It was as if they materialized out of the stones. At the time I thought that impossible.

"We were greeted by a man whose graying beard reached to his knees, while the forepart of his head was shaved clean from ear to ear. In one hand he carried a long staff carved from the wood of the ash. He said his name was Mac Coille, meaning 'the Son of the Wood,' and further identified himself as the chief druid. Before I could offer an innocent explanation for our visit he told me its true purpose. Yet he showed no anger. He accepted our arrival as inevitable and seemed untroubled by it. Quite the contrary, he offered us the hospitality of a guesthouse and promised to show us almost anything we wished to see. A few of the most sacred rituals might be denied us, but everything else was wide open."

"Only someone supremely confident of his power," I commented, "would grant you such access."

"That was my conclusion too, Ainvar. I privately told my men to cause no trouble, but to be wary. For several days we wandered at will around Tan Ben y Cefn. At first I was merely curious; before long I was baffled. Although every member of the community obviously had a specific function to fulfill, I could not determine what those functions were.

"In front of the temple, different druids spoke daily on a variety of both esoteric and practical subjects. Their audiences were encouraged to ask questions, but even the simplest query might elicit a complex response that took up half a morning.

"In addition to the lectures we also witnessed incomprehensible rituals. Some had results so astounding we doubted the evidence of our senses."

"Such as?"

"I saw a druid stand atop a rock and hold up his arms. He gave a peculiar cry and the birds of the air swooped down to him in their hundreds, covering his head and shoulders, fighting for perches on his arms, blanketing the earth at his feet until he stood amid a feathered flood. He did not feed them, he did not even speak to them."

"He was being *with* them, Probus," I explained. Knowing that would mean nothing to the Roman mind. "Give me another example."

"An elderly female druid carrying a parcel wrapped in deerskin hobbled to the edge of a bog. While my men and I watched, she crouched down and chanted under her breath for a long time. Then she stood up again, with considerable effort and creaking of joints, and unfolded the deerskin. A tumble of bones fell out, at least a dozen of them. Yet she caught each one *separately,* in midair, and flung it out onto the bog. That crippled old woman!

"Wherever a bone fell," Probus added in a voice still tinged with amazement, "on the following day a flower bloomed."

I longed to ask if the bones were human, but kept silent.

"Then there was the matter of food. We were very well fed during our stay, though the druids did not hunt game or cook meat. They subsisted, as far as I could tell, on fish from the streams, and fruit and nuts and root vegetables, and cheese they made from a herd of goats. And the most delicious bread I ever tasted."

"They grew wheat on Mona?"

"As far as I could tell, the answer is no, Ainvar. We never saw a wheat field or any other cultivated crop. What we did see were round ovens made of clay, presided over by druids who brought stones of a specific size from a nearby stream and put them into the ovens first thing every morning. When the sun stood overhead they opened the ovens and took out loaves of bread. Golden, crusty loaves of moist bread. A man could live on that bread alone.

"I looked into the ovens after they took out the bread. There were no stones inside.

"None of the magic I saw is explicable, Ainvar. Yet I was aware that every action resulted from another as naturally as a flower bud unfolds from the heat of the sun."

"Naturally," I echoed.

"You sound as if that is important."

"It is. The 'magic' you witnessed was accomplished through an understanding of the natural world that doesn't conform to your limited perceptions."

Probus started to say something; stopped; gave me a long, thoughtful look. "I hope you will explain that statement to me sometime. Meanwhile we must take pity on our young friend here." With his eyes he indicated Labraid. "He can hardly stay in his skin for eagerness to hear the part about himself."

## *chapter* XXVIII

"MY MEN AND I SPENT SEVEN DAYS AT TAN BEN Y CEFN," PROBUS continued, "observing everything and understanding practically nothing. For all we learned we might as well have stayed on Albion. We could not even determine the exact population of Mona. 'They come and they go,' Mac Coille said.

"Then one morning he announced, 'Two who have visited here before will be returning soon; we must make ready to welcome them.' Although I did not know it at the time, he was talking about Labraid and Cormiac Ru."

I turned to scowl at Labraid. "You should have mentioned meeting the druids before."

"We didn't meet them, Ainvar; not the first time anyway. From the sea the island had looked uninhabited. I ordered one of the boatmen to stay with the boat while the rest of us went ashore with the leather waterbags. We explored only long enough to find a stream, but we didn't see anybody. We filled the bags and hurried back to the boat because I wanted to sail on before the wind turned and—"

I held up one hand. "Be quiet for a moment. Let me think."

Our two young men had landed on Mona and departed again without ever encountering the druids. Some time later, the chief druid had referred to them as "two who have visited here before"—according to Probus, who was precise in his language. This meant Mona's druids had been aware of the pair when they first visited the island. Yet they had not revealed themselves.

The reason, my head commented, was rooted in the philosophy of druidry. Cormiac and Labraid had been seeking only water. They required nothing from the Order of the Wise on that occasion, so the druids had not interfered.

To interfere without being asked can distort the Pattern.

Labraid looked as if he were about to explode with the effort of keeping quiet.

"Perhaps we should let him tell his own story now," Probus suggested.

With a grateful grin, the young man prepared to launch himself into a highly colored and probably rambling discourse. I forestalled him. "Let's keep the string straight, shall we? Where did you go when you left Mona?"

"We went to sea, of course, where I was an excellent—"

"But where did you *go,* Labraid? It's been two years since you left Hibernia. Where were you all that time?"

"At sea, mostly."

"I don't understand."

"Keep it simple," Probus advised in a kindly tone, demonstrating insight. Friendship might work with Labraid but exasperation never would.

"We set sail for the east, skirting the southern coast of Albion thanks to my understanding of the stars. But when we entered the waters that separate Albion from Armorica things started to go wrong." Labraid's tone changed abruptly. It was the first time I had ever heard him sound subdued. "We ran into a fleet of Roman warships. They didn't have much trouble overpowering us, and by sundown we were galley slaves."

"You were actually on a Roman ship? Where did you go, what did you see?"

"I have no idea where we went, Ainvar, and I never saw much of anything. On the rowing deck your only view is the sweaty back of the man in front of you. You smell nothing but the stink of the men around you. You hear nothing but the thudding of the oars and the pounding of the drum that beats out their rhythm over and over and over again until your head feels like it's going to burst. On the rowing deck you can't tell if it's night or day. It's always hot, though; you can't imagine how hot. How stifling. A lot of men simply die where they sit, so there's always a need for replacements. As soon as we were brought on board Cormiac and I were clapped in leg irons and then chained to a rowing bench."

Labraid Who Sails the Seas. One should be careful when choosing a name for oneself. That Which Watches has a sense of irony.

"I thought we were on one of Caesar's warships until the other rowers told me Caesar was dead and we were under someone else's command. They said, 'It doesn't matter who's in control, it will make no difference to us.' They were right. There's only one kind of life for a galley slave. You row until your muscles are on fire, then they take you down into the very bottom of the boat and you're given some food—never enough—and a chance to sleep—not long enough—and then they take you back to the rowing deck and it starts all over again.

"Most of our urine came out in sweat. What didn't ran into the bilge at the bottom of the boat and we had to put our feet in it. If we broke the rhythm of rowing they beat us. Briga saw my scars, she'll tell you how bad they are."

I took a good long look at Labraid. He had grown as big as his father, and even gaunt and battered, he was a physically impressive man. Whatever hardships he had endured had only made him stronger.

He interpreted my appraising gaze correctly. "I fought back, Ainvar."

"I'm sure you did. What happened to the boatmen who'd accompanied you?"

"I never knew. It was only by chance that Cormiac and I were left together. We were chained together at the ankles, so we rowed the same oar," Labraid added through gritted teeth.

That explained a lot.

"When I realized I was so strong that being a galley slave wasn't going to kill me, I almost wished it would. The monotony was terrible. And it was no good trying to talk to Cormiac; you know how he is."

I did know. Cormiac spoke only if he had something worth saying.

"Eventually we were transferred to another warship. Different slave-masters but the same life. The ship took part in several battles but we didn't know much about them; we worked like oxen in the steamy half dark while above us warriors sounded trumpets and tried to kill one another. That was a frustrating experience, I can tell you. Once or twice we came near to sinking. I thought we might have a chance to escape then, but they never unfastened our chains. Galley slaves go down with the ship," he added bitterly.

"At last we put into a port where the galley slaves were taken off and thrown into holding pens. There was a lot of yelling and cursing but it didn't bother me; it was bliss not to hear that drumbeat night and day. The food was bad but there was plenty of it. Cormiac thought we were being rested and fattened up for a reason. He said we must be on the losing side and whoever was in command was trying to hoard his resources."

A shrewd guess, my head observed. If Cormiac Ru survived his injuries he would make a fine leader for our clan.

For Labraid I had other plans. "Where were you at this time?"

"In a *pen,* Ainvar! Timber and iron bars. Weren't you listening to me?"

"But where was the pen? What harbor, what town?"

"Somewhere in Iberia," he said impatiently. "I don't know where, it didn't matter. All that mattered was escaping. Which we did, thanks to my cleverness. I told the others that I had a plan and they should follow my lead, then late one night I threw myself on the ground and shouted that something was wrong with my belly. I kept howling until the guards came running; I sounded very convincing. When they opened the gate of our pen—there were twenty of us in each pen—we rushed them. About half of us got past and scattered like rats. Cormiac and I hid under a wharf until the morning, then I scouted around and found a merchant ship being loaded with cargo. The two of us sneaked aboard and concealed ourselves until we were out of sight of land. Then I made a deal with the captain. I know how to strike a bargain and the captain knew a good man when he saw one."

"I'm sure he did," I said dryly. "What about your chains? I assume you were still wearing them. How did you explain those?"

"Oh, Cormiac broke them off long before then," Labraid said dismissively. "With a rock or something.

"I arranged for us to work for our passage as independent seamen. Crewing a cargo vessel is hard work and willing men aren't that easy to find. It was an ideal situation for us. The merchantman was going to sail north as far as

Armorica, then turn around and head south again, passing through the Pillars of Herakles to the Mid-Earth Sea. Once we got that far I was certain I'd be able to find your daughter. But Cormiac changed his mind and began insisting we return to Hibernia. He'd lost his nerve."

I doubted that. Never in his entire life had the Red Wolf lost his nerve.

"I'm beginning to tire," the Roman interjected. "Shall we go back to the lodge for a while?"

In truth, Labraid was the one who was tired; he had become very unsteady on his feet. If I had made the suggestion he would have refused, but since it was his friend he complied. He kept on talking, though. "I could have gone to the Mid-Earth Sea without Cormiac, Ainvar; I didn't need him. But I'm not one to abandon a member of my own tribe. I planned for the two of us to steal a rowboat when we reached the point nearest Albion and slip away in the night."

"How would you know when you were nearest Albion? And how, for that matter, did you intend to find your way back to Hibernia?"

"I have an excellent sense of direction," Labraid said loftily.

Probus caught my eye. As surely as if I heard him speak aloud, I knew we were thinking the same thing. The only way to obtain an accurate account of this episode would be from Cormiac Ru.

Which must wait until he was stronger.

After we returned to the lodge Labraid continued his narrative, relating more than I wanted to know about his exploits. Not only relating but reiterating, elaborating, and exaggerating, in exhaustive detail. According to him he had single-handedly engineered their escape from the merchant ship with no assistance at all from Cormiac Ru.

"Did you not feel it was dishonorable to desert," I inquired, "after the captain had treated you so fairly?"

He scoffed at the suggestion. "Men jump ship all the time, Ainvar. It's expected."

"Was that when you were injured? Was there a scuffle before you got away?"

"We weren't caught in the act, I'm far too clever for that. We were over the side and gone before anyone knew."

"Then how did you acquire your wounds?"

"Fighting the Romans, of course. I was brilliant in battle, you should have seen me. I had no sword, not even a meat knife, only fists and feet, but I was as quick as a—"

"Fighting the Romans? Do you mean Probus?"

"Oh no, not him! I can tell you about him later, Ainvar. First you must hear how I reached the coast of Albion. Not one man in a thousand could have done it. We only had a little boat meant to row officers ashore, and there was a terrible gale blowing. The waves were like mountains crashing over us. But I'm amazingly skillful at sea, so I . . ."

At some point my ears stopped listening, leaving my imagination to fill in the details. Which I am sure it did with more accuracy than Labraid's hyperbole.

He fell asleep suddenly, between one word and the next.

"Pick him up and put him in his bed, Grannus," Briga instructed. "He's overexerted himself; I was afraid of that. For the next two or three days he's not to leave this lodge. Stay right with him so he doesn't. And don't you tempt him to go outside again, Ainvar!" she added to me. The charge was unjust, but when a wife wants someone to blame a husband is a convenient target.

Before I went to my bed there was something I had to do.

Cormiac Ru appeared to be asleep. When I bent over him he opened his eyes. "Ainvar," he whispered.

"How do you feel?"

"Better than yesterday."

"I'd like to ask you something, then. Am I right to assume your swords were taken from you when you were captured by the Roman warships?"

"They were."

"And the sword you lost . . . was my father's?"

"I'm sorry, Ainvar."

"It's of no consequence, I just needed to know."

"It is of consequence. Your daughter and your sword. I wanted to bring them both back to you."

"You've come back to me, that's all I needed."

And it was true.

The following morning was bitterly cold; the wind off the sea slipped icy fingers through the walls of wattle and daub and ran them up our spines. With Grannus guarding the doorway, Briga kept all three of her invalids indoors. I was free to wander around on my own and talk to anyone who would talk to me. In this way I enlarged my knowledge of the region.

Thus I learned that the estuary of the Liffey provided one of the few breaks in the mountainous, forest-clad, natural bulwark that encircled Hibernia, embracing the fertile central plain. The people of Dubh Linn were in an ideal location to carry on seagoing trade, yet I was told they preferred to fish. "Everything we need is already within our reach," said a cheerful woman as freckled as a blackbird's egg. "Why would we want to give our wealth to strangers trying to sell us what they don't want?"

One often encounters wisdom in unexpected places. When we were home again I would tell my students—many of whom would never travel this far in their lives—about the Gaels of Dubh Linn.

How odd to realize that we, who had been the Gauls, who had traveled the length and breadth of a land vastly larger than Hibernia, now made our home on an island where a day's journey was considered a sizable undertaking, and our grandchildren might never see the sea.

Life expands and then shrinks. And then expands again, like some great creature breathing.

I walked as far as the neck of a peninsula that jutted out into a great bay. The bay was large enough to accommodate hundreds of trading vessels, but only a few fishing boats were visible, hugging the shore. As I gazed at the incoming tide I tried to convince myself that Gaul was still out there, somewhere. I could no longer remember the way the light fell on the fields, or the fragrance of the vineyards.

Even when we stand still, the past runs away from us.

At last I roused myself from my reverie and went searching for someone who might answer the riddle that had been tormenting me ever since we arrived: the identity of the thing that had screamed in the night.

"It's one of *them,*" I was told by a toothless old fellow I found mending his fishing nets. Having mentioned "them," he looked fearfully around, then got to his feet and performed the curious ritual of spitting in four directions, turning solemnly as he did so. It was astonishing that a dried-up old man had so much spit in him.

"Who do you mean by 'them'?"

He looked me up and down. "You're not from around here, are you." A statement, not a question.

"I come from a place far away."

"Then maybe you don't know about the good people."

"Good people? You act almost as if you're afraid of them. Why should you be afraid of good people?"

He gestured to me to bend down until my ear was level with his mouth. "They aren't really good," he whispered. "We only call them that so we don't make them more angry with us than they already are. They can do terrible things."

Suddenly I understood. "Are you saying it was one of the Túatha Dé Danann?"

He took a step backward and made wild gestures with his hands. "Don't do that, you'll call her!"

"Call who?"

"Rígan's *bean sídhe*!" he cried, using the Gaelic for "fairy woman." With these words his nerve broke entirely. Pulling his cloak over his head, he scuttled away from me as fast as he could.

I found Rígan at the Black Pool, where a score of small boats were undergoing winter repairs. Both men and women bustled around them, each to their allotted tasks. Men cut out and replaced damaged bits of timber framework. Women mended the leather hides used for covering the boats. As I walked up, the men were exchanging improbable fishing stories. They fell silent when one of the women began to sing. A song matched to the rhythm of the sewing, a song so perfectly crafted that music and work became one and the same.

Rígan was standing off to one side, though whether supervising or merely observing I could not tell. When he saw me he gave a nod of greeting and beckoned me to join him. We spoke of Cormiac and Labraid—and Probus, though I did not mention the Roman by name. Rígan expressed interest in their progress. "Will you be taking them home soon?" he asked me several times.

Since I could not yet answer his question, I asked one of my own. "What can you tell me of the bean sídhe?"

Rígan stiffened. "Where did you hear about that?"

While I related my brief conversation with the old man Rígan stared past me, wearing the grim expression I had seen on his face the night we arrived. The look of a man expecting disaster.

"Is it true, Rígan? Is there such a thing as a bean sídhe?"

His shoulders slumped. "Oh yes, I'm afraid there is. More than one, in fact. Quite a few clans of the Gael have a bean sídhe. They attach themselves to a direct descendant of the sons of Milesios, and when that person is about to die the bean sídhe screams. Some call it a wail of grief. Others say it's a shriek of triumph. Either way, it's horrible." Rígan shuddered.

"I myself," he went on, "am in a straight line leading back to Ir the Visionary, who saw a god leap out of the sea. Ir was the cleverest and the most noble of all the sons of Milesios. His brothers were . . ." he began counting on his fingers, "Éber Finn the Warrior, Amergin the Bard, Éremon the—"

"Many times grandfather of Fíachu of the Slea Leathan," I interrupted. "Which means that Fíachu might have a bean sídhe."

"He probably does."

"He never mentioned her to me, Rígan."

"I never talk about mine, either. I only wait. And listen. I heard her the night you came here."

"So did I. And . . ." I paused, struck by the wonder of it. "And so did my wife and our friend."

Rígan was ashen-faced. "I shall not live to see the next full moon, Ainvar."

"How can you be certain?"

"One is always certain when the bean sídhe cries. Besides, I have five brothers, all of whom want to be chieftain, and matters are coming to a head. I'd suggest you return to the Plain of Broad Spears as soon as you can."

# *chapter* XXIX

RÍGAN HAD GIVEN ME SOUND ADVICE AND I MEANT TO TAKE IT. I was grateful for the kindness he had shown us, but I had seen all I wanted of war. Men killing other men for the sake of ambition makes no sense to me. In nature there is no model for ambition.

When I returned to the lodge, Cormiac was sitting beside the fire with the others. He was pale and a little shaky, but clearly much improved. The look Briga gave me warned that I must not tax his strength. I limited our conversation to a cheerful greeting, then chatted with Labraid long enough to determine that he too was getting well.

I drew my senior wife aside. "Rígan says there's going to be a clan war here, and very soon. I think we should be on our way before that happens. Will Cormiac be able to travel in a couple of days, if he sits on a horse?"

She glanced over her shoulder at him. "I can't say, Ainvar. He's an amazingly strong man, but he suffered appalling injuries and he's still in a lot of pain. Are you sure Rígan's right about the war?"

"I have good reason to believe him." I did not want to go into details. There were too many things I needed to think through in the quiet of my head.

Although I had been speaking for Briga's ears alone, the Red Wolf overheard. "I can do it, Ainvar. I can sit on a horse."

"If you're going to ride a horse I want one, too!" cried Labraid.

Briga assumed her sternest expression, which did not fool anyone. She could be strong but never stern; it was a mistake to confuse one for the other. "Both of you are going to stay right here for at least two more nights, war or no war. After that, we'll see."

"What about me?"

Briga turned toward Probus. "You're able to travel now if you have someplace to go."

"I don't."

Labraid said, "You old fool, you'll always have someplace to go. Wherever I am, you are welcome." He put his hand on the other man's shoulder. Not an extravagant gesture, nothing of the sort one would expect from Labraid. Yet it spoke more eloquently than all his words.

For the first time in his life the Speaker was thinking about someone else.

The old woman was restless that night. She twisted her gnarled fingers into fantastic shapes and paced the floor. "I can't seem to settle," she complained.

"Perhaps it's the wind," I suggested.

She seized on my words. "That's it, the wind!"

She continued to wind and rewind her fingers. After a while Grannus said, "Maybe it's something you ate."

"That's it, something I ate!"

She kept on pacing.

"Sit down, woman!" the old man roared at her.

Her nervousness infected us all. No one slept much. At last Briga, with her head pillowed on my shoulder, whispered, "Perhaps we could leave in the morning, Ainvar; if we're very careful and travel slowly."

And so it was.

At dawn I made my way to the pen that held our horses, along with the tribe's milk cows. The gray and the chestnut were standing head to tail, dozing. The dark horse stood a little apart with his head up, watching for me.

"We're going home," I called to him.

Until that moment I had, quite sensibly, intended to put Cormiac on the gray horse because it was the gentlest. Labraid would be given the temperamental chestnut—let him boast of his horsemanship then!—and Briga would ride my horse, whom I had no doubt she could handle.

But when the dark horse threw up his head and came trotting toward me, everything changed. I looked into his eyes and everything changed.

The old woman gave us food for our journey. Rígan's women provided sheets of well-worn linen which Grannus tore into wide strips for Briga, who used them to bind Cormiac's broken body tightly enough to give him some comfort. Lastly we wrapped both our young men in blankets. Probus declined to accept one. "I am accustomed to having only a cloak," he said.

It was harder than I had expected to say good-bye to the old couple. They had two great virtues: They had been generous to us, and they had not interfered. Such people are to be commended.

I gave them a pair of arm rings of hammered silver that young Glas had made for me.

When all was in readiness I brought the horses to the door of the lodge. "You'll ride this one," I told Labraid, indicating the gray. "Probus, you're familiar with horses. Will you take the reins and lead him?"

"I don't need anyone to lead my horse!" Labraid protested, but I ignored him. I handed the reins of the chestnut mare to my senior wife. "You'll enjoy her," I predicted. Briga laughed and stroked the animal's neck. "I know I will, Ainvar."

Lastly I turned to the dark horse. "Grannus, help me lift Cormiac onto this one. Gently, now."

The dark horse stood as if carved of stone. Although we hoisted Cormiac up as carefully as we could, I saw him go white with pain. I assured him, "We'll only go at a walk. I'll hold the reins, and Grannus will be right beside you every step of the way in case you get dizzy or lose your balance. But you can trust this animal to let no harm come to you. He's fit for a chieftain."

With an effort of will Cormiac made his broken body relax so he could settle into the curve of the horse's back and adapt his legs to the spring of the horse's ribs. He, who had never ridden a horse before, became part of one. Seeing him absorb some of the creature's strength and splendor, I might almost have been looking at Vercingetorix again.

"I'm ready," said the Red Wolf.

Our little procession slowly moved away from Dubh Linn. One step at a time, which is how everything happens.

Rígan came to the gates to watch us go. He lifted a hand in farewell but I suspect he was not thinking about us. He was already anticipating the thrust of a sword in his belly.

There are few easy endings to Thislife.

We had made the journey from the Plain of Broad Spears in a long hard day and part of a night, but I suspected it would take at least seven days to return, with many stops along the way and the nights reserved for sleeping. There would be plenty of time to hear the rest of the story from our three adventurers. First, however, I wanted to be alone in my head for a while.

Labraid denied me that chance. We had barely passed the rock outcropping when his complaints began. He was too warm, we must halt and unwrap his blankets. Then he was too cold and needed more blankets. We had not gone much farther when he announced that his shoulder was hurting. Next he claimed a pain in his head.

The end came when he demanded the horse Cormiac was on. "My father was a great chieftain," he reminded us unnecessarily, "so I should be riding the best horse."

"You are not riding any horse," Probus pointed out. "You are only sitting on one. So what does it matter?"

"It matters to me. Ainvar, you knew my father. If he were here today, you know he'd want me to have the best horse."

Through clenched teeth I replied, "Yes, I knew Vercingetorix from boyhood. In his entire life I never heard him complain, yet since we left Dubh Linn you have done nothing else. If Rix were here today he would be ashamed of you."

Labraid lapsed into an affronted silence.

Probus glanced in my direction, and winked.

Incredibly, I found myself actually liking a Roman.

SOUND CARRIES ON THE RIVER. ALTHOUGH WE WERE NOW SOME LITtle distance from Dubh Linn an appalling noise, one we had not heard for many seasons, reached us. The sudden din of battle. The shouts and screams of men doing their best to kill one another.

Briga reined in her horse. "Should we go back and try to help Rígan, Ainvar?"

Labraid forgot his aches and pains in an eyeblink. "I can do it! Just give me a sword!"

"No," I said firmly. "What is meant for him will not pass by him, and we will not interfere. Let's go, Probus."

The Roman tugged the reins of the gray horse and we rode forward again.

I longed to reflect on the implications of the bean sídhe, but Rígan's fate was too distracting. So I asked Labraid, "Do you feel like talking?"

"I feel like fighting!"

"I appreciate that, but we're not going back. I was hoping you'd tell us what happened after you deserted the merchant ship and before you met Probus."

I did not have to ask twice.

"We rowed the boat for a long time—I did most of the rowing, of course, since I'm stronger—but finally we caught sight of land. Huge white cliffs rising straight up out of the sea. There were tremendous breakers but I managed to land us safely on a shingle beach. After we'd rested, I went hunting and found enough small game to feed us and—"

"What did you use for weapons?"

"Oh, Cormiac made some," Labraid replied offhandedly.

I looked over my shoulder at Cormiac Ru. "Out of what?"

"Driftwood. Stones. The thongs of my sandals."

"And you took part in this hunt too, I suppose?"

"Yes."

Ignoring this exchange, Labraid said, "As soon as I provided food we got back in the boat and made our way south along the coast. For days and days and days. The edge of Albion is very rough and broken, extremely difficult to navigate, but I did. When we saw smoke from fires we didn't go ashore in case there might be Romans."

"Albion is inhabited by Celtic tribes," I informed him. "Your chances of encountering Romans would have been small."

"That's all you know! Just listen. Eventually we rounded a great finger of land that sticks way out into the sea and headed north again, across what appeared to be a very wide river mouth. At night I studied the stars, trying to determine when we should change course for the west. Finally I was just about to give the order to Cormiac when we were hailed by a group of men onshore."

"Hailed in Latin," Cormiac added.

"I'm telling this," Labraid testily reminded him. "I shouted back at them before I realized they were speaking Latin. At once a large boat put out after us. We tried to outrun them but it was no use. They forced us onto the land and attacked us. There were at least fifty of them, Ainvar, with breastplates and helmets, and . . ."

"There were twelve," said Cormiac.

". . . and the only weapons we had were clubs and spears."

"Why did they attack you?"

"Labraid waved his spear at them."

"I was only trying to be friendly. Anyway, we had to fight for our lives. I don't know how many men we killed, but it was a lot."

"Nine," said the Red Wolf.

"You killed nine Romans?"

"I killed my share!" Labraid stressed.

Cormiac looked down at me. "He did."

"When we saw our chance," Labraid continued, "we ran for the boat and put out to sea. We were almost dead ourselves by that time. We couldn't even pick up the oars, we just let the tide carry us where it would. After a long time we washed up on the shores of Mona."

Briga, who had been listening to this with as much fascination as I, asked, "How did you know it was Mona?"

"We didn't know the name of the island, not then, but we landed exactly where we'd landed the first time."

Probus said, "Was that not an amazing coincidence?"

There are no coincidences, just unexpected glimpses of a hidden Pattern.

"We crawled out of the boat and simply lay on the beach for a while, amazed to find ourselves alive. Then some men came out of the trees and walked toward us. They had tonsures like you used to wear, Ainvar. I tried to explain what had happened to us and ask for their help but I couldn't tell if they understood me or not. They picked us up as if we were children and carried us off into the forest. I'm not sure what happened then; Probus can tell you."

I knew Labraid was exhausted—not because his shoulders were sagging, but because he willingly relinquished the narration to someone else.

The Roman obliged. "When the druids brought them to Tan Ben y Cefn, both men were in dreadful shape. Labraid was unconscious and Cormiac could not speak. One of the druids knelt beside them and made signs in the air with his hands, and eventually Labraid revived, but he made no sense. He kept talking about 'killing thousands of Romans' and slashing his arms around. My men were alarmed. Anicius wanted to kill them both immediately but Mac Coille intervened. 'On Mona there are no enemies,' he said. He insisted that the two Celts—for such they obviously were, their language gave them away—be taken to a guesthouse and given food and drink and healing.

"As for us, I felt we had learned all we could there. We had left the garrison insufficiently manned for a longer stay, so I announced that we would set sail for Albion on the following day. Anicius began to argue with my decision; I had to remind him who was in command. Then he told me we should take the two strangers with us as prisoners of war. We had not captured them in a war, I pointed out; they had nothing to do with us, they were guests of the druids. Anicius insisted they were enemies of Rome, condemned by their own words, and it was our obligation to dispatch them.

"I had seen far too many enemies 'dispatched' for my liking. But you will understand all you need to know about Anicius when I tell you he loved to remember what I most wanted to forget."

"I knew someone like that once," I remarked. "A man called Aberth, who took his greatest pleasure from the extinction of life."

"There are such men, Ainvar. Perhaps I was a bit that way myself when I was a boy. I was curious about death and eager to observe the process without ever relating it to my own potential for pain."

"Killing another creature does not add one drop of its life to your own life span," I said.

"I doubt if Anicius ever made that discovery. I had known him for a long time, and though I did not like him very much, I thought he was a good soldier. It seems I misjudged him.

"During the night he spoke secretly to the other members of my company and convinced them that I had grown soft. From there it was but a small step to persuade them that he should replace me."

As the last despairing cry of the murdered chief of Dubh Linn still echoed along the waters of the Liffey, I glimpsed the Pattern with perfect clarity.

# *chapter* XXX

"WHAT DOES IT MATTER WHO IS CHIEF AND WHO IS FOLLOWER?" Briga wondered aloud. "Pain and joy and death come to all."

"Of course it matters," Labraid said irritably. "Women simply don't understand these things."

Labraid made many foolish remarks; I could not be bothered to reprimand him for every one.

Probus continued, "When I arose in the morning Anicius and the rest of the company were waiting for me, but fortunately so was Mac Coille, who got to me first. 'Your men mean you harm,' he warned me.

"As soon as I saw their faces I knew he was right. They wore the look of absolute innocence men assume when they are guilty. They gathered around me in much the same way I imagine the assassins gathered around Caesar in the Senate. Anicius began by suggesting I needed to 'delegate responsibility' for a while in deference to my 'exhaustion,' for which he claimed to feel sympathy. The cold expression in his eyes belied his words. The other men still had their weapons concealed, but his hand was on the hilt of his gladus.

"Strangely enough, the druids had begun to gather in a large circle around us. Their movements were so inconspicuous I did not notice at first. They took no action, just stood and watched. I do not think Anicius was even aware of them. Keeping his eyes fixed on mine, he demanded I surrender the prisoners to him.

"When I replied that I had no prisoners, he turned around and began ordering the others to fetch the two Celts. In that moment he saw the druids. He shouted at them to stand aside.

"They did not move. My men reached for their swords and brandished them openly, but still the druids did not move.

"Mac Coille told Anicius, 'You cannot take our guests without their permission. Let us ask them what they want.' When the chief druid called their names, Labraid and Cormiac, leaning on two of the druids, emerged from one of the guesthouses. Mac Coille asked if they wished to leave with the Romans. They both said no.

" 'There's your answer, Anicius,' I told the rebel. 'If anyone is to be taken prisoner, it is you, for trying to lead a revolt against your commanding officer. That is a capital offense.'

"But the scoundrel had been more successful than I realized. When he leaped at me with his sword in his hand, the other men joined him. My own weapon was still back in the guesthouse; I had not carried it on my person since the first day. I braced myself and prepared to go down fighting.

"In the final moment before they closed over me, I heard a deep voice say, 'You have to ask for help.' So I did. I shouted for help at the top of my lungs.

"Mac Coille instantly thrust his long wooden staff into my hands. I gripped it with all my strength and began to lay about me with what proved to be a most effective weapon, even against the Roman gladus. I took only one blow to the chest with the flat of someone's blade. Meanwhile, Anicius was doing his best to drive his sword into my belly, but the druid's staff parried his every thrust. I am good, Ainvar, but that ash stick was better. It clung to my palms like my skin, and of its own volition swung and smashed and scattered the comrades who had suddenly become my enemies.

"Out of the corner of my eye I saw the circle of druids change its configuration and form into a passageway: two rows of men and women facing each other, with an open space between them and the forest visible in the distance. 'Take our two friends with you!' Mac Coille shouted to me.

"I had never run from a fight in my life and was not about to run from this one. Yet I had no choice! The staff plunged down the passageway like a runaway horse, dragging me along behind. I could neither drop the thing nor resist it. The passage widened as I ran, and I felt, rather than saw, the two injured men being urged along after me. By other druids, I assume. Then I heard angry cries as my men—my former men—attacked them.

"I whirled around. The staff was willing to stop its headlong flight long enough to allow me to swing it at our pursuers. While I fought them back, Labraid and Cormiac stumbled past me, covered with blood."

"That's when you cried, 'Run for the forest!' " Labraid said. "I didn't want to, I wanted to stay and fight, of course, but—"

"The trees closed around us," said Cormiac.

"They did." Labraid sounded awestruck. "Long before we reached the safety of the forest the trees . . . except they weren't trees, they were druids . . . or had been druids . . . but suddenly they were trees . . . were all around us. Crowding so close that nothing could get between them."

"Except Probus," said Cormiac.

"Well, yes, Probus soon joined us. He pointed straight ahead with the staff and ran forward and we followed him."

"You three ran into the forest?" I asked, trying to follow the action. "Was this the same vast forest you described to me earlier, Probus?"

"It was."

"Then how did you find your way through it without a guide?"

"By following the druid's staff," said the Roman. "It led us all the way to the sea."

Labraid took up the narrative. "We finally came out of the forest just above the beach where we'd left our little boat. By that time we could hear men crashing about in the trees behind us, and I wanted to go back and fight them but Probus insisted we get into the boat instead. He pushed it out into the water, then climbed in after us and we set out."

"For Hibernia," said Cormiac.

"You three, two of you badly wounded and one with a broken rib, traveled all the way from Mona to the harbor at Dubh Linn in a small rowboat with no crew? How can that be?"

"I propped the staff at a forward angle in the prow," Probus replied, "and the boat followed it. That is all I can tell you."

Even I, who had seen and done great magic in my time, felt the gooseflesh rise on my body. "Where is the druid's staff now?"

"The incoming tide washed us onto a strand below Dubh Linn. I used the staff to lean on as I got out of the boat. Some boys who were gathering birds' eggs nearby noticed us and came running to help get the other two out. In the confusion I must have dropped the staff in the water; I never saw it again. The rest you know, Ainvar."

I regretted the loss of Mac Coille's staff as I had regretted surrendering the torc of Vercingetorix. If I had heard this tale while we were still at Dubh Linn, I would have been on my hands and knees at water's edge, searching.

"Does any of this make sense to you?" Probus asked me.

"It does."

"Then can you explain it so I can understand it?"

"That would take a lifetime," I told him with perfect truth.

"Perhaps you can tell me this, at least. If the druids were vastly outnumbered—by a very large army, for example—would they still be able to cast their spells, or whatever it is they do?"

"I can't answer that, Probus."

"Oh, I think you can. That is what happened in Gaul, is it not?"

"If we'd had enough warriors we would have won!" Labraid cried.

Probus looked up at him. "I disagree. The problem was not the size of the Gaulish forces, but their lack of discipline and organization. They had no clearly defined channel of command. Once Vercingetorix was captured, the outcome was inevitable."

My head agreed with him. Caesar had defeated us not because his warriors were better, but because they fought as one man. The Gauls, being Celts, fought singly, each in his own fashion. They had failed to learn from nature.

I had once seen a swarm of ants, moving to a single pattern, overrun and devour much larger beetles, each of whom was armed with savage pincers.

Labraid would have argued with me, but he did not argue with Probus. Instead he lapsed into silence, which was soon interrupted by a series of rhythmic sounds like the soft little grunts of suckling piglets. Probus, who was still holding the reins of the gray horse in one hand, put up the other to steady the gently snoring man.

We walked on.

"You seem genuinely fond of Labraid," I remarked to the Roman. "I'm glad for his sake, yet puzzled, too. He's not a very likable man."

Probus chuckled. "I was born old and Labraid will never grow up. The symmetry appeals to me."

We walked on.

My head sought new ways to occupy itself. I began thinking of my students in the glade, and then of my own children. Dara and Eoin and Ongus and Gobnat. Cairbre and Senta and Niav. My head painted glowing pictures of them clustering around me, laughing with joy because I was home.

From time to time I turned to smile at Briga. She smiled back at me. A man could wrap himself up in that smile and stay warm for all of his life.

My Briga. Princess and healer and mother . . . my questing head seized on the concept of motherhood. How incredible the diversity that was born of woman!

Was a creature such as Caesar born in the natural way? Or was he an unnatural alloy of the vile, the vicious, and the avaricious? For years my head had sought new ways to express my loathing for the man. It had reached a point where my hatred was a greater burden than its cause. "How long can one hate a dead man?" I did not realize I had spoken aloud until Briga asked, "Are you talking about Caesar?"

"I suppose I was."

"I never hated Caesar," she said. "I pitied him."

*"Pity!"* I was outraged.

Briga fixed her blue eyes on mine. Deep wells, those eyes. Briga herself was a deep well, walled with mystery. "I used to hate the druids, Ainvar, until I realized that the threads connecting you with them made you what you are, a man I could trust and love. So I stopped hating them. In fact, I stopped hating altogether and I feel much better for it. Hatred is a poison and should be expelled from the body."

She held my gaze until I understood that pity was exactly what I should feel for Caesar. I, who would be content with honey on my bread and the gleam of firelight on Briga's hair and the laughter of my children, must pity a man of such unappeasable appetites that he was driven to annihilate multitudes in a vain effort to assuage them.

All this I discovered while Briga looked at me with infinite love shining out of her eyes.

We walked on.

The journey seemed endless. Sometimes we talked among ourselves; more often, we were silent.

I was thankful to be left alone in my head.

But my thoughts kept returning to Caesar. Whom I must no longer hate. Caesar, who had been such a large part of my personal Pattern. Why? For what purpose had his life been entangled with mine? If life was a lesson, what lesson was I meant to take from him?

In his wake Caesar had left hundreds of thousands of dead Gauls. Mountains of bloated, blackened, decomposing bodies had lain rotting beneath the sky. Men, women, even tiny children, liquefying and seeping into the soil. I had furiously blamed the Source for allowing such things to happen. Perhaps that was when the loss of my faith began, like rot setting into damp wood.

But then . . . think, head. Think back. Step by step.

The living Carnutes had possessed courageous hearts and skillful hands; they had hopes and dreams and memories. Yet their dead bodies had been disgusting. Shapechanged by Caesar into horrors.

As we walked on, my eyes reported the first signs that winter was dying. Tiny blades of new grass were peeping up through the old. Hard green buds were forming on otherwise bare branches. Holding life locked inside . . .

And the answer came to me.

The missing component in those dead bodies was *spirit.*

A body could be slain but even Caesar had no weapons for destroying the spirit. Spirits were sparks of the Great Fire of Life, born of the immortal Source. The fact of their existence was proved by the fact of their departure.

I had blamed the Source for permitting horrors.

A simplistic assertion, and totally wrong.

The Source had not failed us. The bodies that died and disintegrated would have done so anyway, sooner or later, returning to the earth to nourish other bodies. Nature feeds on that which perishes.

But that which lives, lives forever. Sparks of the Great Fire.

When Rix and I lay on our backs on summer nights all those years ago and gazed at the sky, we had been observing the Infinite that is part of us all.

My lips formed a silent song of thanksgiving. Not because Cormiac and Labraid were alive, and not because Caesar was dead.

But because the Source Is.

We Are.

## *chapter* XXXI

NOTHING HAPPENS ON THE PLAIN OF BROAD SPEARS WITHOUT everyone soon knowing. As we approached our clanhold, we discovered a large number had gathered there to greet us. In the forefront were my children: Dara and Eoin and Ongus and Gobnat, Cairbre and Senta and Niav, waving in wild excitement.

I signaled a brief halt to savor the moment. What I had lost was only a shadow in the sunshine of what I had gained.

Probus said, "How are they going to react to me, Ainvar?"

"Don't worry about it. Most of them haven't the slightest idea who or what a Roman is. Besides, you're our friend."

And he was.

Friends and family crowded around us. Perched atop the gray horse as if on a pedestal, Labraid began to relate, with extravagant gestures, his own version of the last two years.

"Grannus," Briga said urgently, "take him off that horse at once and carry him into our lodge. He's in no condition for this."

Before Grannus could comply he was shouldered aside. "My son!" Fíachu exclaimed as he reached up for Labraid.

The chief of the tribe gave the rest of us a pleasant though perfunctory greeting; it was obvious he could not wait to carry Labraid in triumph to his own stronghold. He looked askance at Probus, however. "Where I go, this man goes," Labraid insisted. "He saved my life."

"Then he shall be honored among us for as long as he lives," Fíachu promised. Facing Probus, he solemnly intoned, "I am Fíachu, chief of the Slea Leathan, the tribe of Broad Spears in the kingdom of the Laigin. I am a direct descendant of Éremon, who, as everyone knows, was the most gracious and the most noble of all the sons of Milesios."

The Roman was a match for him. "I am Probus Seggo, son of Justinius, magistrate of Genova, and formerly an officer in the legion of . . ."

I left them to it and entered my lodge.

Lakutu was waiting for me with her face scrubbed and shining, and the belt Glas had made for her firmly fastened around her waist.

I spent the rest of the day happily crowded into my lodge with both of my wives, all of our children, and Cormiac Ru. Briga put the Red Wolf to bed almost at once. I had thought I wanted nothing so much as to lie down on my own bed and rest, but I was wrong. Time may be fluid, but on rare occasions you can trap it in your heart and extract every drop of pleasure. One should never sleep through those moments.

Shortly before sunset Probus appeared at our door. He entered almost shyly; accepted the basin of water for washing; greeted us each in turn. Niav last.

He could not seem to look at her.

Briga whispered to me from behind her hand, "The Roman was smitten with Lakutu's daughter the moment he saw her."

I had not noticed, but if Briga and I always made identical observations there would be no need for two of us.

My wives pressed hospitality upon Probus. He was given a loaf of bread for his right hand and a hunk of cheese for his left, and a pitcher of mead was set beside him. To my surprise, he began to devour the food like a starving man.

"Didn't Fíachu prepare a feast for you?"

"He did, Ainvar," Probus replied around a mouthful of cheese. "Labraid is probably still enjoying it, but I lost my appetite. Fíachu threw some of his cousins out of their lodge in order to give it to Labraid until a new lodge can be built for him. The dispossessed family is very unhappy, and I am not comfortable with the arrangement myself."

"You're welcome to stay with us for as long as you like," my senior wife assured him.

"That is most kind, but you appear to be very crowded here already." Probus swept the room with his eyes—looking at everyone but Niav.

She, on the other hand, kept her eyes fixed on him.

A gentle dew formed on the Roman's forehead.

Niav smiled the tiny smile of a woman with a delicious new secret.

I told Probus, "Normally there are not so many people in this lodge. There are several other lodges in the clanhold as well; I'm sure we can make you comfortable. We owe you a great debt and are eager to repay it any way we can."

"There is one way. . . ." He hesitated.

"Tell me."

"Work magic for me, Ainvar."

Only once before had I heard the request so baldly put. On that occasion I had been unable to oblige Duach Dalta. There was no reason to believe my gift had returned since then, and the last thing I wanted was to be humiliated in front of my family. "You already saw magic on Mona, Probus; greater magic than anything I might show you."

"I know what I thought I saw, but I need to be convinced it was possible."

"If your mind is closed, nothing can convince you," I told him. As I spoke, my gaze accidentally fell on Briga. Her eyes widened at my words.

"Please, Ainvar," Probus urged. "Work magic for me. I trust you."

A Roman trusted me, and I liked him. The world is rarely what we expect.

Taking Probus by the hand, I led him over to Niav. "Let's begin by having the two of you get to know each other. Sit down here, Probus, and talk with my daughter for a while."

Probus obediently seated himself next to Niav, who blushed furiously and smiled that tiny, delicious smile. The Roman forgot his cheese and bread; even his cup of mead. He forgot everything but the huge dark eyes of Lakutu's daughter.

There is more than one kind of magic.

The following day I told Keryth about the strange stars in the Black Pool.

"Have you ever seen anything like that before, Ainvar?"

I rummaged among my memories. "When the Great Grove of the Carnutes was burning . . . it's hard to describe this adequately . . . I saw the blazing oaks turn into pillars of stone. Above them rose a spire like the tallest pine tree in the world."

"Aaahh." The parchment-thin skin on Keryth's face folded into pleats, so that for a heartbeat she looked her age. "I believe you've seen a vision of the future, my friend. In fact, you have twice glimpsed the future."

"I'm no seer."

"The future is not the sole possession of prognosticators, any more than only the bards can compose poems or only the healers can heal. We simply have a more highly developed gift."

"But what I saw doesn't make any sense, Keryth."

"That's because the future is beyond current comprehension. We won't understand it until we're there."

I prefer mysteries I can solve in Thislife. One all-important mystery remained for me. In time I intended to learn the answer.

# *chapter* XXXII

Cormiac had survived the journey in better shape than anyone expected. Ensconced in comfort in my lodge, with both of my wives to fuss over him, he gained strength rapidly. By Lughnasa, Briga assured me, he would be whole again except for his scars.

We all have scars of one sort or another.

Mine were deep inside.

Just as I had made a conscious decision to stop hating Caesar—at which I succeeded sporadically—my head informed me I should stop agonizing over the loss of my gift. Knowing what one should do and being able to do it are not the same thing, however. The more I tried not to think about magic the more the subject haunted me.

Although I never shared these thoughts with her, my Briga knew. She—who had never acknowledged druid magic—selected a branch from an ash tree and took it to the Goban Saor. At her instruction he fashioned a staff perfectly suited to my height. On one side she had him carve a most singular face: ageless, mysterious, wise. When Briga presented the staff to me I looked at it twice before recognizing the visage as my own.

At the next change of the moon Fíachu announced the creation of a new title for Labraid. The Speaker Who Sails the Seas—a title he no longer used, to my amusement—was to be known in future as the tanaiste, the chief-in-waiting.

Dian Cet and Morand devised an elaborate ceremony of conferring for the new tanaiste; one almost but not quite the equal of a chieftain's inauguration. Before the ceremony began the tribe was served a splendid feast. After gorging themselves on Fíachu's food and drink the Slea Leathan could hardly refuse to accept his chosen successor.

SOMETIMES I THOUGHT ABOUT KERYTH'S PREDICTION OF A PEOPLE starved for time and space. I hoped that this once Keryth was wrong.

AT BEALTAINE, NIAV AND PROBUS WERE MARRIED IN OUR CLANHOLD. Afterward we danced around their fertility pole, but they did not remain with us for long. On the day they departed, I told Probus, "I salute you as a free person."

It was better than being a citizen of Rome.

Probus took my daughter to Dubh Linn and settled on the north shore of the great bay. There he established a trading post, doing business with anyone who made the journey across the sea from Albion or even beyond. From the beginning the venture was a success. Probus was, as he said himself, uniquely qualified.

IN THE CLANHOLD OUR LIVES SETTLED BACK INTO A COMFORTABLE routine. It was heartening to see how much my people were contributing to the larger tribe. The marriage laws that had begun with Dian Cet and Morand were enlarged as other wise heads joined the ranks of the brehons. Among them they determined that a sixth-degree marriage resulted when a woman is abducted and prevented from returning to her people. The seventh degree was a soldier's marriage, the casual union between a man away from his clanhold and a woman he meets along the way. An eighth-degree marriage took place when one partner deceived the other in order to gain sexual access. Forcible rape constituted the ninth degree of marriage, and the tenth occurred when there was sex involving persons whose heads are not capable of understanding what they do.

The last pronouncement of Dian Cet forbade the building of any settlement "in the shape of the towns of Caesar."

"After this," the old brehon announced, "I shall leave the making of law to younger men and women."

I protested. "But you are as wise as ever; probably wiser."

"My head is filling up with cobwebs, Ainvar," Dian Cet replied, with no indication of regret. "I have devoted my life to my people. Now I want to sit back and enjoy the last of it for myself."

When I shared his words with Briga, she said, "He's earned his rest. The wheel of the seasons turns only one way, but that's as it should be. Change is life. You are still growing, Ainvar; growing inside, where it counts." She added with a self-deprecating chuckle, "On the other hand, I am growing old."

"That's not true. Young is *who* you are, not *what* you are. My Briga is forever young."

"Oh, you." She gave me a playful shove, but her cheeks were pink with pleasure.

We marked the turning of the wheel with four great feasts: Imbolc, Bealtaine, Lughnasa, and Samhain. During every season new faces appeared while old ones faded into memory. Labraid married Aislinn. They were still enjoying their time of honey-feasting when the old king of the Laigin died.

At the funeral feast Seanchán recited a lengthy lament for the dead man. Dara leaped to his feet to lead the applause. I thought Briga gave him a nudge in the ribs with her elbow first, but I could not be certain.

Later my eyes observed the two bards walking side by side. Their heads were close together; they were lost in an animated discussion about the composition of poetry. Both men were enjoying it.

When Fíachu was elected as the new king of the Laigin, Duach Dalta conducted the inauguration ceremony.

Sometimes we teach our children, and sometimes they teach us. After the inauguration I made a point of telling Duach Dalta, "You have a splendid sense of ritual, the best I've ever encountered. The kingdom of the Laigin is fortunate in you."

He looked surprised but could not fail to recognize my sincerity. "Speaking of praise, Ainvar—I was thinking of asking your son Dara to compose a praise poem in honor of the new king. Do you approve?"

Briga had said, "Change is life." And it is.

AS SOON AS HE WAS FULLY HEALED, CORMIAC BEGAN TO ROAM. HE went farther and farther afield and stayed away for longer and longer. I kept meaning to ask the question that had haunted me ever since Dubh Linn, but whenever he returned to us I forgot. There was so much else to keep me occupied. My life was filled to the brim with family and students and those riches that cannot be bartered but glow in the heart.

My children were seeking mates for themselves and there was excitement in the air. Furtive visits to Fíachu's stronghold; longer journeys to other clanlands; a shimmer of shy glances; a secret touching of hands. Of lips.

Before long I would have grandchildren to tug at my cloak.

THEN, WHEN I THOUGHT HER LONG PAST CHILDBEARING, MY BRIGA worked the greatest magic of all. She presented me with a new son. We called him Bran, for her brother, whom the druids had sacrificed.

Almost as soon as Bran could talk he was asking questions. And such questions! One day I found him crouching beside a pool in which a golden ball was floating.

"What's that?" the child asked, pointing in fascination.

"A reflection of the sun."

He looked up at me with innocent eyes. Briga's eyes. "What's the sun?"

"A symbol of the Great Fire of Life."

Bran cocked his head to one side. "Why is life?"

Why is life. Children are both the question and the answer.

"Nature is our teacher in all things," I told the little boy. "Just as water reflects light, the purpose of life is to reflect the Source."

And it is.

THE NEXT TIME CORMIAC RU RETURNED TO OUR CLANHOLD HE WAS accompanied by a princess of the Deisi; the daughter of Cas the Curly-

Haired. She was a fair-haired girl with a soft hoarse voice like the purring of a cat. They told us they planned to be married.

"We'll have a new lodge built for you and—"

"I think not, Ainvar," Cormiac said. "I've found a place that fits me like my skin and I intend to raise my family there."

"On the Plain of Broad Spears?"

"No, in the kingdom of the Deisi. I have permission to take up a clanhold in the mountains there."

The last thing I expected was that Cormiac would leave us permanently. Briga was as shocked as I was; she looked so heartbroken that I reminded him, "You once promised you would never be far from me and mine."

"I won't."

"But I don't see how—"

"I always keep my promises, Ainvar. Always."

And that was that. The Red Wolf had to be taken on faith.

Shortly before he left us for his new home I took him aside. "There is something I must ask you about. When Briga and I came to Dubh Linn, you told us that Maia was dead."

"She is."

"How could you be so certain? It's bothered me ever since."

"The woman told me. Showed me, in fact."

"What woman? Who are you talking about?"

"She came to me in my dreams." A faraway look crept into Cormiac's eyes. "Night after night she transported my sleeping self for a great distance. Night after night I saw Crom Dubh running with little Maia in his arms. Night after night I watched everything that happened, until at last I was forced to accept that I was seeing the truth. Your daughter never went through the slave market, Ainvar. She sickened and died on the bank of a river in Gaul. Crom buried her where the water sings."

My heart was thundering. "What woman showed you this?"

The colorless eyes met mine. "She was small and slender and pale. Her feet never touched the ground, yet she danced. When she spoke I could hear silver bells."

## *chapter* XXXIII

THE RED WOLF WOULD NEVER NEED BRIGA'S VIRILITY POTION. HE produced a veritable litter of sons. They called the firstborn Cas; the second was named Eoin. Ongus was the third son, then Cathal, Anluan, and a pair of twins called Mahon and Lorcán. Next came Cormiac Óg—young Cormiac—and finally another Bran. Following the tradition of the Gael, each boy would be expected to pass his name on to the next generation.

Cormiac Ru was putting his stamp on Hibernia.

As for me, the seasons were passing more quickly than they should. I would be willing to swear there were fewer days in each cycle of the moon, and winter came earlier and earlier.

I rarely traveled far from our clanhold anymore. One day, however, I felt an urge to wander. Without saying anything to anyone—Briga would have fussed at me—I took my warmest cloak from its peg, picked up my staff, and went outside. Frost silvered the grass. As I walked away from our lodge my footprints were briefly etched in time.

There was nothing in particular to do, no place I had to be. Sulis was conducting the class in the glade that morning. There were even several young ones who were training to become teachers when the older generation was gone.

My feet chose a path for me, ambling toward the mountains. Once or twice I turned around to enjoy the sight of my footprints leaving an unmistakable pattern behind me.

A pattern . . .

The third time I looked back, there was a second set of prints on the frosted grass.

I gave a violent start.

Not far away from me stood the silver wolf. By my reckoning he had to be very old indeed; it was astonishing he had survived for so long.

Neither of us moved.

He was alone. I could feel his absolute aloneness. Whether in his old age he had become an outcast from the pack I do not know, because it was a matter of indifference to him. He accepted without regret whatever nature brought.

All are truly alone when their time comes to die. I do not know if that was my thought, or came from the wolf.

For a timeless time we stood looking at each other in mutual understanding. Then he turned and went his way and I went mine.

AINVAR'S BODY WAS TRULY OLD. WHEN I PUT SOMETHING DOWN I HAD to remind my eyes to watch closely and my head to remember exactly where I put the object; otherwise I might never find it again.

The house of my spirit was falling down around me. Becoming too dilapidated to live in.

The morning came when I awoke with the certain knowledge that it would be my last morning in Thislife. Perversely, I felt stronger than I had in a long time. It was a gift, and I used it well. First I gave Lakutu a fond hug. "Egypt," I whispered.

She pulled back and looked at me. Her eyes were sunken with age and cobwebbed by time. "Why do you call me that, Ainvar?"

"Because you are everything that is rare and exotic. I may never have mentioned it before, but that's how I've always thought of you."

Briga had gone to the spring to fetch water. Walking slowly, for walking had become difficult, I came up behind her. "Magic," I said.

She turned around. "I didn't know you were there, Ainvar. What did you just say?"

"Magic. You practice magic every day, you know."

Her nose wrinkled with a laugh. "I do know, you old fool. Did you think I didn't?"

For one splendid, fiery moment I glimpsed the Absolute.

Then it was time to go.

THE FUNERAL WAS ONE OF THE LARGEST EVER HELD ON THE PLAIN OF Broad Spears. Everything was done as the dead man would have wished, a perfect balance of Gaul and Hibernia.

When the last stone had been placed on the cairn Briga addressed the assemblage. "So passes Ainvar of the Carnutes," she intoned, adding with pardonable pride, "the greatest of all druids."

Placing her hand on the cairn, she whispered, "We will meet again, dear spirit. Some other time, some other place."

Caressing the strings of his harp, Dara, bard of the Slea Leathan, recited a lament for Ainvar. Then exactly as father and son had planned together, the lament shapechanged. Sorrow melted into beauty. In a voice of purest gold the bard sang of the magical island of Hibernia, of sweet water and green grass, of red deer and silver wolves and immortal spirits.

And most particularly of Eriu.

*Remember us.*

## about the author

Novelist MORGAN LLYWELYN was born in New York City of Irish and Welsh ancestry. Shortlisted in 1976 for the United States Olympic Team in Dressage, she then turned her energies to exploring her family history in Ireland and Wales. Her first novel, *The Wind from Hastings,* was a selection of the Doubleday Book Club. With her second novel, *Lion of Ireland: The Legend of Brian Boru,* Llywelyn made the *New York Times* bestseller list and captured an international audience she has enjoyed ever since. After the death of her husband, Charles, in 1985, she moved to Ireland, the source of her inspiration. An Irish citizen, she lives in the countryside north of Dublin.

Since 1978, Llywelyn has created a substantial body of work chronicling Ireland and the Celts. Although her novels primarily are mainstream historical fiction, many of them include a depiction of the druidic culture that was central to Celtic and early Irish society. *Druids,* originally published in 1991, won her many new readers for its combination of meticulous historical research with breathtaking magic.

Llywelyn has won numerous literary awards. She was named Exceptional Celtic Woman of the Year; is a founding member of the Irish Writers' Centre and past chairman of the Irish Writers' Union; a director of the Irish Copyright Licensing Agency; and has served as a member of the judging panel for the highly prestigious International IMPAC Dublin Literary Award.

## *about the type*

This book was set in Garamond, a typeface originally designed by the Parisian typecutter Claude Garamond (1480–1561). This version of Garamond was modeled on a 1592 specimen sheet from the Egenolff-Berner foundry, which was produced from types assumed to have been brought to Frankfurt by the punchcutter Jacques Sabon.

Claude Garamond's distinguished romans and italics first appeared in *Opera Ciceronis* in 1543–44. The Garamond types are clear, open, and elegant.